A
MARKED
SOUL

A MARKED SOUL

ELIZABETH SEDELL

SOUL FERRIER BOOK 1

For Abbey

PLAYLIST

BY CHARACTER

Claire Woods
I Don't Care, Apocalyptica

The Superior
Lose Control, Teddy Swims

Billy Blake
Whatever It Takes, Imagine Dragons

Johnny Snake Demon
Highway to Hell, AC/DC

Mark
I'll Be There for You, The Rembrandts

Destiny
Made You Look, Meghan Trainor

Nancy
Best Friend, Brandy

Scott
Feelin' Way Too Damn Good, Nickelback

Gabriel
Runaway, OneRepublic

CHAPTER 1

My lungs held my breath as Mrs. Hanover's exhaled her last. There was something about the moment of death that seemed to make time stop. The lights above the hospital bed flickered and dimmed. The ever-present beeping of life support machines abruptly halted, filling the air with a choking silence.

I stood against the wall, watching the doctors and nurses quietly scurry about the room. They spoke to the family members in hushed tones and moved the now useless equipment into the hallway. Mrs. Hanover's adult children stood by her bedside, still squeezing her hands as they wept.

"What's happened here?"

The curious voice came from beside me and I knew that I was the only one who had heard it.

"You died, Mrs. Hanover," I whispered, not wanting to draw anyone's attention just yet. "Your children are grieving."

Mrs. Hanover's soul looked much as she had in life. Her light brown hair still surrounded a face lined with life, but now there was a lack of tension in her shoulders and a soft ethereal glow surrounding her.

"Ah, that explains it," she said casually, her gaze flicking around the room as though she'd never seen it before. "How did it happen?"

"Motorcycle accident."

She scoffed. "Greg must have loved that. He always said riding them was going to kill me someday. I guess he was right."

I nodded my head slowly, unsure how I should respond. Shuffling from across the room drew my attention back to the bedside. The doctors and nurses were offering condolences before filing out the door. Greg and his sister were left standing by their mother, much as they had been for the past several days. In fact, Greg was still wearing the same shirt he had been when I'd met him yesterday.

"Who are you?"

My attention flicked back to Mrs. Hanover's soul. Her face was scrunched in utter concentration as she tried to place me in her former life.

Flashing a quick smile, I shook my head. "We've never met before, Mrs. Hanover. I'm Claire Woods. Your son contacted me so he could speak with you."

She bobbed her head up and down a few times, then suddenly stopped. "And why can you speak to me?"

"I'm a soul ferrier."

The bobbing began again as she replied, "Well then, nice to meet you, Soul Ferrier Claire."

A soft chuckle fell past my lips. I dipped my eyes down to the scuffed tips of my shoes, wanting to avoid staring at Greg and his sister. They deserved to have this time. Everyone deserved a moment to process the death of someone they loved.

A rushed huff of air flew out of Mrs. Hanover's soul. "Honestly, I expected more of the grim reaper than this."

Lifting my head, I raised a quizzical brow at her. She flicked her hand at me and said, "You don't look like a harbinger of death. If anything, those big brown eyes and blonde hair make you look like Bambi."

"Bambi?" I hissed, my voice coming out louder than I intended. "And I'm not a harbinger of death. I'm here so your kids can talk to you."

"So, you're a medium," she stated.

"No, a soul ferrier is something more than that."

The soul beside me responded with a dismissive shrug of her shoulders. Explaining my gift was always difficult. I had been knowingly and unknowingly talking to souls my entire life. Trying to define something so innate within myself was like someone else explaining why they were a gifted athlete or a musical prodigy. I didn't know why I could do what I did, it was something that just was. A sudden voice cut through the room.

"Greg, what is that woman doing?"

My attention abruptly shifted back to Mrs. Hanover's bedside where both of her children were now staring at me. Greg's eyes were red-rimmed and curious, while his sister's were hard and narrowed.

"Honestly," the sister continued, whipping her head around to face her brother, "it's not enough that we had to watch our mother die this way, but you had to invite this *freak* here to witness it?"

Greg sighed and rubbed his hands down his face. "She helped Harry's family."

"And you just believed him?" she spat. Then, her eyes swept over me. "You could at least pretend to be speaking to our mother. Light a candle or something for all he's paying you."

She swiped furiously at her cheeks and then crossed her arms. Greg raked his hands through his hair and curled down into himself. I was used to people disbelieving in my abilities, but the dejected way Greg looked pulled at something in my chest. Sucking in a breath, I stepped forward, retort ready, when a cool breeze blew past me.

"Now, Ronnie that is quite enough," Mrs. Hanover's soul said.

The sister, Ronnie, screamed. As her mother continued toward her, she tripped over her own feet and landed unceremoniously on the floor.

"What the hell is this?" she cried; eyes wide.

I stepped beside Mrs. Hanover's soul and placed a tentative hand on her shoulder. The magic inside me pulsed and my entire body came alive with the contact. The soul stopped abruptly as her face went blank. With a shudder, I dropped my hand and shook out the tingling feeling spreading up my arm.

"Souls only appear to those they wish," I said, offering Ronnie my hand. She briefly glared at it before looking back at her mother. Her body stayed rigidly glued to the spot on the floor. Greg came around the bed, almost walking through his mother to get to us.

"Ronnie, what's the matter?" he asked, crouching down beside her.

Her eyes flicked from her brother to me, back and forth before finally settling on me. In a breathy voice she asked, "Why can't he see her?"

"As I said before, souls choose who they appear to."

With a sharp inhale of breath, I reached my hand back out to Mrs. Hanover's soul. The moment my skin touched hers, my magic reawakened. A tingling sensation rushed through me as though every cell of my body was infused with power that was flaring to life. Euphoria flooded me and pushed me to take control of the being beside me. To infuse the empty shell with purpose. My purpose. I fought that overwhelming sensation, working to keep my hold over Mrs. Hanover's soul as light as possible.

"Would you allow your son to see you, please?"

Asking was unnecessary as my magic compelled her to obey, but I preferred the illusion of civility over the reality, especially in front of other people. I knew she had complied when Greg stumbled backward onto the bed and cursed.

"What is happening?" he breathed. He lifted a trembling finger toward his mother while his widened eyes turned to me. "Is that…is this real?"

"Yes, Greg, it is me. I'm so glad you are here."

A choked sob sounded from his lips. His eyes sparkled with unshed tears as he took in the soul before him. "You were in an accident, of course I would be here."

Mrs. Hanover's soul waved a dismissive hand at him. "Well, I know how that wife of yours can be."

Greg stepped back as his brow furrowed. "Natasha? Mom, you love Natasha."

His mother guffawed incredulously. "No one likes her, dear. Isn't that right, Ronnie?"

Ronnie, who was still lying on the ground, stared wide eyed back at her mother. Her eyes flicked to her brother and then back to curiously scan the being before her.

Clearing my throat, I stepped forward. "Perhaps I should have mentioned that although souls have most of their memories, they return somewhat lacking in inhibitions."

"Honestly, Greg," his mother continued, leaving Ronnie be on the floor as she faced her son, "I should have told you that a long time ago. You deserve someone kind and hardworking." She smiled over at me. "Someone like Claire, here. Perhaps you should ask her on a date."

My eyes widened as I choked on a laugh. Feeling a need to change the subject, I said, "Perhaps now would be a good time to ask your questions, Mr. Hanover?" I nodded quickly at Greg. "You can speak to her as you normally would. I'll just be waiting outside if you need me."

I heard him say 'thank you' but I was already spinning away and walking toward the door.

Once outside the room, I leaned my head back against the wall and sighed. My magic was still buzzing. I took several deep breaths in through my nose and out through my mouth. Using my magic always created a pull within me to utilize more. It was as if the well of power inside me needed me to reach out and feel every soul possible. Feel, and control.

I don't want her anywhere near him.

The words pounded into my head. Memories flooded back in with them. My brother, young and pale. Too pale. He was lying on a bed in the middle of a room like Mrs. Hanover. My parents were arguing while I stood unnoticed in the doorway. I was young, but not so young as to not understand the words my father was hurling at my mother. Words about me. The words that pushed my mother to leave me at home the last day my brother was alive.

Shaking my head, I focused on the bustling sounds of activity around me. The quiet chatter at the nurses' station and the constant beeping and whirring of hospital equipment filled my ears. Slowly, the memories faded and my power receded.

"Tough day?"

The deep voice ripped me out of my thoughts. Turning toward him, I felt my power rising along with a chill that skated up my spine. He looked like a tall man with dark, greased back hair, but the magic in my veins saw him for what he was. A demon.

"Can I help you?" I asked, keeping my voice as even as possible. My hands fell instinctively down to my pockets, hoping to find a key or something with which to defend myself. The only thing I found was a tube of Chapstick. *Fantastic.*

"Claire Woods?" he asked, casually dropping his shoulder to lean against the wall. He crossed one sneaker over the other and grinned down at me.

I pushed off the wall, creating some space between us, then nodded. Every hair on my body stood on end as my eyes scanned him for signs of movement. He stayed inhumanly still for a few moments, staring back at me, before he huffed out a breath and said, "I've got a job for you."

Replying almost instinctively, I said, "Thanks, but I'm not interested."

Demons lived to trick humans, so I had no intention of entering into a deal with one.

His brows rose. "You're not even a little curious?"

If I was honest, yes, I was curious. A demon had never before offered me a job. I wasn't aware of any skill that I possessed that the being before me couldn't do himself. Perhaps there was some secret Soul Ferrier magic I was unaware of, but never having met another, I could only guess what that could be.

"Listen," I started, before glancing down at the nametag on his aqua colored scrubs. "Johnny, thanks, but no."

His eyebrows rose as he said, "Johnny?"

I lifted a tentative finger toward his chest. Slowly, he tipped his head downward. A wicked cackle slipped past his lips before he said, "Johnny is letting me *borrow* this."

Ew. I didn't know if by *borrow* he meant the scrubs or Johnny's whole body. Knowing that demons donned human skin to hide themselves in our world led me to believe it was most likely the latter, but I wasn't going to ask. I also knew better than to ask him for his name. Demons' true names were a closely guarded secret because a human in possession of a true name could summon a demon and demand a favor. Failure to comply with the request led to some unpleasant side effects, or so I've been told.

"Fine. Whoever the hell you are, the answer is no," I said clenching my teeth together and giving him a forced smile.

The color green slowly bled across his irises. The hairs on my arms rose in response. Apparently, I had seriously annoyed him with that comment. Pissing off a being ten times faster and stronger than me wasn't the best idea, but I didn't think he would do anything to me in public. It also told me something more about him. The color of the flare was unique to each type of demon and green meant the one before me was a snake demon.

His hand snapped out and wrapped around my wrist. In a gravelly tone he said, "I didn't ask if you were interested, Ferrier. I need you to find someone for me."

I twisted my left arm and pulled my wrist through the gap between his thumb and fingers. His eyes widened at my sudden release and my lips pulled up into a sneer. That's right, I'm not a damsel in distress, demon. I would never be as strong as them, but I had learned a few things to at least defend myself against them.

More green expanded across his irises as he bared his teeth at me. Just then, the door behind me opened and Greg stepped out into the hallway. He started at the sight of us standing so close together.

"What's going on here?"

His eyes darted between us, before settling on the demon with a hard set to his brows. "Everything okay, Miss Woods?"

While I appreciated his sense of chivalry, this wasn't a battle for Greg. The vast majority of humans were unaware of the demons among them and after seeing the soul of his dead mother earlier, I thought it best for him to stay oblivious on this one.

Slipping past me, the demon extended a hand toward Greg. With a slick smile plastered across his face he said, "Hi, I'm Dr. Jonathan Leslie, pleasure to meet you. I was speaking with Miss Woods about a patient of mine who is interested in retaining her services."

Greg looked down at the offered hand but didn't take it. His eyes narrowed back at the other man. "And that requires you to invade her personal space?"

My lips quirked up at the edges and a feeling of warmth spread through my chest. I wasn't sure what had motivated Greg to feel so protective of me, but considering how most people felt about me after witnessing my gifts, I wasn't going to question it.

The demon's head quirked to the side. "And why are you so interested in Miss Woods' personal space?"

Rolling my eyes, I stepped between them, facing Greg. "Mr. Hanover, how can I help you?"

My skin crawled with unease at having my back to the demon, but I had faith he wouldn't do anything with another human present. Greg clearly didn't know what Johnny was and there was a powerful being who would be pissed if another human was let in on the secret without good reason. I shuddered as a memory tried to surface in my mind. Forcing it away, I instead turned my focus to Greg's face. He remained silent with knitted brows for a moment, and then he huffed out a resigned sigh.

"We're done speaking with my mother," he said, pausing to audibly clear his throat and glare over my head. "We were wondering if you could escort her out?"

I smiled genuinely back at Greg. "Of course."

Eyes still glaring past me, he moved to step back into the room to retrieve his mother. I spun around to see Dr. Leslie leaning back against the wall, examining his fingernails.

"I don't know how many more ways I can convey to you that I am not interested," I spat.

His shoulders jostled against the wall as he chuckled. "Probably the same number of ways I could tell you I don't give a shit about your interest."

The slick grin that spread across his face caused my stomach to roil. Disregarding my revulsion he continued. "The person I need you to find is a girl. She's been missing a couple of weeks."

Gritting my teeth I shoved my hands through my hair and huffed out a breath. "Is she dead? Is that why you are here bothering me?"

He shook his head. "No. In fact, I hope she's very much alive."

Before I could reply, the door behind me opened and Greg returned with Mrs. Hanover in tow. She beamed over at me and swiveled her head quizzically toward the demon. Upon seeing him, her smile fell.

"What is that?" she asked, her voice barely a whisper.

Greg's attention snapped to the doctor still leaning casually against the wall. Not wanting him to get any more ideas about Dr. Leslie, I latched onto Mrs. Hanover's wrist and gently pulled her into my side. My magic pulsed to life as I said, "That's a doctor, Mrs. Hanover. We were just chatting."

With my touch, the concern on her face melted away. Her son was less easily placated, as evidenced by the scowl still on his face, but before he could ask anything I said, "I'll escort her out."

I pulled Mrs. Hanover down the hallway, leaving the two beings staring at each other. My hope was that Greg, having released his mother into my care, would return to the room and leave the suspicious Dr. Leslie alone. As we reached the end of the hall, I pushed my finger onto the button to call the elevator. My fears for Greg were quickly allayed by the appearance of the demon at my side.

"You didn't let me get to the best part, Ferrier. I offer payment I know you can't refuse."

His brows lifted suggestively. I laughed derisively and his eyes flashed green as he glared over at me. "Not that, human." He took a few breaths in, seemingly needing to compose himself before he whispered, "I hear you have issues with The Superior."

Cold panic washed over me. That was a name I didn't want to hear. We had come across each other only once before, but it had been enough for me. Pissing off the most powerful demon this side of Hell's Gates had not been a smart idea. I liked to think that I mostly knew how to learn my lessons.

The elevator doors opened, and I hurried inside with Mrs. Hanover. The demon's hand shot out and wrapped around the metal.

"I don't know what you're talking about," I said far too breathlessly.

He slipped inside with us and pressed the button for the lobby. Once the doors shut, he stepped in front of me and leveled his eyes with mine.

"I know his weakness."

"Bullshit." The word slipped out.

Johnny sucked in a sharp breath. "I would be destroyed for even speaking of it."

I rolled my eyes. There was no way I was falling into this trap. As far as I knew, The Superior didn't have any weaknesses, and even if he did there was no way I wanted to be the possessor of that information. Having any further involvement with that demon would not be good for my health.

Sensing my hesitation, he said, "You will never get another chance at this information."

The doors slid open behind him into the main lobby of the hospital. With so many people bustling about I felt confident as I turned back to him and said, "Look, Johnny, I have no interest in this job offer. I want nothing to do with The Superior. My answer is emphatically no."

He stood in the elevator and as the doors began to close, he flashed me a wicked smile. "We'll be in touch."

CHAPTER 2

The soul and I stepped out into the wintery air. November in Western Pennsylvania meant dropping temperatures and blustery winds. I zipped my coat up, nuzzling down into the insulated layers. My right hand pushed into a pocket, while my left stayed connected to Mrs. Hanover. She was unaffected by the weather and looked happily out at the busy street. As she had died at UPMC Presbyterian, we were soon walking along Fifth Avenue in the bustling Oakland neighborhood in the city of Pittsburgh. Students and professionals clogged the sidewalks as people made their way between the universities and lunch spots. The sun was shining high in the sky which helped to somewhat distract from the cold day.

Mrs. Hanover glided along beside me as we skirted behind Hillman Library and walked toward Schenley Park. Having worked often enough in this area, I knew there was a portal not far into the park. We walked together in silence, which I was grateful for, as it gave me time to adjust. Sucking in deep breaths, I let the world around me become clear. I spent so much of my life actively ignoring the spirits. Most people didn't like that I could see them, so I did my best not to. Now they were a steady stream along my subconscious, like any other pedestrian on the street. In this moment, however, I needed to see where we were going.

With my newly heightened awareness, I could see a few souls walking nearby, heading in the same direction as us. I smiled at an elderly woman's soul who held her hands in front of her as if she were accustomed to a walker. We reached the portal just as another soul crossed through. The portal stood twenty feet tall, a massive opaque arch that shimmered and fluttered in a phantom breeze. The temperature in the air dropped as we stepped closer and I could hear faint whispers. They tickled like a gnat across my ears.

"Okay," I said, turning to face Mrs. Hanover, "Here we are."

She simply stared at me, so I released her arm. Mindfulness once again filled her face and she looked nervously between me and the portal.

"What's on the other side?"

"The Otherworld."

She shook her head at me. "I meant, what's over there?"

I shrugged. "It changes. You could go through the same portal seven times and each time you would see something different. Except for The River. That's always in the middle leading to The Gates."

"The Gates? Well, now that sounds good."

Wincing, I said, "Not those gates."

I'd never seen color drain from a soul's face before. Mrs. Hanover looked stricken and it was a complete surprise after her attitude in the hospital. Perhaps, the conversation with her children had opened some old wounds, making her question herself.

"Do I have to go through right now?"

"No, you can stay here, but eventually, we all have to go through. The Otherworld is the gateway into the Afterlife."

Her lower lip trembled slightly as she asked, "Can you come with me?"

A deranged laugh burst from my lips before I could stop myself. "I could, but, um, let's just say the being in charge over there and I don't get along so well. He *asked* me very kindly to never come back again." Asked was being generous, but I didn't want to frighten her. I wanted to emphasize that The Superior was not someone to be crossed.

Mrs. Hanover's eyebrows rose. "You don't seem the type to be easily scared off."

I locked eyes with her, letting the full weight of my feeling show as I whispered, "You've never met someone like him."

A beautiful face flashed in my memory. Waves of lustrous dark hair falling across eyes that blazed with red. I shook the image away and smiled. Worrying Mrs. Hanover's soul wasn't helping either of us.

Nodding behind me toward a bench I said, "Come on, let's take a few minutes."

We sat and chatted amiably. Being this close to the Conservatory meant there was a fair bit of foot traffic going by. For a time, we simply watched as the world went by. Wind blew through the trees in cold bursts and I bounced my knees to keep blood pumping through my body.

After enough time, Mrs. Hanover's soul smiled over at me and nodded. I started to rise with her, but she placed a hand on my knee and gave a small shake of her head. She needed to embark on this next phase in her journey alone, and she knew that now. A returning smile tugged at my lips and I watched her glide across the grass. No one noticed her, except for me. A moment before she stepped through the portal, she looked back over her shoulder and gave me a wave. I returned the gesture, despite a few odd glances from passersby, and watched as she disappeared from this world.

A heaviness settled in my chest at the loss of her spark, but I knew this was an inevitability. There was no life without death and therefore there was no sense in me grieving for her. My sympathies would be better placed with her remaining family members.

Sucking in a breath and wiping a few traces of dampness from my cheeks, I pulled out my phone and saw that I had a few missed calls from my office. I called it my office, but it was more like a glorified closet. I paid an exorbitant amount in rent to the owner, who seemed to be under the impression that I was peddling witch spells out of his building.

My fingers would freeze while holding the phone for the duration of a call, so I walked back to my car before dialing. I started the engine of my small hatchback and bounced in my seat as the heaters started blasting air into the cabin. Once they'd quieted down, I flicked out my phone and dialed.

"Claire Woods, finder of lost souls."

I rolled my eyes, "Mark, I told you not to answer the phone like that." Putting the phone on speaker, I tossed it onto the dashboard and started rooting around in the back seat.

"No," he said, drawing out the word dramatically, "Technically, you told me to stop saying 'soul wrangler,' 'find your soulmate,' and 'put your souls at ease."

A laugh bubbled out of me before I could stop it. Mark was the perfect assistant. He was instantly likeable, never batted an eye when I talked about souls and demons, and let me pay him a barely livable wage.

Tossing a gym bag onto the floor I mumbled, "Okay, that may be true, but I'm trying to appear professional here, Mark."

"Professionalism comes second to profit, Claire."

I scoffed. He had a point. My hand landed on a grocery bag and I ripped it open only to find it was full of trash. A huff of exasperation fell out of me.

"What are you doing?" he asked.

"Looking for some chips. I missed lunch."

"I know I sent you out the door with some this morning. It was in a blue bag."

My eyes wandered over the contents of my backseat, hoping that a bright blue bag would suddenly appear before me. Considering the mountains of items that were currently in the back of my car, it was highly unlikely. I couldn't afford to live in the city proper, so when I drove into work, I packed everything I could possibly need into the car.

A groan slipped past my lips just before I felt a brush of magic coming from my passenger seat. I flicked my attention over and saw the blue bag sitting on the seat. My hands snatched a full bag of Doritos out of it and hurriedly ripped it open.

"Mmm," I moaned as I stuffed a chip into my mouth, "Thanks, Nicky."

A scoff sounded through the phone. "Twenty-five years old and still believes in Santa Claus."

"Hey," I spat, rolling my eyes and searching the bag for the most perfect chip, "I needed a name for whoever sent me this stuff and when you are eight there is already a magical being who delivers gifts, so I logically assumed they were one in the same. Excuse me for being a whimsical child."

A boisterous laugh barked through the line. "I know, I just like taunting you about it because I am in fact secretly jealous."

I scoffed and shoved another chip into my mouth. The magical whoever or whatever that randomly gifted me things had long since been a mystery I'd given up on solving. The items had started arriving shortly after my powers had first manifested. Initially, I hadn't noticed anything odd. I'd just assumed that the items had been there, something I'd simply overlooked. Then, I noticed when I pleaded for things, sometimes I would feel a tingling brush of magic just before stumbling upon the object of my desire. I probably should have been more concerned about it, but the gifts were always helpful, so at some point I'd decided to stop asking questions.

"Back to business," Mark said, pulling me out of my memories, "How'd it go with the Hanovers?"

"Fine," I said, not feeling like mentioning the demon. "What'd you call about?"

There was a beat of silence before he said, "We got an interesting call about an hour ago."

I sat munching my chips and wishing I had some water. My hand reached into the bag and I smiled when I felt the cool metal of a Yeti and pulled it out. After I took a sip, I noticed that Mark still hadn't said anything.

"Mark?"

A hurried inhalation came across the line. Oh no.

"Well, you see, I wouldn't be telling you about it, except that they just kept offering me more money. It was just so much, that I felt like, I mean, you need money."

He was rambling. This was going to be something bad.

"Just spit it out, Mark."

"It was a retrieval call."

Deafening silence filled my car after he finished speaking. I sat, not breathing or moving as a wave of dread washed down my spine.

"Mark, no," I whispered as my pulse pounded in my ears.

"Look," he continued, his voice soothing, "I know you have this rule that you don't go into The Otherworld anymore, but it's so much money, you have to at least consider it."

I tossed the chip bag into the passenger seat, my appetite suddenly gone. "I can't spend the money if he kills me."

"He never said he'd kill you."

"What do you think he meant by never come back, Mark?" I shouted at the phone.

Silence filled the car again. I sat rubbing my forehead. Mark didn't need to tell me the value of retrieval jobs. When I had been doing them, business was good. Not everyone was like Greg Hanover who knew when his mother was being removed from life support and was therefore able to contact me before she died. For most people, it was more sudden than that and by the time they got to me, their relative had been dead for at least a few days. Souls could wander in our world for a time, but most of them crossed through the portals fairly quickly. That meant if their family wanted to talk to them, I had to go through a portal and retrieve them. Those jobs were more dangerous and more difficult, so I was able to demand exorbitant fees for them. After I had been *asked* never to return by The Superior, my business had taken a nosedive. Requests for retrieval jobs still came in, but my life wasn't worth the risk. Apparently, whatever sum of money this person had offered was worth my potential loss of life in Mark's opinion. Part of me didn't want to know what that amount was.

"Listen," Mark said, his voice low and empathetic, "I told them you don't do retrievals anymore and they kept offering more money. And from what they told me, this guy shouldn't be hard to find. He wasn't a complete asshole, but enough of one that I assume he's waiting by The River. All you have to do is find the dock he's on and pick him up."

Finding a soul in The Otherworld took some understanding of their character in life. Squeaky clean or despicably dirty souls were impossible to intercept. They were on the fast track to The Afterlife and I rarely even saw those souls. The rest milled about in The Otherworld for a time determined by something or someone greater than myself. What I did know, was the more selfish a person was, the quicker they found The River.

It sounded like whatever information Mark had been given led him to believe this client was less than saintly. I trusted his judgement. Mark had been working with me for five years now and for three of those I'd done retrieval jobs. Somehow in that time, his knowledge of The Otherworld had reached a level that rivaled my own.

Interrupting my thoughts, Mark blurted, "The amount they offered was more than you made last year."

My eyes widened.

"Plus, what I made last year."

I let out a low whistle. That was some serious money, and I could use a good payday. Now I understood why Mark was pressing so hard for me to take it.

"Where and when did he die?" I finally asked. It didn't hurt to hear all the pertinent information.

"This morning at 4:31 at UPMC Presby."

That meant he would have gone through the portal I just left. Pressing the ignition button, I turned off my car and huffed out a resigned sigh.

"Send me the info," I said, before pushing open my door and stepping back out into the cold.

CHAPTER 3

As I walked around to the back of my car, my phone pinged with the email from Mark.

Information from Client:

William Blake, 58 years old

Cause of Death: car accident, serious head trauma, most likely caused by Mr. Blake being intoxicated while driving and not having fastened his seat belt properly

Relations: Wife, Marie, 30 years old. Ex-wife, Donna, 45 years old. Children: William "Billy" Blake, III, 26 years old, Charlotte Blake-Ferguson, 23 years old

Client: Billy Blake. Claims his father was an alcoholic, non-abusive. Ran a bait shop in the Strip District.

The information was sparse, but considering the time Mark had to collect it, it wasn't bad. Slipping the phone into my back pocket, I opened the trunk of my car and took in the mostly empty space. A flashlight and blanket were tucked into a side panel while a heavy black box was strapped at the back. I leaned forward, unhooking the straps and then walked the box back toward me. My fingers brushed across the keypad and then I lifted the lid. A sigh fell out of me as I looked down at my retrieval supplies. Several attempted maps, assorted pens, a change of clothes, a pair of rain boots, a pair of hiking shoes, a machete, and under it all a small plastic case. I pushed all the other items out of the way and pulled out the case. Inside was a six-inch-long steel knife with a plain carbon fiber handle. The blade was in decent shape considering it had been packed away in my trunk. I grabbed the leg sheath out of the box and then pulled my cleaning supplies out from under the floor.

As I dragged the rag over the blade, I opened the picture of William Blake that Mark had attached to the email. Mr. Blake had neatly combed salt and pepper hair. His olive complexion was a bit ruddy from his alcohol abuse as well as a bit swollen in the cheeks and nose. His rather large ears stuck out unevenly from his head and a few moles dusted his face and neck. Overall, he was a rather generic looking fifty something man, except for his eyes. They were dark and despite the smile on his face, his eyes didn't match. There was a darkness there and something told me there was a lot more to William Blake than being a bait shop owner.

After I finished cleaning the blade, I put away the supplies, locked the box and reattached it to the back of the trunk. I tucked the knife and sheath into my jacket and walked back to the portal.

People shuffled past me through the park, their days continuing like normal while mine was about to be turned upside down. For two years I had stayed away. Mark was right that The Superior hadn't specified what he would do if I returned. I would have to rely on that defense when the time came because I knew the instant I stepped through the portal, The Superior would know. The Otherworld was his domain and things didn't happen there without his knowledge. Dread churned in my gut as I stared up at the shimmering gate before me. The accompanying phantom breeze of the portal brushed across my skin and stirred the strands of my hair like a welcoming caress. The magic inside me rose at the close proximity of The Otherworld. I focused my thoughts on the stack of bills currently sitting on my kitchen counter, the bucket under the sink in my office that caught the drip that leaked through the inches of duct tape, and I thought about Mark. This job would help with those bills, allow me to hire a plumber, and give me the funds I needed to keep Mark. As I sucked in a breath and stepped through the portal I thought, "I just need to find Mr. Blake without being seen by any demons and get paid before The Superior has a chance to kill me. Piece of cake."

I emerged into a thick jungle. The air was heavy with moisture and heat. Pulling down the zipper, I removed my jacket and tossed it and my sweater onto the ground by the portal. I stood in a tank top and jeans and still I felt beads of sweat beginning to form along my hairline. Pulling the knife and sheath out of the jacket, I quickly strapped the sheath to my leg and inserted the blade with a practiced twitch of my hand. The knife was my last line of defense after avoiding, running, negotiating, and whatever else I could possibly think of in the moment. I didn't mess around with the beings of The Otherworld if I could help it, and I would do a lot to help it.

A drop of sweat slid down my neck and I wiped it away with my hand. All around me were massive green leaves, twisting vines, and tall trees. The sun barely peeked through the dense foliage of the canopy.

"I should have brought my machete," I said absently to myself. I never knew when I went through a portal what environment The Otherworld would provide. The portal's location along The River was constant, but what the world looked like changed. I wasn't sure if it was a reflection of the last soul to have entered or some whim of the place itself. I'd been through this particular portal several times and it had never before been a jungle.

A small backpack dropped onto the ground in front of me. Pulling open the top, I saw a machete and a bottle of water with a sweatband and a hair tie wrapped around it.

Smiling blissfully upward I said, "Thank you, Nicky."

I pulled out the machete and wrapped my hair up into a bun and off my neck. With the sweatband sliding onto my brow, I was set for my trek through the jungle.

Thirty minutes later I was sick of the color green. My arm hurt from swinging the machete through the dense vegetation and despite being in another world, there were still bugs. I slapped at a black speck on my arm and then wiped my damp hand on my jeans.

"I could use a guide through this jungle, Nicky," I shouted toward the sky.

Nicky didn't respond as I pushed through a cluster of leaves into a rare clearing. I sighed with relief and slid the backpack off my shoulders. Tossing the machete into the grass, I pulled out the water and guzzled half of it down.

A twig snapped in the jungle behind me. Without thinking, I pulled my knife and whirled around. A man in a white linen suit stepped into the clearing. His dark brown hair was cut rather short, but I could still see flecks of gray at his temples. Warm brown eyes regarded me above the most rigidly straight nose I had ever seen.

"Miss Woods, you shouldn't be here."

His voice, like always, was a beckoning embrace. It soothed the edges of my frustration and made the itch of my sweat disappear. I wasn't sure if Gabriel was aware that his angelic presence altered everything around him. Perhaps one day I would ask him.

Sighing, I returned the knife to its sheath and said, "Now isn't a good time, Gabriel."

Gabriel stepped closer to me, his gait not at all bothered by the vines and tree branches along the jungle floor that had been tripping me since I began this hellish walk. He lifted my machete off the ground and held it out to me handle first. The corners of his eyes creased as he smiled. "So good to see you, Miss Woods, now please, leave."

My hand snatched the blade away from him as I rolled my eyes. "I would love to do that, Gabriel, but as you can see I am lost in this infernal jungle."

He raised a hand indicating the direction from which I had just come. "The portal is fifty yards back that way. I would be happy to escort you."

"Fifty yards? That's it?" I spat before letting out a very undignified groan. Tucking the water bottle back into the backpack, I slung it over my shoulders and pulled out my phone. The picture of Mr. Blake was still open and I turned it toward the angel.

"I just need to find this guy and I'll be out of here."

His eyes flicked down to my phone and then back to my face. He shook his head. Gabriel might have desperately wanted me to leave, but he wouldn't lie to me.

"Fine," I said, lifting the machete to point in the direction he'd appeared from. "Is The River that way?"

Something shifted in his eyes as he debated about answering me. I didn't have time to waste while he considered telling me or not. "Look, I'm not leaving without him, so the faster I find him, the faster I get out of here."

A muscle jumped in his cheek. I grinned, showing him all my teeth and slid my phone back into my pocket. After another moment, he sighed and flicked his head in the direction to my right.

We walked silently for a few moments, with me swinging the machete back and forth through the understory. Sweat glistened on my arms as I swiped a hand across the back of my neck. Looking over my shoulder, I saw Gabriel moving effortlessly through the jungle with not a single drop of sweat or dirt on him. "To be an immortal," I sighed.

"How's that?" Gabriel asked.

"Nothing," I said, continuing my swinging. "So, Gabe, how's business?"

Looking over my shoulder, I saw him bristle. "You know very well that I do not condone your use of that name, nor do I accept your implication that my given purpose is a *business* venture."

I laughed. Ever since I had known him, which had been from the moment I first stepped through a portal, he had always been strict in his decorum. He appeared in suits, hair perfectly coifed, and he insisted on calling me Miss Woods despite my insistence that Claire was fine.

"Sorry, Gabriel," I said, emphasizing the last two syllables, "How have you been?"

A downed limb obstructed our path. Without hesitation, Gabriel offered me a hand and helped me step on top of it. I jumped down and peered back, watching as he gracefully vaulted over the tree.

"I am divinely blessed," he said, continuing easily, "I am always well."

"Uh-huh. And how have your souls been?"

He tsked. "Few and far between."

I nodded. Gabriel was an escort. The most righteous and good among us were greeted on the other side of the portal by an angel. Those exceptional souls were guided straight into the afterlife, skipping through the purgatorial plain of The Otherworld. I'd once asked him who warranted such treatment, but all he would say was only the best among us. An intentionally vague answer, so I dropped the topic. Apparently, some things were meant to remain a mystery until death.

Speaking of death, I asked, "Any trouble with the other side?"

Gabriel's voice dropped into a menacing tone. "They are no *trouble* for me. It is you and your safety that concerns me. He surely knows you are here by now."

The amount of revulsion that Gabriel spewed upon referring to The Superior was enough to make me shudder. Angels by nature detested the demons, but there was something else to Gabriel's relationship with The Superior. It had to be something personal. Any time I even hinted at asking about it, he vehemently shut down my inquiry.

Pushing past another large, broad leaf, relief washed over me as I finally saw the edge of the jungle. A few steps in front of me, there was a line of trees and then an open field of tall, green grass. With a sigh, I walked out of the jungle and raised my hand to block the sun. My eyes took a few moments to adjust to the sudden brightness, but soon enough I was able to see The River in front of me. The surface of the water sparkled as it flowed ponderously along.

"I believe I see him," Gabriel said from beside me.

Following his line of sight, I saw a small wooden dock about sixty yards away. A cluster of souls milled about the simple platform. From this distance, I couldn't see William Blake myself, but I trusted Gabriel, so I started across the grass toward the dock.

Once we were closer, I got my first glimpse of William Blake. He stood patiently waiting, hands clasped in front of him as his head swiveled to take in his surroundings. My shoulders relaxed at the sight of him and I grinned at Gabriel before stepping onto the platform.

"William Blake?" I asked as I stepped in front of him.

With a touch of humor, he said, "Who's askin'?"

I smiled and said, "I need you to come with me for just a bit, Mr. Blake."

His grin faded a little as he looked back over the water. "No can do, love, I got a ride comin'."

Under my breath, I whispered my thanks to the universe. Once souls boarded the boats, they didn't get off until they passed through The Gates. The information the client had given Mark was clearly lacking because souls that went straight to the boats were definitely assholes.

Filing that piece of information away for later, I reached out my hand and clasped Mr. Blake's forearm. My powers pulsed to life inside me and swept across my hand into the soul. His face went blank, and I started leading him off the dock.

Gabriel stood at the bottom, but his attention was fixed upriver. Glancing past him I saw what he was staring at and felt a chill wash down my spine. A boat was chugging down the middle of The River toward us.

All of the boats were driven by demons, and I couldn't afford to be seen by one right now. My hand squeezed Mr. Blake's forearm and I dragged him off the dock. Gabriel helped us down and then followed closely behind me. I ran in a crouch, keeping my head level with the tips of grass. My legs started to burn from the prolonged squat, but I kept pushing myself forward. Sweat ran into my eyes but through the blur of my vision I could see the tree line was just ahead.

"Hey, you!"

I froze at the unfamiliar voice. The trees were so close and yet still too far away. Most of me was hidden by the grass, but my hand extended upward to maintain my hold on Mr. Blake. Behind me, I heard the boat engine shift down into an idle. They had reached the dock.

"Hey," the voice called again, "I'm talking to you. What do you think you're doing here?"

A ringing began in my ears as my stomach dropped. I had been so close and yet my first retrieval job in two years was about to end in failure. That massive paycheck would be going back to the Blakes and undoubtedly, I would be getting a visit from The Superior. All in all, I was worse off than I had been when I started this day.

My knees dropped into the dirt and I pivoted around. Instead of seeing The River, however, I almost ran into the backs of Gabriel's legs. He stood tall with his hands on his hips, blocking me from sight.

"I am free to go wherever I wish," Gabriel shouted with an air of authority in his voice.

"You know the rules," the voice spat back, "Docks are off-limits to your kind. Keep your righteous asshole where it belongs, angel."

Gabriel bristled. "I would recommend a course in manners if I thought there was any chance the concepts could penetrate that incredibly thick skull of yours."

There was a beat of silence before the voice responded, "Take your trash and get out of here."

My muscles tensed at the demon's tone. One of Gabriel's hands moved to the center of his back and he flicked it in a shooing motion. Shifting forward I breathed, "Thank you," and then turned toward the trees. I heard a whoosh of air and the fluttering of feathers. Gabriel had opened his wings. Popping up onto my feet, I adjusted my grip on Mr. Blake's arm and then bolted for the trees.

CHAPTER 4

The trip back through the jungle was faster than my initial foray. My previous ministrations with the machete had left a clear path I was easily able to follow. Once we exited the portal, I'd called Mark and arranged a meeting with Mr. Blake's family.

I now stood in the middle of Homewood Cemetery, shivering inside my large coat. The sweat from being in The Otherworld still clung to my skin making me shudder with every passing breeze. The sun set several hours ago, and the temperature had dropped precipitously.

Mr. Blake's soul stood beside me, a mildly amused expression on his face. The three individuals whom we'd met at the cemetery were currently huddled together, arguing in hushed tones and gesturing rather vigorously in our direction. I couldn't find any amusement in the situation as the undercurrent of violence rolling off William "Billy" Blake, III had been choking me since I first laid eyes on him.

The whispered argument suddenly ceased, and Billy turned to stride toward us. He trailed a hand through his dark, greased back hair as he approached. "You want to run that by me again?"

Like his father, he had a slight New York accent. He stood several inches taller than me, with his willowy frame clad in a long tan peacoat that perfectly matched his oxfords. His previous smile had made his large ears jump, but there was nothing genial in his expression now.

Clearing my throat, I repeated, "Souls only appear to those of their choosing. Give him a moment and maybe he'll change his mind."

After Mr. Blake's soul's first refusal to appear to his family, I had almost instinctively offered my assistance, but the look on Billy's face had given me pause. Eyes that had before appeared friendly, quickly took on a deadly calculation. His gaze trailed over me, assessing my worth and I realized I did not want to know what happened to people he found wanting.

"*Maybe* he'll change his mind?" He spat, stepping closer to me with his hands fisted. "Maybe? I'm not paying for no fucking maybe."

"Can't she just make him? She must be able to do something," a female voice said from behind Billy.

He turned and faced his mother. Despite their height difference, the ex-Mrs. Blake still managed to look down her nose at her son. Her hazel eyes held a keen sharpness as she stood with her arms crossed and her cosmetically inflated lips pursed. The air ruffled the layers of fur she was wearing as she shifted in her shiny black boots that somehow, despite walking through a cemetery, had not a single speck of dirt on them.

"Well?" she said, eyes lighting on me as her perfectly manicured brows rose. "Before we freeze to death in this *place*."

The location wasn't my choice. For some reason, my clients seemed to think that cemeteries were the only appropriate place to meet their recently deceased. This was not my first meeting in this cemetery, and I doubted it would be my last. Frankly, I would have preferred meeting at any one of the restaurants down the street. What little energy I'd acquired earlier from the chips, had been burned through by my trek in the jungle.

I sighed and placed my hand on Mr. Blake's forearm. There was still a niggling feeling in my stomach telling me I shouldn't do this, but I needed the money and I was beginning to be concerned about what Billy would do if I didn't make his father appear.

"Mr. Blake, allow your family to see you, please."

A moment later, Billy's sister let out a startled gasp. Her mittened hands flew to her face as her eyes widened. The reaction was one I'd seen countless times before, but the one on Billy's and his mother's faces surprised me. Something sinister gleamed in their eyes as their lips twitched upward. I shivered as the weight of my situation settled onto my shoulders. My gaze darted around the empty cemetery as I swallowed down my rising panic.

Billy strode forward, leveling his gaze with his father. "Thought you could get away with it, didn't you?" I stood as still as possible next to Mr. Blake, but Billy's gaze pivoted over to me. "We need a minute here."

Another shudder ran through my body, and I attempted to play it off as a chill by wrapping my free arm across my torso. I shook my head. "If I let go of him, he'll leave."

There was a small chance that wasn't true, but if Billy Blake looked at me the same way he was looking at his father, I would high tail it back to The Otherworld without a second thought.

Billy stepped into my personal space. "Then order him to stay."

I shook my head again. "It doesn't work that way."

His lips twitched as he lifted his right hand onto his hip. The movement pulled his coat open revealing the gun strapped to his side. "Why don't we try that again. Make. Him. Stay."

A shaky breath fell out of me. "Trust me, I would if I could, but if I release him, he will no longer follow my orders." As almost an afterthought, I added, "We signed a contract, so anything discussed here is confidential."

Doubt-filled eyes flicked over me. Billy continued assessing me for several moments before his sister pleaded, "Please, Billy, let's just get this over with and let father be at peace."

He took a step back but didn't acknowledge his sister. His attention was fixed on his father. If there had been love between these men at some point, it was no longer evident.

"Where is she?"

Billy's voice was a low whisper that hummed with violence; however, Mr. Blake's soul had left all his cares behind when he died. He smiled back at his son and said, "I'm not tellin' you."

An exasperated sound flew out of Billy's mouth before he raised his fists into his father's face. "That's my fucking money, old man, and I don't care about some whore you screwed getting any of it. Tell me where she is!"

"It doesn't matter where she is," Mr. Blake said, undeterred by his son's threats, "Cause the money's not goin' to Delores. It's goin' to our daughter."

A choked sound came from one of the two women. The ex-Mrs. Blake's face suddenly came into view as she pushed her son aside to glare at her former husband. "You mean to tell me there is yet *another* woman *and* a child?"

Her hand shot out incredibly quickly to slap across the soul's face. I could have told her that physical violence toward souls by humans was pointless, but she soon realized it herself when her hand passed through his head. She jumped back in horror, shaking her hand out before wiping it against her coat.

"You," she said, turning to face me, "Do something."

My magic flared in response as if reminding me that I could exert more power over souls than simply commanding them to speak. The desire to bend the soul to my will and open its mind so I could extract its secrets rose like a tidal wave inside me. I sucked in a breath and mentally pushed the power down, reminding it that I was in charge. Sweat broke out across my brow.

"I can't," I said, my voice coming out slightly hoarse.

The ex-Mrs. Blake scoffed. "Charlotte, you're up," she called to her daughter over her shoulder.

Charlotte Blake-Ferguson hadn't really caught my eye before. She'd mostly remained a shadow cowering beside her mother, but now, I watched as her brother grabbed her by the arm and dragged her forward. Her eyes blinked furiously as tears spilled down her face. She shook her head back and forth, the word 'no' repeatedly falling past her lips.

Billy yanked her one last step forward and said, "This is for the good of the family, Charlotte, now do what's best for your family. Remember them? Your two sweet girls and that shit for brains husband of yours we got back at the house?"

My heart broke at the look on Charlotte's face. Her eyes were wide, cheeks pale and traced with tears. She nodded her head at her brother then turned to look at her father's soul. With a cascade of dark hair blowing around her face, she wrapped her arms around herself and her bright pink, puffy coat. It struck me that I hadn't really noticed how much she looked like her father until now. The same heart shaped face, olive complexion, and mischievous eyes. Where Mr. Blake's had been cunning and ruthless, however, Charlotte's appeared more intelligent and calculating.

"Papa, please," she pleaded, her voice low and soft. "Think of your granddaughters. Think of me. Please."

The soul simply stared blankly back at her. Emotional appeals were pointless. Once someone died, they changed. Their priorities shifted and it frequently meant the concerns of those left behind were inconsequential to them now. Mr. Blake's soul did, however, wish to protect this other child. He must have felt a strong sense of devotion or perhaps love for his other daughter for it to still motivate him this way.

Charlotte's face fell as the realization that her father wasn't going to comply finally hit her. She turned pleading eyes over to me and with the pain that look caused in my chest, I felt some of my resolve begin to crumble. She was a mother and a wife being threatened with the lives of her loved ones by the people she called family. It was disgusting and I wanted to help her.

Billy shoved her aside violently and then reached out to grab me. I stepped back quickly, and his fingers snatched the air in front of me. He grumbled low in his throat. "Fix this. Now."

My desire to help Charlotte receded as I faced her brother. My pulse raced in my ears as I shook my head back and forth. "I can't do it."

This time, Billy darted more quickly, and I wasn't able to avoid his reach. He pulled me forward and seethed in my face. "What the hell am I paying you for? He hasn't given me shit. I *need* that information and I need it now."

A tendril of defiance brewed in my stomach and rose up as I spat out the words, "Short of torturing him, I don't think I can get you that information."

He dropped his hold on me and lifted his arms triumphantly upward. "Finally, something useful. Get to it."

I blinked slowly. Something in me hoped that I hadn't heard what I thought I had. The look in Billy's eyes, that wicked gleam of success, told me I'd heard right.

"I'm not going to torture anyone."

Each word I spoke, I emphasized with vehemence. I would not be bullied into doing this, not for anyone.

Billy scoffed and then paced back and forth a few times. He lifted a finger to point at me. "You're gonna give me what I want." He paced a few steps again then he abruptly turned, ripping his gun from his side holster to point at me. "You're gonna give me what I want, or I'm going to fucking kill you."

"Billy!" I heard his mother shout from behind him. With my heart hammering in my chest, I stood as still as I could. My lungs constricted as I forced myself to take only small breaths for fear that any greater movement would cause him to pull the trigger.

"Please," I breathed.

The ex-Mrs. Blake charged forward into her son's line of view. "If you kill her, how are we going to get the money?"

Perhaps I would laugh at her complete lack of sympathy later, but for now I was struggling to hear anything as a ringing had started in my ears. My vision became flecked with spots and I realized I may pass out.

"Don't worry, ma," Billy said, his attention never faltering from my face. "She'll do it because she knows how serious I am."

A tear slipped through my lashes. The look on Billy's face told me I wouldn't leave this cemetery alive. My mind raced, trying to think of a way to save myself from this mess. If by some miracle I survived, I would be sure to thank Mark for convincing me to take this job. Billy and I were locked in our standoff, when a voice came from behind me.

"I can do it."

A new wash of icy panic flooded down my spine. My breath hitched in my throat and I had to force myself to keep my attention on the man in front of me. It had been two years since I'd heard that voice, but I'd never forget it.

Heat gently licked up my backside as The Superior glided up beside me. I could see his tall frame in my periphery, and I willed myself not to flinch at his nearness. Billy kept his gun trained on me, but his eyes flicked to the demon beside me.

"Who the fuck are you?" Billy spat.

The Superior took several steps forward, placing himself between me and Billy's gun. Some of the tension in my body eased at no longer being forced to stare down the barrel. I wasn't sure what would happen if Billy shot The Superior, but something in me doubted it would kill him.

"Of course, my help is conditional," The Superior replied, continuing as if Billy hadn't spoken. "I will extract the information from your father and you will either pay Miss Woods double your agreed upon amount or you can owe me a favor."

Billy scoffed. "You work with her then? I see, it's all a game to con me out of more money."

Indignation rolled through me. I stepped forward, a retort ready on my tongue, when The Superior stretched out a hand to block me.

"If I wished to play a game with you, William Blake, I have far more suitable ideas. As for Miss Woods, I am simply offering her my assistance in this matter."

Without thinking, I stepped closer to The Superior and hissed in his ear. "No, I do not want your assistance. I do not accept this favor."

Being indebted to a demon was bad enough, but being indebted to this particular one would likely be the death of me. I knew why he was here, and I'd rather suffer his rage at defying his orders than owe him a favor.

Abruptly, he spun around to face me. His movement stirred the air around us and I was suddenly engulfed in his scent. It was an intoxicating mix of wood, leather, and smoke. His full sensuous lips were tilted upward in a mischievous smile. My gaze flicked down to those lips and when they returned to meet his warm brown eyes, I saw something there I didn't quite recognize. He looked sinister, but also playful in a way that caused a fluttering sensation low in my belly. I wanted to look away, but my eyes were drawn to him. Fixated on him. He was without doubt the most beautiful being I'd ever seen.

"I've been looking for you," he said, the wind tousling his dark wavy hair across his forehead, "But interrupt me again and I will be forced to remove you."

I swallowed and willed myself to speak. "I do not accept this favor."

"Fear not, Miss Woods, you may consider this one a gift."

My eyes widened and before I could voice my protest, he turned back around to Billy.

"What will it be, William?" he asked, completely ignoring me.

Billy asked, "What kind of favor?"

A contemptuous snort fell from my mouth and The Superior cut a glare over his shoulder at me. "Perhaps you would feel better waiting in your car, Miss Woods?"

The tone of his voice brooked no argument. Not having much choice, I turned around and walked to my car.

CHAPTER 5

My fingers drummed the steering wheel as I waited in the enveloping heat of my car. Air whistled through the vents as I idled on the roadside. The Superior and the Blakes stood only a few steps away, but I tried to ignore them. Whatever was happening out in that cemetery no longer involved me. I highly doubted that Billy had agreed to pay me double, which meant I had done all of this for nothing. Less than nothing, as I now had to figure out what a gift from The Superior meant.

I leaned forward, huffing out a sigh. Something hard pressed into my stomach and I remembered I'd tucked my knife into my jacket when Mr. Blake and I had left The Otherworld. Extracting it, I tossed it into the seat beside me. Never before had I needed a weapon for protection from a client. I realized that the thought of using it hadn't even crossed my mind tonight. Not that it would have been any help against Billy's gun, but the thought disturbed me. It had been reflexive to pull the knife earlier in The Otherworld when Gabriel had appeared and yet in the graveyard, I had forgotten all about it. Perhaps I needed to reevaluate my sense of self-preservation.

Pulling my attention back to the cemetery, I looked over at Billy. He prowled in front of his father's soul, his face set in a hard line. Unease swirled in my gut as I wondered where we went from here. He had threatened my life, and I doubted he was simply going to move on from it. I made a mental note to file a restraining order on my way home.

The group suddenly split apart, with the Blakes walking toward their car and The Superior and Mr. Blake's soul remaining behind. I pushed the ignition switch to turn off the car and walked out to meet them. The air outside felt even colder than before, so I burrowed down into my coat and thrust my hands into my pockets. As I approached, the Blakes' car faded from view.

"You may go."

The Superior's voice broke through the stillness. For a moment, I mistakenly thought he spoke to me, but then I saw the soul suddenly stiffen. He turned and immediately walked away in a determinedly straight line.

Realizing I was now alone with the demon sent a wave of goosebumps skittering across my arms. I kept my eyes on my shoes as I waited for him to speak. When he finally did, they weren't the words I had expected.

"The son intends to kill you."

He said it as a statement of fact that did nothing to assuage my own concerns about Billy. Sighing, I replied, "Seems like it."

I could feel his eyes on me, but I kept mine downcast. My teeth worried at my lower lip as I pondered my predicament. Billy would be back, but he was a problem for later. Right now, I needed to be rid of the demon before me.

"You said you were looking for me?"

Another breeze whirled through the cemetery causing me to shudder.

"You need not fear," he said, his voice closer than it had been a moment ago. "I will take care of Billy."

My head snapped up at his words. "No, I don't want to owe you anything."

He was standing much closer to me now and I could see the spark of amusement in his eyes. "Nothing will be owed. Billy and I have struck a deal and I shall see it through."

I stepped back, considering his words. My stomach churned as I wondered to what Billy had agreed. Part of me felt that he deserved it, but another part of me couldn't condemn another human being to the machinations of the being before me. The Superior struck fear into the hearts of other demons. I didn't want to think what horrors he could inflict upon a human.

Swallowing, I finally said, "Ok, but that still doesn't tell me why you were looking for me."

His head tipped to the side as he studied me. He looked perfectly calm, his face blank as his eyes traced me up and down. I didn't know what he was hoping to find, but I started to squirm under his intense scrutiny. Finally, he put me out of my misery.

"You spoke with a demon earlier today. Tell me what happened."

I had assumed he was here to scold me for entering The Otherworld against his wishes. Thinking back on my earlier conversation with the snake demon, I remembered his offer of information on The Superior. Was that why he was here? Did he think I had taken the deal and now had something to use against him?

Clearing my throat, I tried to think of the best way to describe my earlier encounter. "I was approached in the hospital by a snake demon wearing a Johnny suit. He said he had a job for me. Finding some girl. I told him no."

He stared at me for several moments, his brow furrowing as he did. Then, very carefully he said, "A snake demon…wearing a Johnny suit?"

My lips quirked up briefly at the look of confusion on his face. It wasn't an expression I'd seen him make before and something about it amused me. "Yes," I finally returned.

His eyes narrowed momentarily before he said, "Why did you refuse him?"

Without thinking, I said, "Because I don't want to work with a demon."

"And why might that be?" he asked in a lowered voice.

Blowing out a breath I said, "Because none of you can be trusted."

I blinked and he was suddenly before me, hair whipping from the breeze of his movement. His eyes blazed as red flared around his irises. Instinctively, my hand reached for the concealed blade in my jacket, but too late I remembered that I left it in my car. The Superior's hand clamped down painfully on my wrist.

"What might you be reaching for, Claire?"

My heart hammered in my chest. "Does it matter? It's not like anything can hurt you, right?"

The red rimming his irises expanded like flames feeding on a burst of oxygen. His face pressed closer to mine as he said, "Now who can't be trusted?"

With a final squeeze on my arm, he released me and took an abrupt step back. My other hand flew up to encircle my throbbing wrist as I sucked in cold gulps of air. His eyes flicked to my hands before suddenly becoming interested in our surroundings. He scanned the trees and the sky, looking at everything but me. It almost seemed as though seeing me in pain made him feel guilty, but I quickly banished the thought from my mind. He was a demon. Their purpose in life was to inflict pain upon mortals.

"You will work for me," he said finally.

A derisive laugh came out of me. "You're joking, right?"

My eyes scanned his profile as he continued to avoid my gaze. His jaw ticked but he said nothing. I waited, but after several moments of continued silence I huffed out, "Fine, then my answer's no. Have a good night."

Spinning on my heels, I took a step toward my car. As I expected, he moved in front of me, with nostrils flaring and eyes narrowed.

"Did you have something to say?" I asked, my tone more sarcastic than I would have expected given that I was staring down a demon. Technically, staring up a demon as he was several inches taller than me, but it had been a long day, and my fatigue was starting to get the better of me.

"If you find the girl for me, I can offer you my protection for your other situation."

His eyes flicked meaningfully back toward the road where the Blakes had been earlier. Despite my concern over Billy's intentions toward me, I wasn't about to make a bargain with a demon.

I shook my head. "No, I'm not indebting myself to you."

He made a frustrated sound deep in his throat. "I said nothing about a debt. It would be an even exchange of services."

The stress of the day, the lack of food in my stomach, and the general fatigue from my current predicament crashed down on me and a flood of words poured from my mouth. "What is it with everyone not understanding the word no today? No, I will not work for Johnny Snake Demon. No, I will not torture souls and finally no, I will not work for you. Ever."

The molten red color surrounding his irises continued to churn as his right lid twitched. The Superior tipped his head, and the resounding crack of his bones rent through the air. I flinched.

"You are allowing your petty human emotions to cloud your judgment, Claire."

I bristled at the chastened tone he used when he said my name. Shrugging my shoulders, I replied, "If that's all you wanted to see me for, then are we done here?"

He crossed his arms over his chest, and I tried very hard not to notice the strain his biceps put on his shirt. His physique suggested he worked out, which seemed a ridiculous notion for an all-powerful demon, and yet the evidentiary muscles were right in front of my face.

"You have very little choice. Either you accept my offer, and Billy Blake doesn't kill you, or you continue this rebelliousness and end up dead along with the missing girl."

That struck me as odd, so I asked, "Why do you assume the girl will die?"

"Dangerous beings are looking for her, and now, by extension you."

I tipped my head back and groaned. "Why me?"

The sky didn't answer. Light pollution blocked out many of the stars, but I still searched for one to wish upon. There had to be one wish, one tiny possible twist of fate, that could get me out of this predicament. I held onto that idea for only a moment longer, before tipping my head back down. The Superior's irises were still outlined in crimson, but less so now. Looking at him now, I noticed that the churning in my stomach had eased while we'd been talking. I assumed that meant I needed to go home, eat, and get to bed.

"Well," I said, before rubbing at the cold tip of my nose, "If I'm going to die soon, I should probably be off to get my affairs in order. Thanks for the heads up."

I beamed at him, then walked around his menacing figure to my car. This time, he didn't follow me.

CHAPTER 6

The dead woman before me was still trying to find her cat.

"Once again, Mrs. Edelman, you can't take your cats with you," I said, rubbing a hand across my face.

I'd been at this for an hour now, and despite my relief at having a more typical job to distract me from the events four days ago, my patience was wearing thin.

Mrs. Edelman cooed, "Where are you Fluffy? It's time for your medicine, my dear."

Reaching out a hand, I tried to grab onto the soul, but the magazine pile beneath me shifted and I tumbled into the overstuffed bookshelf on my left. My shoulder slammed into the shelf and several books toppled down on me, but I didn't fall. I really didn't want to fall in this place. Stacks of papers, clothes, and trash covered the floor from years of Mrs. Edelman's hoarding, and I didn't want to think about what else I would find down there if I fell.

"Careful, dear, that's how poor Gloria broke her foot."

I huffed indignantly back at her. Gloria's broken foot was why I was the one crawling through this stinking mess.

"I know, Mrs. Edelman, that's why I'm here. Your grandchildren realized you were still in the house when you pushed that stack of books onto Gloria."

Mrs. Edelman sniffed. "She threatened to burn down my house."

I nodded in support while secretly agreeing with Gloria. The smell alone upon entry had hit me so hard I'd spent the first few minutes dry heaving. The structure of the house was undoubtedly suffering as well, and the city had labeled the dwelling a health hazard.

Bypassing that I instead said, "They want you to be able to move on, away from this house. Please, won't you take my hand?"

Inching forward slowly, I extended my hand again.

"Fluffy still needs his medicine," she said before disappearing through a wall of boxes at the end of the hall.

Shoving off the bookshelf, I let out a frustrated groan. "Fluffy isn't here! Your grandchildren have your cats!"

I balanced myself against the wall as I lifted my right foot out of the debris on the floor. A silken garment with questionable brown stains came up with my shoe. Another bout of nausea turned in my stomach while I attempted to flick the clothing off my foot. I made my way slowly down the hall until I reached the stack of boxes through which Mrs. Edelman had disappeared.

The stack went all the way to the ceiling. Peeking left and right, I saw the narrow passageways Mrs. Edelman had built in life to navigate through her home. Not knowing what was on the other side of this wall, I figured I needed to choose a way around, but then something soft brushed against my left leg. Thinking it must be one of her fifteen cats, I looked down, only to find a massive rat. I screamed. Loudly. Abruptly lifting my foot away from the creature, put me off balance, and I fell into the stack of boxes. The top two fell to the floor and exploded open, dumping out an assortment of Christmas decorations.

My breaths flew rapidly in and out as I lay partially over the boxes. I had shifted the entire stack and now that I had, I noticed a strip of molding on the wall. The stack was in front of a doorway. Why would she have closed off a room? Pondering that, I pushed on the stack and managed to drop a few more boxes off the top. Stepping onto the remaining boxes, I reached down for the doorknob and hoped that the door swung inward. While twisting the knob, I shoved my shoulder into the door. It moved a crack. After repeating the process a few more times, I managed to make a gap into the room large enough for me to fit through. Stepping down from the stack, I entered the dark room.

There was hardly any light, so I reached out to the wall hoping to find a light switch. Finally bumping across one on my left side, I flicked it upward only to remain in darkness. A meow sounded from the other side of the room. Shuffling my feet along the floor, I kept my hands on the wall and made my way to the corner. Going along the next wall, I found a window covered by heavy drapes. I pulled them aside and shielded my eyes from the sudden brightness. Sunlight poured into the room that was empty except for an area rug, Mrs. Edelman, and me.

Mrs. Edelman stood transfixed by the middle of the rug. I watched her lips part as she made a meowing sound.

With a tentative step toward her I said, "Mrs. Edelman?"

She said nothing. I moved closer to her, stepping onto the edge of the rug. My power vibrated so painfully in my body that I was forced to step back.

"Mrs. Edelman, what did you do in this room?"

Her head tilted upward and the fear in her eyes sent my pulse racing. I walked forward, until I felt my power surge again, then I moved to the right to see if it continued in a line. The same prick of strange energy hit me. I repeated the movement, and found that my power surged all along the edge of the area rug. When I reached out to Mrs. Edelman, that same painful sensation hit me again.

Standing as close to her as I could, I asked, "What is under this rug?"

Slowly, she turned her head to look at me. "I'm sorry."

With the tip of my shoe, I kicked the area rug upward and managed to get a corner of it to fold over itself. I gasped. Flowing, black demonic script covered the floorboards under the rug in what looked to be a circle. A summoning circle.

My eyes flew wide. "Please tell me you didn't use this."

An answering thump sounded from the underside of the floor. I bolted for the door, avoiding the middle of the room as the pounding from beneath me intensified. My hand latched onto the wood of the door as I heard the splintering crack of the floor behind me. Looking briefly back, I saw a gaping hole and only darkness within it. Mrs. Edelman stood beside it staring at me, her face blank. I turned back to the door and squeezed my right hip through the opening. Another impact sent the entire floor buckling. I lost my footing and with one last crash of wood, the floor opened wide and I fell into blackness.

CHAPTER 7

My back crashed into something hard, and air surged out of my lungs. I gasped in my next breath, wincing from the pain. Looking up, I could see the shimmering outline of a portal. Somehow, there had been a portal to The Otherworld under Mrs. Edelman's house. I wondered how that was possible until a low rumbling growl sounded through the darkness around me.

Right, there was a demon. Slowly, I pushed myself into a seated position. The ground beneath me was soft and full of shifting granules. Sand. I grabbed a fistful of it and waited while silently pleading for some light. A familiar sensation of magic touched my right hand, and I slowly stretched outward until I brushed against something metal. Wrapping my fingers around it, I felt the cold cylinder and realized it was a flashlight. I whispered my thanks to Nicky before pressing the button that flooded the other side of the chamber with light.

A yelp slipped past my lips as I took in the other occupant of the cave. The fact that I was sitting in a cave was less concerning to me than the massive cat-like demon standing a few feet away. Calling it a cat was somewhat generous. It stood on four legs, had a tail and whiskers, but otherwise the abomination before me was something entirely demonic. Small beady black eyes looked me over as drool dripped from its long, razor-sharp teeth. Its ears were massive and protruded above its head of spikes like a donkey's. From the ground, I had to look far up to see its face, and I guessed that if I stood, I would only reach its shoulder.

Very slowly I pulled my knees up to my chin. The demon tilted its head, regarding my movement before it said, "Don't try to run."

Its deep voice rumbled the stone walls around me. I sucked in a shuddering breath. "What do you want from me?"

The demon sat down on its haunches, and I could see that it had a mostly human torso. The contrast of skin and fur caused my stomach to turn so I moved the light back to the creature's face.

"I want you to sit here until they arrive."

They? One demon was bad enough, I wasn't going to wait for more to show up. With a burst of speed, I launched onto my feet. The demon shifted to the left and growled menacingly back at me. I flicked the flashlight past the creature and saw a dark tunnel. *Thank you for showing me the way out.* Shifting my weight forward as if readying myself to run, the cat demon fell for my feint and lunged toward me. My left hand swung around, and I tossed my fistful of sand into its face. The creature yowled and rubbed furiously at its eyes, while I darted past it and into the dark tunnel.

My steps were sluggish at first, sinking into deep sand, but eventually the ground beneath me shifted upward and became solid rock. Unfortunately, that meant my pounding footsteps echoed all the way down the tunnel. An enraged roar shook the walls around me, and I picked up my pace.

A pinprick of light appeared ahead of me, and I pushed myself hard toward it. I was panting by the time I burst out of the cave and into the brilliant sunlight. Tears tracked down my face as I blinked furiously, trying to adjust to the sudden brightness. The air around me was hot and dry and I felt the grit of sand coasting across my skin in the breeze. Finally, my vision cleared enough for me to see my surroundings. I was in a bazaar filled with wooden walls and brightly colored canopies. Each shop was brimming with different wares and food that spilled out onto the narrow street. I made my way through to the crossroad at the end. Two identical paths lay to either side of me. A crash sounded behind me, followed by a frustrated roar as the demon leapt from the cave and slammed into the first stall. I ran to the left.

My feet pounded on the sand slicked stone as I weaved around the cluttered streets. Ahead of me the path was blocked by a large wooden cart. Air rushed in and out of my lungs, burning down my throat as I raced toward it. When I reached the wagon, I dove under it and popped back up on the other side. I was immediately hit with the smell of rot coming from the decaying cabbages that filled the cart. Bile rose in my throat as movement at the end of the street caught my attention. The cat demon came hurtling around the corner, its massive wings banking expertly through the narrow space.

"What kind of fucking cat are you?" I shouted, before I took off down the next street. Looking up, I saw that all the shops looked exactly the same. Great, I thought, I'm trapped in a maze with a flying demon. I cursed under my breath at the sight of another wagon filled with cabbages blocking the path. Dropping onto my knees, I ducked my head to slide underneath the obstruction. A massive paw clamped down on my shoulder and several spots of sharp pain shot across my back. I slammed down onto the street and looked up into a muzzled demon face.

"I told you not to run."

The demon lifted its claws to its lips and a pink and black tongue darted out to clean off my blood. I groaned and turned my head away. A loud pop sounded through the air. Turning toward the cat demon, I screamed as I watched its face, now covered in a bright green gel, melting as if it were covered in acid. Two more pops sounded, and the cat was hit twice more. I scrambled away from him and whipped my head around to search for the assailant. Something shifted at the end of the road. A large dark blue canopy was suddenly filled with a massive snakehead with two glowing green eyes. Slowly, the snake moved out of the darkness, and I felt my heart spike up in my chest. The demon was so massive, its body struggled to fit down the narrow pathway. As it slithered closer, its body collided with the walls of the bazaar. The sun glistened off its blue-green scales as its overlarge head came down to inspect me. It graced me with a quick flick of its tongue before moving to assess its victim. The cat demon didn't move. The snake opened its mouth and worked its throat until it produced a ball of green venom which it shot at the other demon. The chest of the cat demon started melting just like its head had done earlier.

Twin pools of swirling green came to stare into my face. Human intelligence examined me through those eyes right before its tongue darted out to touch me again. I flinched away from it. A horrible rasping hiss choked out of its throat. "You don't look happy to see me again."

I tilted my head and narrowed my eyes. Then it hit me. "Johnny Snake Demon?"

The demon made that terrible hissing sound again and I realized he was laughing at me.

"Sure," he said, laughter still present in his voice, "We can go with that."

Dropping onto my butt in the sand, I looked him over. "Gotta tell you, I prefer the Johnny suit."

The head snapped back as if slapped. Then he opened the gaping maw of his mouth wide and flicked down two massive fangs. His red tongue danced between them and then he winked at me.

"Impressive," I said flatly.

He retracted the fangs and then flicked his head to the right. "Come on, there's a portal this way." Despite the wall of bazaar stalls, the snake demon plowed straight through them as if they were paper.

Continuous crashing sounds and a cloud of dust marked his path. Pushing myself upward took far more effort than it should have. The wounds in my back were starting to throb and the heat from the sun beating down on me did nothing to ease the pain. Sweat trickled down my face as I took my first tentative step. The path of destruction left by the demon was easy enough to follow, if not slightly treacherous, from the piles of debris. I moved slowly and purposefully along, focusing intently on my feet.

As I walked, I had time to consider my situation. There was no way that Johnny's appearance was random. Either he was working with the cat demon and had killed him to indebt me to him, or he had followed me. I didn't care which it was, because either way, he had just saved my life, and that meant a debt was owed.

Finally, I took one last staggering step and saw the snake wrapped around a portal. "After you," he said, elegantly gesturing with the tip of his tail. Shuffling forward, I adopted a limp and visibly winced several times. If he believed I was injured, perhaps I could surprise him on the other side of the portal. After stepping through, I was welcomed back by the night sky and a blast of cold air. The cool breeze froze the sweat on my skin and eased the throbbing of my wounds.

Strong hands wrapped around my arms from behind. "I have someone who can patch you right up," Johnny whispered into my ear. His grip tightened uncomfortably.

I started shivering. It was November, and I was outside without a jacket, but that wasn't the cause of my reaction. There was no way I was going anywhere with him. I stuttered out, "N-No, thank you."

"You don't mean that." His silky voice sent a shudder down my spine. He brushed his nose along my neck. "And afterward, we can have a little chat about that job you're going to do for me."

A strangled cry squeaked out of me. My back was beginning to hurt in earnest, and the cold air had stuck my shirt into my wounds. I had bled more than I realized. All thoughts of running faded from my mind as I desperately tried to think of another plan.

The click of a safety being disengaged sounded from my left. I blinked and then the gunshot blasted through the air. The hold on my arms dropped as Johnny fell to the ground behind me. My ears rang as I turned to see a tall man holding a smoking pistol mere feet from me. His eyes were a crystal-clear blue set against long, jet black hair that was shaved along the sides. Most of his free skin was covered in tattoos and or piercings and I knew that when he smiled, he had the brightest, whitest teeth.

"Mark, what the hell are you doing here? With a gun?" I shouted.

He flicked the safety back on and tucked the pistol into the band of his black jeans. Then he raised a finger to his lips. "Stop yelling."

His words were muddled as if they came through water. I pointed angrily at my ears, but the motion pulled the injured skin on my back. A yell tore from my mouth and Mark dove to my side. I heard him cursing when he saw my wounds.

"Hospital?" he asked, when he came to stand in front of me again.

I shook my head. He glared at me, then took out his phone and pulled up one of his contacts. Turning the phone to me, he showed me the name and I nodded. He shook his head several times before he tapped a button on the screen and lifted the device to his ear. Gesturing toward his car, he extended a hand to help me balance while holding the phone with his other shoulder.

Mark's lips moved, but his words were still muffled. Glancing briefly over my shoulder, I saw the portal and a pool of blood. Johnny's body was gone. Apparently, a gunshot to the head wasn't enough to kill a demon.

"He's going to be so pissed," I whispered.

Hanging up the phone and shoving it into his pocket, Mark pulled me gently forward. "That's a problem for another day."

His words were slightly easier to hear this time. "That is a massive problem, Mark. What the hell were you thinking?"

He walked backward in front of me, continuing to balance my hands while occasionally checking the path behind him. "I was *thinking* you were in trouble."

I ignored the condescension in his voice. "How did you find me anyway?"

Mark's head flicked behind him. "Mrs. Edelman's house isn't far from here. When you didn't check in after the job, I came by. I saw your car, but no you."

A warmth spread through my chest, and I smiled. "Best assistant ever. But seriously, you should probably lay low for a few days. You did shoot a gun in the middle of a populated area."

We stepped onto the street and Mark clicked the button to unlock his truck. Moving around to the passenger side, he opened the door to the back. I paused with my hand on the doorframe. Something brushed across my senses, and when I looked down the street, I saw Mrs. Edelman. Her soul stood in the flood of a streetlight, but she made no move toward me. She simply stood and stared as I climbed into the car.

"Hi, Nancy."

I plastered the biggest smile I could muster onto my face as I leaned heavily into Mark's side.

Nancy stood in her doorway with her arms crossed and her eyes narrowed. She was still wearing her scrubs and her usually tame, tight curls were a frizzy mess. I was guessing she'd just come off a long shift at the hospital.

She pursed her lips as she looked me over. "What did you do?" she asked, her tone scolding.

Wincing, I turned and showed her my back. "*I* didn't do anything."

With an eyeroll, she stepped aside and gestured for us to enter. I walked over to her kitchen table and sat down. Nancy came up with her medical bag and dropped roughly into the chair beside me. Mark parked himself on her couch and started searching for the remote.

"What did this to you?"

Avoiding her eyes, I deflected. "Does it look that bad?"

"A demon," Mark called from the couch, not looking back at us while he scanned through Nancy's apps. I glared at the side of his head. Nancy raised her brows at me, but when I said nothing, she went to work assessing my injuries.

"Shirt's ruined," she replied, "Might be easier for me to just cut it off. That okay with you?"

I nodded and she rose and walked down the hallway that I knew led to her bedroom. She returned with a new shirt that she placed on my lap. Sitting back down, she pulled out a pair of shears from her medical kit and made quick work of the fabric across my back. She threw the useless heap onto the floor.

"Fine for me to unhook your bra?" she asked.

"Yeah," I said, then tentatively asked, "How bad is it?"

Nancy shrugged before placing the scissors back in her kit and started rooting around for her next tool. "Four incisions, each about five inches long, mostly shallow cuts. I'll need to stitch a few spots, but otherwise we just need to clean them and bandage them."

A sigh of relief flew out of me, right before Nancy jabbed me with a needle.

"Some local anesthetic," she said simply.

"A little warning would have been nice."

A second jab stung me, and I winced. Nancy leaned into my peripheral vision. "Oh, I'm sorry, would you rather go to the hospital and have someone stitch you up there? You know, someone who is actually being paid for their time?"

"No," I sighed, "Thank you for helping."

Nancy smirked and thankfully set down the needle. "Now while that sets for a bit, you can pay me back by telling me everything."

Her chair screeched in protest as she slid it across the kitchen tiles. She bounced giddily in her seat while her eyes bore into mine.

"Sometimes I forget how insane you are," I said in response.

She slapped playfully at my knee. "Come on, tell me what you did to piss this demon off."

I scoffed. "How do you know I pissed it off? Maybe I was just in the wrong place at the wrong time."

Mark chose that moment to chime in. "I don't know, he looked pretty pissed right before I shot him."

Nancy almost fell out of her chair. She looked at me, wide eyed with an almost deranged smile on her face. "Okay, now you *absolutely* have to tell me everything. Tell me or else I'll start stitching before the anesthetic sets in." To emphasize her point, she poked me roughly in the back with her finger. I yelped.

"Your demon obsession is unhealthy."

The gleam in her eyes didn't dim as she moved to rest her chin in her hands. I had expected this response and if I hadn't needed help with the wounds on my back, I would have never involved Nancy. While being a talented physician, Nancy also had a fascination with the demonic. Our first encounter had been under similar circumstances, when I'd gone to the emergency room for a broken wrist. If I hadn't also been soaking wet on a perfectly sunny day, she might not have questioned me so hard. As it was, Nancy found my story suspicious and had followed up at my office several days later. She'd discovered my talents and instead of running off assuming I was insane, she'd dropped down into my client's chair and spent the entire day questioning me about my life. After that, she kept coming back and somehow that had morphed into friendship.

"Fine," I said with a sigh and proceeded to tell her everything while she stitched my wounds. I told her about my first encounter with Johnny Snake Demon and my subsequent trip through Mrs. Edelman's floor. Purposefully, I neglected to mention anything about The Superior. His involvement in all this was still a mystery to me and until it became necessary, I didn't want Nancy getting any ideas about him.

After she finished stitching and cleaning my back, Nancy placed some bandages over my wounds and gave me some pain pills. While I pulled on the shirt she'd given me, she said, "Why don't you go lay down for a bit?"

She flicked her head toward her guest bedroom. "That way Mark can go home, and I can keep an eye on you."

Mark was currently snoring on the couch. Glancing down at my phone, I saw that it was past eleven at night. Nodding, I stood, feeling pleasantly numb and suddenly very tired. I walked down the hallway and just managed to pull off my pants before I fell into the bed.

CHAPTER 8

A knock sounded on the door. With a groan, I rolled over in the bed only to wince as I turned onto my back. My injuries felt tender as I slowly maneuvered myself over to the bedside table. I looked at the time on my phone. Six in the morning. Glancing out the window, I saw that it was still dark outside. Rubbing my hands down my face. I mumbled, "Yeah?"

The door swung open slowly and Nancy's head popped in. "Hey, I'm heading to work in a bit, but I wanted to check you before I went."

I sat up and nodded. She pushed into the room and set her medical kit down on the bed. My clothes had been ruined or dirty, so I'd slept in what Nancy had given me. Looking down, I saw I was wearing a faded *Elf* shirt. I snorted. "Of course, you put me in your tacky holiday pjs."

Nancy dropped onto the bed beside me. "For someone asking me for free medical care, you're being awfully judgmental. Now lift up your shirt so I can change your bandages."

While working to remove the bandages, she commented, "Everything is healing nicely. Demon must have cleaned his claws beforehand."

Wincing at the memory of my last moments with the cat demon, I mumbled, "Yeah, thank goodness."

"I'll clean you up and get you rebandaged. You should be good to head to work after."

She worked quickly and quietly. The longer her silence stretched on, the more I suspected something was off. Clearing my throat, I said, "Thank you, again. For, well, for everything."

"No worries."

Looking back over my shoulder I saw her pull some fresh gauze out of her bag. She turned determinedly back to her task. Perhaps she was simply focused, but a small seed of worry started to grow in my stomach.

After a few more minutes she said, "Finished. You can find another less offensive outfit to wear in my closet. I'll meet you in the kitchen for some coffee."

She stood abruptly and left the room. With a sigh, I stood from the bed and walked across the hallway. Nancy's bedroom was minimally furnished. There was a bed, two nightstands, and a dresser. Heavy blackout curtains and a stock painting of a field were the only things on the walls. Spending so little time at home, Nancy never cared to decorate. I stepped into her closet and found a gray sweater dress and threw it on.

I walked into the kitchen to find Nancy sitting at the table, clasping a mug in her hands. Her eyes lit up upon seeing me and I watched her lips twitch, trying to contain a smile. Sitting in the chair opposite her, I shifted nervously in my seat.

"Nancy, what's going on?"

Pressing her lips together, she rose from her chair and grabbed another mug of coffee. After she set it on the table before me, she sat back down and crossed her legs. "You had a visitor."

"What?" I sputtered.

Her lips finally spread into a wide grin. "A visitor. Last night after you fell asleep."

I lifted the coffee and blew across the top, trying to think who it could have been. No one immediately came to mind, so I shook my head back at her. Slipping a hand into her scrub pocket, she produced a small white envelope. She placed it on the table and slid it toward me. My name was scrawled on the front in elegant cursive.

For a moment, my heart stopped. I blinked several times before looking at Nancy. She was practically bouncing in her chair. There was only one thing that made Nancy that excited.

"Was it a demon?" I managed to ask in a calm tone.

"Yes!" She practically screamed the word at me.

"Nancy," I sighed, "Most people don't consider that to be a good thing."

She waved her hand dismissively. "Most people are boring. Now this? This is exciting."

I rolled my eyes and took a sip of my coffee. The burn helped to ground me as my mind raced. Assuming the note hadn't been left by a yet unknown third demon, that left me with two options. One of those had been shot in the head yesterday. He had gotten away from that injury, somehow, but I doubted that after that he'd be the type to leave an elegantly written note. That left me one option.

With a resigned exhalation, I set down my coffee mug and picked up the paper. "Did the demon give you a name?"

Looking over at Nancy, she bobbed her head several times, then propped her elbows onto the table. She set her chin in her hands and smiled at me. "You have some explaining to do, my friend. How could you neglect to mention that you know *The Superior*? And oh, by the way, he's *gorgeous*?"

I brought my free hand to my forehead and stared incredulously back at her. "He dropped it off himself? He was here?"

Nancy nodded. "He stopped by a few hours after you went to sleep."

My mind raced. The Superior had been here. He'd spoken to Nancy. Nancy. I had put her in danger by coming here. The thought of demons using my friends against me had never even crossed my mind. My stomach sank low as guilt weighed down my shoulders.

"Did he threaten you?" I finally asked.

She scoffed. "So, you're just going to ignore my questions, then? We're not going to acknowledge the godlike man in your life?"

I glared back at her. Nancy scooped up her coffee and took a sip. She leaned back in her seat and patiently waited for me to continue.

"Fine," I said with a huff, "He's attractive, but he's not a man, Nancy. Don't forget that."

"Not a man, but a super sexy demon, excuse me," she said, before glancing down at her watch, "Oh shit, I have to go soon. Open it!"

"Nancy," I shouted, setting my mug down so forcefully, some of the liquid spilled over the top and onto my hand. I grabbed a napkin and started wiping it up. "This isn't a joke. Did he threaten you?"

She stood and ran some water over a paper towel. Returning to the table, she placed the cool towel on my hand and shook her head. "He was fine. Nice, even. He didn't want to wake you, so he left the note instead."

Her tone was calmer than before. I nodded, satisfied that she was now taking me seriously, and flicked the note open.

I warned you of the danger.
You will accept my assistance the next time I see you.
-S

"Damn," she said, reading the message over my shoulder, "I was hoping it was a love letter."

I snorted derisively and she laughed.

"Come on," she said, moving to place her mug into the sink, "I can drop you off at your car before I head to work."

She left me alone in the kitchen while she finished getting ready. I stared down at the words on the paper. The Superior may not have threatened my friend, but there was no missing the threat here. This situation with the demons wasn't going away and if the gashes across my back were any indication, the beings chasing me weren't above using violence to gain my cooperation. How far would they be willing to push me to get what they wanted?

Crumpling the note in my hand, I tossed the paper into the trash and headed toward my room. If I was going to be forced into taking this job, I needed to find out some more information. Luckily, my car was currently parked outside of the house of a soul that I'd been wanting to question anyway.

An hour later, I was once again knee deep in Mrs. Edelman's shit. I'd checked every room and still there was no sign of the mischievous soul. There was a chance that she had gone through a portal, but after seeing her last night, I had a sneaking suspicion she was still around.

"Mrs. Edelman," I called out to the room as I shifted a mountain of clothes to the side. There was a window a few steps in front of me, so I clambered through the hoard to reach the sill. Sliding it open, I sucked in a lungful of crisp, fresh air. The smell in the house had not improved and I chided myself for not grabbing a mask at Nancy's before we left.

Movement near my car caught my attention. Glancing down, I saw a figure hunching down by the driver's side.

"Can I help you?" I yelled.

The figure jumped as if startled, then walked around to the front of the car. A soft glow told me it was a soul before I could see their face. Once they moved closer, I saw who it was and smiled. Mrs. Edelman.

I made my way downstairs with some difficulty, but I eventually managed to reach the front door. Thankfully, I was able to retrieve my coat and mittens after having left them behind yesterday. Stepping onto the porch, I turned to face Mrs. Edelman, with my arms crossed over my chest.

"I'm sorry," she said.

The desire to latch onto her and force her to answer my questions rose in me like a tidal wave. I suppressed that urge in favor of sucking my teeth and narrowing my eyes at her.

"You're sorry?"

She nodded her head vigorously and I noticed that her hair was thinner than it had been yesterday. Her eyes were sunken, and her face was gaunt. Souls never usually looked good or bad, and they certainly didn't change, but somehow, Mrs. Edelman looked worse than she had yesterday.

"Yes, I needed to speak with you before I left."

Her current state still intrigued me, but I returned my attention to my questions. I said, "Speak with me? Like explaining what the hell that was yesterday?"

She visibly shook as if cold. "I made a deal with the wrong people. They were going to take my house. I had to do something."

I nodded but stayed silent.

"I didn't want to leave my house, and when my kids showed up and threatened to burn it down, well, I panicked. I found someone who said they could help, but they said a human had to draw the circle. I gave them my son's information. They reached out to him, claiming they could free me from the house if he drew it. He didn't know any better."

My lips twitched downward as I clenched my jaw. "You contacted demons because you didn't want to cross over and then willingly used your son to summon a demon?"

Her hands clenched into fists at her sides. "They were going to level my house!"

"You're dead!" I seethed, throwing my hands out to the side. "And now your son is in danger."

"No," she countered, stepping forward, "No, they said once he summoned the demon, it would lie in wait under the house until he contacted you. His part in this is over."

I rolled my eyes but didn't say anything. She was getting to the part of the story I was most interested in, and I needed her to keep going.

"They promised me if I led you to the circle, the demon would capture you, but nothing bad would happen."

My hands rose to clasp onto my head as I shook it back and forth. "Oh, Mrs. Edelman, how could you be so naïve?"

"I didn't think they could break their word once given, and then they go and rip up my floor after saying they'd protect my house."

Tilting my head back up, I stared incredulously back at the soul. Her fists were on her hips now as she looked over the house looming behind me. Apparently, the wellbeing of her home trumped my own. Perhaps if it had been an exceptionally nice house, I could have forgiven her for that, but as it was, I needed a gas mask to enter her home.

"But you see, I overheard them talking," she continued, unconcerned with my current feelings toward her. "And I heard them say a few things about you. They said they needed you to find the girl because there's a connection between you."

With a shake of my head, I stepped closer to her. "What connection?"

The soul before me shrugged, "I don't know, but they said you, the girl, and someone called The Superior were all connected."

My body went rigid. Air fled from my lungs as my pulse started to pound in my ears. "What?" I whispered.

Mrs. Edelman nodded. "That's what they said. Judging by your face that must mean something to you." Stepping forward, she attempted to place her hand upon my shoulder, but she passed through leaving a chill in her wake. "I'm sorry they hurt you. And now I hope you make them sorry for wrecking my floor."

With that, she moved around me and went inside the house. I stood there, blinking slowly. There was a connection between me and The Superior? Not only us, but the missing girl, too? I couldn't fathom a connection between myself and the demon, but I did know what it meant. I was well and truly fucked.

CHAPTER 9

The words on my computer screen blurred. I rubbed my eyes with the palms of my hands while stifling another yawn. Looking at the clock in the bottom corner, I saw that it was after five. A glance out the one small window in the office told me it was already dark outside. The lights from the businesses across the street already blazed.

With a sigh, I finished inputting my hours into the spreadsheet and sent an update for tomorrow to Mark. He'd been out of the office since I'd been injured, lying low in case Johnny Snake Demon showed up. At the time, it had seemed like the best idea, but weirdly, even after only three days I was starting to miss his presence in the office. I stretched my arms upward and felt the slight tug of the wounds on my back. They were scabbed and healing, but they occasionally felt a bit itchy.

One last tap on the screen and then I shut the laptop and slipped it into my bag. Switching my office shoes for snow boots, I stood up from my chair and moved to the tiny coat closet by the door. My ridiculously puffy jacket was a welcome barrier to the cold air outside.

On the drive home, my attention darted to every movement along the roadway. Neither Johnny nor The

Superior had approached me in three days. I knew they would eventually and until one of them showed, I was jumping at everything. My research into the missing girl hadn't turned up any answers either. Searching the missing persons lists, I hadn't seen anyone familiar. Perhaps she hadn't been officially reported yet. I didn't have enough information on my own to find her. At this point, I had more questions than answers, but I was coming to terms with the fact that I was somehow inextricably involved.

Pulling into my driveway, I parked the car and pressed my fingers into the crease between my brows. Tension radiated through my head and shoulders. My stomach grumbled as I grabbed my bag and took my phone off the charger. I stepped outside and inhaled the crisp night air.

A figure sitting on my front porch moved to stand. The night was dark and I hadn't left any lights on, so I couldn't see anything other than a dark outline. While peering up at them, I missed the person behind me.

"Turn around slowly."

The hairs along my skin rose at the familiar voice. As I shuffled around, I hit the emergency call button on my phone and tucked it into my jacket pocket. Sucking in a breath, I lifted my arms as I was once again confronted with Billy Blake's gun.

Most of his face was cast in shadows, but there was enough light for me to see his satisfied smirk. "Hello, Miss Woods."

I swallowed. "Hello, Mr. Blake."

His gaze quickly flicked past my shoulder. He nodded his head, and I heard footsteps descending my front stairs. The person from the porch was moving up behind me. The privacy afforded to me by my tree-lined property suddenly felt suffocating. Unless someone pulled into my driveway, no one could see what was happening to me.

Billy stepped closer. "What game are you playing at?"

Shaking my head slowly, I said. "I don't know what you're talking about."

He chuckled. "You think I don't know a setup when I see one? I'm supposed to believe that demon friend of yours just happened to show up? Bullshit."

The tension in my body escalated as I tried to form a coherent reply. My arms started to shake as I continued holding them in front of me. Explaining to Billy that I wasn't friends with that demon would get me nowhere.

I licked my lips. "I don't want anything from you, Billy. I just want to go home."

Billy spat on the ground. "What's your cut?"

Raising my brow, I carefully shook my head back and forth. "What cut?"

"The money, bitch, how much are you gettin'?"

Irritation trickled up my spine. "I'm not getting anything. If you recall, your deal wiped away my fee."

"You walked away from that fee awful fast once your demon friend showed up."

I was starting to lose feeling in my fingertips. Billy was still pointing his gun at me, but he was talking, which had to mean he wanted something from me. I hoped whatever it was, it was enough motivation to keep him talking. My emergency call had to be connected by now, but I needed time for the authorities to arrive.

"What do you want from me?" I asked simply.

He narrowed his eyes and ran his tongue along his teeth. Somewhere in my yard a bird cried out. "I want my money."

My head tipped to the side. "What money?"

His nostrils flared before he dropped the gun and grabbed my coat with his other hand. He fisted the fabric and pulled me into his chest. I could smell the cigarettes on his breath as he spat, "What money? My fucking money! That demon got my father to tell me where his bastard daughter was, but when I go to find her, guess what? She's gone, along with my money."

The bird called out again, louder this time. Billy glanced up and his eyes narrowed. He looked at his companion. "What the hell is that?"

I tried to turn and see it for myself, but Billy tightened his hold on me. With his other hand, he raised the gun over my shoulder. A chill washed down my spine. Whoever or whatever he was pointing the weapon at wasn't coming from the road where the authorities would be. I tried twisting again and Billy moved his gun to the center of my chest.

"Come any closer and I'll shoot her."

Sucking in a breath, I slammed my eyes shut and waited. There was a shuffling sound from behind me, then an inhuman shriek. I shuddered at the noise just before something collided into my back. I tipped forward, falling as Billy's gun shifted upward to my shoulder. Pain exploded across my chest with the resounding bang of the weapon discharging.

Billy's eyes flew wide as we collided. Our momentum carried us all downward until we landed in a heap on the ground. I cried out as the weight on top of me pressed onto my wounded shoulder. Blood poured hot and slick from where I had been shot. My breaths came quick and short as I fought against the pain. Kicking my legs, I tried to free myself from the middle of the macabre sandwich I'd landed in. Suddenly, the weight on my back was gone and I felt myself being gently rolled off Billy. I landed beside him, and my face turned in time to see his eyes widen with horror right before he was thrown upward into the air.

Cool air fanned across my face as I continued to pant on the ground. Rocks and asphalt pressed into my skin as I searched the world around me. I didn't see or hear anything. Slowly moving my right hand downward, I found my pocket and pulled out my phone. The screen was black, but the call to emergency services had been placed. Dropping it next to my face, I attempted to push myself upward into a sitting position. Pain shot through my side and my vision swam with black spots. I managed to flip onto my back. I stared up at the stars and tried to focus on simply breathing in and out. In and out. The wetness of my blood continued to trickle across my chest. I'd have to buy a new coat. I loved this jacket. In and out. In and out.

Something slammed into my side. Blood splattered across my face as I started to roll down the driveway. My vision flashed with white as pain shot through me. I bounced along the asphalt, unable to control my movements. The last thing I saw was the giant boulder at the end of the drive. My head slammed into it, filling my world with darkness. I heard screaming, followed by maniacal laughter. Then, nothing.

CHAPTER 10

A sudden jolt of pain told me I was alive. Everything was dark as I worked to open my eyes. My lids were heavy as though coming out of a very deep slumber. Finally managing to open them a crack, I was assaulted by blinding light. I tried to lift my left arm to block the offensive brightness, but it was mostly unresponsive. Attempting to move it had caused another sharp stab of pain in my chest. I groaned.

"Wait, I'll get the lights."

The voice came from somewhere to my right. It took me a second, but then I remembered.

"Mark?"

My tongue smacked loudly in my dry mouth. That single word had dragged its way up my throat and ended in a croak. I opened my eyes again and saw that the room was now more suitably dim. Blinking rapidly a few times finally brought Mark's face into focus.

"Want me to raise the bed a little?"

I nodded, not wanting to try my throat again. The mechanical whir of the bed started, and it carefully pushed me upward. More pain went through my chest. When the bed stopped, I unsurprisingly discovered I was in a hospital room. The memory of being shot by Billy Blake was clear, but what had happened afterward was not.

Looking to my right, I watched Mark settle into the visitor chair by my bed. His eyes were rimmed in dark circles and his hair was uncharacteristically disheveled. I opened my mouth to ask him when he'd last slept when I noticed the windowsill behind him. On it was a huge vase full of flowers. The beautiful bouquet was filled with carefully arranged blooms that looked ridiculously expensive. Mark followed my line of sight and looked back at me with a serious expression. "You've had an admirer while you've been out."

My eyes widened as I tested out saying, "Who?"

The word was more understandable than earlier, but the attempt caused me to start coughing. Mark walked around my bed and poured some water from a pitcher. He handed me the cup with a long straw, and I happily took a sip.

Mark sat back down and said, "Well, he wouldn't give me his name, looked at me like I was a bug, and is definitely not human."

I spluttered and coughed. There went my brief hope at normalcy. My dating life had never been stellar, but for a few seconds there I had been able to delude myself into thinking a man had sent the flowers. With the stark reality of my circumstances thrown back in my face, I sighed and stared at the vase.

"He is also the most attractive man I've ever seen," Mark added almost absently.

Dammit. I rolled my eyes upward and dropped my head back onto the pillow. There was one demon who always seemed to get that description. I heard Mark's smile in his voice as he said, "Looks like you might know who that is."

Clearing my throat, I managed to say, "Superior."

"Woah."

My eyes were on the ceiling, but I could feel the tension ratchet up in both of us at the mention of that name. Rolling my head to look over at him I said, "Tell me what happened."

He leaned forward, his brow pinched and his eyes serious. "You got shot."

I gestured rudely at him, and he laughed.

"Dispatch got your call. They could only hear muffled voices and then the call disconnected, but you know, once they get a call they go. Once they got there, they found you at the end of the driveway, bleeding from several places and what looked like a massacre on your front lawn. They got you patched up. Bullet went through your chest, clean out the back. Luckily, they got you here in time. Been in surgery for the past several hours."

"How long have I been out?" I asked, happy to hear that my voice was almost back to normal.

Mark pulled out his phone. "It's noon, so not quite a day."

Almost a day. I'd lost almost a day of my life, and yet, I had been fortunate. If I hadn't hit the call button on my phone, I shuddered at the thought of where I would be. Reaching to set the water cup on the bedside table, my arm felt leaden. I felt weak and the throbbing in my shoulder was starting to compete with the ache in my head.

Mark shifted forward, grabbing the cup and setting it down for me. "Don't move so much."

He settled back into his chair and scratched at the shaved part of his head. A crease formed in his brow as he asked, "What happened?"

I swallowed and cleared my throat. "Billy." The word came out with less difficulty, so thankfully I was able to continue. "He thinks I stole from him, so he shot me."

Mark was chewing on his bottom lip. His eyes widened and then dipped away from mine. "I'm so sorry, Claire. This is all my fault."

Shifting in the bed, I attempted to turn to face him, but the movement sent a sharp pain through my left side. I grabbed my shoulder and twisted toward him as best I could.

"None of this is your fault."

His eyes briefly met mine, before darting away again. "If I hadn't forced you to take that job, none of this would have happened."

I stretched my fingers out to him, but only managed to lightly brush his knee. "Mark, you are not the one who shot me, Billy is. He's the only one to blame in all of this."

He still wouldn't meet my eyes. With an exaggerated sigh, I said, "Fine. If you wish to assuage some of your guilt, could you call a nurse for me? My head feels like it's about to explode."

A huff of laughter fell out of him, and he looked up at me with watery eyes. With a swipe of his hand across his cheeks, he rose and stepped out of the room.

I was alone for a mere moment, before a nurse came in followed by Mark and two police officers. While the nurse checked my vitals and attached an IV of pain medication, the cops asked me questions. I told them everything except my suspicion that my blurry savior had been a demon. They were familiar enough with Billy to know he had enemies, but the amount of blood at the scene seemed to give them pause. After several rounds of questions, the nurse returned to inform them that I needed rest. They closed their notebooks and told me while they searched for Billy they would be stationing a guard outside my room. I nodded my thanks.

As the officers were leaving, the nurse came over to fluff my pillows. She smiled down at me and whispered, "Your boyfriend's here."

Looking up at her, I noticed her cheeks were flushed. My lips parted, ready to ask her what the hell she was talking about, when my door swung open.

The Superior stepped in, and I instantly understood why my nurse had been so flushed. His dark hair was brushed back, but with tendrils of it breaking free to frame his face. He was wearing a hunter green turtleneck underneath a long charcoal colored coat. Everything on him looked expensive and tailored to fit him perfectly, but it wasn't his outfit that had drawn her in. He was smiling. His entire face looked warm and welcoming, and my jaw dropped at the sharp transformation.

The nurse stepped in front of him, chatting so quietly I couldn't hear her. He smiled down at her, and she giggled before brushing a strand of hair behind her ear. She gestured toward me and then stepped out of the room. The Superior turned that dazzling grin toward me before his eyes slid to my right. Mark had settled back into the visitor's chair beside me and was currently chewing on a candy bar. All the warmth and congeniality instantly melted from The Superior's face as his eyes flashed with red.

"Get out."

He said the words in a low tone that sent shivers down my spine. Mark froze like a deer in headlights. Sucking in a fortifying breath, I gestured with a hand toward Mark and said, "He's my guest. I want him here."

The Superior paid no attention to me as he took several steps further into the room. Heat washed over me as he stopped next to Mark and glared down at him. Mark shifted uncomfortably for a moment, before shakily rising from his seat. Looking over at me, he gestured toward the door. "I'll just be going."

I opened my mouth to object, but he shook his head. He grabbed his bag off the floor and stepped carefully around the demon. Mark was tall, but The Superior had a few inches on him. He was currently using every bit of that height difference to stare menacingly down at Mark. Sweeping around the end of my bed, Mark placed a hand on my foot and gave it a quick squeeze. "I'll just go grab something in the café." He threw his bag over his shoulder and left.

With a sigh, I said, "That was rude."

Refusing to look at The Superior, I instead stared longingly at a fruit bowl the hospital staff had brought in. It was sitting on my bedside table, which was unfortunately just slightly out of my reach. I licked my lips and wondered if I could reach it with my foot.

Hands appeared around the table and pushed it closer to me, then held out a fork. Snatching it quickly, I mumbled, "Why are you here?"

The bed dipped beside my legs, and I looked up in horror to see him sitting down beside me. I shifted over and glared at him, but his attention was focused on the machines around the bed.

"Human medicine is fascinating," he said. I watched as his gaze shifted to follow the tube of medicine down to my arm. He poked the spot where the IV was placed in my skin and I flinched with a pained yelp. "If not somewhat barbarous."

His attention shifted to my face as his eyes scanned my injuries. They flicked back and forth across my head then down to my shoulder. I was wearing a gown, but the searing look on his face made me feel like he could see right through it.

Searching for a distraction, I turned and grabbed the fruit bowl and started unwrapping it. I did so with some difficulty as I was left-handed, and my left arm was still mostly useless. "Yeah, I guess it can be," I finally replied.

I speared a large piece of watermelon and popped it into my mouth. The juice felt cool running down my throat, and I reveled in the sweet taste on my tongue. There had been a lingering medical taste in my mouth that the water hadn't been able to wash away.

"You have been injured. Again."

Looking up, I saw he was staring intently at me. I swallowed the fruit and picked up a grape. "I have, but this time it wasn't a demon. It was Billy Blake."

His eyes flashed with red as a muscle in his jaw ticked. The temperature in the room rose a few degrees and I squirmed uncomfortably. Noticing my movement, he sucked in a deep breath and as he slowly released it, the air around me cooled back down. I'd never actually seen him use his powers, but if his mood swings gave off that much heat, I wasn't sure I wanted to. His ability to flick them off and on like a switch was incredible.

"Billy will be dealt with," he said, his eyes falling to my arm again. "I am presently here for you."

A strawberry caught my eye near the bottom of the bowl, so I dug around for it as I said, "Here for your thank you?"

"My what?"

Finally freeing the berry, I stabbed it with my fork and brought it to my lips, buying myself some time. I set the bowl and fork on my lap and my right arm fell back onto the bed. Warm skin tentatively brushed across my fingertips. I looked up to see The Superior staring intently downward as he continued touching my hand.

"Your thank you. For saving me," I said, pulling my fingers away from him into a fist. He seemed unbothered by the movement, as he reached out and gently turned my hand over. His finger brushed along the inside of my wrist. I swallowed as I felt my heart rate quicken.

He kept touching me as he looked up to meet my gaze. "It was not me."

My eyes widened and I blinked several times. He went back to examining my arm. I tried to focus on remembering what I had seen and heard that night, but my attention kept bouncing back to the fact that The Superior was touching me. His touch was gentle while being almost uncomfortably warm. He poked the needle in my arms several times, and I had to resist the urge to slap him away.

"Ouch, that hurts," I hissed.

He abruptly stopped and moved to picking at the tape holding the needle. This time, to my surprise, I did slap his hand away. "Stop that."

His lips twitched slightly upward, but he moved his hands back to his side. "My apologies. And as far as your thanks go, I believe you owe it to, what did you call him? Johnny suit demon?"

"Johnny Snake Demon."

"Yes," he said, his lips momentarily stretching into a grin, "Johnny Snake Demon."

I cursed under my breath. "That's twice now he's saved me."

The Superior looked up at me and all humor on his face died instantly. "You are quite seriously indebted to him then. This is a problem."

Nodding, I attempted to raise my fingers to my chin, in a contemplative gesture, but The Superior's hand snatched my wrist and held it down on the bed. His other hand started picking at the bandage on my arm again.

"Hey, I told you that hurts." I tried to squirm away from him.

He looked at me, while maintaining his firm grip on my forearm. "Will you accept our arrangement now?"

"What?" I breathed, feeling a burst of pain in my shoulder from fighting to free myself from him. It was a useless effort, so I settled down for a moment and stared at him.

"Do you accept the terms of my agreement?"

I shook my head. My breaths were coming quickly now as fear slowly built in my belly. His face was serious, but I saw something like doubt flash across his eyes. It was so brief that I could have been mistaken, but then I sucked in a breath as he peeled the bandage from my arm and ripped the needle free.

"This is going to hurt," he said just before a fiery pain exploded across my right forearm.

CHAPTER 11

My heart pounded as sweat slicked my brow. The pain in my forearm was sharp and intense, overriding any discomfort I felt from my injuries. I held my eyes tightly shut, but tears still dripped from the corners. A cool, soft towel dragged gently across my forehead.

I flicked my eyes open. Blinking several times, I noted that I was on my side, but still in the hospital bed. Abruptly, I sat up and smacked away the towel.

"What did you do?" I demanded, watching The Superior set the cloth on the end of the bed. Looking down at my forearm, I let out a strangled cry. I shuffled backward in the bed, trying to make space between myself and the demon beside me. My elbow slammed into the bedside, but I barely felt it as I stared down at my skin. From below my right wrist to just about my elbow there was a swirling trail of black ink. It was a mix of lines and symbols I didn't recognize made with a strange iridescent ink that was tinged with red along the edges. The Superior laid his hand across it, and I felt a welcoming burst of heat trail along the tattooed lines and into my body. I looked up into his face and slapped him.

"What did you do?" I repeated, my breaths coming in and out in short bursts.

His head was still turned from the impact of my slap. Slowly, he returned his gaze to my own and I saw that his eyes were brimming with red. "I need you alive and since you are too reckless to consider your own safety and accept my bargain, I have made one for you."

I raised my hand to slap him again, but he caught my wrist.

"Don't," he whispered, his eyes molten. His fingers dug painfully into my wrist, while I yanked uselessly against his hold. "Now let me finish healing you."

"Healing me?"

"Yes," he snapped as he released my wrist. "Or did you not notice there is no longer a hole in your shoulder?"

With a start, I shrugged my left shoulder and felt nothing unusual or painful in the movement. Reaching up with my hand, I pulled the collar of the gown down a few inches and stared at my skin. It was still covered in a large bandage, but when I poked at the flesh, it felt solid.

"What is this?" I asked, my voice shaking slightly.

"An agreement."

"That's not an answer," I said, my voice rising to a shout. Glaring back at him, I felt heat pricking the backs of my eyes. "What. Is. This?"

We sat silently staring at each other for a moment before The Superior extended his hand out to me. "Let me finish healing you and I will answer."

Hesitantly, I placed my arm into his palm. I immediately felt warmth flowing from his hand into my body. There was a subtle push of power, as heat coiled around my forearm, head, and shoulder. I could feel my body absorbing the magic like a battery charging in the sun. What had felt intrusive at first, now felt invigorating.

"Finished," The Superior said after a few minutes. He removed his hand from my forearm. I immediately felt the loss of his warmth, but his power still coursed through my veins. My body thrummed with the influx of energy that was greater than anything I'd ever felt.

The Superior cleared his throat and said, "It is my mark."

It took me a moment to register what he had said. When I did, a dose of panic mixed with all the adrenaline coursing in my veins. My chest squeezed uncomfortably as I brought my hands up into my hair. I started shaking my head and mumbling 'no' under my breath.

"Claire," The Superior said calmly, "It's not the mark of a servant."

I looked up at him, trying to see if there was truth in his words. His face was much as it always was, a stoney mask of indifference. And yet, there was something in his eyes. Whenever I looked at him before, his gaze met mine with a challenge. Right now, though, he was struggling to maintain my eye contact.

"This is something different," he continued, turning his attention to straightening his jacket on his lap. "Something stronger."

He shifted his position and crossed his arms over his chest. "It's the mark of a bond. It's how I was able to heal you."

His nervous fidgeting was doing nothing to calm my own unease. Whatever was bad enough to make him uncomfortable could not be good. "You're still not telling me something," I said, turning my arm over to look at the strange marking. "What bond is it?"

"A strong one," he said, finally turning his head to look at me. "A very rare one."

The spot where I had struck him was red now and I was contemplating if I could get away with slapping him again. My eye twitched as I asked, "And why have you forced this bond on me?"

His shoulders rose and fell as he took a deep breath. "You were being difficult."

I crossed my arms over my chest and narrowed my eyes. "Difficult? I was being *difficult*?"

"I can remove it after you find the girl."

The words hit me like a slap. Throwing the sheets off the bed, I rose abruptly to my feet. "Blackmail. You think you can blackmail me into working for you?"

A cool breeze across my backside reminded me that I was wearing a hospital gown and nothing else. I fisted the fabric closed at my back and then gestured with my other arm toward the door. "Get out."

He stared at me, blinking slowly several times, before rising smoothly to his feet. "Very well, I shall leave you for now, but I will be back to collect you this evening."

"Collect me?" I scoffed, "I intend never to be near you again."

Suddenly, he was directly in front of me, his fingertips trailing lightly across my newly marked skin. "Run as far away as you like. The bond will allow me to find you. Always."

My nostrils flared as I glared up at him. His heat enveloped me and whereas before it had felt stifling, my body now yearned to lean into it. I took a small step back. "Then I will have to find my own way to get rid of it."

His eyes searched my face before his lips spread into a wide satisfied smirk. "See you tonight."

I clenched and unclenched my fists in my lap while listening to the drone of the car radio. Who even listened to the radio anymore?

"So," Mark started while keeping his eyes on the traffic around us, "Are we going to talk about what just happened or pretend like all of this is normal?"

Bouncing my knee, I checked the side mirror for what felt like the hundredth time. "Normal," I finally said with a sigh, "Completely normal."

Mark grumbled something under his breath but didn't press the issue further. It was dark out, but it was still early in the evening. Early enough, I hoped.

See you tonight.

The words played over in my head, and I started drumming my fingers against my knees. After The Superior had left my room, I'd burst into action. I texted Mark to get his ass back to my room and then Nancy asking for a change of clothes. She had been on shift at the hospital and luckily for me doctors always have a change of clothes hidden away somewhere. With the mark safely tucked away in Nancy's jacket, I had informed the hospital staff that I was leaving. They had many questions, none of which I would answer and finally, after several hours of arm twisting and threatening to call my nonexistent lawyer, I was released against medical advice.

"Are you sure you don't want to talk about it?" Mark asked, drawing my attention back to the present. It was difficult, but I summoned the necessary energy to turn my head toward him. His brow was furrowed as he turned the car off the highway.

I appreciated his concern, but I couldn't focus my thoughts enough to articulate what had happened. At least not yet. Shaking my head I said, "Not right now. I just want to get home and…think for a bit."

Drink for a bit, was what I meant. Crawl into a hole under my covers for a bit was also likely. Thinking was honestly the last thing I planned to do once I got home. I just needed to get there. My eyes swept back to the police car that was following us. Talking my way out of a hospital stay hadn't applied to my police security detail. They'd insisted upon escorting me home. At least they'd remain in their car.

We turned onto my street and Mark asked, "Do you want me to keep the office running for a few days?"

I groaned. Work was the last thing on my mind. With a shake of my head, I said, "I think closing down for a few days is acceptable. I did get shot after all."

He gave a forced laugh while turning into my driveway. We moved forward, stopping by my front steps and I shuddered at the sight of them. My eyes were immediately pulled toward the porch, memories of a shadow standing there playing across my mind. Stepping out of the car, I saw the signs of the police investigation. There was an outline where I had been found, with blood still staining the rock. Markings on my driveway indicated footprints or tire tread, I wasn't sure. Small, numbered flags peppered my front lawn.

"Do you want me to stay with you?" Mark asked gently from beside me.

Tears pressed into the backs of my eyes, but I shook my head. He really was the best assistant. Mark tried to hold my arm to help me walk, but I felt fine. Better than fine as whatever The Superior had pumped into me was still circulating through my veins like a stimulant. That, mixed with my anxiety, had me practically sprinting to the door.

"You're sure you're okay?" Mark repeated.

I gave him a reassuring smile and nodded emphatically. "I'll be fine. Thanks for looking out for me."

Mark deserved some rest, so I shooed him off the porch and toward his car. I waved as he backed out of the driveway. With a twist, I turned to my door and headed inside. Plopping my bag onto the floor, I engaged all my locks and marched into the kitchen. I pried open the cabinet above my refrigerator and eyed the bottles inside.

I sighed at the sight of the half empty container of vodka. "Nope," I said, pulling it down and setting it onto the counter, "Not going to be enough."

Grabbing a glass and a can of Sprite from the fridge, I mixed half of the can with a generous free pour of vodka. I sipped at the drink while I opened an alcohol delivery app on my phone. With the day I'd had, I was going to need way more liquor.

CHAPTER 12

The bottle slipped from my grasp and fell with a thud onto the carpet. Trying to pry my eyelids open proved difficult and my tongue felt like sandpaper. Why was I awake?

Someone pounded repeatedly on my front door.

Stretching out a hand, I searched the coffee table next to the couch for my phone. Seven in the morning on Thursday. How was it Thursday already?

The knocking continued, growing more urgent as a voice called, "Claire, I know you're in there!"

I licked my dry lips and found little relief from it. Sitting up, I found a glass of water and took a swig. I pressed upward onto my feet and shuffled to the door. With some fumbling, I found the lock and pulled the door open the tiniest bit. It was forcefully swung open into my face as Nancy barged her way into my house.

"Good, god, Claire," she said, after I shoved the door closed again. "It smells like a bar in here."

Nancy was dressed for work with her first aid kit in hand. Her eyes took in the state of my living room and then turned to look at me. She pressed her lips into a line.

"I'm fine," I said with a wave as I started working my way back to the couch. Thankfully, my small ranch style house meant I didn't have far to go. I had a small entryway that opened directly into my living room which in turn opened to the dining and kitchen area. A bottle clinked against my shoe as I made my way to the couch.

"Like hell you are," Nancy spat, "The last time I saw you, you had just been shot and practically concussed and now you look like you've been on a six-month bender."

I dropped onto the couch and Nancy sat beside me. She grabbed my face and flicked my eyelids down. Squirming out of her grasp, I reached for a bottle on my coffee table. Nancy snatched it away.

"Talk to me. Now," she said, setting the liquor on the floor next to her feet.

Eyeing it, I said, "Give it back."

She shook her head. "What the hell has happened to you?"

I lunged for the bottle, but she headed me off and shoved me back onto my seat. Even at my best I didn't think I could ever take Nancy. Sometimes she had to strongarm people in the ER, so she wasn't one to skip arm day at the gym.

"Since when do you need a drink this badly?"

My head whipped around, and I glared at her. "Since I learned how badly it pisses him off!"

Crossing my arms, I huffed out a sigh. It was childish, but the past few days had exhausted me, mentally and physically.

"You need to tell me what the hell is going on," she said quietly. "You're scaring me, Claire."

I turned, retort ready on my lips, but I stopped when I saw her. Brows furrowed and worrying hard at her bottom lip with her teeth, the concern on her face caused a twinge in my chest. I sucked in a deep breath and tried to push out my anger with the exhalation.

"I'm sorry. It's been stressful."

She nodded and waited patiently for me to continue. I pulled the hoodie I was wearing tighter around my body and then realized it was the same one I'd borrowed from her five days ago. It didn't seem possible that it had been that long since we'd last talked.

"Let's see, since I last saw you," I started, kicking my heels up onto the coffee table, "I left the hospital against medical advice. Then, Mark drove me home. Thankfully we got here when we did, because a couple minutes later The Superior showed up. I watched him flip his shit all over my yard because he couldn't get into my house."

Nancy raised her hand, to halt my story. "Wait, how come he can't get inside?"

I beamed over at her. "This building used to be a church. Blessed ground means no demons allowed."

She laughed. "Clever. Very clever."

My smile widened. The house certainly was not perfect, but I had to pat myself on the back for having the foresight to buy a holy structure. Thank goodness that congregation had grown and needed a new building.

"Anyway," I continued, "He stormed off. Then the next night he showed up with a battered and bruised Billy Blake, who he promptly handed over to the police. They took off and The Superior set up his own security detail around my house." I rubbed at my temples. The relief at seeing Billy being taken away in handcuffs had been short lived as a new source of frustration had turned up. "The stupid sentries have been a nightmare. They talk all night long, very loudly, throw things against my house, and constantly call my name asking when I'm coming out."

Nancy huffed. "Well, that's rude."

Pulling my fingers through my hair, I groaned. "I'm going stir crazy and I'm going to run out of food soon."

"Why don't you get something delivered?"

"I tried, but the demons just stole it," I complained. "I even tried meeting the delivery person on the front porch, which is still part of the holy ground, but the second I step outside, they tell The Superior and he shows up and calls me a child and tells me how ridiculous I'm being."

"I was wrong before," she said, leaning back and crossing her arms, "This is all fucking rude as hell. What could he possibly want from you this badly?"

With a wince, I said, "It's complicated. A conversation best had with a drink."

She raised her brow dubiously. "I have work."

"Coffee?"

Nancy leapt to her feet. I went into the kitchen and tossed some beans into the grinder. After getting the coffee maker started, I went back into the living room and found Nancy tidying.

"You don't have to do that," I said.

She brushed past me with several bottles in her hand. She placed them on the kitchen table before heading out to the garage to retrieve my recycling bin. When she returned, she slid the bottles from the table into the bin and went back into the living room. Grabbing a trash bag, I went to join her on the floor.

"How could you have drunk this much in less than a week?" she sighed as she fished a bottle out from under a chair.

"He won't let me get drunk," I said absently, while cautiously opening a takeout container. Pancakes, thankfully not smelly, but definitely trash. I tossed them into the garbage bag and then looked over at Nancy. She was staring at me.

"What do you mean he won't *let* you?"

Right, I thought with a wince. "This is the thing we need coffee for."

She set the recycling bin down and moved in front of me. "Tell me now."

With a resigned sigh, I slowly pushed up my right sleeve. Nancy's eyes grew as wide as saucers. She tipped up her head and our gazes locked. "Oh. My. God. He marked… he, The Superior, he…gave you his mark. Oh my god. Oh my god."

Nancy continued reciting her pleas to a higher power while I walked us into the kitchen. Her reaction was worse than I had expected. I settled her into a chair and poured two cups of coffee before returning.

"You gonna be okay?" I asked as I slid a mug toward her.

Her fingers snatched the mug, but her eyes continuously trailed over my exposed forearm. I self-consciously rubbed at it.

"It's beautiful."

"Chains are never beautiful."

She looked up at me and winced. "Sorry, I just meant, the lines and the look of it. Why did he give it to you anyway?"

Without looking at it, I pushed my sleeve back down. "He's using it to blackmail me into working for him."

"Hmm," she said contemplatively while lifting her coffee to blow across the top, "Well, not much is known about the mark, but I can tell you what I do know. It is an incredibly sacred bond. All demons will know what it means when they see it and that it ties you to The Superior. Only the most powerful demons are even able to make the connection. I've never seen one or ever heard of anyone actually having one."

Lifting my own mug to my lips, I took a tentative sip. Near scalding. Perfect. "That's not much information, Nancy."

"No shit," she said with a derisive snort. "I told you not much is known about them. What did he tell you about it?"

I shrugged. "It's a bond. Something strong that allows him to find me no matter where I am and allows him to heal me."

Nancy's eyes widened and her jaw dropped. "He can heal you? Oh, this is fascinating. What else?"

"Nancy," I said, snapping my fingers in front of her face, "Focus! You're upset with the demon who did this to your best friend, not fascinated by him."

Her eyes narrowed in a mock scowl. "Right. I hate that guy."

With a laugh I said, "Thank you. That's better."

Then she placed her elbow on the table and placed her chin in her hand. "So is the drunk thing because of the healing?"

A growl-like sound reverberated in my throat. Nancy's lips twitched upward for a moment, but she said nothing. "I don't know what it is exactly, but I came home the first night intending to get shitfaced and I drank, and I drank and nothing happened. Well, I did pee a lot. Then he showed up at my house ranting about not letting me drown myself in alcohol." My eyelid twitched as I took another sip of coffee. "So, obviously like a mature adult I took that as a challenge."

Nancy snorted into her coffee. "Hey, you know who you should ask about this? Tabitha."

She was lucky that I didn't have any coffee in my mouth, otherwise I might have spat it across the table at her. "I am not going to some demonic cult leader for advice, Nancy."

Lifting her hand, she pointed toward me with an exaggerated flourish. "First of all, it is not a cult. It is a group of like-minded individuals who enjoy learning about demonic culture."

"Cult," I fake coughed into my hand.

Glaring at me, she lifted another finger and pointed it at me. "Second, those non-cultish people might be able to help you right now, so perhaps you should speak a little more kindly about them."

I smiled sardonically at her. "I think I'd rather stay here trying to get drunk."

Nancy dropped her hand exasperatedly, then looked at her watch. "Damn, I should get going, but hey, I do have one more piece of info."

"Spill," I said, half-heartedly.

"That mark," she said leaning forward and flicking her eyes toward my forearm, "That is The Superior's true name."

I sat completely still for several seconds. It was possible that I had heard her wrong or simply misunderstood. The serious look on Nancy's face told me I'd heard her right. Jerking up my sleeve, I stared down at the swirling black mark.

"Can you read it?" I asked, desperation thick in my voice.

She leaned forward and inspected it closely. My breath stayed locked in my lungs as I waited for her response. Finally, with a shake of her head, she said, "Sorry, Claire, I can't."

Sinking back into my chair, I pushed the sleeve back down and sighed. "It's okay. It was worth a shot."

I should have known The Superior's true name wouldn't be easy to decipher. If he'd thought I could easily read it, I doubted he'd have put it on my arm. Knowing his true name would mean I could demand a favor from him and that was not something to be taken lightly.

Nancy pulled out her phone. "Let me take a picture and show Tabitha. Couldn't hurt right?"

With a shrug, I pulled the jacket sleeve back up and she snapped a few pictures. When she was satisfied with them, she tucked the phone back into her scrub pocket. She gulped down the last of her coffee and rose to put the mug in my sink.

"Listen, I know that being a reclusive drunk has been your MO for the past few days, but have you given any thought to what you are going to do next?"

"I don't know," I said, rubbing my eyes with the palms of my hands, "But if I don't get some sleep soon, I may be forced to work for him."

She hummed. "Well, if you are thinking about folding, might as well get something out of it."

Meeting her gaze, I asked, "What do you mean?"

"I mean he wants something from you, so why not get something from him in return? Make some kind of arrangement. He knows you can't stay in here forever, so why not come out on your own terms?"

My own terms. Even my sleep addled brain could tell this was a fantastic idea. I just needed to think about what I wanted in exchange for my cooperation.

Nancy chuckled at the look on my face. "There you go," she said, swiping a hand across my shoulders on her way to the front door. "Oh, and maybe take a shower. You're bordering on smelling worse than my patients with gangrene."

I glared but failed to find anything to throw at her before she stepped out the door.

CHAPTER 13

An ear-splitting screech jolted me awake. Heart racing, I sat up in bed and for several moments just listened. The sound didn't happen again, and I couldn't see any movement in the darkness around me. I tossed back the covers and flicked on my bedside lamp. Glancing at my phone, I saw it was just after seven at night. At least that meant I'd gotten a few hours of sleep.

Yawning, I dragged a hand down my face. "Time to get this over with."

After Nancy left, I'd spent some time cleaning and thinking. I realized she was right. The demons weren't going away and if I was going to be forced to work with one of them, it might as well be on my terms. Partnering up with The Superior wasn't my favorite idea, but not knowing anything about Johnny Snake Demon, I figured it was better to go with the devil I knew.

I rose from bed and padded across my room toward the closet. While pulling on a sweater, I heard the screech again. It was surprisingly loud even coming from outside. I wasn't sure what could be making that shrill, high-pitched sound. Nothing I'd ever heard before sounded quite like it. Either way, I needed to find one of the sentries so I could put my plan into action.

Walking into the kitchen, I peered out the window over the sink. My gaze was met by a pair of large, yellow eyes.

Something was nestled in the tree near the center of my yard. Wings fluttered around a dark shadow as the creature blinked. A prickling sensation started at the base of my spine. There were creatures in The Otherworld called demonkin and if they crossed into our world they inhabited animal skins, instead of human. All of the previous sentries had been demons in human skin, but perhaps The Superior had sent a demonkin this time.

The thought offered me little comfort as I moved into the living room to gather my coat and hat. After I was bundled, I peeked out the front window. Squinting my eyes, I could just make out the line of trees by the road. Everything was unusually quiet. There were no animal sounds. No leaves swayed in the breeze. There was just stillness. The prickling at the base of my spine increased as I flicked on the porch light. A shadow darted around the corner of my house.

My breathing quickened as I tried to blink the image away. Maybe all this time trapped inside was affecting me worse than I thought. Now I was seeing things. Although Nancy had given me a full evaluation before she left. She'd said that despite being so recently near death I was a picture of perfect health. Except for the showering thing.

"Relax," I told myself, stepping back from the window, "It's probably just a sentry who didn't want to be seen…for some reason."

Having spent the week avoiding the sentries, it felt odd seeking one out. I moved through my house, hoping the demon was simply out back. Whoever they were, I knew they all had direct lines to The Superior and I needed one of them to call him for me. Next time I saw him, I guess we needed to exchange phone numbers.

I stepped around my dining room table toward the sliding glass door. My hand was flicking up the lock, when I stumbled back with a yelp. The large pair of yellow eyes now stared at me from the base of my porch steps. It looked like some kind of owl, but it was huge, about the size of a labrador. Locking eyes with it, I noticed the yellow color was swirling around its irises like a toxic cloud. Definitely not a normal bird. Maybe it was a new sentry.

Tapping on the glass, I shouted, "Hey, can you call The Superior for me?"

The creature's head swiveled, then it opened its beak and let out a loud shriek. I stumbled over one of my dining room chairs, but caught myself before I fell. Crouching, I shuffled across the floor and slammed my back into the cabinets beneath my sink. The bird continued its call, loud and strong for another moment, and then its rhythm changed to something undulating. It sounded like a fire engine that was getting closer and closer, but several times louder. I covered my ears with my hands and peeked around the side of the cabinets. The creature's head was still swiveling as it sat at the base of my stairs. From the corner of my eye, I caught a sign of movement from behind the bird. Something glided across the grass in a smooth line. It stayed just inside the shadows before taking cover behind a tree.

Finally, the bird stopped screeching, and a deafening ring started in my ears. "Well, this is not good," I said to myself, although the sound was muted. "Who the hell are these people?"

Billy Blake, Johnny Snake Demon, and The Superior all flashed before my mind. Any one of them could have orchestrated this, but I doubted The Superior had. He'd approached me several times now and this wasn't his style. I started wondering where he was and whether he could get to me in time if I needed him. Realizing that I was thinking of The Superior for aid made something cold sink in my gut. I pushed away the feeling and focused on what I needed to be doing now. If these weren't The Superior's people, then they were most likely sent by one of the other two. I'd been injured by both before, so I needed to find some protection. With a curse under my breath, I remembered my knife was still in my car.

"Nicky," I whisper shouted to the world around me, "I left my dagger in the car, could you send it to me please?"

My eyes searched the ceiling above me, until I felt the familiar prickle of magic at my side. Smiling, I looked down at my dagger. It wasn't much, but at least I had a weapon.

"You're the best, Nick," I called, and was pleasantly surprised to find my hearing was back to normal. "Any way you can do your delivery trick with The Superior?"

Nick didn't answer. I was on my own. Dropping my knees to the floor, I pivoted slowly to look out the glass door again. The bird was gone. My yard was empty. Leaning further out from my hiding place, I still couldn't see anything. There were no darting shadows, no arriving sentries, no signs of anyone.

A series of heavy knocks sounded on my front door. Sliding back behind the cabinets, I whipped my head around and scanned the front windows. My pulse raced and I clutched the dagger to my chest. I couldn't see anyone, but if someone was on the porch, that meant they weren't a demon. That meant they could get inside my house. A tremble started in my body as I tried to steady my breathing.

"Come on outside, now," an unfamiliar gruff voice called from the other side of the door.

I scoffed but said nothing. There was no way I was going outside now. Readying myself for an attack, I dropped one knee to the floor but kept my other foot planted. My eyes kept both the front and back doors in my peripheral vision and my knife was now resting along my thigh. Adrenaline pounded in my veins as I fought to keep my body still.

"We don't want to hurt you, sweetheart, but we got a job to do."

My lips twitched in disgust. Did he assume calling me sweetheart would somehow endear me to them?

Something crashed into the sliding glass door. I shifted my body against the cabinets just before one of my patio chairs flew through the door and into my dining room table. Glass sprayed in all directions, and I ducked my head to avoid getting cut on my face. A few sharp stabs of pain skittered across the backs of my hands, but otherwise, I was unharmed.

Two figures, wearing all black and tactical gear, burst in through the remnants of the glass door. The first one saw me and lunged. I waited until I felt their hands on my back, then stood as fast as I could, driving my shoulder into their middle while stabbing forward with my knife. An oomph sounded through their mask as my body connected with theirs and then they let out a sharp cry of pain when my blade sank into their armpit.

Stepping back, I pulled the blade free and watched the person drop to their knees. I kicked them as hard as I could in the chest. Training and instinct overtook all thought as I evened out my breaths and focused on my next opponent. This figure was bigger, and now I'd lost the element of surprise. They looked down at their fallen comrade, who was writhing and clutching their side, then back at me.

"She's got a knife. Roads is down. Call medic."

The woman, clearly speaking to someone else through a radio, used an unaffected, practiced tone. Great, sounded like she'd had training, and she wasn't alone. The odds were not in my favor.

"Stand down."

It took me a moment to realize she was talking to me now. With a quick shake of my head, I flicked the blood off my blade and angled it toward her.

"Seriously?" she sighed, before pulling a taser from her belt, "Let's not make this any worse of a situation."

"Oh, I'm sorry," I said with a flourish of my empty hand, "Did I hurt your friend while the two of you broke into my house?"

As I finished speaking, I darted toward the doorway. My skills with a blade were no match for someone with combat training and armor. I'd gotten lucky with Roads, and I didn't think that would happen twice. Glass shards crunched under my feet as I made it onto the back porch. I took the first step down, then jumped onto the grass. Heavy footsteps sounded from behind me as I started running for the trees. My breaths sawed in and out of my lungs as my feet pounded on the ground. I had no idea where I was going, I just knew I had to get away from these people.

"Incoming!"

There was a shout from somewhere behind me. My steps faltered at the sound. Something massive slammed into my back, and I fell forward. Air whooshed out of my lungs as my body collided with the earth and a heavy weight landed on top of me. I briefly saw arms beside my head, before the weight lifted and hands grabbed the back of my shirt. I was wrenched upward onto my feet.

"Move," a woman's voice hissed into my ear.

She pulled hard and I fell backward into her chest. I dug my heels in as she started dragging me back toward my house. Why was she taking me back? Not knowing her intentions and only managing to dig divots in my grass with my heels, I started flailing my limbs. I kicked and punched backward, managing on occasion to hit something solid. If she wanted a willing hostage, she wasn't going to get one. Despite my efforts, the woman was incredibly strong and soon we were back at my porch steps.

"Climb, or I will drag your ass up these stairs," she ordered.

Getting my feet under me, I took a tentative step backward. She tugged hard on my shirt, and I stumbled, catching myself with my hands. I rose, trying to find my balance, and that's when I saw him.

"Move!" the woman shouted desperately as she threw me onto the porch. I landed on my side, turning my head back to look for him. Our eyes connected and I sighed with relief.

The Superior walked slowly across my yard. He moved with an unhurried steadiness that did not match the chaotic pulse in my veins. His hair waved in a calm breeze and his face was a blank mask. In his long gray coat, dark jeans, and stylish loafers, he looked like a man out for an evening stroll. All except for his eyes. They glowed with a fiery fury that even I could see. I hadn't thought it possible to look so relaxed and pissed at the same time.

The woman with me wrapped her fingers around the back of my neck and dragged me onto my knees. I winced as her fingers squeezed. Reaching up, I tried to pull her away, but then she pressed a gun to my temple. With a shuddering breath, I slowly dropped my hands. The Superior's eyes widened momentarily, but then his face hardened as he turned to look at my captor.

"Hurting her is the last mistake you will ever make," he said simply.

She scoffed and pressed her barrel more firmly into my temple. "I know you can't get to me in here, so how are you planning to stop me?"

Shudders wracked through my body. The adrenaline from earlier was wearing off. It left me feeling cold as I realized that I was once again faced with someone trying to kill me and having only The Superior to stop them. I'd felt safe here because the demons couldn't enter, but it wasn't a demon currently holding a gun to my head. Once again it was a human threatening my life.

"I may not be able to reach you," he said, casually stepping closer, "but they certainly can."

He moved so quickly I couldn't track him. Then something dark and about the size of a basketball hurtled through the air and smacked into my captor. She fell backward, but kept her hold on my neck, pulling me down with her. Another object flew through the air above me and slammed into her. A rage-filled scream spilled from her lips as she shoved my body upward. Crouching behind me, she angled me in front of her as a shield. Pressing my hand down to balance myself, I felt something warm and sticky. I looked down and saw a pool of blood. A horrified scream fell out of me as I traced the source of the blood to the object The Superior had thrown. It was a severed head. There was a second one just past my captor's foot. Both were still wearing black masks and a pair of goggles.

Bile rose in my throat, and I worked to swallow it back down. Two more heads landed on the porch beside me with a heavy, wet thump. I pressed my clean fingers to my mouth and squeezed my eyes shut. My captor scrambled on the ground behind me, her grip never faltering on my throat. I could feel her ragged breath along the back of my neck.

"I believe I am missing one," The Superior said. I slowly opened my eyes and saw he was meticulously cleaning blood from his hands with a small white towel. He dropped it and then stared just over my shoulder. I assumed he was locking eyes with the woman. The deranged expression on his face made me shift uncomfortably away from her.

"Plenty of time to find him later to complete the set," he said with a flourish of his hand to indicate the other heads. "Now, if you tell me something useful, I will make your death quick."

Her hand shook on my neck.

"Tell me who hired you."

I waited, willing her to answer him and end this. She shoved me forward and released my neck before turning and bolting into my house. My hands slammed into the wood of the deck before my gaze lifted to The Superior. He rolled his eyes and then something bright flashed in his hand before he threw it. I heard a thump and then a crash.

Wet, gasping sounds came from inside. I turned to see the woman thrashing on the floor. Not thinking, I jumped to my feet and ran to her. Her hands clutched at her throat as blood pumped in rivers down her chest. Bending closer, I saw the tip of the blade protruding from the middle of her neck. I gasped and took several steps away from her. My eyes searched around me for something useful. Finding a kitchen towel, I grabbed it and pressed it into the woman's hands. She clutched it to her throat, and it was immediately soaked with blood.

"If you wish to speed along her death, I suggest you remove the knife, Claire."

My head whipped around to see The Superior standing at the base of the porch steps.

"Why did you do this?" I asked, my voice full of accusation.

He crossed his arms over his chest. "Why did I kill the people attempting to kill you?"

"They weren't going to kill me," I spat, holding my trembling hands over the woman's. Her movements were slowing, but she still took wet gasping breaths. Leaning forward, I reached around to the back of her neck. I found the knife handle and wrapped my fingers around it. Her eyes shifted to mine just before I gave it a sharp tug and pulled the blade free. Blood poured as I tossed the knife onto the ground. Placing my hands back on top of hers, I watched her struggle to breathe for a few more moments.

"What did you think they were planning to do with you?" The Superior asked, his voice sounding unfazed as the woman before me sucked in her last breath. I watched as she exhaled slowly and then went still. The only movement, her blood flowing across my floor.

I rose to my feet, ignoring the soul now standing in my dining room. A high-pitched ringing started in my ears as I made my way to the kitchen sink. The water ran pink as I scrubbed the blood from my hands. I stood there for a long time, willing the soul to leave. Finally, I turned off the water and found myself alone in the house. Stepping onto the back porch, I saw The Superior still patiently waiting for me.

With a sigh, I said, "They didn't deserve this. No one deserves this."

His eyes narrowed. "And yet I am deserving of your contempt for my actions? I, who came here to save you. Save you *again*, Claire. Why am I met with the disdain these people deserve?"

The words hit me like a brick in the chest. He'd never spoken to me like this before. I wanted to shout that he wasn't being fair. That they were different, but that wasn't it. I knew what I truly meant by that. They were human and he was not. Looking back at him now, seeing his eyes rimmed in red, I realized he never stood a chance. From the moment I'd first met him, I'd judged him based on the actions of a few other demons. I didn't do that with humans, so why had I done it with him? Why didn't he deserve to be regarded based on his actions alone? Granted, he had marked me without asking and he had decapitated at least four people tonight, but he had also saved me. Again.

Stepping back inside, I retrieved one of my deck chairs and placed it at the top of the stairs. I sat down and clasped my hands together in my lap. "You're right. I'm sorry." Adjusting my position in the chair, I dipped my gaze down to his chin. "Thank you for saving me."

He nodded, but I could see tension still radiating through his body. Pulling out his phone, he tapped the screen a few times, then lifted it to his ear.

"What are you doing?" I asked.

"Calling cleanup," he said, matter-of-factly, "They have a lot of work to do."

With that, he turned away from me. I guessed that meant this conversation was over.

CHAPTER 14

An hour later, there were people swarming all over my house. I didn't recognize any of them, but they each gave me a deferential tip of their heads as they passed. One of them placed bandages on my hands and inspected my neck. A bruise was likely, but otherwise I was physically unharmed.

Not wanting to be in the way or see the bodies being removed, I stepped out onto the front porch. Wrapping my jacket tightly around me, I sat on the top step and stared out into the night. I wasn't surprised when a few minutes later The Superior appeared before me.

He kicked at the bottom step and said, "Of course you would have a blessed house."

I chuckled, then wrapped my arms around myself. My fingers clenched and unclenched in my gloves. Despite having washed them several times, I still saw the woman's blood on them. Hiding them in cloth helped, but the images still played in a loop in my mind.

After a few moments of silence, I asked, "What are we going to do?"

His gaze briefly met mine, before he looked past me into the house. "My people will take care of everything. There will be no evidence left behind."

Clearing my throat, I said, "That's not what I meant."

The Superior looked at me. "What did you mean?"

I squirmed at the intensity of his gaze but pushed myself to continue. "We can't keep going on like this. With us at odds and whoever this is sending people to kidnap me."

"Agreed," he replied, his tone not conveying any of his emotions.

Something more was going on with the missing girl, but I would have to figure that out later. For now, I needed to be somewhere safe. I needed to be where I knew Billy Blake couldn't find me and where Johnny Snake Demon wouldn't dare go. All of that pointed to The Superior. I didn't like admitting that I felt safer with him, and I sure as hell wasn't going to admit it to him.

"I've got a deal for you," I said, leaning forward to place my elbows on my knees. Now it was time to see if Nancy's idea paid off. "Truthfully answer five questions for me and I will try to find this girl for you."

His face twisted into what I thought was a look of surprise, before going blank. "No."

I groaned. "Four questions?"

He thought for a moment. "Three questions answered, but I get to choose which ones I answer."

"That kind of defeats the purpose, don't you think?" I said with a scoff.

"I want you out of this house, Claire," he said, his eyes flashing red. It was subtle and only for a moment before they returned to their warm brown. "Three questions of my choosing or I simply burn your house to the ground."

My jaw dropped as I stared at him. If I hadn't been, I wouldn't have noticed the slight twitch of his lips.

"Was that a joke?" I asked astounded.

He shrugged. "Three questions and you come out. Deal?"

"Fine," I said, scooching forward on the step. I lifted my right arm to him and said, "You said this was your mark. I know it's your true name, so what might that be?"

His eyes stayed on mine as he said, "No."

I rolled my eyes back at him. My assumption had been that he wouldn't answer that one, but I still had to try. So many questions raced through my mind, but I had to pick the right ones. I had to get the most out of this arrangement and The Superior was smart. He would dodge the truth as much as he possibly could.

"Okay," I said, straightening my spine, "Next question, what exact power does the mark give you over me?"

He continued staring at me for a moment. Finally, he lifted his right index finger. "One. You already know this. It gives me a vague sense of your location at all times. The sense is magnified if you are injured. It also allows for a transfer of power."

Before I could respond, my skin sparked with a warmth. I looked down at my arm just before the heat expanded, racing through my body, igniting every nerve and muscle. Rising to my feet, I felt my skin buzzing as if I had drunk twelve cups of coffee. I felt ready to run a marathon. The Superior smiled.

"The power goes both ways."

I tilted my head curiously before I felt something cold blooming in the center of my chest. It felt as if a ball of ice had been planted there. Slowly, it started spreading throughout my body. All the energy and warmth I'd felt a moment ago was violently yanked away from me. I sucked in a ragged breath as my diaphragm struggled to contract. My knees shook and then the muscles of my legs gave out and I collapsed. Sounding like a fish out of water, I struggled to breathe as I turned my head toward The Superior. He reached out a hand, flexing against the barrier of the holy ground, and the cold spreading through me suddenly stopped. Slowly, he pushed warmth back into me. Eventually, I felt strong enough to sit back up.

The power he held over me was stronger than I thought. Despite the returning warmth, I couldn't stop shaking. Looking over at him, I felt the familiar trickle of fear that I hadn't felt since he'd first saved me from Billy. Without thinking I sputtered out, "When this is all over, is this how you'll kill me?"

His head tilted to the side, and he looked at me with an emotion I couldn't quite place. "Two. I have never, nor will I ever, desire your death, Claire. And if it is the desire of any demon, I will kill them."

A strange thrill swirled low in my belly. I fought against the feeling. "How can I possibly believe that's true?"

"Because it is true."

I scoffed and stiffened my spine. My body was finally feeling normal again. "While we are connected, maybe, but once the mark is gone—"

"Once it's gone, that will still be true," he snapped, cutting me off before I could finish. His jaw ticked and his eyes were suddenly swimming in red. I wasn't sure what I had said that had upset him so much.

"Why?" I breathed, "Why do you want to protect me?"

His gaze flicked away from mine. "You've had your three answers."

"What? No, I haven't," I said indignantly.

"'How can I possibly believe that's true?' was a question, Claire. That was three asked and answered, whether you choose to believe my answer or not." He paced in a small circle, then looked back up at me. "Let's go."

I swallowed, then sat there staring back at him for some time. Thinking back over my words, I realized I had been careless with my questions. I'd known I'd have to be careful, but the power transfer had really rattled me. With a resigned nod, I rose to my feet.

"Let me grab my bag."

"Your things are already being packed for you."

Despite the deal we'd struck, I still couldn't make myself take the first step toward him. I'd always assumed he was powerful, but that demonstration had been something else. My fingertips still tingled with the memory of my life being sucked out of me. I didn't meet his eyes, not wanting him to see my fear. My instincts screamed as I took one tentative step toward him. Focusing on my breathing, I managed to take another step. Then another. When I reached the last step, The Superior lifted his chin and extended his hand to me. Slowly, I lifted my own hand and set it into his warm palm.

Pulling me gently down onto the grass, he clasped our hands together. "Thank you," he said and when I looked into his eyes I saw sincerity there.

Licking my lips, I asked, "So, what now?"

He kept a tight grip on my hand as he led me down to the driveway. A large, blacked out SUV sat idling at the entrance.

"Now, we get to work."

We reached the vehicle, and The Superior opened the rear passenger door. He gestured for me to enter while moving his hand from my grasp to the small of my back. Trust between us was going to take time.

"Where are we going?" I asked, as I stepped inside.

"My home."

My eyes widened. "Your home?"

He nodded. I shifted in the seat and scanned the yard around him. Maybe I still had time to run. There had to be time for me to reconsider.

As I worried at my lower lip, the words tumbled out of me. "Well, but shouldn't we go to an office or something? I could go to my office and work from there. That would work, right?"

The Superior stepped forward and pulled the seat belt toward me. With shaking fingers, I managed to take it and latch it.

"Claire," he said softly. He waited until my eyes rose to meet his. "Your office is not safe and being there could endanger your assistant. The hallowed ground of your home did not stop the humans from entering. Until all other threats are neutralized, the safest place for you is my home."

His words made perfect sense, but something in me still resisted. "I just didn't think it meant…living together."

"It's for the best," he said with a shrug.

A man jumped into the front seat. Spinning around, he dipped his head toward me and said, "I'm Jeffrey. Nice to meet you, My Queen."

"Queen?" I sputtered, turning questioningly to look at The Superior.

The demon gave me a small smile. "Yes, now that you will be among my people you should know that bearers of the mark are known as their demon's queen."

My lips twisted, but before I could open my mouth to ask one of the many questions I suddenly had, he slammed the door shut.

The car sped along the highway, but I was aware of little else in the world around me. The reality of my situation kept crashing into me, causing ever increasing waves of panic. I was on my way to The Superior's house. To not only live with him, but help find some missing girl, a task I had never done before in my life. All of this after being attacked by a demon, shot, and having to watch a woman bleed to death on my dining room floor.

Beside me, The Superior seemed unfazed as his fingers slid across his phone screen. At one point, he'd stifled a yawn, but other than that the ride had been silent for the past twenty minutes. Pulling off my gloves, I flexed my fingers, feeling the tape from the bandages pulling on my skin. The mark on my arm suddenly heated. A moment later, I was removing the wrappings to find clear skin underneath.

"Thank you," I mumbled, my gaze flicking over The Superior's profile.

He nodded but said nothing. His fervent attention to his phone brought a realization to my mind. No one knew where I was. Reaching into my jacket pocket, I pulled out my own device and hurriedly typed out a message to Nancy. I assured her that I was safe, but that I wouldn't be home for a while. Hesitantly, I added that I had decided to accept the job with The Superior. After Nancy, I emailed Mark with similar information.

Opening my calendar, I sighed. "I'm going to have to do some work tomorrow." My clients had been willing to accept a delay for my hospitalization, but things were starting to pile up. A quick scan of my bank accounts further confirmed that I needed to be working again.

At first, I thought perhaps The Superior hadn't heard me. I loudly cleared my throat and repeated myself. He ceased scrolling and looked over at me. "What work is required of you?"

I shrugged. "Just some jobs I had lined up before all of this."

His attention returned to his phone as he said, "Tell them you have to cancel."

My eyes widened and I scoffed. "I've signed contracts. I can't just cancel. My business would suffer."

He quirked his brow then turned back to face me. He clicked off his phone and set it in his lap. "How much would you need?"

Not wanting to assume he was saying what I thought he was saying, I asked, "How much would I need for what?"

The Superior waved his hand between us. "This is technically a job, correct? I can simply compensate you for your jobs lost, the contracts broken, plus whatever you wish to charge for assisting me in this matter."

He was in fact saying what I thought he was. I set my jaw and glared back at him. "I'm not breaking those contracts. It isn't about the money." Or it wasn't *only* about the money. "My business and my clients matter to me."

"Fine," he huffed out, "We can draw up a contract for this job. You will think of an amount to be paid, and you will refuse to take on any new clientele until our business is concluded."

He held his hand out to me. I stared at it. "What?"

Dropping his hand, he leaned his head back on the seat. "You are technically working for me. I should pay you for your services. How much would you normally charge?"

I shook my head. "I've never been hired for something like this. I have no idea if I'm even capable of finding this girl, so, I have no idea."

Our gazes locked for several seconds and I shifted uncomfortably in my seat. We were too close together for this amount of eye contact.

"You will work out an amount for me to pay." He said with finality. I opened my mouth in protest, but he raised a silencing hand. "You will not take on any new clients until after we are finished. I will assist your present clientele. Fair enough?"

"What?" I sputtered.

He crossed his arms over his chest and said, "If you will not come up with an amount, I will."

"No," I said, the word shooting out of me before I could stop myself, "I meant my present clients. *You* are going to help them?"

His eyes flashed with red, and his jaw gave a small tick of annoyance. "I have more power over souls than you, Claire, I assure you, I can handle it."

Raising my hands in a placating manner I said, "That's not what I meant. I just…I just didn't expect you to want to *help* people."

"I don't," he said, the red in his eyes fading away. He turned his attention back to his phone before he said, "I am doing it to help you."

My heart fluttered in my chest. I quickly dropped my gaze and pretended to type something on my phone. Feelings I'd never felt for the man beside me tried to build in my chest. Something like curiosity and interest tinged with desire. I squashed them down. He was only helping me to get something in return. There was nothing about this that was done out of the goodness of his heart or out of any affection toward me. This was a business arrangement. He'd made that very clear.

"Okay then," I finally said, extending my hand out to him. "You've got a deal."

He looked briefly over my face, then shook my hand and we returned to staring in silence at our devices. I tried paying a few bills, but the stress of my life was overwhelming me. Instead, I played a simple game on my phone and when that became tiresome, I looked out the window. The world was still dark, but I could make out the occasional passing building or copse of trees. I wondered how far The Superior lived from me.

At some point, I must have fallen asleep. I realized this when something hard under my head kept shifting up and down. My eyes fluttered open and I noticed the car had stopped and the driver was gone. The thing under my head continued to bounce and with a sudden sinking horror I realized what it was. Bolting upright, I dragged my hands down my face and glued my side to the car door. The Superior smiled wryly at me. His gaze flicked over my cheek where I assumed there was a red imprint from where I had fallen asleep on his shoulder. I slapped my hand over the damning patch of skin.

"You snore," he said with a mocking twist to his lips.

My jaw dropped and I stared at him aghast. The corners of his lips twitched higher just before he stepped out of the car. Pivoting, I reached for my own door handle and stepped outside. All my embarrassment quickly fled as I gawked at the world around me.

I stood at the edge of a circular gravel drive. In the middle was a massive marble fountain with a statue of a woman delicately playing a small harp. Music floated from unseen speakers as the crystal-clear water burbled and cascaded through the levels. White lights shone from the depths of the water and along the edges of the gravel drive. Trees lined the other side of the gravel all the way down the driveway until it connected with the main road some distance from where I stood. There looked to be pillars and perhaps a gate at the entrance, but it was so far away, I couldn't be sure. Spinning around, I faced The Superior's house, although calling it that was an understatement. I had assumed he had money. He was always dressed impeccably well, but this was beyond even my imagining. The house sprawled in every direction before me. Upward, it climbed at least three stories and to my left and right further than the trees and hedges would allow me to see. Light brick covered the façade and black shutters adorned each of the massive windows.

The Superior came around the SUV and gently placed his hand on my lower back. He guided me up the front steps and I gasped at the large fountain set into the wall. It was a beautiful piece of glass, full of different colors woven into intricate patterns, that rippled like a flag in the wind. Small rivulets of water flowed across its surface, highlighted by lights along the sides. The faint trickling sound of the water as it reached the bottom created a wonderful sense of calm.

"This is beautiful," I whispered.

The massive wooden door to my left was pulled open and a man dressed in a tuxedo stepped out. He tipped his head, and I saw his attempt at covering a small bald patch.

Guiding me past the man, The Superior and I stepped into the entrance. My mind didn't think it could be further stunned by his home, and yet, I was once again standing with my mouth hanging open. I stepped onto the cream-colored marble floors in my salt-stained snow boots. The foyer was two stories tall, with a grand chandelier hanging above me and twin staircases curving ever upward before me. There was a large table between them, with a huge vase full of artfully arranged white flowers. Everything was muted in color because you were meant to look at the walls. There, filling every available space, were some of the most beautiful paintings I had ever seen. Varying sizes, styles, and colors, all mixed together on the walls in a masterful design that took my breath away.

My eyes found The Superior's and I noticed he had been watching me. He raised his brows and said, "May I take your coat?"

I nodded as my fingers moved numbly over the buttons. His place was so unexpected that my brain felt like I was looking at something in a dream or through a lens. I gave my jacket to The Superior, and he handed it back to the man by the door.

"Do you require anything else, sir?"

The man's voice was warm and professional with a hint of an accent. The Superior gave a small smile and waved a dismissive hand at him. "That is all, Martín, thank you."

Glancing over my shoulder, I saw Martín bow and then turn and walk into a room right beside the entrance.

"Come, this way," The Superior said, as he once again placed his hand on the small of my back. It felt warmer than before because I no longer had the extra layer of my jacket between us. Something felt too intimate about him having his hand there while he was showing me around his home, but I didn't shy away from his touch. There was a part of me that found it comforting and I actually needed the help, as I couldn't take my eyes off the walls. We entered a hallway, and it was just as full of artwork as the entrance had been. Turning down another, I let out a gasp, as the marble walkway expanded, and the walls were replaced with floor to ceiling windows. Set before each one was a sculpture. Again, the mediums and colors were all different and yet somehow cohesive, like in a museum.

"Who arranges all this stuff?" I asked, pointing at an ancient-looking vase.

The Superior cleared his throat and indicated a set of double doors at the end of the hall. "I do," he said simply.

He pushed open the doors and stepped into the interior space. Compared to the rest of the house, this space was simple. Comfortable. Still, stylishly designed, but a more functional space. There were only a few pieces of art in this room. Mostly paintings of musicians or portraits. There was a kitchenette with an island and barstools off to the right. A large sitting area with a fireplace to my immediate left and a long table and chairs in the back. Two hallways led out of the room, one to the left just past the fireplace, the other to the right, past the bar.

The Superior turned and faced me. "You will be staying here. Your room is down the right hall. There is a small bath down there, but the main washroom is down the left hallway. There should be any toiletries you require in one of the bathrooms."

I stepped toward him and tilted my head. "What do you mean, 'you do'?"

He blinked back at me, looking puzzled for a moment, before understanding dawned. "I meant in answer to your question about the arrangements. I do them."

"All of them?"

"Yes."

My brows lifted. "Artfully arranging things doesn't seem like typical demon activity."

He stepped closer to me and inhaled deeply. His voice lowered as he asked, "And what would you know about typical demon activities?"

I shivered. There was something in his tone that suggested things that made my face heat. Taking a step back I forced out a small chuckle. "I just assumed destroying beautiful things was more in line with a demon's nature."

His eyes darkened and we stood staring at each other. The space felt too small and warm all of a sudden. Finally, a small smile spread across his lips. "Perhaps, but I am not typical. Nor would I ever harm something so beautiful and irreplaceable."

He spun on his heels and marched down the right hallway. After a deep breath, I followed him. He gestured as we passed a small bathroom and linen closet then opened the back door into a beautifully appointed bedroom. There was a large bed centered in the middle with floor to ceiling windows draped with cream-colored curtains. A floor length mirror stood in one corner along with a wooden desk. Behind the bed was a walk-in closet. There were a few clothes set on a bench in the middle of the space and several more items in the dresser drawers.

"Whose room is this?" I asked, running my fingers along the empty hangers.

"Yours," he said, with an air that it should be obvious.

I rolled my eyes back at him and said, "Then whose stuff is this?"

He looked at me curiously. "Yours."

"Oh," I said, picking up one of the items from the bench. It was a silky red camisole with thin straps and a hemline that would leave very little to the imagination. My eyes flicked up to The Superior who looked unfazed by the provocative garment in my grasp.

"I had them bring in some night clothes for you since your own will not arrive this evening. Are they not sufficient?"

Rolling my lips, I clenched my mouth shut and tried not to laugh while shaking my head. "They're fine," I said, clearing my throat loudly while gently placing the camisole back down. "Thank you."

His eyes continued to flick between my face and the clothes on the bench, but he eventually accepted my words and walked toward the door. I followed him, wringing my hands together. "Thank you, again. For everything."

He turned with his hand on the doorknob. His head dipped in a small nod before he said, "You're welcome. Goodnight." With that, he stepped out of the room and clicked the door shut behind him.

CHAPTER 15

I awoke the next morning feeling surprisingly refreshed. It definitely had something to do with the ridiculously comfortable bed I was lying in. Sunlight streamed in through the cream curtains as I turned over to bury my face in the pillows. I wondered if I could get away with stealing some of them when I went back home. The thought of home pulled me out of my reverie. I sat up and huffed out a sigh as I wondered what I should be doing.

Flinging back the covers, I went into the closet in search of something to wear. There still wasn't much, but a clean simple sweater worked on top of the jeans I'd worn last night. The jeans needed to be washed, but I had only seen sweatpants in the drawers. Something about parading around The Superior's home in sweats didn't feel right.

After getting dressed, I decided to venture out into the great room. I tugged nervously at my sleeves. For the first time since I had been given the mark, I would be around people who would appreciate its significance. I wasn't sure how I felt about that yet.

When I stepped into the main living space, I found it empty. With a chance to explore, I wandered down the hallway by the fireplace. I reached the first door on the right and gave it a tentative knock. There was no answer, so I pushed in. My mouth nearly dropped to the floor. The bathroom was massive. I suspected my entire kitchen, living, and dining rooms could fit inside. On a raised dais to the left, was a tub that looked large enough to fit five people. Running along the entire right wall was a marble counter. The two sinks sat below a long mirror wrapped in an elaborate iron frame. In the middle of the room, was the largest shower I had ever seen. Three glass walls enclosed the space with a stone wall and ceiling holding several shower heads and dials. A small entryway into a changing space was situated between the shower and tub. I was tempted to jump into the shower, but my budding caffeine headache needed to be addressed first.

Regretfully, I left the beautiful bathroom and went back into the hallway. The door at the end of the hall was locked and when I knocked there was no answer. Moving back into the main space, I searched the bar area for a coffee maker. Not finding anything, I pulled open one of the double doors and resolved to find the kitchen. A woman leaned against the wall, but upon seeing me she swept into an elegant bow.

"Good morning, My Queen," she said in a cheerful voice as she rose. "The Master is busy this morning, so I'll be escorting you. I go by Destiny. I am The Master's second in command."

She smiled brightly and I felt my heart skip a beat. The demon before me was stunningly beautiful. Her fire red hair was pulled into a high ponytail leaving her large green eyes fully exposed. They were the purest emerald color I'd ever seen. The rest of her face was a perfect balance of soft full lips and chiseled cheeks and jawline.

"Would you like some breakfast, My Queen?"

I shuddered at the title. "Coffee and something small would be nice."

With a nod, she turned and beckoned me to follow her. Watching her body sashay down the hallway I realized it wasn't just her face that was gorgeous. Ample curves met at an impossibly narrow waist. For a moment, a sickening, twisting sensation gripped my stomach as I wondered what exactly it was Destiny did for The Superior. My eyes narrowed at her backside as I opened my mouth to ask, but then I snapped it shut. I was feeling jealous. It didn't make any sense as I had no claim to The Superior. I had only just met the demon before me and yet the clenching sensation in my gut didn't ease.

Shaking my head, I tried instead to focus on the route we were taking. We traveled through several different hallways from last night, but these, too, were filled with priceless pieces of art. The Superior's admission that he arranged them still struck me as odd. It felt out of character for him and yet that thought reminded me that I didn't really know that much about him.

Destiny stepped around a corner, and we were greeted by the smells of coffee and frying bacon. The kitchen was befittingly massive like everything else in the house. At the back, a wall of windows looked out onto a green lawn. There were several long tables set up next to them and a handful of people currently milled around them. They all stopped and stared as Destiny and I entered the room.

Seemingly unfazed, she turned to me and said, "Coffee bar is over there. Fully self-serve. The Master has three chefs on staff for breakfast and they can make you anything you like. I'm feeling like a waffle. Would you like one?"

Looking across the room, I saw the massive island and cooktops the chefs were working behind as people lined up at the counter to place and receive their orders. The place felt a bit more like a cafeteria than a home kitchen, but there were a lot of people around, so it made sense. I wondered who everyone was, but then realized I hadn't answered Destiny.

"No, thank you," I said quickly. "I think I'll just start with some coffee."

"Of course, My Queen."

She turned to leave, but I held up my hand. Destiny raised her brows but said nothing. "Could you not call me that?" I asked tentatively.

Destiny shrugged and gave a small laugh. "Sure. What do you want to be called?"

"Claire is fine."

"Okay. Anything else, Claire?"

I smiled and shook my head. She walked off in the direction of the chef's island and I headed for the elaborate coffee bar. There were a few carafes of coffee and tea, and after finding a blonde roast, I grabbed a mug. Next to the bar was a small table with trays of fruits, cereals, bagels, and pastries. Grabbing a small plate, I looked over the fruit, trying to decide what I wanted.

"You must be new."

The voice came from beside me. I hadn't noticed anyone standing there a moment ago. Glancing up, I met the eyes of the young man standing a little too close to me. He was several inches taller than me with light brown hair and a scruffy chin. I gave him a small, polite smile then moved my attention back to the fruit.

"I know everyone here and I know I would remember someone as pretty as you."

Disgust immediately churned in my gut. Was this guy seriously hitting on me? Who hit on people over fruit bowls? I glanced over at him and saw that he had a stupid grin he probably assumed was suggestive plastered onto his face.

Turning toward him, I asked, "Does this crap usually work for you?"

He took my words in stride and gave a small laugh. "Actually, it does. You know, what with the type of women who end up here."

I glared back at him. The presumption that the only woman who would be here would be morally loose grated along my spine. True, I had made a lot of assumptions about demons and their human servants myself, but I was trying to change that. Besides the fact that he was wrong about me, I balked at his audacity to use that misguided opinion to prey upon the women here. With a scoff, I turned away from him and grabbed a large scoop of pineapple. To my dismay, he didn't take the hint.

"I'm Trevor," he said, keeping the smile on his lips. "What's your name?"

Blowing out a loud breath, I stepped further down the table and grabbed an asiago bagel. Turning around, I scooped up my coffee mug, said, "I'm not interested," then proceeded to the corner with the toaster. He followed me, so I abandoned the bagel and decided to search for Destiny instead. I found her sitting at the end of one of the long tables. She waved when she saw me, and I quickly made my way over and took the seat across from her. The shriek of a chair being pulled out filled my ears and I groaned as Trevor plopped down beside me.

I looked over at Destiny, thinking I would say something about the idiocy of some men, but the look in her eyes stopped me. They were flushed with violet flames and a cruel smile curled her lips.

"What do you think you're doing here, Trevor?" she asked, her words filled with venom.

His smile faltered slightly, but he was otherwise undeterred. "I was just trying to get to know our new friend here."

"Ew," I said loud enough for him to hear.

Neither of them reacted to my comment as their attention stayed fixed on each other. I wondered what kind of demon Destiny was. She was looking at Trevor as if he was prey. Tasty prey. I couldn't remember ever having seen a demon with a violet eye flare.

"No one wishes to know you, Trevor," Destiny finally said, "Go away."

There was a warning there, but Trevor simply settled back against his chair. He was either used to being threatened or simply choosing to ignore it. Either way, I was beginning to think Trevor had a death wish. I sipped at my coffee and grabbed a piece of pineapple, wanting to push myself as far away from the conversation as I could.

Trevor crossed one leg over his knee and placed a hand on the back of my chair. "I just want to know her name, is all. And if I were you, I'd watch that tone. I am one of The Superior's subjects, so you can't just threaten me."

I swallowed my fruit as my widened eyes bounced between them. My knowledge of human servants was very limited, so I found it interesting that Trevor regarded himself as The Superior's subject. He also seemed to think this afforded him some protection even from demons who worked for The Superior. I wasn't sure how true that was, and I wouldn't have been willing to test it if a demon was looking at me the way Destiny was currently looking at Trevor. Her smile fell just before she launched herself across the table. I expected her to see her body collide with Trevor's, but she landed in front of me, and seized my right arm. She shoved the sleeve of my sweater up, exposing the mark on my forearm.

"You want to know her name?" she asked, holding my arm out to him. "Not yours."

Destiny gracefully slid back into her chair and crossed her arms over her stomach. Trevor abruptly stood up from the table. I looked over at him and all the color had drained from his face. He stumbled backward, tripping on the leg of the chair before catching himself. Mumbling several apologies, he practically ran out of the kitchen.

Looking around, I saw everyone was staring at me. No one would meet my eyes. I slowly pushed my sleeve back down and covered my head with my hands. Heat rose in my cheeks at the continuing silence.

"Was that necessary?" I whispered when Destiny's gaze met mine.

She looked around the room, as if noticing everyone for the first time. "Get back to it!"

The sounds of chairs sliding, and feet shuffling began again. The ring of the order bell sounded, but people were only speaking in hushed whispers. Destiny nodded, satisfied, and then brought a massive piece of waffle up to her mouth. "If it keeps you safe, then yes, it was completely necessary."

Destiny shoved the huge bite into her mouth and gave a satisfied moan. I blinked over at her. She finished chewing, then said, "Look, surprise, sur-fucking-prise, not everyone who belongs to the master is a good person. There are terrible people who rightfully get mixed up with demons and Trevor and his friends are some of those people. You don't want them taking an interest in you, and that mark will keep them far away."

I peeked behind me and saw a group of men huddled together staring at us. They quickly averted their gazes, but not before I saw the look of contemptuous rage in their eyes. Turning back to Destiny, I shuddered. "Why does The Superior even have people like that?"

She was chewing through another large bite of waffle before she could answer. Her voice lowered as she said, "Would you rather they were out on the street? Once they're servants to The Superior, they have strict rules they have to follow, and the Master doesn't tolerate any of their shit. Their sick and twisted fantasies better stay fantasies or else they get a nice long visit with The Superior."

For some reason, I couldn't imagine The Superior torturing people. It made sense that there was some punishment for disobeying the rules, but I couldn't picture

The Superior being the one to mete it out. Even with my assumptions about what he'd done to Mr. Blake's soul back in the cemetery, the demon I knew didn't seem like the type to torture his servants. Once again, I was reminded that I knew very little about him.

"Besides," Destiny continued, "It's not like people like that aren't destined for The River anyway, you know?"

I did know. The souls of the worst people I'd ever encountered always moved with a singular purpose. They were undeterred and almost unaware of the world around them as they made their way to the boats. Once a soul boarded, they didn't get off until they went through The Gates.

The image of Billy Blake popped into my mind. I had attempted to save Billy from being a servant to The Superior, but now I was wondering if The Superior had planned that all along. Perhaps he had been watching Billy for some time and had used me to finally trap him.

"I'm going to get another waffle," Destiny announced, bringing my attention back to the present. "Do you want anything besides pineapple?"

There was a derisive tone in the way she said *pineapple*. I looked up to see her smirking down at me. Humor glinted in her eyes as she took in the sad state of my breakfast. "I like pineapple," I said.

She shrugged. "And I like giving head, but that isn't enough to satisfy me, now, is it?"

My eyes widened as I snorted with laughter. Destiny offered me a wink and then swept away from the table. When she returned, both her hands held plates ladened with waffles, whip cream, and strawberries. I don't think I've ever liked someone more.

CHAPTER 16

After breakfast, Destiny walked me back to my room. I was taken aback when I opened the closet and found all my clothes hanging or neatly folded into drawers and my shoes placed in racks. My heart started pounding at the sight of my entire wardrobe in The Superior's home. Something about that made it feel too real. So much more final. I was officially moved in.

Darting back into the hallway, I found Destiny leaning against the wall. "Destiny," I said, grabbing her by the arms. Alarm flared to life in her eyes at the note of panic in my voice. "Do you have a gym?" I asked.

Her brow quirked. "What?"

"A gym," I repeated, releasing her arms to press my fingers through my hair. "I need to go for a run and since I don't know where we are, I figured a treadmill would be best."

She glanced down at her phone screen. "The Superior is going to be back to collect you soon."

Her words made the bubbling panic in my chest rise to a full stream. My fingers massaged my chest as I said, "Please, I just need a few minutes to work out some of this tension."

Destiny regarded me for another moment, before she nodded. I whispered my thanks to her, then ran back into my room to change. Once I was appropriately dressed with my hair in a bun, I went back out to meet her. We walked the short distance to the gym, and I happily clambered onto a machine. Destiny took up her perch leaning against the wall by the entrance.

The belt of the treadmill turned, and I took several long, deep breaths. I walked for several minutes and then finally increased the speed enough to break into a light jog. As my feet pounded against the machine, music drummed in my ears and my head finally quieted down.

I'd never liked change, not since the tumultuousness of my childhood. Discovering I could talk to souls didn't go over well with everyone, especially my father. My mother seemed to understand, or at least, accept what I claimed to be, but she never once stood up for me when it came to him. When he said he didn't want to see me anymore, she packed me up and moved me in with some of her relatives. When they grew tired or scared of me, she sent me somewhere else. Always further away from him. Never once did she offer to come with me. When I turned eighteen, I was finally done and moved out on my own. I'd been on my own ever since. Seeing all my belongings simply appearing in The Superior's house had hit an old, damaged nerve. My life was still so easily uprooted.

After twenty minutes of running, I finally felt the waves of panic subside. This didn't mean anything. My house was still mine and I would go back to it just as soon as this was over. My life was not changing forever. Lowering the speed, I started a cool down walk, happy to feel the trails of sweat gliding across my skin as my heart thundered.

With my workout complete, I cleaned the machine and Destiny and I walked back to my room. She nodded at me from the hallway as I closed the main door. Stepping around the bar, I searched for a glass. When I found one, I filled it with water from the tap and gulped down several swallows. I sighed contentedly as I returned to the sink for a refill. My music still blasted in my ears as I drank. My eyes glazed over as I sipped the water while staring across the room at one of the portraits.

A hand lightly brushed my elbow. I jerked the same elbow backward, connecting with a solid wall of muscle, while letting out a startled scream. Pulling my ear buds out, I spun around and came face to face with The Superior.

"You scared me," I spat, taking a few steps away from him. Hurriedly, I wiped my hands across my damp forehead and clasped my chest. Turning, I spotted my water glass rolling across the bottom of the sink.

"My apologies," he said, "I didn't know how else to alert you to my presence."

I waved a hand at him. "You could have said something, or waved, not just come up and grab me."

My heart already pounded with adrenaline from my run, but now it felt like it was trying to beat out of my chest. The Superior's lips flicked briefly upward. He was wearing a gray turtleneck sweater that somehow looked thick and cozy and yet still highlighted the broadness of his shoulders and hugged the muscles of his arms. His black slacks and shiny black loafers completed the casual yet sophisticated ensemble. An errant strand of dark hair fell across his brow, and I fought the urge to brush it off his stupidly handsome face. Who looked that good just hanging around their house?

"Apologies," he repeated, "But I did call your name several times."

"Whatever," I groused before wiping my brow again. "What do you want?"

He crossed his arms over his chest and leaned his hip against the bar. "If you recall, we have work to do."

Looking down, I took in my sweaty gym clothes. "I don't suppose I have time for a shower?" I glanced up in time to see his jaw tick.

"You were aware I was coming, were you not?" he asked with a note of annoyance clear in his tone.

"Yes," I huffed, "But, I needed to clear my head after breakfast, okay?"

He stepped toward me, his eyes sharpening on me as red swirled to life around his irises. "What happened at breakfast?"

A chill flooded down my spine at the dangerous gleam in his eyes. Not fear for myself, but at whatever switch had just flipped inside him. He'd gone from a mildly annoyed client to a vengeful demon in the blink of an eye. I swallowed, not sure what brought on this level of malevolence.

"It was nothing," I said, feeling fresh drops of sweat along my skin as the temperature in the room slowly climbed upward. "I was just weirded out by seeing all my stuff here. That's all."

He tilted his head slightly to the side as he continued studying me. His nostrils flared as he sucked in a deep breath and as he exhaled, I felt the room grow slightly cooler. "Fine. Go shower."

I looked at him quizzically, but when he didn't say anything more, I stepped around him and headed for my room.

"Oh, and Claire," I heard him call just before I entered the hallway. Turning, I looked back at him. He was still leaning against the bar, but the rigid set to his shoulder told me his feelings didn't match the casual pose. Once our eyes locked, he said, "You're a terrible liar."

Rolling my eyes, I ignored his jab and went to shower.

I cleaned and dressed as quickly as I could. The call of the magnificent shower in the other hallway was strong, but I didn't think The Superior would give me enough time to truly enjoy it. To be fair, my hall bath was also large and luxurious, just less so in comparison. Back in my sweater and jeans combo, now complete with wet hair, I headed into the main living space.

The Superior sat at the table. When he saw me, he pulled out the chair next to him and slid a stack of papers in front of it. Sitting down, I looked over the official documents with small colored tabs sticking out along one side.

"Your contract," he said while gently placing a pen beside my left hand.

My eyes wandered over the pages. "Most of my contracts don't look like this." I said while shuffling the papers. A handful of pages were usually sufficient for my previous jobs, but this stack looked closer to fifty. When I got to the payment section, I stared at the amount. I blinked several times, thinking that the extra zeroes had to be my imagination. Nope, they were there. I thrust the offending number into The Superior's face. "What the hell is this?"

Seemingly unperturbed, he glanced down at the page that was nearly brushing the tip of his nose. "I assume you're talking about your fee?"

"Yes," I answered as I set the paper back down on the table. "It's way too much."

"Perhaps you undervalue yourself."

I stared hard at him trying to determine if he was teasing me, but his face remained neutral. "I've never done anything like this before. I don't know what to charge, but even if I guessed, it wouldn't be anywhere near that amount."

Twisting in his seat, he turned to face me more fully. He dropped one elbow behind the back of his chair. "Then tell me an amount. The money doesn't matter to me."

"Must be nice," I mumbled, while scratching out the first number. Drumming my fingers, I tried to think of a more reasonable one. "What sort of job does a demon overlord have anyway?"

He sighed. "To put it simply, I have properties and investments. I even hold some patents. I have been alive long enough for some of those things to accrue rather massive amounts of wealth."

Giving up on thinking of a figure, I tossed the pen down onto the table. The Superior plucked it up and began writing something in that elegant script I'd seen before in his note. When he finished, his large hand placed the pen next to mine. The number was still too high, so I grabbed the pen and scratched it out.

"So basically, generational wealth, but every generation is really just you?" I said and wrote down a number that was half of what he had written and tossed the pen back down.

With a shrug, he scribbled down something else. I looked at it then nodded my head.

"Finally," he said, pushing the papers further back on the table, "I will have my lawyers make the changes this afternoon. Now, to business."

My brows rose and I straightened up in my chair.

"What all do you know about your power?"

I sucked my teeth. "Well, not much, honestly. I mean, I never even had a name for what I was until the first time I met a demon. He spat it at me like it was an insult."

The Superior's lips quirked upward for a moment before he moved to cross his ankle over a knee. He brushed briefly against my leg under the table, and I felt heat radiate through my body from the contact. "Ferriers and demons have a…complicated past."

"You've known other ferriers?" I asked, leaning toward him.

He nodded. "Yes. It is my understanding that your power is meant as a balance to that of the demons. We create an unnecessary obstacle to the afterlife whereas you are meant as a guide. I believe some of the earliest ferriers actually drove the boats on The River."

I was sitting far forward in my seat, enraptured as he spoke. Never before had anyone told me anything about ferriers. My life had been a series of blunders in discovering my powers. The first time I went through a portal had been a truly horrifying experience. I had fallen in the woods and passed through the portal as I rolled down the hill. When I finally stopped, I had no idea where I was or if I could get back. That had been the day I met Gabriel.

My mind whirled with questions, but I made myself focus. "Okay, so how does that translate to me finding this girl?"

The Superior shifted in his seat. "Although your powers are not limited to The Otherworld, how did you find souls there in the past?"

Shrugging my shoulders, I replied, "I found out what type of person they were, then I retraced their steps."

His brow rose. "Let me ask you this: have you ever sought to find a soul in The Otherworld and been unsuccessful?"

The answer to that question wasn't a surprise to me. I knew I had a one hundred percent success rate with my retrieval jobs. It just hadn't occurred to me that my power had something to do with it. I had assumed it was because I hadn't done that many and that Mark and I had thoroughly researched our targets. Although my last job disproved that because I'd had hardly any information on William Blake and I'd found him relatively easily.

"No, I haven't," I finally admitted, "But that's in The Otherworld with dead people."

"As I said previously, your powers are not limited in the way you think."

I chewed my lip for a moment then said, "Okay, assuming I have this ability, I have no idea how to *turn on* that part of my power."

He rose gracefully from his chair and extended his arm. "That's where I come in."

CHAPTER 17

The Superior pressed open two large wooden doors and we stepped into a beautiful library. Every wall but one was covered from floor to ceiling in books. The room was two stories tall with a balcony running around the middle. Several ladders leaned against the shelves and in the far corner a small metal staircase led up to the balcony. Light poured in from a domed glass ceiling and the wall of windows. A large fireplace burned wood to my left as I stepped into the center of the room.

Spinning in a circle, I took in the sights and smells around me. The fire popped and I breathed in the smoky scent. The Superior made his way across the room to a desk where a man sat. Following slowly behind, I let my fingers brush the high backs of the chairs in the room. One held a plush white blanket that was quite possibly the softest thing I'd ever felt. I mentally marked its location so I could steal it into my bed later.

We reached the desk, and I smiled pleasantly down at the top of a man's head. His unkempt strawberry blond waves were covering his face, but I did see a pair of glasses balanced precariously on the tip of his nose.

"Master, what can I do for you?" he asked, not deigning to look up at either of us.

The Superior cleared his throat as if to begin speaking, but then his phone started ringing. He pulled it out of his pocket and upon seeing the screen let out a growl-like sound deep in his throat. Chills skittered down my spine and the hairs on the back of my neck rose in response.

"What?"

He spat the word with such vehemence that I was thankful to not be the person on the other line. Lifting his index finger, he gave me an apologetic look and took several steps away to continue his conversation in private.

Stepping forward, I extended my hand under the man's nose. "Hi, I'm Claire."

"That's nice," he mumbled, then slid his book out from under my hand and turned the page. Slowly, I retracted my arm.

Drumming my fingers on my thighs I asked, "What's your name?"

"Toby," he said absently, still not looking at me. I started to wonder if after the breakfast incident with Trevor, The Superior had warned his subjects against interacting with me. Looking back at the demon, I saw him pacing in a tight circle with his free hand clenching and unclenching into a fist at his side. The call was not going well by the looks of it, so I turned my attention back to Toby.

"So, what is it you do here, Toby?"

That got his attention. Finally, his face tipped upward, and I was greeted with rapidly blinking blue eyes set over lightly freckled cheeks. His lips were too big for his face, and they were tipped into a slight frown. "I keep the Master's books."

I smiled and nodded. Perhaps Toby wasn't one for conversation. Trying again, I said, "Mm-hmm, and how long have you been working for him?"

"Is there something I can help you with?" he asked in a flat tone.

Before I could answer, The Superior returned, fuming and with his eyes a sea of red. "I have to go," he said bluntly. "We'll have to do this later."

"Do what, exactly?"

A small flicker of hesitation flashed across his eyes. "I have a private library that may contain texts that better define your powers."

My eyes widened as I gawked at him. "If those books exist, then tell me where they are right now, and I will go find them."

Not only were there books that talked about my powers, but they were somewhere in here? I needed to find them. What other information did they contain and who wrote them? Stepping closer to The Superior, I crossed my arms and glared at him, daring him to come up with a good enough reason that I couldn't go find the books myself.

He pressed his fingers to his forehead and said, "It's not that simple."

"Bullshit," I scoffed. "I am perfectly capable of finding some books. And even if you use some archaic demon alphabetizing system, I'm sure he can point me in the right direction."

I lifted a finger and pointed at Toby, who was now watching us with some interest. The Superior's jaw muscle ticked as he looked between me and Toby. When his eyes connected with the librarian's, I saw his face soften slightly. With a strangled sigh, he pulled a ring of keys from his pocket and set it on the desk. "Toby, I need some books from the private library."

Toby straightened up in his seat. His eyes gleamed with excitement. "Of course. Which books?"

The Superior leaned down and wrote some things down on a piece of paper. He came back to me and extended a hand as though to lead me out. I pushed his arm away and said, "I'm going with him."

His right eyelid twitched as the flames around his eyes began to flicker. "No, you are not. Toby is perfectly capable of finding the books on his own."

With a shrug, I stepped around him. There was no way I wasn't going along to search for those books. "Who doesn't love an extra pair of hands?"

Just as I passed him, The Superior's fingers lashed out and wrapped like a vise around my wrist. He pulled me close to his body. Heat radiated off him and I got a whiff of that smokey, woodsy scent I'd smelled on him previously.

"I don't have time to explain this to you, but no," he hissed close enough to my face that I could feel his breath on my cheek.

A soft chuckle slipped past my lips. The sound caused The Superior's eyes to momentarily dart down to my mouth before snapping back up to my eyes.

"Here's the thing," I said, "You've already played your hand. I know you won't kill me to keep me from going and based on the number of times you've healed me, I don't think you'll hurt me either. Judging by your reaction to that phone call, there's somewhere else you urgently need to be, which means you're either going to have to drag me along with you or lock me in my room because nothing is stopping me from getting those books." I was smiling when I finished speaking and was surprised to find The Superior looking at me with intense interest. His eyes scanned my face as heat continued to build around me. Whereas before it had felt oppressive and frightening, this time it was more comforting, like wrapping myself in a blanket straight out of the dryer.

"Well?" I prompted.

His lips quirked upward as he said, "Hang on, I'm still thinking about locking you up."

My eyes rolled as I gently pulled my wrist from his grasp. He let me, but our eyes stayed locked together. With a sigh, he said, "Fine. You may assist Toby, but Claire, there are rules. First, don't hurt Toby."

I laughed, thinking he was joking, but he leveled his gaze at me. "Fine," I said, raising my hands in placation.

"Second, know that I am very particular about my library. Do exactly as Toby says at all times and do not touch anything without his approval."

"Fine," I said again, but when he raised his brow at me, I continued, "I won't touch anything unless Toby tells me I can."

He nodded approvingly. "Toby, Miss Woods will be accompanying you."

Toby scooped up the key ring and paper and stood from behind the desk. He started searching through the keys on the ring while The Superior stepped closer to me.

"Give me your word, Claire," he whispered.

"What the hell is in there?" I asked, letting my anger at his distrust through. "I give you my word, I'm not going to hurt your books or Toby."

He lightly gripped my elbow. "Last thing. There are books in my private library written in demonic script. They are dangerous for humans to read. Do not read them."

I raked my fingers through my hair and gave an irritated groan. The pad of his thumb grazed the underside of my chin, pulling my gaze upward to meet his. His eyes flicked with concern as he said, "Promise me, Claire."

My heart thumped heavily in my chest as I stared into that beautiful face. With his heat still enveloping me and the curiously rough texture of his fingers against my skin I felt my resolve fading. I managed to nod. With that, he pulled away and swept out of the room.

Turning to face Toby, I felt my cheeks burning. What the hell had just happened? I had always found The Superior attractive, but this had been something different. Something stronger. A cold wash of fear shot through me as

I once again wondered how much power the mark gave him over me. Could he manipulate my emotions? Glancing over at Toby, I decided I had one more reason to search The Superior's library.

"Wait for me," I called as I hurried across the room.

Toby leaned under the desk and must have pushed a button because a wall of books suddenly slid aside revealing a set of stairs.

"Wow, a secret passageway in a library. How cliché."

He ignored my comment and pressed the shelf further inward revealing more of the stairway. Toby stepped through without a second glance and I hurried to catch up with him.

CHAPTER 18

Toby's medium frame descended the stairs ahead of me. For a hidden stairway, it was rather beautifully designed. The corridor was wide and well-lit by brightly burning sconces along both sides. Wood creaked under my feet as we made our way downward. It didn't feel like we were heading into a basement, and yet I knew we had to be below ground. At the bottom of the stairs, I passed under an intricately carved archway and entered a cavernous room. It almost rivaled the main library in terms of space, although the ceiling wasn't quite as high. The floor was poured concrete, but it was covered in lush rugs that warmed the space considerably. There were no windows nor fireplace, but the same cozy chairs sat around the room. Walls ladened with books soared upward toward another glass dome.

"It's a fake ceiling," Toby said, following my upward gaze. "It typically mimics the sky outside. Controls on the wall can make any kind of day you'd like, or it can simply emit natural light."

He walked over to the far wall and started typing on a screen. He turned and smiled at me before nodding toward the ceiling. Slowly, the blue sky filled with gray clouds. Then, small specks started to appear and then they slid toward the edges. Raindrops. It looked so natural that I never would have guessed it was fake.

"It's beautiful," I said, then turned my attention to the books around us. Stepping toward the nearest shelf, I started reading the spines. My fingers itched to run along the spines, but I remembered my promise to The Superior and kept my hands clasped in front of me. The shelf I stood in front of contained mostly philosophy and art. Moving along, I found sections of history, politics, and memoirs. Then I came to a shelf that had my jaw dropping to the floor.

Toby, who had entered a small adjoining room, returned to the main space holding two flashlights. I bolted across the room, gesturing wildly behind me. "Toby, is that what I think it is?"

Tilting his head to look around me, Toby found the object of my sudden excitement. "Ah, yes, first edition of Pride and Prejudice by Jane Austen."

My eyes flew wider still. "It's signed!"

Extending a flashlight toward me, he nodded. "That is the Master's first edition Regency romance shelf."

"Toby," I said, bringing my hands together in front of my face, "The way you just said that makes it sound like he has several first edition shelves."

He looked at me curiously. "He does."

"What?" I screamed.

Adjusting his glasses as though my outburst had unsettled them, Toby said, "The Master collects all books of importance."

My mind was reeling as he pressed the flashlight into my hand. Toby turned and walked back toward the small room he'd been in previously. I followed, wondering why I was so surprised by this revelation. It wasn't like I knew anything about The Superior before coming here. Why was it any time I learned something about him, I felt so stunned? I pondered that for a moment before realizing it was because the things I was learning made him feel human and for some reason that bothered me.

"This way," Toby said, interrupting my thoughts. I wanted to ask what the flashlight was for, but I quickly saw the answer. He had opened a doorway into another stairwell. This space looked tight and poorly lit. Stepping inside, I saw sporadic bulbs hanging from a wire near the top of the ceiling. The walls were carved rock at first and then just smooth earth as we descended further. The stairs were ancient slats of wood that looked hastily put together. Some steps were larger than others while some slanted to one side or another. I kept one hand on the wall, trying to maintain my balance as I made my way down the uneven steps. Toby was unhindered by the odd stairs and ended up several paces ahead of me.

When I reached the bottom, he was waiting for me. "Thanks for waiting," I said, accidentally brushing some dirt from hand onto my jeans.

"I couldn't see the keyhole."

He lifted the ring of keys, and I shined my flashlight on them. His fingers flew through the keys, clearly looking for some marker, while my gaze wandered behind him. There was a barred metal gate built into the tunnel walls. It looked ancient, but sturdy.

"Got it," Toby exclaimed, lifting the key and turning toward the gate. I followed him, lighting the keyhole.

"How old are these tunnels?" I asked.

Toby twisted the key and the thunk of the bolt coming free echoed through the small space. He pushed the gate inward, and the screech of unoiled metallic hinges assaulted my ears. Toby stepped through and gestured for me to follow. Once I was on the other side, he closed and locked the gate. Looking around the earthen tunnel, my breathing quickened as the small space started feeling slightly oppressive.

"Old."

My head jerked toward the sound of Toby's voice. He had the ring of keys in hand again and looked up at me with a bit of annoyance. "Light, please, Miss Woods."

"Sorry," I said, shining the light. Looking over my shoulder, I saw we were only a few steps away from another gate. The tight feeling in my chest increased as I looked from one locked door to the next. "You can call me, Claire, by the way."

"No, thank you," he replied without looking up.

I gnawed anxiously at my lip, but Toby seemed unbothered by the small space. He found the next key with the same speed at which he'd found the first and we were soon repeating the process with the second gate. And then the third. With each successive gate, I felt my pulse rising.

"Where exactly are we going?" I asked.

Toby shined his light down the pathway. There were no more gates and at the very end, I thought I could see stairs.

"Almost there," he said as he set off.

I followed and felt a wash of relief when my feet started up the stone steps. They were worn and imperfect, but in better shape than the wooden stairs. Part of the way up, the dirt walls turned to stone and once again lights dotted the ceiling. We climbed up and up. Sweat broke out across my brow, and yet the stairs continued. Eventually, I asked Toby if we could take a break.

Leaning against the cool stone wall I looked over at Toby who seemed unbothered by the climb. "Sorry," I said, panting slightly, "I ran this morning, and I didn't eat enough breakfast for that and a hike."

It wasn't a lie. Not only was I thirsty, but I was suddenly starving. I sincerely hoped we were almost to the top. Glancing up, it was too dark to see very far. What I did see were more stairs. I looked over at Toby. He was tracing the lines of the steps with his flashlight, following them up and up, until the light became too faded and then he moved back to the beginning.

"Do you like working for The Superior?" I tried.

That got his attention. His eyes flicked up to mine. "I love it."

Smiling, I said, "What do you love about it?"

His face beamed and he suddenly looked years younger. "He has the best books. Not just the special editions, but rare books. Books I'd never even heard of, in all kinds of languages. And not just Classics, but all books and he lets me read them."

An idea popped into my head, and I acted on it before I had a chance to think better of it. I pushed back my right sleeve and held my arm out to him. "Have you ever seen something like this before?"

He stepped forward, intrigued. Shining his light onto my skin, his face moved incredibly close to me. His eyes fixed on the marking for several moments, then he abruptly straightened. "I believe I have."

My heart leapt. "You have?"

Nodding, Toby indicated further up the stairs with his flashlight. "If I have seen it, it would be in the Master's private collection."

"Well, then," I said with a smile, pushing off the wall, "What are we waiting for?"

We ascended the remaining stairs until we came to what I thought was a dead end. Toby pointed upward with his flashlight, and I saw the trapdoor above us. We repeated the process of finding the key with my guiding light. Toby climbed a ladder built into the wall to unlock the door and then thrust his shoulder into it to pop it open. Light poured through the opening, and I stepped back, shielding my eyes.

Once I finally adjusted to the brightness, I climbed the ladder and pulled myself up onto the wood floor. Toby watched me and then shut the door behind me. Spinning in place I felt completely disoriented. We were in a luxurious wood cabin. Windows filled the wall to my left and the view was breathtaking. The cabin sat on a small hilltop overlooking the rest of the estate. The Superior's home sprawled on the ground before me along with several smaller outbuildings, all surrounded by lush trees. I could imagine him standing up here, observing his empire. Behind me was a small state of the art kitchen with stainless steel appliances that shined like new. To the left, there was a bedroom and a bathroom. To the left of the kitchen was a curved archway. Toby passed under it and disappeared into the room beyond. I followed him a moment later and saw that the back of the cabin was entirely made up of the library.

Small, rectangular windows filled the narrow space between the shelves and the ceilings. Every wall was filled with books and several freestanding shelves stood in the middle of the room. A table sat to the left of the entrance. Toby set the ring of keys down on top of it along with the paper The Superior had given him.

"Okay," I said, clapping my hands together, "Where do we start?"

CHAPTER 19

I spun the desk chair around for what felt like the thousandth time. The sound of Toby's footsteps shuffling through the aisles reached my ears and once again, I felt like ripping my hair out. At the start, we'd had a discussion as to what qualifications I had to assist in the search. Underwhelmed by my lack of skill with foreign languages and basic cataloguing methods, Toby had placed me in front of a shelf and asked me not to stray beyond it. The books had all been in English, although some were in an older variant. After a few minutes of flipping through them, I'd concluded that none of them contained the information we needed. My hasty assumption had gotten me sent off to sit and wait and I'd been here ever since.

Rising abruptly from the chair, I walked into the kitchen. I prayed there was something to drink in the fridge. Upon opening it, I found several bottles of water. Twisting off the cap, I took a drink and then turned to stare out the window. We had been here for a couple of hours. The sun was beginning to sink into the distance. The prospect of returning to the tunnel that connected us to the main house didn't thrill me, but neither did spending another hour sitting here.

After finishing my water, I placed the empty bottle on the counter and went into the bedroom. It was simply furnished, with a massive bed and two end tables. The large windows overlooking the estate continued in this room, but there was a haze to them. I suspected there was a film on the glass that kept the room private. Searching the bedside tables, I found all the drawers were empty. The closet was similarly unimpressive, so I walked back to the library. Toby was immersed in his work and barely aware that I even existed. I walked through the shelves and around to the back of the room. One wall of books continued down a skinny hallway that I hadn't noticed before. Stepping into the hall, I turned to see a door that blended seamlessly into the wall. I pulled on the handle, but it didn't budge.

"Toby?" I called, but heard no reply.

I went to where I'd last seen him and gently tapped him on the shoulder. With a start, his wide eyes turned to regard me.

"What's behind that door in the corner?" I asked, gesturing to where I'd just been.

Adjusting his glasses, Toby blinked at me. "Storage?"

"Are you asking me or telling me?"

He shrugged and returned to scanning the titles on the shelf. I tapped him again. He jerked just like he had before.

"Can I take the key ring and see if one of the keys unlocks it?"

His nose scrunched as he studied me. "Why are you asking me?"

I smiled. "Because The Superior said to get your permission before I touched anything."

"Fine, whatever," he said, with a wave of his hand, dismissing me.

Almost tripping in my haste, I snatched the key ring off the desk and ran back to the door. I was confident the key I needed was on the ring, I just had to find the right one.

Picking one key to start with at random, I slid it into the lock and wiggled it. The first key was not the right one. Nor was the second. Neither were the eighteenth or nineteenth keys. Finally, after I had stopped counting and almost broken a key in the lock, I found the right one.

The wood of the door groaned as I pushed it open. Inside was dark, so I searched the wall for a light switch. Finding it, I flicked it upward. It looked like an old linen closet. There was hardly enough room for one person to turn around inside, especially since there was a large trunk taking up most of the floor space. The walls inside the closet were also filled with shelves; however, the books in here were very different. Each shelf contained the same thin, black, leather-bound books and each one had a number down the spine. The condition of the books varied. Some were wrinkled with wear while others looked shiny and crisp. My finger trailed along a shelf before I selected a random book and pulled it out.

The number on the spine read 1881. Holding the soft bound book in my hand, I realized it was a journal. The number was a year. I opened it slowly to a random page and saw handwriting I instantly recognized. It was the same as the note Nancy had given me from The Superior.

I stared down at the page and read:

July 8, 1881

63
Slavery still rampant. Natives are being pushed out.

I have added two more subjects to my employ. One, a woman named Dorothy will be of great use for her values are strong but her mind easily corruptible. The man, Jonathan, will bear watching.

July 11, 1881

62
Sins still abound. Demons run much of the world.

Ethel has left my employ. Our arrangement completed;
she had no reason to remain. She will be missed. Jonathan
has been asking questions. He was disciplined. Watching still
required.

Elina is sick. I hope she will be well again soon.

I dropped to my knees, the journal bouncing out of my
hands to lay open on the floor. With a tentative hand, I
flipped through the pages and saw they were all the same.
Filled with journal entries. My eyes travelled upward as I
took in all the books around me. There had to be hundreds
of them.

Reaching up, I grabbed another book. It fell open in my
hands and I saw the same methodical record keeping. I
grabbed another and another. Each one was the same as the
one before. A date, followed by a number, a brief
description of current events, and then a longer section on
people. His people, who he knew by name and even
expressed remorse over losing. My mind spun as I rocked
back onto my heels.

Who the hell was The Superior? The first time we'd
met, he'd scared me so badly I hadn't been able to return to
The Otherworld for two whole years. My business had
suffered. My life had suffered and yet here he was, showing
so much care and sympathy for people. I couldn't get these
incongruous pieces of The Superior to fit together in my
mind.

I shoved the pile of journals away from me. My arms
wrapped around my knees as I rocked on the dirty floor. I

had seen flashes of tenderness and kindness in him myself, but I could never forget the day we met.

I'd known the job would be difficult from the outset. Families of the victims of a serial killer wanted a chance at finding their lost loved ones. I'd known catching his soul would be difficult. The moment his soul materialized, he would be moving toward a portal. He was scheduled for execution, so we all gathered together in the room, and waited. The second I spotted his soul, I snatched his arm, but he'd fought me. His soul wanted to get to The River, and it pulled him so fiercely that he almost broke free from my grasp. I'd poured all the magic I could muster into getting him to stand still. Even then, his eyes continuously darted away and I could feel the tension vibrating through him. The families asked their questions, and I'd held him for as long as I could. Even in death, he wouldn't give up all of the locations of the bodies. My power was drained, but I'd still wanted to see that he made it through the portal. I needed to know that the world was safe from someone like him. We'd stepped through and that was the first time I saw The Superior. He'd been all fire and fury. His frustrated shouts had thundered around me, making my ears ring. His fingers had wrapped around my arms, burning my skin with his scalding heat. His demons had encircled me, snarling and laughing as I'd stood there trembling in terror.

"Never again."

Those had been the only words he'd spoken to me, but they had been enough. I'd stayed away, always keeping my distance from the demons. Until now. Looking down at the books, I realized I now somewhat counted as one of The Superior's subjects. Perhaps that was why I'd seen some kindness from him.

"Having fun?"

The sound of an unfamiliar voice coming from directly behind me caused me to jump and scream. Turning around,

I saw a man I'd never seen before, leaning in the doorway. His sandy colored hair fell over sea green eyes that stared mischievously down at me.

Rising to my feet, I brushed the dirt off my hands. "Who the hell are you?"

"Scott," he said, extending his hand. I stared hesitantly down at it, but didn't take it. He finally dropped his hand with a chuckle, but he didn't move out of the doorway. His eyes roved over me and everything else in the room. When his gaze came back to meet mine, it held a humor that I felt was directed at me.

"What?" I asked, really wishing he would back up.

He tilted his head and crossed his arms over his chest and said, "Don't mind me. I'm just trying to put it all together."

"Put what together?"

"Why there's a woman in the forbidden closet with the keys, and a body outside on the floor."

CHAPTER 20

"What?" I cried before I shoved him in the chest. He fell backward and I bolted into the library. Running around, I searched the shelves until I saw Toby, lying sprawled on the floor with a book still grasped in his hand.

"Oh my God, what happened?" I shouted as I fell to my knees and pressed my fingers to his neck. There was a slow but steady pulse. A sigh of relief flew past my lips.

"He's alive," Scott said, coming to squat on Toby's other side. "Probably read too much demonic script, because you wandered off and left him to do all the work."

I glared over at him. "I didn't *make* him do all the work."

He cut me off with a wave of his hand and said, "You might want to close that door. The Master is on his way."

Jumping to my feet, I ran back to the closet. I grabbed the journals and hurriedly placed them back onto the shelves. When I finished with the books, I snatched the keys off the floor and locked the door behind me. Scott was still squatting by Toby when I returned. He smirked at me when I tossed the key ring onto the table. Who the hell was this guy?

"What are you doing here?" I asked, taking a few steps closer to him.

"Looking for you. The Master assumed you'd be back by now. I see why you were delayed. You were busy snooping, but did you have to involve poor Toby here?" Scott tsked and shook his head shamingly at me.

"I didn't do this," I spat, coming back to kneel beside Toby. Thankfully, his chest still rose and fell in a regular rhythm. It almost looked as if he were sleeping. "I didn't even know reading demonic script did this to people."

"Uh-huh. Is that the story you're planning to go with when he gets here?"

"How did you even get here? We have the keys." I said, shifting onto the floor while continuing to check the open doorway in the floor. The Superior hadn't arrived yet and I couldn't understand why he'd sent this man ahead of him.

Scott pulled a ring of keys out of his pocket. "You honestly thought he had only one set? You should know your demon better than that, My Queen."

I scoffed but said nothing as my eyes were drawn to the book still clasped in Toby's hand. His thumb was stuck between the pages. Gently sliding it out, I pulled the book into my lap and opened it. I gasped at the drawing of a forearm with scrawling black script on it. It was a picture of a demonic mark. Toby had fallen into this coma-like state because of me. The realization hit me hard, and I felt a pit forming in my stomach. My hand reached out to clasp Toby's as I stared down at the page. Lines of black symbols, that I assumed had to be demonic script, filled the space around the drawing. I needed to find a way to translate the text, preferably without The Superior finding out.

Rising to my feet, I took the book over to the desk and pulled out a scrap of paper I'd seen earlier. I fit it between the pages and placed the book on the stack with the others. My eyes found Scott's. He watched me with a curious expression, but there was no judgment there. I heard the light sound of footsteps and turned in time to see The

Superior enter the room. His eyes swept the space and when they landed on Toby they immediately bled with red.

"What happened?" he asked, his voice deadly low. He stood unnaturally still and in the ensuing silence, I could hear my pulse in my ears.

"I don't know," I said honestly.

In an eerily slow motion, The Superior tipped his head up. His gaze locked on mine, and I flinched. Heat swirled around my body as I struggled to hold his gaze. "Why don't you know, Claire?"

I fiddled with the sleeves of my sweater. "I was doing something else."

He stared at me for several moments, then turned back to Toby. Kneeling down beside him, The Superior gently wrapped his fingers around Toby's wrist. I focused on steadily breathing in and out as The Superior continued checking Toby's vital signs.

"What did you find when you got here?" he asked, looking at Scott.

"Toby was lying here like this, and the Queen was MIA, sir. I found her researching in the back. She seemed genuinely surprised by Toby's status."

Scott's response had been surprisingly vague. I didn't know if he did it to cover my tracks or if it was normal for him to omit details when talking to The Superior. Something told me it was the former and I didn't like the idea that I now owed him. The Superior mulled over Scott's words for a moment before he reached under Toby and easily lifted him into his arms. He stood and quickly closed the distance between us. Toby lay limply across The Superior's chest, and I struggled not to cringe with guilt as I looked at him.

The Superior lowered his voice and said, "You broke your promise."

With tears starting to well in my eyes, I said, "I'm sorry. Is he going to be, okay?"

His gaze searched mine, looking for some sign of deception, but he wouldn't find any. I genuinely felt responsible for what happened to Toby.

Accepting whatever he saw in my expression, The Superior nodded. "He will improve once I get him to the infirmary. This is the consequence of humans reading demonic script." He leaned his head to the side, looking around me to the desk. "Hopefully, whatever he found was worth it."

Turning, I stared back at the stack of books. "I don't know what he found. I just know he didn't think I was a good assistant and clearly, I am not."

I forced out a small chuckle and looked back at The Superior. There was no humor on his face. "So many things in which you are *clearly not* good."

His tone sent a shiver down my spine, but I said nothing as I focused on simply holding his gaze. The world around me still felt like an oven and his eyes glowed like embers. This mistake had cost me some trust, and for some reason, that bothered me. The Superior's and my interactions may have confused me, but I had seen nothing but steadfast dedication when it came to his people. No matter how I felt, I knew that was true, and I had hurt one of those people after swearing I wouldn't.

My cheeks reddened as I mumbled, "I'm sorry."

The Superior's nostrils flared as he forced out a breath. He spun in place and started walking toward the exit. "Scott, collect the books and take her to her room."

Scott bowed and The Superior left. I stared at the empty space for a moment, feeling my stomach drop even further. He had ignored my apology and it stung. Scott let out a loud whistle. "You're a lucky one, aren't you?"

Striding across the room, he came to stand beside. He flicked his brows at me before he turned and started piling books into his arms.

"What are you talking about?" I hissed.

He continued stacking the books as he said, "He's fucking pissed because he knows you're lying."

"I'm not lying," I said before remembering he knew the truth.

A full belly laugh poured out of Scott. It was a deep, happy sound, and it lightened something within me when I heard it. "You are," he continued while stacking the last few books into his arms. "And you're terrible at it. Seriously, when you suck that much at it, maybe don't try lying to a demon."

"You lied, too," I retorted because I apparently couldn't think of anything clever to say.

"No, I didn't," he said somewhat seriously. "I omitted facts. I didn't lie. There's an important distinction there, Your Majesty."

He walked toward the tunnel entrance and then bent to set the stack of books on the floor. Dropping down next to it, he hung his legs into the tunnel and then jumped. "Toss me the books," he shouted from the bottom.

Rolling my eyes, I walked over and saw him standing at the bottom with a flashlight between his teeth. He flicked his hands at me and so I started gently tossing the books down. The last one I threw with a little extra force, and he grinned around the flashlight at me when he caught it.

I hopped down next to him and took the light out of his mouth. He flexed his jaw a few times, then said, "Thanks. Did you bring the keys?"

With a groan, I climbed back up and retrieved the keys off the desk. I found my flashlight by the desk chair and then returned to the tunnel with both items. Somehow, I managed the necessary acrobatics of closing and locking the door while holding keys, a ladder, and a flashlight. Scott helped by shining light onto the lock and on the rungs as I made my way down to him. When I reached the bottom, he tucked his flashlight away and adjusted the books in his arms. He set his chin on top of the stack to stabilize it and smiled over at me.

"Need a hand?" I asked while shining the flashlight over the stack.

He shrugged. "Light the way and manage the keys and we'll be good."

We started down the stone steps with some difficulty. I was twisted awkwardly, trying to keep a light for Scott behind me and a light in front for myself. Eventually, we squeezed together on the steps, so I could switch to using one flashlight.

When we hit the first gate, I shined the light on the key ring and said, "Please tell me you know which key it is."

"Hold 'em up?"

I moved them closer to his face.

"Yeah, you see that brass one?"

Rolling my eyes, I forced out a fake laugh. "Oh, you mean all of them?"

"Just trying to loosen things up, Your Majesty. They have numbers. Should be twenty-two."

Popping the flashlight in my mouth, I used both hands to flick through the keys. The numbers were small and some were starting to wear, but they did at least appear to be in order. Finding the one labeled twenty-two, I moved to the gate and opened the lock. Scott stepped through and I locked it behind us.

We walked side by side again as I directed the light. After a few moments, I said, "My name is Claire, by the way."

Scott glanced at me. "I know."

"Then call me Claire."

"I don't think so," he said with an exaggerated chuckle.

Turning to face him, I gave him my best hard stare. "Stop calling me Your Majesty."

That easy smile spread across his lips as he leaned closer to me. "Apologies, My Queen."

I groaned in frustration, and he laughed. "Destiny called me Claire."

"So?" he replied, shifting the stack of books in his arms. "She's his number two and a demon. She can get away with that shit."

"And who the hell are you?" I demanded, struggling to contain myself. My eyes scanned his face, trying to learn something about the man I was stuck with underground. He smirked down at me, his entire demeanor relaxed, but there was something deeper behind his eyes. The Superior trusted him enough to give him his keys and to leave me alone with him. Despite how he acted, Scott had to be someone important.

"Look," he finally said, "As much as I love being with you in a dark hole in the dirt, can we just move this along?"

That wasn't an answer, but it seemed to be all he was willing to give. I nodded, and we started toward the next gate. We walked in silence and when we reached the gate, we repeated our earlier process to proceed through it.

After locking up behind us I said, "What about Miss Woods?"

Scott huffed. "Fine."

I smiled triumphantly up at him. "So, Scott, how long have you been with The Superior?"

My arms swung as I walked, making the beam of light dance across the ground. The floor was mostly level dirt down here, so I was less worried about tripping. I was also feeling the press of the earth around me and searching for a distraction.

"A while."

"Uh-huh," I said, kicking a small pebble with the tip of my shoe, "And how long is that? Are we talking years? Decades?"

Scott looked over at me, a flicker of annoyance clear in his eyes. "A long time."

I popped my lips, and it echoed in the small space. Liking the sound, I did it again. And again. "What kind of work do you do for him?"

We reached the next gate and after giving me the number Scott asked, "What the hell are you doing?"

Looking up at him, I rattled the keys. "Looking for the key."

"No, why are you asking me all these questions?"

With a shrug, I continued searching the ring. I found the right key and proceeded to unlock the gate. It was the last one and I could feel the tension in my shoulders starting to ease. We would be on our way back to the surface soon. "Just making conversation."

Scott moved through the open gate and stopped beside me as I locked it. "Then why not ask me about movies or something?"

"I don't know," I said with a nervous laugh, "I've never spent time with a human servant before, so I was curious."

"Curious about what?" He was standing still, staring down at me. His face hardened.

Trying to wave off the tension, I gestured awkwardly over at him. "About everything. What do servants do and what do they get out of it? Why the hell you people willingly tie yourselves to a demon? Stuff like that."

He stiffened and his face jerked back as if I had slapped him. His voice was low, all the good humor from earlier gone as he said, "Yeah, why would anyone tie themselves to a demon?"

My cheeks flushed as I realized what I'd said. I started back pedaling, not understanding exactly what had gone wrong. "No, I didn't mean like me."

"Right," he said, stepping closer to me, "You're different. Sorry we didn't all get the same option to fuck him instead of serving him."

I stumbled backward. My back hit the dirt wall, and I slid down, stopping in a crouch. Dropping my hands onto my knees I stared back at him. "I wasn't trying to insult you, I just wanted to learn."

"Oh, you want to learn?" he said, sarcasm lacing his words. He shifted the stack of books and turned to better face me. "Well, first rule of thumb, don't ask people about their service. It's private, between them and The Master. If people want to tell you, let 'em, otherwise, don't ask about it. Second, we're not all here by choice. It's a mixed lot of us. Some like it here, some don't. Some like The Superior, some don't. It's the same as any other group of people. We're still humans."

Part of me wanted to protest that I wasn't saying any of that. I wanted to say I never assumed any of those things about human servants, but then I stopped myself. Maybe I had made some of those assumptions. Stress about the situation had played a part in my rambling questions, but that didn't change what I had said. A weight started in my chest and pushed down into my stomach.

"Scott," I said, pushing myself up from the wall, "I'm really sorry. I guess I never let myself think that way. Thank you for telling me."

He nodded but his irritation was still evident. We started walking again. I put all my concentration and effort into holding the flashlight steady in front of Scott. When we reached the stairs, I huddled against the wall, giving him as much space as I could to freely move up the steps. When we reached the small room off the lower library, I turned off the flashlight and breathed a sigh of relief. We were still below ground, but the space around me felt cavernous and bright compared to the tunnel.

Moving into the main space, Scott set the book stack down on a table and stretched out his arms. "Ok, I feel like I kicked a puppy. I'm sorry."

My jaw dropped. "No, you shouldn't feel bad."

"But I do," he said, lifting a hand to stop me. "You're a queen now and I should be happy you want to learn more about your people. I shouldn't assume because you're sleeping with a demon that you know all this."

"I'm not sleeping with him," I huffed, placing my fists on my hips. Realizing that made me look like a petulant child, I instead crossed them over my chest.

"Oh yeah?" he said, his earlier humor once again lighting his face. "You have seen him, right?"

I narrowed my eyes, and he gave a small chuckle.

"I'm a handsome guy, but I'm enough of a man to admit I'm second best when he's in the room."

My lips lifted upward, and I couldn't keep myself from laughing. "Second best? So humble."

He ran a hand suggestively through his hair and winked at me. I tossed my head back and laughed harder. This man was something else, but I appreciated that he wasn't holding our earlier conversation against me. Scott lifted the stack of books again and nodded toward the stairs. I followed him.

"You're his queen and you're pretty, excuse me for making the assumption."

His back was to me as we climbed the steps, so thankfully he couldn't see the color rising in my cheeks at his flirty words. We stepped into the main library, and I was struck by an idea. When Scott turned to me, I said, "I will excuse everything if you give me that last book Toby found.

And if you don't mention anything about it to The Superior."

He regarded me for several moments. His eyes lazily made their way up and down my body before he smiled. "Deal."

I stepped forward, moving toward the exit, but he shifted into my path. "A book in demonic script isn't going to do you much good without a translation."

My brow scrunched. I hadn't thought about that. Scott lowered himself and he was suddenly close enough that I could feel his breath on my skin. "If only you had the keys to the lower right-hand drawer of Toby's desk. There could be a translation book in there."

He abruptly straightened and with a wink he said, "I'll just go ahead with these ones, while you lock up. Key sixty-three should work."

I smiled as I watched him leave before remembering that I already owed him for not telling The Superior about the journals. Looked like I would now owe him for two things.

CHAPTER 21

The book of translations felt like fire in my hands as I made my way down the hallway. It had been as easy as Scott had said, but carrying the contraband back to my room made me feel uneasy. I assumed everyone I passed knew what it was and was silently judging me for having stolen it. In reality, there were very few people in the hallways and most of them smiled at me before politely tipping their heads.

After ducking around the last corner, I hurried down the corridor of windows that led to my room. I stepped inside and quickly shut the door behind me. Scott stood by the table with his trademark smirk. I held the book up triumphantly and he passed me the book with the mark. He nodded and then left.

I walked back to my bedroom and searched for a good hiding place. All the drawers seemed too obvious and there weren't enough clothes in the closet to really cover the books. I settled on the tried and true and tucked the books under my mattress.

Moving back into the main room, I sat down at the table and wondered how long it would be before The Superior returned from the infirmary. A glance at the clock on my phone told me it was late afternoon and the rumbling in my stomach reminded me I was starving. I drummed my fingers on the table for a few minutes, then thought to hell with it, and went in search of food.

The hallways were still fairly empty as I made my way toward the kitchen. Getting lost once or twice, I was thankful for the people I did see, as I had to use a few of them for directions. Everyone was very friendly, and I was reminded of Scott's words. Not everyone here was a bad person. People like Toby were here because they were really good at something.

Stepping into the kitchen, I made my way to the expansive island. A chef greeted me while he swept a rag over the counter. I asked if I could make myself a sandwich, but he quickly dismissed that notion in favor of making one for me himself. When he slid the finished plate over to me, I thanked him profusely then headed to the refrigerator to grab a drink. I carried a can of Coke and the plate with the delicious looking sandwich and fresh chips down the hallway.

This time, I made it to the room only getting lost once. I kicked my door shut behind me and settled in to eat at the table. My stomach continued to growl as I popped the top on the can and took my first bite of the turkey sandwich. The food tasted amazing, and I quickly devoured everything on my plate.

I sat sipping the Coke when I decided to reach over and look at the books Toby had found. There were maybe a dozen books and most of them looked fairly old. A few were in languages I couldn't read, and even one in English I couldn't read, because I had no idea what the book was saying. It was lines and lines of text with charts and graphs. Nothing about the book seemed to relate to me or my power and even a search of the index didn't tell me much about it. The last book had a beautiful symbol embossed on the front in gold filagree. I wondered whether or not the gold was real before opening it to a random page. More symbols filled the white space and I let my eyes drag across the lines of script. My head felt heavy after the events of the day, so I leaned my head onto my hand. I flipped through the pages, on occasion seeing a symbol or two that looked similar to something I'd seen previously. Something in me thought to remember them. Absently, I thought I should grab a pen and notepad.

"What do you think you are doing?"

The voice startled me, but the words came to me as if through a dense fog. I heard them, but they weren't clear. Slowly, I turned my head and saw The Superior staring down at me. His eyes were alert and focused while his hand reached out and gently cupped my face. Warmth immediately spread through my body. I wanted to lift my arm to bat him away, but my body suddenly felt as if it were weighed down by lead. My head tipped further into The Superior's hand as my whole body slumped over. His other hand rose and rested on the other side of my face. Warmth enveloped me, slowly pushing away the haze. Slowly, I felt strength returning to my muscles. My lungs finally were able to fill again, and I was able to unhinge my jaw and force out a word.

"What?"

The Superior's hands were still on my face, so I saw his lips briefly twitch upward. "I told you not to read the demonic script."

Understanding washed over me. My mouth was dry, but my tongue was working better as I said, "I had no idea that's what it was."

I looked down at the offending book and immediately closed it and shoved it across the table. The Superior released me and took a step back and I wished he hadn't. His chest was bare and glistening with water droplets. The perfection of his face was matched by every chiseled inch of his exposed skin. Flawless rigids of muscles spanned across his chest and down the ripples of his abdomen. The beautifully defined muscles across his stomach directed my eyes down to the white towel that was wrapped low around his hips.

"Woah," I said, not even trying to hide the fact that I was ogling him.

He squatted down and reached out a hand to clasp over my own. "Claire, do you feel alright?"

A laugh bubbled up in my chest, but I stuffed it down. He was concerned that I was still being affected by the demonic script. I didn't think he needed to know that it was his bare chest that was currently knocking me on my ass.

"I still feel a bit weak," I said honestly, and then wanting to change the subject asked, "Were you in the shower?"

Standing back up he rested one hand on the knot of his towel and nodded. "I felt your heartrate plummet. I didn't know what was happening."

"Oh, sorry," I said, squirming in my seat, "I didn't know either."

His fingers found the offending book and brushed across the cover. "Didn't I tell you not to touch anything without permission?"

He looked over at me and raised his brow. I glared back. "I said I was sorry. Don't you have a shower to finish or something?"

The Superior smiled and then moved a hand through his wet hair. Drops of water skated down the curve of his back, drawing my eyes down the planes of his body. "You wait here, and I will get dressed. Don't try to read anything while I'm gone."

I glared at him, but he turned away from me and started walking down the left side hallway. Bolting upright from my chair, I followed him.

"Where are you going?" I asked, my heart rate spiking as my mind turned over the possibilities.

"I believe I said I was going to get dressed," he replied without slowing his pace.

"But this is my room."

He stopped and spun around so abruptly, he had to grab me by the shoulders to stop me from plowing into him. "Is it?" he asked with an amused look on his face.

Flinching away from his grasp I said, "When I got here, you told me this wasn't anyone's room."

He lifted a finger and pointed back toward the main room and said, "The room at the end of that hallway is reserved for my queen." Then his finger brushed along my chin as he turned my head to the left and said, "Whereas this room has always been mine."

My heart continued pounding in my chest as he went into the room at the end of the hall and gently shut the door. I took several deep steadying breaths while I turned and walked back into the main space. When I'd first arrived here, I'd known there'd been something off about my room. The Superior had been too cagey when I'd asked whose room it normally was, but I had been tired. I'd accepted his answer and moved on. Now I knew I'd been sharing this space with him. I didn't want to be this close to him especially when I remembered the books currently hidden under my mattress.

I sat with my hands clasped on the table, waiting patiently for The Superior to return. My earlier shock at our shared living space was dying down.

The Superior returned soon after he'd left, dressed and wet hair combed back. He was wearing a pair of dark gray chinos and a cream-colored sweater. His bare feet padded across the floor and for some reason I fixated on them. Never would I have thought to be in a situation where The Superior was comfortable enough to take off his shoes and socks. Staring at him now made me decidedly uncomfortable.

He took the seat next to me and briefly looked through the stack of books. With a nod, he turned his attention to me. "I'll look through this later. Hopefully one of them will be helpful."

"What exactly are you hoping to find?"

Reaching behind the stack, he grabbed a folder I hadn't noticed. "Information on your powers. Particularly as to how you use them to locate subjects."

I gave him a questioning look, but he was focused on the folder in his hands. "Do you really think it's in one of those books?"

"No, but I am hoping to get enough information to get us started," he cleared his throat and then pulled something out of the folder. It was a picture. He slid it across the table to me. "This is the missing girl. Her name is Monica."

Looking down at the picture, I saw a young woman with bright golden colored hair smiling while holding up her middle finger. Her eyes were narrowed, so I wasn't entirely sure what color they were, but they looked mischievous. She appeared to be in a restaurant or bar as the lighting was low and there were several blurry figures in the background. I stared for several minutes longer, but despite what Mrs. Edelman had told me about our connection, I didn't recognize her.

"What do we know about her?" I finally asked.

Eyes still fixed on the folder, The Superior sucked in a deep breath. "She has been under my care since she was born. Not as a servant, but still under my care. Her home life was difficult. She has struggled, to say the least. She frequently makes rather poor choices, most recently in her choice of boyfriend."

My shock surely showed on my face, but he wouldn't know because he still wouldn't look up from the table. A feeling of dread slowly started to pool in my belly. There was something to this story that The Superior didn't want to share with me, but I clamped my lips shut and willed him to continue.

"The boyfriend was becoming an issue. He was a violent man, and I suspect he hurt her on more than one occasion. I attempted to remove him, but Monica protested. In turn he threatened me by implying his affiliation with a powerful demon. Obviously, I was not cowed by his threat and may have let slip my own true nature."

I gave a small huff of laughter. "Let slip?"

His eyes flicked up to mine and they held a wicked gleam. "Boys should know not to tempt monsters."

At his words, a chill rolled down my spine and the hairs on my arms rose. I realized my reaction wasn't entirely based on fear. I flicked my gaze away from his, feigning a need to stretch my neck in hopes he wouldn't see the color in my cheeks.

"Anyway," he continued, leaning back in his chair, "The boy somehow learned who I was, and he and his demon friend got the bright idea to kidnap Monica to blackmail me. She is not someone to underestimate, as they quickly learned when she escaped. After three days of searching, they contacted you."

I stiffened in my chair. "Why me?"

He clasped his hands together on the table. "I believe they are aware of a connection you are not."

My head slowly shifted back and forth as I waited for him to continue. When he didn't, I managed to ask, "What connection?"

Emotions warred across his face. The sight of him hesitating set every nerve in my body on high alert. Finally, his lips parted, and I heard words I never expected to hear.

"She is your sister."

CHAPTER 22

I sat stunned, my mind momentarily blank. My heartbeat pounded in my ears as The Superior's words played over and over in my mind. Looking up at the demon, I could see his face was once again an indifferent mask. Any sign of his earlier contrition gone.

"I don't have a sister," I finally managed to reply.

"She's a half-sister. Your father's daughter."

When I raised my brows at him, he shook his head. "He doesn't know about her either."

Shaking my head, I reminded myself that my father and I were never close, so it was possible. After abandoning me to a childhood spent bouncing from home to home, my mother had settled into life with my father. Apparently, it hadn't been what she'd wanted, and soon after, they'd divorced.

"How old is she?" I asked, trying to place when this could have happened.

"Twenty."

She was five years younger than me, which meant that she was conceived shortly after my parents separated. It was possible that he'd met someone in that time, but it wasn't something I wanted to think too much about. My thoughts went to another question.

"How do you know her?" I asked, studying him closely.

"I told you, I've cared for her since she was born."

"Why did you care for her?"

"That's not the issue at present."

An evasive answer. He didn't want me to know something. I turned my attention back to the picture. Staring more intently at her face, I guessed I could see some resemblance. Her hair and mine did appear to be a similar shade of blonde. Perhaps what he was saying was true and this woman was my sister. Curiosity built inside me as I continued staring down at her. If she was who The Superior claimed she was, I wanted to meet her. Regardless of who she was, I knew she needed help. There were demons chasing her and she was fleeing a domestic violence situation.

Still there was something giving me pause. The Superior was being too evasive about her. There had to be more to their relationship that he wasn't telling me.

I crossed my arms and leaned them onto the table. "Why are you telling me this?"

His eyes narrowed and his face grew suspicious. "You said you researched your clients in order to increase your chances of finding them. I assumed it might be relevant in finding a living subject as well."

"And if I hadn't said that? Would you have told me I had a sister?"

Our gazes locked and I tried to keep my face neutral and my breaths steady. A burning rage was starting to simmer inside me as I saw the flicker of doubt in his eyes.

"No."

The word felt like a slap. My insides felt infused with fire as my muscles tensed. I kept my voice as calm as I could. "No? You didn't think I'd want to know that the woman you hired me to find is my sister?"

"I didn't think it necessary."

I stood abruptly. The fire inside me was no longer willing to be contained. "It doesn't matter what you fucking thought! It matters that she's my sister and you knew all this time and were never going to tell me."

Turning away from him, I marched into the kitchenette. My breath was sawing in and out of my body and I needed something to cool me down. I searched the cabinets for a glass so I could get some water.

"You will find no alcohol here."

My body went rigid. Slowly, I rose and stared at The Superior who was standing on the other side of the bar. His eyes held the barest hint of red and that only served to further fuel my own anger. "What did you just say to me?"

He crossed his arms over his chest. "We don't have time for this again. We need to focus on finding Monica."

I slammed my hands down on the counter. The Superior didn't even flinch. "And *why* do we need to find her?"

"I can't allow her to be taken."

With an irritated groan, I asked, "Why?"

His answering silence snapped something inside me. The dam holding back the last of my emotions broke. Sweeping my hands off the counter, I turned and started walking toward my bedroom. Anger bubbled in my belly. How did he expect me to do this job when he was hiding important information from me? Information I needed to find Monica and news that literally just turned my world upside down. I wanted to contemplate what it meant that I suddenly had a sibling, but all I could focus on was The Superior. He had acted like he'd told me my shirt was ugly. Like I should have taken a moment to absorb the insult, then turned around and started working.

Tears started to prick the backs of my eyes. I needed to find my sister, but for the moment, I needed space from the demon more. As I made my way down the hall, I could hear his footsteps behind me. Perhaps he did care for his servants and for my sister, but I was an employee. He only cared about what I could do for him. The mark on my arm sent a faint flicker of heat through my body. I whirled to face him.

"I don't know what you are trying to do, but stop it." His lips parted to respond, but I cut him off. "You know if you wanted to keep track of Monica so badly, why didn't you put your mark on her?"

He stiffened, then flicked his gaze away from me. "That wasn't an option."

"Why not?" I shouted, stepping closer to him.

His eyes stayed averted from my own and I watched his jaw muscles tick, but he said nothing. Pushing my sleeve back down, I took the last few steps to my bedroom and thrust open the door. I quickly grabbed my purse and jacket. While shoving my feet into my boots, The Superior came into the room.

"Where do you think you are going?"

"I'm leaving," I said, rising from the bed.

He moved to block the doorway. "You know I can't allow that."

Stepping forward, I pushed my arms into my jacket and moved my left hand into the front pocket where I'd finally remembered to hide my dagger. "I'm not asking."

"We have a contract."

"Do we?" I asked with a teasing smile. "I don't recall signing anything."

"Claire."

"I'll be back later," I said as casually as I could as I stepped close enough to him for my jacket to brush the front of his shirt. As fast as I could manage, I pulled out the knife and pressed the tip into the front of his pants. His midsection jerked slightly backward, but he stayed planted in the doorway.

"Move."

Our eyes met and I saw a rage that matched my own simmering in his eyes. "Do you honestly think you could defeat me in a fight?"

I shook my head back and forth. "No, but I'm pretty quick. I think I could at least nick you and are you really willing to gamble with your manhood?"

His nostrils flared as we stared at each other for several long minutes. I could see him thinking over my threat, but eventually, he relented and stepped aside. With an exaggerated twist of my wrist, I put the dagger back inside my jacket and then zipped it closed.

Stepping past him, I felt a surge of heat in the air for a suffocating moment. He'd been containing all of it during our spat and with this last straw it was released like a tidal wave. The Superior quickly tamped it back down before he said, "I *will* see you later."

The cold night air brushed against my skin while I sucked in a deep breath. Looking out into the dark night, I let out a small sigh of relief. The Superior had let me go. I'd half expected him or one of his flunkies to tackle me before I got to the front door. Tucking my hands into my coat pockets, I quickly realized why he had let me go. I didn't have a car, and I had no idea where I was. On the way here, I'd fallen asleep, so I knew I was somewhere near Pittsburgh, but that was about it.

Glancing up at the stars, I decided that even a stroll in the moonlight would be helpful in clearing my head. I took the steps down to the gravel driveway and walked around the fountain toward the main entrance. Stones crunched under my boots and the breeze tossed my hair. The property was quiet, with only the sounds of the wind in the trees and the gentle splashing of the fountain. A car engine roared to life somewhere in the distance.

I walked toward the road, trying to push my thoughts of The Superior out of my mind. He cared about his people, but for some reason he didn't see me as one of them. I was here to do a job and the sooner I finished, the sooner we could separate. The mark on my arm had to be the reason for my conflicted feelings, so I needed to focus on getting rid of it.

With a deep breath in, the image of my sister came to mind. She was out there somewhere, hiding from demons. Was she scared? Was she hurt? My mind turned over the possibilities until the sound of a car drew near. Looking over my shoulder, I saw a set of headlights coming toward me. I groaned as I stepped to the side of the driveway. A dark gray sedan slowed to a stop in front of me. A familiar face smiled out at me from the driver's side.

"Need a lift, Miss Woods?" Scott asked with a wink.

I glared back at him and asked, "That depends. Did The Superior send you out here to babysit me?"

He pretended to look affronted at the question, but then he shrugged his shoulders. "I know where the bars are and I'm willing to take you there, isn't that enough?"

My anger faltered slightly at the mention of a bar. I could definitely use a drink. I stepped forward and put my hand on the door handle. "Fine, but I'm drinking alone."

Scott saluted me and I rolled my eyes, then got into the car.

CHAPTER 23

The bar wasn't far from The Superior's estate. Although I wasn't going to admit it out loud, I was glad Scott picked me up. There was no way I would have found this place otherwise. We'd turned down a few unmarked roads until we'd finally pulled into a large dirt lot. A few light poles ringed the edges, but none of them gave off much light. The spots were more theoretical than marked, so Scott did his best centering his car between two trucks.

Stepping around the back of the car, I gazed up at the building. It wasn't much to look at. In a former life, it was probably a barn. There was a cupola and a large door taking up most of the front of the building. The white paint was peeling and the few windows there were, were either frosted or incredibly dirty. A small side door was propped open with a rock.

I looked skeptically over at Scott, who only laughed. "Come on, you'll love it."

We made it to the entrance and Scott gestured me inside. I stepped inside and immediately stopped in my tracks. The inside was beautifully refurbished. Sleek, polished wood covered the floors. Large wooden poles rose from the middle of the room up to the two-story high roof. Each pole was wrapped with lights and surrounded by a circular table and stools. There were a few other tables, a few booths along one wall, and a large open space that appeared to be setup for music and dancing.

Scott directed me toward the back where the bar was. The entire wall was covered in a mirror and glass shelves that held countless bottles of liquor. Lights illuminated the shelf so well that it appeared to shine like a star in the otherwise dim space.

Country music, blaring television stations, and patrons created a chaotic mix of sound around me. Occasionally there was a shout, but overall, it had a relaxed, casual vibe. Sliding onto a stool at the bar, I waved at the bartender who was conversing with an older couple at the other end. I glared at Scott when he took the seat next to me.

"I said I wanted to be alone," I reminded him.

"Come on," he said, with a crooked smile, "You won't even know I'm here."

"Fine," I said, sitting back down on my stool as the bartender walked our way. "You can stay as long as you stop calling me Miss Woods. That shit is annoying."

Scott chuckled. "Fine. It was Claire, right?"

Rolling my eyes, I turned and focused on ordering a drink. I went for a rum and coke and Scott asked for a beer. While we waited, I let my eyes drift over the bottles behind the bar. When the bartender slid our drinks over, I smiled at him and turned to look over at one of the televisions.

There was a football game on, but it didn't draw my attention like I'd hoped it would. As I felt the burn of alcohol on my tongue, my mind still spun. All this time The Superior had known I had a sister. He'd spoken to her, spent time with her, and had never once thought to mention us to each other. Not only that, but her connection to The Superior had gotten her into this mess. What was their relationship anyway? He'd said he'd cared for her since her birth, but that was about it. Sounded almost like a godparent. A demon godfather.

I chewed on my straw, while I continued to sip and think. Soon I was sucking bubbles and air from the glass, so I set it back down onto the bar. My eyes connected with the bartender, and he nodded at me in acknowledgment. When I turned back toward the tv, I saw Scott out of the corner of my eye. He was studying me too closely for my liking.

"What?" I asked, turning to face him.

"That straw took quite a beating," he said, inclining his bottle toward my empty glass. I looked back at it and noticed the numerous teeth marks and twists now adorning the straw.

"Want to talk about it?" he asked, tipping his head back to drink from his bottle.

"I told you I didn't want to talk."

He shrugged, "In my experience, most people say that when they need to talk."

"I'm mad at your boss," I said, thanking the bartender as he handed me another drink. "And since he sent you to watch me, I don't feel comfortable telling you anything."

A small frown touched his lips as he said, "He asked me to watch you, not talk to you, so anything we say is between us. Besides, didn't I prove myself trustworthy earlier when I didn't rat you out for being in the closet?"

Admitting he made a fair point would probably stroke his ego too much, so I simply shrugged.

He scoffed. "And how's that translation book working for you?"

Well, he had me there. Despite my reservations about his loyalties, I did feel like I could trust Scott. I didn't know if that was because he had kept those secrets for me or if I was beginning to be affected by the alcohol. As the warmth of the liquor continued to spread through my body, I decided I didn't care.

"Fine," I said, setting my glass on the bar. "You know, the woman he hired me to find? Turns out, she's my half-sister. I've never had a sibling and he's known all this time, and he never said anything. The only reason he's telling me now is because he thinks it'll help me find her faster. Like, what the hell? Who does that?"

Scott let out a small laugh before taking another sip of beer. "Sounds about right."

"What's that supposed to mean?"

He set the bottle on the bar with a small clink. "Look, does it suck that he did it? Yes, it does, but you're thinking about it wrong. The Master isn't a man, so you can't hold him to human standards. He's a demon, so he thinks in weird, twisted demonic ways."

I scoffed and dug my fingers into the edge of the bar. "And that's supposed to make it all okay?"

Scott held up his hands in placation. "No, I'm just reminding you he's not a man. He doesn't think like your past boyfriends."

A disgusted sound fell past my lips. "First of all, he is *not* my boyfriend. Second, I don't care how he thinks, he should have told me."

"What do you call it then?" Scott asked. "Demon mate?"

I waved my hand at him and emphatically shook my head. "Ugh, you're making it sound worse and worse. Attached, let's say we're attached."

"Attached," he said, drawing out the word. "I think that sounds worse. Like you've been glued together or something."

My head tipped back as I laughed. Scott chuckled beside me, but I knew he didn't fully understand how close to the truth he was. "Well, what did you call his previous mates?"

Scott looked at me as though I'd suddenly sprouted a second head. "He's never had one."

The alcohol was making my head feel light. I waved my hand again. "You're trying to tell me he's never had a girlfriend?"

He took a sip of his beer, then shook his head. "I'm not saying that. I'm saying I've never seen a woman live with him. I've certainly never seen someone marked as a Demon Queen."

Despite the pleasant numbness of the liquor, my heart started to pound at his words. Nancy told me the mark was rare, but for some reason, hearing it from Scott hit differently. Maybe it was because he was a human servant, which meant he actually spent time in the presence of demons, whereas Nancy's knowledge was mostly theoretical. Either way, I was once again wondering why The Superior had given it to me.

"You've really never seen another one?"

Scott shook his head.

"Have you ever heard of one?"

He shook his head again.

"Thanks," I said, grabbing a menu and looking over some of the food. "You've given me something new to obsess over."

Sliding his empty bottle back onto the counter, he said, "Glad I could help." He rose from his seat and braced his hands on the bar. His tall frame slowly bent down, bringing his lips close to my ear. "Why do I get the feeling you and The Superior barely know each other?"

My head turned slightly toward him, causing my hair to brush his lips. "So what if we don't?"

He smiled as his eyes bounced across my face. "If you're being held against your will blink twice."

I cackled with laughter. He licked his lips, and his grin grew. Was he flirting with me? I held my eyes wide open as I stared back at him. "I am here of my own free will."

Technically, the mark had been against my will. I still wasn't happy about that part, but I had made the choice to take this job. Granted, that had been after numerous threats upon my life, but Scott didn't need to know all those details.

His fingers trailed lightly down my shoulder as he said, "Good. At least this way I get to spend some time with you."

He was definitely flirting now. Not for the first time, I wondered what his position was with The Superior. I doubted that he would be happy to hear Scott speaking to me this way. Then again, we weren't really involved, so maybe he wouldn't care.

Scott gave my shoulder a squeeze and stepped back. "I'm going to use the restroom."

I nodded and watched him walk toward the other side of the bar. My eyes trailed down his backside and the slight jump of my pulse told me I liked what I saw. Scott was an attractive man, and I didn't hate his flirting. It was dangerous and would go absolutely nowhere, but for the time being I allowed myself to enjoy it. When he made the turn around the bar, he looked back at me and winked. I laughed into my drink. That man was trouble.

CHAPTER 24

My eyes were still glued to the spot where Scott had been. Several minutes had passed and I still didn't know what to think of our conversation. I tried to tell myself that maybe it was just his personality. Either way, he had distracted me from my thoughts about my sister and The Superior. I was grateful to him for that, so I waited patiently for him to return.

The game on the tv kept playing as I slowly nibbled my fries and sipped from my drink. I had a decent buzz going when a man slid into the stool beside me.

"Well, hi there."

He smiled down at me and I gave him a brief, uninterested nod back. I'd never seen him before, and I didn't like how close he was. His head was covered in a ball cap, and he wore a loose hoodie and jeans. Turning away from him, I waved at the bartender for my check.

The man beside me spun around in his chair, kicked his legs out and propped his elbows up on the bar. He brushed against my side, and I shrank away from him. When he leaned toward me, I unabashedly glared back at him. His lips tipped into a smile before he said, "That boyfriend of yours has been gone a *long* time."

With a quick nod, he rose from the chair. My eyes followed him as he walked out the front door. Instantly, my stomach dropped. Fumbling in my purse, I found my phone and checked the time. Shit. It had been a while since Scott left.

I waved frantically at the bartender. He glared at my impatience but handed me both Scott's and my checks. I scribbled out a signature on them and abruptly stood. My head swam slightly, so I grabbed the edge of the bar to steady myself. After regaining my equilibrium, I scanned the crowd, desperately hoping I'd spot Scott. I didn't see him anywhere.

The restrooms were down a narrow side hallway, so I headed that way. Part of me thought that maybe Scott was sick. Another part of me knew that didn't explain the strange man who had approached me. When I reached the men's room, I tapped on the door. There was no answer, so I knocked more forcefully. After the silence that time, I slowly pressed the door open and peeked inside. Only the disgusting smells of a men's bathroom at a bar greeted me. There was no one inside and no signs of a struggle.

My heart started to pound as my eyes bounced around the room. Where could he have gone? The rising panic was clearing away some of the haze of the alcohol, but my thoughts were still sluggish. I needed to find Scott or some evidence of where he'd gone. Looking down to the end of the hallway, I saw a door that led out to a patio. I could see lights and a few people smoking. I walked to the exit and the moment I heard the door click shut behind me, I knew I'd made a mistake.

"Try to run and your boyfriend gets it."

Cold night air whipped through my hair as all the people outside stubbed out their cigarettes and turned to face me. I sucked in a breath and felt my body tremble as they all took a step closer to me. The man who had spoken stepped up behind me and grabbed my arms. A whimper slipped past my lips as he pulled me into his chest.

"Make a sound and we'll kill you both."

I swallowed but said nothing. The man holding me took it as an invitation to keep talking and I wasn't going to stop him. "See, you might not remember us, but you and your demon friend got several of our buddies killed last night."

If these people worked with Johnny Snake Demon, then their threat to kill me was a lie. I knew their boss needed me alive, which meant I just needed to buy Scott and I some time until The Superior could come save us. Oh, and think of a way to contact The Superior.

The group closed in around me and they pulled me away from the bar toward the parking lot. I'd been told not to scream, but they hadn't said anything about hitting. Turning slightly in my capturer's hold, I kicked toward the shin of one of the group members. He saw me at the last second, so I only managed to graze him. They moved in closer, boxing me in so I couldn't get enough of a wind up to do any damage. Too late I remembered the knife tucked in my jacket. I had to hope they gave me an opening to get my hands on it.

We made it to the parking lot, and I saw we were walking toward Scott's car. Five men crept out from the shadows surrounding it. They were all heavily armed and I had to swallow down a gasp. This did not look good. The man who had spoken to me at the bar stepped into the light and grinned at me.

"We just want to have a little chat with you, sweetheart."

Ugh. Why did random men call women that? I scowled back at him only causing him to laugh.

"You got spirit, I'll give you that." He nodded to another one of the men who pulled out a key fob and clicked it. Scott's trunk popped open. My eyes shot to it as the man from the bar said, "You're going want to cooperate or else your boyfriend isn't going to make it."

A horrified scream tried to burst out of me, but I had to choke it down as I looked at Scott. Or at least, I had to assume it was him. The clothes were right, but the mangled bloody pile of a person was indiscernible. His face was beaten and bruised, and his limbs were sitting at odd angles tucked into the car. I watched his chest, praying to see signs of rising and falling, but I was too far away.

Pain built in my chest as tears sprang from my eyes. I jerked against the hold on my arms, but it was solid. The man with the key shut the trunk, and I let out an objecting sob.

"Wait, please," I cried, but they ignored me.

"Let's take a walk," the man from the bar said as he stepped in front of me. He nodded to indicate the field next to the parking lot.

The man holding me shoved me forward, but I stumbled onto my knees. Several hands dragged me upward and I was forced to walk away from Scott. I wanted to scream. I needed to fight, but I didn't have training for anything like this. There had to be a way for me to get help. Judging by the amount of blood on Scott's body, I didn't think he had long. I had to do something.

Then, as if a switch had been flipped in my brain, I remembered the mark. The Superior had told me it worked as a tracking device, but hadn't he also said it alerted him if I was injured? With a sigh, I decided there was only one way to find out.

I took a steadying breath and forced my elbow back as hard as I could. The man behind me doubled over and let out a grunt. I lifted my right foot and kicked into his shin. His hold momentarily lightened, but still not enough for me to free my hand. My foot came around and slammed into someone's knee. That person immediately went down, clutching their injured leg. Thank you for making yourself a prime target, I thought, right before I kicked him in the shoulder and sent him rolling into one of his buddies.

Hands wrapped tightly around my body in a bear hug. I thrust my head backward and felt it connect with something hard. Happily, the alcohol was still dulling my senses, because I knew that was going to hurt in the morning. The person behind me cursed and then spun me around. I grinned like an idiot at them, and they slapped me across the face.

My head whipped to the side as pain exploded across my cheek. I didn't think it would be enough, so I turned back to the man and kicked out toward his groin. His hands snatched for my leg while he twisted to the side. I missed, but thankfully, he had released my arms. Pulling out my knife, I grinned wildly back at him.

"Stop that unless you want to get yourself killed," He spat at me through his mask.

I charged. Either he was going to injure me enough to summon The Superior or I was going to win this fight. The odds were not in my favor as my body sailed forward. Seeing me coming, the man dodged to the side, then extended his arm and slammed it into the side of my head. I dropped to my knees and gasped. My vision was momentarily fuzzy, and my ear was ringing from the impact. Spots dotted my vision, and I wondered if he could have given me a concussion. I'd have to ask Nancy.

Fingers dug into my coat, hauling me upward, and smacking my knife out of my hand. My head swam and pain bounced through my skull. I stuck out my tongue to wet my lips and winced when I tasted blood. At some point I'd cut myself.

"That's enough," someone in front of me said, "You're not getting away, so all you're doing is hurting yourself."

A psychotic bubble of laughter fell out of me as the mark on my forearm heated. The Superior had gotten my message. Now I just needed to buy some more time. No problem. I spat my blood at the man in front of me. "I'm not going anywhere with you."

"Fine," he said, crossing his hands in front of his belt. "We can talk here."

"What do you want?" I asked, swaying slightly on my feet.

The man in the baseball cap stepped closer to me. "We were hired by a third party to find you and offer you a job."

I slowly nodded my head, and said, "I am familiar with your third party, and I have already told him to go fuck himself."

His nostrils flared and I simply smiled back at him. "The job offer was non-negotiable."

"Well then I will definitely not be taking it," I said, letting my words slur together slightly.

He smiled, but it wasn't a pleasant expression. It held the promise of violence if I continued to refuse him. "Burns," he shouted to someone behind me. "Call him and tell him we will be delivering the package."

My legs faltered. I had seen enough true crime documentaries to know you never allowed yourself to be taken to a second location. Ideas scrambled together in my brain as I tried to come up with a plan. "Wait," I blurted, "I'll work with him, but only if he meets me here."

The man looked at me skeptically, so I kept talking. "Look, I'm willing to meet you halfway here. Call an ambulance for my friend and I'll stay here and wait for your client. You don't want to drag me all around town and I don't want to be kidnapped, so just have him meet me here."

His lips twitched, and I almost thought he was going to smile, before he reached into his pocket and pulled out a gun. He aimed it at my head and said, "The time to willingly accept has passed. You're coming with us now."

"No," I shouted as fresh tears filled my eyes.

Whoever was holding me tugged me violently backward and I fell against them. I opened my mouth and screamed as loud as I could. My feet flew into the air, trying to connect with anyone I could find. I flicked my head back again and again, hoping to hit something as my arms were tightly pinned to my sides.

The gun was thrust into my temple. "Shut up right now or I will kill you."

Something inside me broke at the familiarity of the situation. How had my life come to this? In the past few weeks I had been threatened on multiple occasions, been shot, marked, and now I was fighting off my second kidnapping attempt. It wasn't fair that I was thrust into all of this. I hadn't even known Monica, and I still didn't know if I could find her, and yet these people were willing to do anything to ensure my cooperation. They wouldn't take no for an answer and adding Billy Blake to the mix had been enough.

All of the fight drained out of me as I stared up at the man holding the gun. His jaw was tense as he watched me for further signs of struggle. I went limp in my captor's hands.

"You can't kill me," I whispered, "They won't let you. They've done all of this to get me to do something I can't even do." Tears spilled down my cheeks. "I can't do it, but they won't leave me alone."

The man before me sucked in a breath, then took a few steps back. He lowered the gun and studied me with an almost sympathetic expression. "Sounds like you're pretty worthless, but that doesn't mean we're not taking you in. Job's a job."

I sobbed into my chest. Nothing I'd done had made any difference. My lip was bleeding and my head was pounding, but I was still being kidnapped. Everyone was taking away my choices and no one gave a damn what I felt about any of it. Sucking in a breath, I filled my lungs and knew that if I had to accept this, I would do the one thing I still could. I screamed. I pushed everything I had into being as loud as I could, hoping beyond hope that someone would hear me and come running. Not to save me, but to find Scott and to save him. I would go on to work for Johnny Snake Demon, but I wouldn't allow my mistakes to be Scott's end.

As if in slow motion, I watched the man in front of me shake his head. He raised the gun and then squeezed the trigger.

CHAPTER 25

"What the hell were you thinking?"

Someone was yelling not far from me. I couldn't remember where I was. Several small things were poking the left side of my face. It was scratchy. I tried to think where I could be.

"Relax, she's not dead."

I knew that voice. It made me start to shake and then I remembered. A gun leveled at my head. That voice had pulled the trigger. My eyes flew open. Things were blurry at first, but after several blinks I saw the world was sideways. The lights from the parking lot were to my right, the bar above me. Blades of grass were to my left under my head. I was lying on the ground, clearly abandoned after having been shot. Somehow, I wasn't dead.

"You shot her in the head, of course she's dead, you idiot!"

Another shudder wracked my body as I recognized the second voice. Johnny Snake Demon. I scrunched my forehead and felt a sharp throb along the left side. Every nerve in my body yelled at me to flee, but my would-be-murderers were still too close. Shifting my eyes downward, I could see blood on the grass beside me. I couldn't tell how badly I was injured, but at least I was alive.

"The bullet grazed her. I just wanted her to shut the hell up."

"You are not getting paid for this," Johnny snapped.

There was a loaded answering silence. My spine stiffened as I tried to breath as shallowly as I could. As long as they continued fighting each other, I had hope they wouldn't notice I was awake.

"I lost good men trying to catch this one. She started screaming and I didn't want that other one showing up."

I heard swift footsteps crunching in the grass. Johnny's voice held a deadly edge as he asked, "What other guy?"

The ground beneath me shuddered. It was subtle, like distance thunder, but it was there. Johnny sucked in a breath. The world shook again. This time stronger than the last. That was weird. Pennsylvania didn't get earthquakes.

Another pulse slammed into the ground and if I had been standing, I probably would have lost my balance. The world around me erupted in motion. Figures blurred past as the air filled with shouts and curses. Hands latched onto my right arm and thrust my sleeves upward. My bare skin filled with goosebumps as it was exposed to the cold air. Fingernails dug into my forearm, and I winced.

"You can stop pretending. I know you're alive."

Johnny Snake Demon yanked me onto my feet. The world spun and my head pounded with the movement. The air felt especially cool along the left side of my face. I reached up to touch it and my fingers came away red. Johnny seethed in front of me.

"You make a new friend since we last talked?"

I wanted to stay silent, but the fear in his eyes sent a wicked, vindictive thrill coursing through my body. Slowly, I nodded my head.

His hold on my arm tightened and the sharp sting in my skin told me his nails had broken the skin. "Please tell me it's not him."

There was a tremble running throughout his body, so much so that I could hear it in his words. I grinned and his face went white. He spun me in his arms and shoved my back against his chest. One of his hands laid across my waist, while the other twisted into my hair. He pulled my head backward and whispered, "Don't move."

The ground gave another shudder, and my knees buckled. Johnny pulled me back up against him and hissed in my ear. Fissures opened in the ground all around us with a deafening crack. Men fell into the holes in the ground with startled screams. The rest scrambled, their running steps beating sporadic paths across the grass. Slowly, we were all encircled by deep fissures. Heat pulsed through my arm.

For a moment, everything went deathly silent. Then a sound like a rushing wind slowly built within the fissures. The world gave one violent shake and then walls of fire exploded upward from the cracks. Blistering heat washed over me, and I cried out. We were surrounded by solid towering walls of Hellfire.

The people who had fallen into the holes were screaming as they burned. It was the most horrific sound I had ever heard. Panic took hold of the remaining people as they ran in circles trying to find a way out. I knew there was nowhere for them to go. There would be no escape.

When the balls of fire formed and shot across the space, knocking people to the ground, I closed my eyes. I couldn't watch, but I could still hear them. The smell of their burning bodies reached my nose. I tried to cover my face with my hands, but Johnny wrenched me backward.

"Stop moving. He's coming."

Johnny's heartbeat pounded against my back. Part of me was happy he was so afraid. The sounds of people dying faded away and the world became nothing but the roar of the flames. Slowly, I opened my eyes. The wall reached high into the night sky. Waves of heat rolled across the open space as embers floated to the stars. Suddenly, the wall in front of me parted and a lone figure stepped through.

The Superior walked calmly into the clearing. He moved forward at a leisurely pace with his hands in his pockets. His body was relaxed but like the night he'd come for me at my house, it was the eyes that gave him away. They glowed a fiery red and held an intensity I had never seen before. He looked murderous. I shuddered when his eyes connected with mine. They quickly swept over my body, assessing my injuries. I winced as Johnny's grip tightened around my waist. The Superior's attention shot to the demon holding me. His nostrils flared and I knew there was no one in the world who would willingly trade places with Johnny right now.

The walls around us dropped with a resounding sizzle. Cool air blew in across my face and I shivered at the sudden lack of warmth. Johnny tightened his grip on my hair, and I gasped as it pulled at the wound on my forehead.

Johnny Snake Demon cleared his throat and said, "If you let me go, I'll tell you who I work for."

To his credit, his words didn't betray the tremble I felt coursing through his body. Johnny and I both knew he was living on borrowed time. The Superior didn't react at first. I didn't know whether he was considering Johnny's words or simply making him sweat. Either way, we waited. The pounding in Johnny's chest grew so intense I was starting to worry his human heart might give out.

The Superior took a small step forward. When he finally spoke, it was a deadly whisper. "I don't give a fuck. You never should have touched my queen."

He tilted his head slightly and I heard a sickening pop behind me. The pressure of Johnny's hold in my hair and around my waist was suddenly gone. Just as suddenly, I was hit with a flood of hot liquid along my backside. I could smell the metallic tang of blood and something sour. My eyes widened in horror as I realized it was Johnny. The Superior just obliterated someone with his mind.

In a blink, he was crouched before me. His eyes were once again brown, but they were wide as they searched every inch of my body. An impressive slew of curses fell from his mouth as he took in my injuries. His gaze landed on my forehead, and he brushed tentative fingers across it. I winced and he jerked his hand away.

"I got here as fast as I could."

My body started to shake as I fell to my knees. I rocked back and forth as I tried to convince myself that I was safe. It was all over, but for how long?

"Claire?"

Tears fell from my eyes as the flood gates of my emotions broke open. I fell forward and screamed. My life had become a series of close calls, of near death, and constant fear. I couldn't take it anymore. Each time that I forced the air from my lungs, I hoped that some of the pain within me would subside. I pushed and pushed, willing the world around me to take on the churning emotion inside me that I could no longer contain. My throat burned as I screamed and sobbed into the ground, trying and failing to find relief.

Strong hands wrapped around my own and squeezed reassuringly. I looked up into The Superior's eyes and saw something I'd never seen before. Fear. Not fear of the situation, like mine, but he was afraid for me. He was so worried that he'd allowed the emotion to show on his face. His lips moved, but for some reason I couldn't focus on anything he was saying.

My eyes drifted toward the field around me. Lying on the ground not far from me was a charred ruin of a body. The remains were still smoking and when I looked at it, I noticed I could also smell it. I covered my mouth with my hand and turned away, trying to press the bile in my throat back down. Looking at my knees, I saw I was kneeling in a puddle. Something thick, red, and glutinous was surrounding me. Johnny. I was sitting in a pile of what was left of Johnny. I turned and vomited.

After I was done being sick, I wiped the back of my hand across my mouth. The Superior's hands gently cupped my face and brought my attention back up to him.

"Claire, can you hear me?" His hands trembled slightly on my face.

I tilted my head and stared back at him for a moment. Finally, I said, "You killed Johnny."

He nodded. "Yes, I did. Claire, are you listening to me? I need you to listen."

My head felt light as he helped me rise to my feet. I wobbled slightly, but The Superior steadied me. His hands once again cupped my face. He hadn't stopped touching me for some time now. No power flowed between us that I could feel. It was almost as if he needed to touch me to reassure himself that I was still here. That I was alive. Truth was, I wasn't fully here. My mind couldn't seem to focus.

"Claire!"

My name came out as a strangled yell. I looked up at him and placed my hands over his. "I'm listening."

"You know snake demons are poisonous, correct?"

I nodded.

"They carry the poison in their blood. Blood which is covering your back."

It took me a moment to understand what he was telling me. When I did, I instinctively pulled my hands away from his and tried to examine my back. He caught my wrists in a blindingly fast movement.

"No," he breathed, "Do not touch it. I am holding it at bay for now, but we need to get the poison off."

I didn't ask for clarification on what would happen if we didn't. There was no need, so I nodded my head, my mind suddenly clear and very focused. "What do we do?"

He gave a sharp nod, then twisted our hands together. "We need to get out of here, but first, do you know where Scott is?"

My heart twisted in pain as the memory of Scott in the trunk flashed before my eyes. I felt a sob building in my chest, but I choked it down and said, "The trunk. He's in his trunk."

The Superior's hand clenched around my own as he made a sound low in his throat. He pulled out his phone and was working through the screens with super-human speed. Without looking at me he said, "We will check on Scott before we leave. Are you alright to walk that far?"

"Yes. I think so."

He finished typing and expertly tucked the phone back into his pocket. His eyes met mine and then trailed upward. "Good. Don't touch your hair."

We started walking toward the parking lot and for the first time I wondered what I looked like. A bruised and beaten mess with blood along my left temple and demon poison covering my back. Maybe it was better that I couldn't see myself.

The Superior helped me over the fissure he'd made in the ground. I'd never seen him use such power before and I wondered what else he could do. Looking over at him I said, "I should be dead."

His body stiffened, but he said nothing.

I tugged lightly on our joined hands. "Why didn't that bullet kill me?"

He kept his eyes on the ground. "I was close enough to heal you."

"You can heal me even when I've been shot in the head?"

The Superior spun in place and we jerked to a stop. He looked down at me, nostrils flaring as his eyes wavered. "What do you want me to say?" I blinked. Confused at his reaction. He took a step closer to me. "You are my queen, and I swore to protect you. Do you need me to acknowledge that I have failed?"

My eyes widened and I shook my head. He looked away from me and his shoulders heaved as he sucked in a ragged breath. "No," I whispered, stepping close enough to him to place my other hand on his shoulder. "That's not it at all. I'm just amazed at what you can do."

He nodded but kept his eyes averted.

"And I wanted to thank you." I gave his shoulder a small squeeze.

"Do not thank me," he said, pulling away from my comforting grasp. "I promised to protect you, and I did not."

"I'm still here," I replied in a small voice.

He said nothing and simply beckoned me to continue walking. We reached the parking lot, and I pointed out Scott's car. I stood by one of the neighboring trucks as The Superior used his elbow to break the driver's side window. He wrenched the door open so forcefully it broke off the hinges. Leaning forward, he popped the trunk release, and I looked away. If Scott was dead, I couldn't bear it.

A moment later, I felt hands brush along my arms. "He's alive."

I opened my eyes and startled a step back as I saw there was a man standing with us in the parking lot. My head flicked toward the man, and I realized it was the bartender.

"You," The Superior said, pointing at him, "Stay here until the ambulance arrives." The bartender dutifully nodded his head. I realized he must be another servant of The Superior's. I didn't have time to dwell on that as The Superior grabbed my hand and pulled me across the parking lot. He reached into his pocket and a nearby black BMW coupe chirped.

"Get in," he said in a voice brooking no argument as he held the passenger side door open. I moved to step in, but then remembered I was covered in poisonous demon blood.

"I'm going to get blood all over your seat."

He huffed out an agitated breath and said, "I don't care. Get in."

With a resigned sigh, I stepped into the car. As I sat back in the seat, there was a squelching sound that filled the car and turned my stomach. I tried to focus on my breathing as The Superior climbed into the driver's seat and we set off.

CHAPTER 26

Try as I might, I couldn't manage to sit still. Every bump in the road or turn of the car sent me sliding around in my seat. I braced one hand against the dashboard and the other gripped the center console. Sucking in deep, calming breaths, I searched for anything to distract me from the sounds and the smell surrounding me. The Superior was tense beside me, and I marveled at the sight of him driving. For some reason, I had assumed he couldn't. There was something so strange about seeing him do such a basic human task. Like seeing him brush his teeth. I looked up at his face and noticed a sheen of sweat on his forehead.

"Are you alright?" I asked, while trying to remember if I'd ever seen him sweat. The strain of holding back the poison must have been immense.

"I'm fine," he said too quickly. His gaze flicked briefly over to me. He inhaled sharply, then dropped his hand next to mine. "It would be easier if I were touching you."

His fingertips lightly brushed the side of my hand. Without hesitation, I placed my hand in his and laced our fingers together. Immediately, some of the tension in him eased.

"You don't have to take it all. I can take some," I said lightly.

He shook his head and his grip on my hand tightened. "No. This was my doing and I will bear the burden."

We turned onto The Superior's road, and I breathed a sigh of relief. I couldn't wait to be clean, and I didn't know how much longer The Superior would last. Seeing him strain to keep me safe sent a pang of guilt through my chest.

"It was my fault," I admitted. "I shouldn't have left."

His attention stayed fixed on the road. He gave no indication that he had heard me, so I stayed silent. We were both wrestling with feelings of guilt. We turned onto The Superior's driveway, and I instantly felt my body relax. The first time I'd come here, I'd felt trapped. Now, I saw it as safety. I still didn't fully trust the demon beside me, but I did believe he wanted to protect me. He fought for me, was currently straining the bounds of his power to save me. I couldn't deny the small leap in my heart at that. Would he sacrifice this much for anyone, or was there something different about me?

I contemplated that as we parked in front of the house. The Superior practically leapt up the stairs and thrust the door open.

"Destiny!"

He shouted so loudly, I felt the house tremble. Destiny appeared mere seconds later. Her hair still fluttering in the breeze of her movement.

"Find a barrel we can burn Claire's clothes in, then meet me in my room."

Destiny looked me over, then nodded and was off. The Superior immediately scooped me into his arms. A protest started to form on my lips, but he cut me off before I could voice it. "You are leaving poisonous shoe prints on the floor."

I looked down and saw the bloody spots on the tile. With a wince, I let myself sink into the comfort of his arms. If I was being honest, it wasn't the worse place to be. His arms were solid and strong around me and he moved with a speed I couldn't have matched.

The Superior briefly stopped to inform someone about the blood in the entryway, then we made it to our room. My mind cursed itself for thinking of it as *our* room, but I didn't have time to think too much about it as The Superior carried me into the large bathroom.

Gently, he set me back on my feet, then went to wash his hands. Glancing over his shoulder he said, "I hope you aren't particularly fond of anything you're wearing because it's all going to have to go."

I shrugged. My clothes were a small price to pay. Looking down at his now ruined shirt, I wondered if he'd felt the same.

Destiny burst into the room easily carrying a massive steel barrel. She placed it in the center of the room and said, "What the hell happened?"

The Superior dried his hands, then came to stand beside me. He spat out a few words in a language I didn't understand, and I saw Destiny's face contort in confusion. They traded those strange words back and forth a few times before Destiny huffed out an exasperated sigh.

"Why the hell would you pop a snake demon when it was standing that close to her?"

He stepped toward her, violence radiating off him as he glared down at her. "You do not question me."

Destiny scoffed. "You know that doesn't work on me. Seriously, what were you thinking?"

The Superior made a sound low in his throat, then said something to her that I couldn't hear. She rolled her eyes and then he moved around her and walked toward the door.

"Fine, fine," she said, stepping closer to me.

The Superior glanced back for a moment, then stepped out of the room.

"Where's he going?" I asked, realizing I was starting to panic at the thought of him leaving.

"He thought you'd want some privacy." She moved closer to me and lightly placed her fingers on my jacket zipper. "May I?"

There was a suggestive tone to her words. She smiled and winked at me. "Sorry, habit."

I was unsure what she meant by that, but I placed my hands over hers, shaking her off. "I can do it myself."

Her grip on the zipper tightened. "Actually, it would be better if you let me. The more poison on your skin, the harder he has to work at keeping you alive. Considering how hard he's already worked at that tonight, I'd say he's owed a bit of a break."

The words felt like a slap. I dipped my eyes away from her and released my hold on her hands.

"Sorry," she said as she unzipped the jacket and pulled it off. "That came out harsher than I meant it to."

She tossed the jacket into the barrel. I shook my head. "No, you're right."

The back of her hand pushed my chin upward. I met her eyes and saw sympathy there.

"I know I'm right, but I shouldn't have said it like that. Sorry."

I nodded at her, accepting the apology. She moved down to my feet and started unlacing my boots. I'd forgotten about them and felt a slight pang of loss when I watched them sail into the barrel. New snow boots were not cheap. Destiny turned back to me and shook out her hands. Sweat now coated her brow. She'd been touching the poison for mere moments and already the strain was showing on her face.

Thinking a distraction might be helpful, I asked, "What did he say?"

Her attention stayed fixed on removing my socks. "Hmm?"

"What did he say," I repeated, setting down my now bare foot and raising the other, "About why he *popped* the demon while he was holding me?"

Destiny tossed the socks into the barrel and turned to face me. There was a smirk on her face.

"What?" I asked, feeling heat flooding my cheeks.

She rolled her eyes and placed her hands on the hem of my shirt. "Why do you *think*?" Destiny tugged the shirt up and over my head. My hair landed on my bare shoulders with a wet plop. I cringed at the feel of it on my bare skin and fought the urge to wipe it away.

Wading my shirt into a ball, Destiny flicked it into the barrel and stared at me. I realized I hadn't answered her question. With a shrug I said, "I don't know."

Her brows lifted questioningly. "And why do you want to know?"

I licked my lips and shrugged again. She stepped forward and hooked her finger into the front of my jeans. It felt too intimate of a touch, and I moved to replace her hands. She batted me away and quickly worked the button and zipper down. "Are you hoping I'll say he couldn't hold his temper at the sight of another demon touching his queen?"

A loud thud sounded on the bathroom door.

Destiny grinned as she slowly peeled my pants down to my ankles. She gently lifted each foot to remove them, then tossed the garment over her shoulder. Her eyes never left mine. Then her fingers grazed the bare skin of my shoulders and traced the edges of my bra straps.

Another bang sounded and this time I saw the door shudder from the impact. I hadn't realized The Superior had been standing just outside.

The demon in front of me smiled and removed her hands. She stepped closer to me and whispered, "Demons don't like it when other demons touch our stuff. The situation was a difficult one because as his queen he needs to keep you safe, but there was another demon touching you."

I tiled my head. "You're another demon and you're touching me."

"I know," she replied and then winked. "He still doesn't like it, though. If you can't tell."

She gave a meaningful glance at the door. Stepping behind me, her fingers moved to the clasp of my bra. I'd been obliging so far, but that was too much for me. Stepping away from her, I turned and said, "I think I can do this next part myself."

Shrugging, Destiny turned and walked toward a cupboard by the sinks. She pulled out a robe and handed it to me. I draped it over my shoulders while Destiny held my hair. Wriggling around inside the robe, I managed to remove my bra and panties and then dropped them into the barrel. I turned to ask Destiny what was next only to see her eyes roll upward just before her body collapsed.

CHAPTER 27

I screamed and the bathroom door burst open. The Superior looked at me, then he saw Destiny on the floor. He knelt beside her and gave her shoulder a shake. "Destiny!"

She moaned and squirmed on the ground. He cursed, then lifted her into his arms. "I told you to be careful, but you were too eager to touch things you shouldn't be touching."

"Sorry, but it was too tempting not to," she replied, but her voice sounded anything but contrite. "Your queen was giving me quite the eyeful."

Her mocking laughter abruptly halted when The Superior dropped her into the tub and turned on the water. She screamed. "That's the cold tap!"

"I know," he said turning to face me with a slightly smug look on his face. "Scrub it off, stupid demon."

His eyes combed over me, and I remembered I was in nothing but a robe. Instinctively I curled my hand into the fabric around my chest. My gaze dipped down to the floor and for a moment we stood like that listening to the sounds of Destiny's protests.

I looked up again and saw The Superior suddenly standing right in front of me. "Your hair," he said, "We need to clean it."

I nodded, then watched him walk across the room and into the back hallway. He returned with a plush, black chair. Placing it next to the sink he began running the water, occasionally testing the temperature. He collected a bottle of shampoo from the shower, then motioned for me to sit down.

"Oh, you don't have to do that," I said while shaking my head.

The Superior turned off the water and collected a few towels from the closet. He lined everything up on the counter, then turned back to me and gave me a small smile. "I insist."

He patted the chair, and I gnawed on my lip. Imagining him running his fingers through my hair set my pulse racing. I pushed my knees together and shook my head. "Shouldn't I just get in the shower?"

Taking a tentative step forward, he extended a hand to me. "The less you touch the poison, the better."

His reasoning was sound, but I still couldn't manage to take that first step.

"Please, let me help you, Claire."

His face was filled with the same guilt that I felt, so I nodded and stepped forward. Settling into the chair, he guided me backward as he gently laid my hair in the sink. The water turned on and he splashed it over my hair. His fingers brushed into my locks, and I had to bite down on my lip to keep a moan from falling out. The nerves in my scalp burst to life with the barest touch of his warm skin. Chills raced through my body as he gently worked out the knots.

"Sorry, I know it isn't the most comfortable," he said, misinterpreting my anguished face.

"It's fine," I said, not liking the slightly breathy quality my voice had taken.

My eyes looked up at his face. He was focused on his task and as his fingers moved water through my hair, I saw him occasionally wincing with pain. He was looking better. The sheen of sweat was gone from his forehead, but the poison was still hurting him. Despite the pain, his touch remained steady and gentle. His fingers grazed along the back of my neck causing goosebumps to erupt along my skin. I pressed my legs together and told myself to focus on something else. Anything else.

He turned off the water and grabbed the shampoo. When he slowly started massaging it into my scalp, I slid forward and almost fell out of the chair. He apologized again for the impromptu setup. Clearing my throat and resettling in my seat, I said, "Seems like you've done this before."

He smiled and I cursed myself for looking at him. When he grinned like that, he was irresistibly handsome. There was also a glint in his eyes that told me he knew it.

"I have at some point, I'm sure," he answered, placing his hands back in my hair. He worked meticulously, brushing through all the strands. I tried not to think about what he was seeing. The memories of my ordeal had been kept at bay since we'd gotten in the car, but I could still feel the press of them in my mind.

A loud plop sounded from across the room. I'd forgotten we weren't alone in here. The Superior's eyes flicked over to the tub and then back to my hair. "Destiny, go put some clothes on."

He said the words so easily that I wondered how often she took her clothes off in front of him. A vicious and unexpected wave of jealousy ripped through me.

"I'm already here," she called back. "I figured I might as well clean myself up."

A look of annoyance crossed The Superior's face, and his eyes glowed faintly red. "Out."

Destiny huffed out a large sigh. Water splashed loudly, then she appeared above me. Her wet hair dripped onto my arm. "How are you feeling?"

I shrugged and hoped that she wouldn't comment on the color currently staining my cheeks. She stepped closer, a crease forming between her brows. Something brushed against the front of my robe, and when I looked down, I saw that it was her breasts. She was still naked. Quickly, I lifted my eyes back up to The Superior. "I'm fine, thank you."

With his fingers still in my hair, The Superior said, "Destiny, get a towel and get out."

She straightened and even with my head tipped back I could see her large bare breasts. I looked over at The Superior, who seemed completely unfazed as he glared fixedly back at her.

"Fine," she said, then she placed a hand on my shoulder. "Sorry about earlier. I should have been more careful."

Destiny moved out of my field of vision. I continued staring at The Superior's face, sure I would see the moment his attention flicked to the gorgeous naked woman parading about the room, but it never did. After Destiny stepped away, his eyes dropped back to his task, and he worked as if her nudity was too mundane to warrant attention.

I scoffed at the thought. There was nothing mundane about what I had seen.

The Superior's attention flicked to me, curious. "What?"

Shrugging, I said, "You don't seem fazed by Destiny's nudity." I didn't care about his personal life, but I couldn't help myself from prying. Something in my gut twisted angrily at the thought of him being with someone. It made no sense. We had no claim to each other, yet I still couldn't take my eyes off him as I waited for his reply.

He laughed and it lit up every inch of his handsome face. His eyes flicked to mine, and I swear I saw them sparkle. I think he knew why I was asking and for some reason, it amused him. "Destiny and I have been together for a very long time. She has many good qualities, but like most of us she has her bad ones as well. Being a bit of an exhibitionist is one of them. Seeing as she's a succubus, I give her some slack for it."

That didn't fully answer my question, but I decided not to press it. "I don't think I've ever met a succubus before."

"Probably best," he said, finally rinsing the last of the shampoo from my hair. "They don't always do well around humans. Destiny is fine, but when they are young, they can struggle a bit with their self-control."

He turned the water off and grabbed a towel. Gently lifting my head, he expertly wrapped it around my hair. He squeezed and patted my head. I sat up and placed my hand on the towel to hold it in place. Not sure what to do next, I raised my brows at The Superior.

Looking me over he said, "You should take a shower. Make sure we got it all."

Before I could answer, his phone buzzed in his pocket. He took it out and excused himself for a moment as he opened the message. A small sigh of relief left his lips. "Scott made it to the hospital. He's in critical condition, but he's alive."

A mix of relief and worry washed over me. I was so happy to hear that Scott was alive, but being in critical condition meant he still had a long way to go. I started gnawing on my lower lip. The Superior brushed a hand over my robed shoulder. "He has a chance now because of you."

I shook my head, feeling the tears starting to well in my eyes. The weight on my shoulders suddenly crashed back down. Guilt swelled in my belly at the memory of Scott crumpled in the trunk. My arms wrapped around my body, and I stared over at the large, empty shower. Something about it looked so barren and cold and I shuddered at the thought of being alone in such a large space.

The Superior placed a hand on my shoulder and gave a small squeeze. "Take your shower. You'll feel better."

He turned as if to go and a soft objecting noise left my lips. The Superior halted abruptly. His back stayed facing me while he waited for me to speak. I didn't know how to voice my feelings. There was no reason I should feel unsafe. I was in The Superior's home. I didn't have to worry about someone coming for me. And yet, thinking about myself being naked, vulnerable and alone set my heart racing.

"Please," I whispered, "Will you please stay with me?"

My body trembled as I waited for him to respond. The memories were starting to flood into my head, and I knew I couldn't hold them back for long. They were going to cascade over me and remind me how weak and hopelessly lost I was, and I couldn't face those feelings alone. I needed him to stay, I was willing him to stay with all my might.

Finally, he turned and said, "Always."

CHAPTER 28

Inviting The Superior to stay had been one thing. Then, I remembered I was going to be naked in a glass shower. I hadn't thought that far ahead and now that we were standing together in awkward silence, I wondered if I'd made a mistake.

Sensing my hesitation, he nodded toward the back hallway. "I can wait in one of the dressing rooms."

My heart lurched at the thought of him being so far away. I found myself pointing toward the cupboard by the sinks. It was far enough away and if he stood on the opposite side, there was a chance he wouldn't see me naked. "Stand there, please."

He walked across the room and then he sank back against the wood of the cupboard. I hadn't noticed how tired he looked. He seemed barely able to stay on his feet. Removing the towel from my head I twisted it in my hands. "You know, I'm sorry, you can go rest."

His eyes fluttered and I could see dark circles underneath them. "Throw that towel in the barrel, then go take your shower."

Leaning his head back, he closed his eyes and crossed his arms, looking perfectly content. There was something so compelling about him then. His hair was an unruly halo about his head. The sleeves of his shirt were haphazardly rolled to his elbows, the cuffs still wet from washing my hair. I realized he'd had to change because I'd gotten poison all over his sweater earlier. He hadn't said a word, just done it and returned to helping me. It was such a simple thing, and yet it meant something to me. The demon before me wasn't anything like I'd imagined him.

I turned back to the shower, deciding to leave my conflicted feelings about The Superior on the other side of the room with him. Grabbing a towel and some supplies from the cupboard, I made my way across the cavernous space. Inside the shower, I arranged my items, gave one more sidelong glance at The Superior, then slipped off my robe. The cool air against my bare skin caused me to break out in goosebumps. I quickly turned to the shower and tilted my head at the screen on the wall. Deciding to bypass it, I grabbed one of the handles and twisted. Water poured from one of the available heads and the screen immediately lit. It displayed shower heads, settings, and temperatures. I played around with it for a moment, before settling on a simple spray of scalding hot water.

Heat bloomed across my skin with each drop. I breathed in the warm mist and let out a sigh. My fingers kneaded through my hair, not feeling nearly as good as when The Superior had done it earlier. As I lathered soap across my body, I felt the tension in my limbs finally starting to relax. I sighed and closed my eyes as I moved my face under the water. Images of the gun in my face and the sound of the gunshot flared to life in my head. With a choked gasp of air, I stepped back, slapping the water off my face, but the memories didn't stop. Billy Blake smirking at me before he shot me. A strange man slapping me across the face. My lip stung with the memory. Then there was Scott. Smiling and flirting at the bar before he became a bloody, beaten mess.

My lungs tried and failed to pull in air. I wheezed as I collapsed onto the shower floor. My head fell into my hands, and I felt my heart pounding as I tried to breathe.

The water suddenly turned off and soft fabric glided across my skin. A warm body pressed into my back, wrapping the towel all the way around me. The Superior's breath brushed against my ear. "Breathe, Claire. Breathe."

I shook on the ground as the tears fell. My body convulsed as I tried to push past the panic, all the while The Superior simply held me, lending me his warmth. There was a part of me that didn't think I deserved his comfort. It was my fault he was drained of his power. It was my fault Scott was in the hospital. I even blamed myself for Johnny's death, because it could have been avoided if I'd just stayed here.

After some time, I grew cold, so I pulled the towel around myself and rose to find a changing room. The Superior nodded, then left to bring me clothes. I stepped into the changing room and immediately wished I'd simply changed in the shower. There was a large, floor length mirror and it was impossible for me not to see the mess that was my face. My eyes were red and puffy. There was a red gash on the left side of my forehead. I touched it gingerly with my fingertips and winced at its tenderness. My hair was a tangled mess from being partially dried without being combed. The left side of my bottom lip was severely swollen, and my right cheek was already sporting an impressive bruise.

At least the mess of my face matched how I felt on the inside. I huffed out a humorless laugh at the thought, but it quickly devolved into sobs. What had my life become? I'd been shot. Twice. I didn't think Billy Blake was involved with the demons searching for Monica. He was just a shitty person and I'd gotten on his bad side. Would he try to hurt me again? What about this other demon who kept hiring people to find me? Even if I managed to find Monica, that didn't mean they would suddenly stop trying to get to her. I needed to find out what was really going on here.

There was a light tapping at the door. I turned. "Yes?"

Eyes averted, The Superior cracked open the door. "I brought you some clothes."

Pulling the towel around my body, I wiped away the tears under my eyes. "Thank you. You can come in."

He stepped into the room and set the clothes on a small stool in the corner. His eyes stayed on the floor as he turned to leave.

"Wait," I said moving closer to him. "Do you, do you think it'll stop?" I sniffled and wiped my nose with the towel. Warm fingers gently pulled my chin upward. The furrow of his brow deepened the longer he looked over my face. I moved to pull away, but he stepped closer and lifted his other hand to cup my chin. His fingers whispered across my lip, my cheek, and my forehead. When his eyes finally met mine, they were trembling. I didn't know if it was from sadness or anger, or perhaps both.

He shook his head. "No. The snake demon wasn't strong enough to have orchestrated this. Someone else was pulling his strings."

My body crumpled at his words. His arms wrapped around me, pulling me into his enveloping warmth. I breathed in his scent and felt my body slowly start to relax. Everything in me calmed with his touch, so I burrowed even deeper into his arms. The strong, steady beat of his heart sounded in my ear. My mind cleared and I was able to focus on what I knew needed to be done.

"We have to find her," I whispered into his chest.

His chin came down onto the top of my head. He hummed his assent, and I felt the vibration buzzing all along my body. The tip of his nose brushed my ear before he whispered. "We will."

I tipped my head up to look into his eyes. "Do you have any idea who Johnny was working for?"

"I have ideas. Nothing conclusive."

"Would everything have been easier if I had simply said yes to them?"

His fingers dug into my back. The softness I'd seen earlier disappeared in an instant. "No," he said in a flat tone.

I shivered but pushed a placating smile onto my face. "I meant, if I did, we'd at least know who they are."

A rumbling sound reverberated through his chest and the temperature of the room slowly started to rise. His fingers trailed across my body and moved to gently cup my chin. "No," he said again.

The word should have made me feel scared, but I reminded myself of what Destiny had said earlier. *Demons don't like it when other demons touch our stuff.* Perhaps I was hitting that nerve again by mentioning working with another demon. Although, I didn't like the idea of being considered 'stuff.'

The Superior leaned back and said, "You should get dressed. You're shivering."

I looked over at the stool and let out a small groan. He could have grabbed anything in the closet. Hell, I would have gladly worn something from his closet, but no, he had to bring me that stupid lingerie. A satiny sleep set that was so inappropriate for winter sleepwear that I wondered if he'd done this as a joke.

"Something wrong?" he asked, genuine concern in his voice. "It was the first thing I found in the closet, so I just grabbed it and returned."

That did make sense. I had put everything else away and left the stupid pile of lingerie on the bench in the middle of the room. My eyes swung over to meet his and I searched his face for any signs of humor. He looked slightly abashed as he realized he was missing something.

"It's fine," I finally said, "Just, well, it's just that I'm rather cold."

To my horror, he grasped the hem of his shirt and pulled it off revealing his ridiculously sculpted chest. He tossed the shirt to me, and I felt his warmth still lingering in the fabric. "That should help until you get back to your room," he replied before turning and leaving.

I dressed as quickly as I could. The small pieces of lingerie would have to serve as my bra and panties until I got back to my room. The Superior's shirt was still warm when I slipped it over my head. I wasn't a particularly small woman, but I still swam inside it. There was a comb tucked into the stack of clothes, so I took a few minutes to work through the tangled mess that was my hair.

When I stepped back into the hallway, The Superior was still there, leaning against the wall. His arms were folded across his bare chest. A thought occurred to me as I took in his tired posture. "Is all the poison finally gone?"

He glanced down at me with his eyes half lidded and nodded.

"You look like you could use some sleep," I said conversationally. I tugged nervously at the hem of his shirt. The panic started to rise again as I thought about sleeping alone in that big room. My eyes flicked up to The Superior. I couldn't read his expression, but when I bit my lip, his gaze immediately dipped to it.

"Stop looking at me like that," he warned.

Heat rose in my cheeks. "Like what?"

"Like you did earlier when you asked me to stay."

My eyes dropped to the floor. Had he really not wanted to stay? The thought sent my pulse pounding with the desire to flee. The tips of his shoes entered my field of vision. His fingers brushed up my arms. "I told you I would always stay with you."

His hands rested lightly on my shoulders as his forehead dipped to brush the top of my head. "If you keep looking at me like I am the only thing that makes you feel safe, I will take you to my bed."

My eyes widened and I swallowed. That thought hadn't crossed my mind, but now that it did, I couldn't stop picturing myself spending the night wrapped in his arms. Part of me knew I would regret it and knew that I was feeling this way because of the trauma I had experienced. There was the other part of me that wondered if there was something more. I had always thought he was gorgeous, but his presence earlier had truly calmed me. Maybe it was all a side effect of the mark, but in this moment, I couldn't summon the energy to care. I wanted this, so I lifted my chin and said, "Okay."

His arms wrapped around me faster than I could blink. A small yelp of surprise escaped me as I was lifted into his arms. He started walking back through the bathroom. I poked him in the chest. "Only to sleep."

A small huff of laughter escaped his lips and the sound of it was so wonderful I felt it flow to the core of me. I started regretting my bold choice, but The Superior kept walking and said, "If that is what you wish, Claire."

I nodded back in placation, but then I wondered if I had wished for more, what would he have said? Suppressing those thoughts, I let myself think about sleep and the more I did the heavier my lids became.

After exiting the bathroom, it was a quick trip into The Superior's room. I was intrigued at the prospect of seeing his personal space, but when we entered, he didn't bother turning on any of the lights. He moved about the space in a practiced grace, setting me easily into a bed with gloriously soft sheets.

I burrowed my head down into the equally inviting pillows and shimmied my way under the covers. A brief gust of air flew over me as The Superior threw another blanket on top of me. I grinned to myself at the added warmth I so desperately needed. My body was heavy with the need to sleep, but I was awake long enough to feel the bed dip behind me followed by warm arms wrapping around me. My body greedily wiggled back into his chest. I sucked in a deep breath and my nose was filled with his scent. My body sank deeper and deeper into the mattress as sleep slowly pulled me under.

Just before I drifted off, I heard The Superior whisper, "You are mine, Claire, and you are safe."

Something told me he hadn't meant for me to hear it, but immediately after, I drifted off into the most comfortable, dreamless sleep of my life.

CHAPTER 29

A throb of pain in my cheek woke me the next morning. My eyes opened to sunlight streaming in through gauzy black curtains. The events of the previous evening played over again in my mind as I brought a tentative hand up to my face. Everything hurt. With a groan, I lifted myself up into a seated position and looked over my shoulder. The Superior was gone. There was a slight twinge in my chest at his absence. Rubbing my chest, I took steadying breaths and told myself that everything was fine. I was safe.

My attention turned to the room around me. I wasn't able to see anything last night. Now, I saw a room very similar to my own. Large windows framed by curtains, a desk in the corner, and the large four poster bed in the middle. Instead of the mirror, there was a tall bookshelf and a plush armchair. Whereas my room was appointed in creams, The Superior's was done in blacks and dark grays.

Sweeping the covers off myself, I stood and stretched. My body was stiff, but it was nothing compared to my face. Gingerly, I examined my lip, cheek and forehead and found each one to be incredibly tender. I decided I should put together an ice pack, but after having some breakfast.

With a yawn, I stepped into the hallway and started toward my room. My steps faltered when I heard voices. I could tell one of them was The Superior, but the other was too low for me to tell. Looking down, I cursed myself for not grabbing some pants from The Superior's closet. As quietly as I could, I spun around on my heels.

"There you are."

Dammit. Turning back, I gave The Superior a small smile, then quickly averted my eyes as color flooded my cheeks. I tried and failed not to think about the fact that I'd spent the night in his shirt and in his arms. Tentatively, I glanced up at him and felt some relief that I saw no judgment in his gaze. He stood with his hands tucked into his gray chinos. His black button up was perfectly sculpted to the arms that had held me all night.

"Come on," he said with a nod of his head. "There's coffee."

I happily followed him into the main space, taking a deep breath to suck in the delicious smell of fresh roasted coffee. My lips parted into a blissful smile until I saw who was sitting at the bar. Blowing across the top of a mug was Nancy. It took me a second to register that it was, in fact, her and then I bolted toward her.

"What are you doing here?" I gasped excitedly while plowing into her.

She returned my hug and when we parted, her critical eyes looked over my face. "You look like shit."

I scoffed. "Thanks for pointing it out, I wasn't aware. Seriously, though, how are you here?"

Nancy's eyes shifted over my shoulder. "He called me."

My head whipping around. The Superior managed to look somewhat sheepish as he pushed a hand through his hair. "I will leave you two to catch up. I need to grab some breakfast."

His fingers brushed along my back as he walked past me toward the door. My eyes followed him and when I looked back at Nancy she had a knowing smirk on her face.

"What?" I asked while walking around the bar to pour myself a cup of coffee.

Putting her chin in her hand she leaned onto the counter. "You know what."

I shrugged. "Tell me how you're here first, then I'll spill."

She took a sip of coffee. "Nothing much to tell. He called me and asked me to come over. How could I refuse?"

My insides gave a little flutter at her words. The Superior had called her for me, but why had he done it? Was he worried about me? Was he just trying to be nice? I sucked in my bottom lip before letting out a hiss of pain. I'd forgotten about the cut.

"Come on," Nancy said, setting down her cup and nodding toward the couch, "Let me take a look at you."

I followed her over to the couch and submitted to her examine. She went through her usual list of vital signs and then she did a slightly more thorough check of my eyes and head.

"Well," she said, setting down her small penlight. "No signs of a concussion. That's good. What exactly happened to you?"

Slowly, I sucked in a deep breath and let the memories flood back in. It took me a moment to sift back through to the beginning. I almost couldn't believe it'd all happened yesterday. Retrieving my coffee from the bar, I sat with Nancy and told her my story. I made it through The Superior's revelation about my sister before needing to take a break.

Nancy's hands gripped my own. "You have a sister."

I nodded and felt tears starting to well in my eyes. Blinking them away, I said, "I have to find her Nancy. Even if she was a stranger, no one deserves to have these people hunting them down."

She squeezed my hands. "I know you can do this, Claire."

With a chuckle I replied, "How can you say that? I'm not even sure I can do this."

"You're stronger than you think. You never give yourself enough credit. Also, I'd be a pretty shitty friend if I said anything otherwise."

Warmth flooded me as I reached over and hugged her. I hadn't know how badly I needed to see a friendly face, but now that I had, I was so grateful she was here. Buoyed by her confidence and a second cup of coffee, I was able to finish telling her everything.

"Wow," she said, pressing a hand to her temple.

I nodded.

"I'm sorry," she said with a wave of her hand, "But I'm going to need you to get to what is clearly the best part of the story."

"What are you talking about?"

She reached forward and gave a small tug on the hem of The Superior's shirt. "The part where you slept with that sexy demon!"

My face was instantly aflame. I'd forgotten I was still wearing his shirt. When I'd told her about last night, I'd mentioned the poison and getting clean, but I had been vague on the details. "I didn't *sleep* with him."

Nancy crossed her arms and rolled her eyes. "Then how did you end up in his shirt?"

I glanced hesitantly at the door. "Look, I'll explain everything, but let's move this to my room so I can get changed."

"Fine," she said, before rising to her feet. "But this better be worth my while."

Walking back into the main room, Nancy was still grumbling that it hadn't been worth her while.

"I told you it wasn't going to be," I told her again, right before I stepped into the main space. I immediately froze and Nancy plowed into the back of me. The Superior sat at the large dining table with a huge spread of food.

He waved a hand over the table and said, "I thought you might be hungry."

Nancy poked her head out from around me. "Always," she said, before pushing me forward. She plopped herself down one chair away from The Superior and motioned for me to take the one between them. I rolled my eyes as I dropped into the seat.

"Thank you," I whispered to The Superior and he gave me a small nod.

Everything looked and smelled delicious. There were egg sandwiches on bagels and croissants, fresh cheese pastries, assorted muffins, a large bowl of fruit, and a fresh carafe of coffee. Nancy was already digging into the food beside me. Peeking to my right, I saw The Superior sat with a mug of black coffee and a chocolate pastry. I stared for a moment, oddly curious to see what food he liked.

While pulling an egg and cheese croissant onto my plate I asked, "Have you heard anything about Scott?"

My conscience still churned with guilt over what had happened to him. Something about us sitting around having a pleasant breakfast didn't seem fair.

The Superior shook his head. "Nothing new this morning."

"I can check on him when I get in tonight," Nancy mumbled from beside me. I looked over and found her stuffing the last of a blueberry muffin into her mouth while reaching for a banana.

"Thanks," I said.

"I do have news," The Superior said, pulling my attention back to him. "I visited Toby in the infirmary."

Swallowing down my bite of sandwich I asked, "How is he?"

The Superior's face was neutral as he took a sip of coffee. I waited for him to reply while my stomach continued to churn. If the guilt kept compiling, I didn't think I'd be able to finish my sandwich.

"He's fine. He'll be back to work this afternoon, but he did mention one of the books that he found in my library."

"Oh?" I said, bringing a glass to my lips to hide the concerned look on my face. Had Toby told him about the book with the mark?

"Yes, there was one that he said mentioned a Ferrier Realm of some kind. He said it would need further translating, but I thought it sounded like a good place for us to start."

I sighed with relief. The books tucked away under my mattress were still secret and now we also had a lead. I took a large bite of my sandwich and considered his words. My eyes wandered across the food on the table before slowly sliding up to The Superior's face. With a start, I saw he had been staring at me. Our gazes locked. Heat started to bloom in my cheeks at the intensity of the eye contact. Slowly, he extended his hand and then gently cupped my chin. I winced at the slight pain of his thumb brushing my swollen lip. The warmth of his power soon flowed across my skin. A moment longer and he dropped his hand. My skin tingled from his power. I raised a tentative hand and brushed it across my cheek. The pain was gone.

"Thank you," I breathed.

"You're welcome," he said with a smile, "I'm sorry I couldn't do it sooner."

My lips rose in a matching grin. His eyes danced down to them, and I licked them almost instinctively. He looked much better this morning. One good night's sleep and all the strain of the previous evening had vanished.

A loud throat clearing came from my left. I turned my head and saw Nancy staring at us. Chin propped on her hand, she had the biggest smile on her face. Her eyes flicked between us. She raised her brows suggestively at me, before turning to face The Superior. "That was amazing. Can you heal anyone?"

His eyes dipped to his plate. "No."

"Can all demons explode things with their mind?" she asked.

I grabbed a cheese pastry and stuffed it into my mouth. I recognized the look in Nancy's eyes. She'd had it the first time she'd come to my office and asked me all about my life. Now, she had a private audience with a powerful demon.

The Superior chuckled. "No."

Nancy nodded and poured herself some more coffee. "How powerful does a demon have to be to make a Queen?"

"Nancy," I warned. She dismissed me with a wave of her hand. Turning, I looked at The Superior and I was relieved to see his eyes were still solidly brown. He wasn't angry with her questions. In fact, he looked somewhat amused.

He leaned forward onto his elbows. "Very powerful."

"Is anyone else powerful enough to make one?"

"There are a few."

Nancy peeled her banana. "Can there only be queens? Like, it seems rude there can't be Demon Kings, too."

The Superior cleared his throat and dipped his gaze down to the table. His shoulders were suddenly tense as his fingers traced the edge of his plate. "In that instance, I believe the term Demon Mate would be more acceptable."

Continuing to munch on her banana, Nancy didn't notice the shift in his demeanor. I nudged her under the table with my knee. She shrugged. "Why can't there be kings?"

"Nancy," I warned again, giving her wrist a squeeze. Finally, she looked over at The Superior. He was still studying his plate.

His voice was barely above a whisper when he said, "Because the one who rules us does not have a pleasant history with kings."

I exchanged a glance with Nancy. The Superior stood abruptly. "Since we are almost finished here, I shall retrieve the books to begin translating."

Without waiting for a reply, he spun gracefully on his heels and walked into the hallway. When I heard the click of the door, I spun to face Nancy.

"Why can't you take a hint, Nancy?"

She shrugged and lifted her hands. "How was I supposed to know that was such a touchy subject?"

"Read the room," I said, sweeping my arms outward.

"God, did it get hotter in here?" she asked as she started fanning herself.

I hadn't noticed before, but now that she mentioned it, it did feel a bit warmer. The Superior must have been letting off some serious steam in his room. Pushing my sleeves to my elbows, I took a few sips of water.

"Oh," Nancy cried, gesturing to my exposed forearm, "I meant to tell you!"

The glass nearly slipped from my hand. "You translated it?"

She scrunched her brow and made a pfft sound. "No, but I did send it to Tabitha. She said she knows a guy that should definitely be able to translate it."

"Okay," I said, sensing there was something more. My fingers drummed lightly on the table while I waited for her to continue.

"He won't be back in town for a few days."

My shoulders dropped and I sighed. "Well, at least that's something, I guess."

"And," she said, drawing out the word. "I made a little discovery of my own."

She bounced with excitement in her seat. I laughed.

"I found something that said that the mark makes both parties super possessive."

"Possessive?" I repeated.

"Yep," Nancy continued. She piled some muffins onto her plate then walked toward the bar to wrap them in a paper towel. "It's supposed to be intense. Like crazy ex-girlfriend keying your car or burning your lawn intense."

I scoffed and walked over to the bar. "I don't feel anything like that."

She looked up at me and winked. "Are you sure?"

"Yes," I said without thinking, because despite my attraction to him, I didn't feel like I held any claim over The Superior. Though after I'd said it, something in my gut twisted sharply.

Nancy was unconvinced. "Uh-huh. Well, I gotta go, but I'll text you once I find out about Scott." She gave me a quick hug and then walked out the door.

CHAPTER 30

The Superior returned shortly after Nancy left. He seemed to have calmed down since our earlier conversation. Even the temperature in the room had returned to normal.

He set the stack of books on the end of the table. The top book he set to the side and opened.

"What do you make of this?" He asked and indicated a line.

Leaning down, I saw his handwriting scrawled across the page. There were notes everywhere, but his finger pointed to a few lines near the bottom.

All souls call out to the ferrier. They offer safety from the demons. To hear the call, the ferrier must be in the realm to listen.

"The realm to listen," I said, looking up at him, "Is that what Toby meant by the Ferrier Realm?"

"I believe so. Does any of that mean anything to you?"

Our eyes met and I shook my head. There was no disappointment in his expression, just a fierce determination. He wasn't going to give up that easily and neither was I.

"The realm to listen," I repeated, "Could that be translated any other way?"

He looked back down at the page and studied it for a moment. "Perhaps. It's the best I could come up with in English."

I scratched my chin. "Hmm, the only other *realm* I've been to is The Otherworld. That doesn't make sense, though. I've been in The Otherworld countless times, and I've never heard anyone calling out to me."

The Superior crossed his arms over his chest. "Perhaps you are thinking too literally. Maybe they haven't called out to you, but you have sensed souls. You yourself admitted to always finding the ones you sought in The Otherworld."

Shaking my head, I sighed. "I don't know. So, you're saying if I go through a portal intent on finding Monica that I will? Even though she's not dead and therefore not even in The Otherworld? I just don't think so."

He stepped closer to me and brushed a tentative finger across the back of my hand. "It's at least worth trying, don't you think?"

It wouldn't be hard to do. My reluctance at entering The Otherworld over the past three years had been because of the man now standing beside me. If he was with me, what did I have to worry about?

"Okay," I said, "Let me just grab my jacket."

His hand lightly wrapped around my wrist and halted me. "Are you sure you're up to it?"

The reminder about last night caused my chest to squeeze, but I knew that I had to keep going. The other demon wasn't going to stop, so neither could we.

"I'm fine," I said.

"Are you sure?" he asked, stepping closer. His thumb pushed under the sleeve of my sweater and swept across my skin. The warmth of his touch left a trail of goosebumps in its wake. He stepped even closer, and I could smell a heady mix of leather and smoke. His eyes danced as a slow smirk spread across his face. "You're looking a little flushed, Claire."

Attempting to laugh it off, I playfully batted his chest with my hand. He clamped his own hand down on top of it, leaving me pinned. I could feel the jumping rhythm of his heart beneath my fingers.

"I'm fine," I repeated, my words a breathy whisper.

His fingers played along the underside of my wrist. "Your pulse is racing."

He was teasing me. Something had shifted between us last night and apparently, he was happy to continue with it this morning. Everything about him now was relaxed and confident. It was a side of him I hadn't seen before and even though I was struggling to process it, that didn't mean I didn't like it.

I smiled up at him. "Maybe because there's a demon with his hands all over me."

His grin widened as his eyes darkened. "You didn't seem to mind these demon hands on you last night."

Any hope I had of my heart rate returning to normal was obliterated with that comment. I tried to focus on my breathing and not the beautiful lines of his face. Was this really happening?

"I was scared to be alone," I finally said.

He gave a small nod and then brushed my hair behind my ear. "Are you scared now?"

Yes, but for a very different reason. "No," I answered, but he raised his brows skeptically. "Because I'm not alone."

His expression softened. "I thought I scared you."

There was a time when that was true. The first time we'd met, he'd scared me so fully that I avoided The Otherworld for years. Now, I thought about him saving me. I remembered the tenderness he'd shown last night as he washed my hair. The look in his eyes right now.

"You did."

I shifted on my feet. We were still pressed together, but he was no longer holding onto me. His grip on my wrist was delicate while his other hand still twisted the strands of my hair.

"Did?" he asked, his eyes dipping briefly down to my lips.

"You saved my life. More than once. I know you need me for this job, but I saw how draining it was for you to touch all that poison and yet you still did it. If you didn't have me, you would have found another way to find my sister. I know you would. You could have let me die, but you didn't."

"Claire," he said, my name passing softly through his lips. "The mark meant I couldn't let you die without dying myself."

It felt like a bucket of cold water had been tossed over me. The mark. I'd forgotten about it. Instantly, I deflated and cursed myself for thinking that any of this was real. The mark connected us, pulled us together and was the reason The Superior was acting this way. My cheeks flushed as I dipped my gaze away from him and took a step back.

His hand in my hair dropped to my right forearm. Slowly, he pulled the sleeve of my sweater up, exposing the mark.

"But even without this," he began, his breath tickling across my skin. I gasped as his lips pressed a gentle kiss to the mark. Goosebumps erupted down my body, and I shuddered.

When he reached the crook of my elbow, he gently released my arm and cupped my face. Heat swam in his eyes. My tongue darted out, instinctively wetting my lips. The movement caught his attention and a small grin flashed across his face. He leaned forward and I closed my eyes feeling nothing but my pounding pulse until those soft lips were pressing against my own. I thought my heart was going to explode. The kiss was featherlight and before I knew it, his lips were gone, and he was pressing his forehead against my own.

My eyes fluttered open as he whispered, "Even if you didn't bear my mark, Claire, I would still save you. I will always save you."

His phone started ringing. I instantly deflated. He stiffened and took a step back, reaching into his pocket. Clearing his throat, he gestured down to it. "I have to take this. Excuse me."

I nodded and when he turned his back, I bolted from the room.

CHAPTER 31

I kissed The Superior. I kissed The Superior. I kissed The Superior.

The thought played over and over again in my mind as I rocked on my bed. I had a jacket clenched in my hands, but I couldn't summon the courage to stand and return to the main room. My pulse was still racing as I tried to convince myself it hadn't happened. The memory of the feel of his lips was there to assure me it most definitely had.

Sucking in several calming breaths, I was finally able to rise from the bed. I had to do this. We needed to get to The Otherworld and see if I could find Monica there. I needed to be a grown-up and face him. The sooner I got it over with the sooner we could get to work.

Stepping out into the main room, I felt my cheeks flushing at the sight of his broad backside. He must have heard me enter because he swiftly turned and smiled at me. He pointed apologetically at the phone in his hands and walked toward the fireplace.

I wandered over to the table and looked down at the books. The page he'd shown me earlier was still open. I stared down at his translation, my fingers brushing over the lines. One of them suddenly struck me as odd.

"What are you looking at?"

The Superior came up beside me, tucking his phone into his pocket while running a hand along my lower back.

I shivered at the familiarity of the touch. Sliding the book toward him I asked, "Safety from demons? What exactly does that mean?"

"Powerful ferriers can control demons," he said simply.

My eyes widened in shock. "What?"

He looked at me curiously. Seemingly unsure if it had been an outburst or a genuine question. He started to repeat himself, but I waved him off. "How?" I asked instead.

"I don't know," he said, shifting the book onto the top of the stack. Stepping away from me, he grabbed a long gray coat off the back of a chair. "But I know it can be done."

Shrugging into the coat, he extended his hand out to me. I simply stared at it. "How? How do you know it can be done?"

His eyes dipped away from mine for a moment. "Because it has been done to me."

"What?"

I practically screamed the word at him. Taking several steps forward, I moved into his personal space, thrusting my chin upward so we were face to face. My head shook back and forth as I tried to fathom using my power to control someone like him. It didn't seem possible. All my life I had felt the pull of souls and the surge of my magic when I touched them, but never had that happened around a demon.

He chuckled as I gripped his wrists. "Will you only be speaking in questions for the rest of the day?"

Ignoring him, I said, "You have to tell me everything." Squeezing his arms, I tried to impress my feelings upon him.

"I understand why you feel that way," he said, a trace of his smile still on his lips. "But that knowledge is incredibly dangerous."

I shook my head. "That's not fair. I have a right to know."

He pulled his arms out of my grasp. It was easy for him, but the tug threw me slightly off balance. His hands wrapped around my shoulders to steady me. "It's too dangerous."

My head continued to shake as I took an abrupt step away from him. He dropped his hands to his sides. I expected him to look contrite, but the slight redness in his eyes told me his anger matched my own.

"You don't get to decide that *for* me."

He stepped closer, all softness in his face suddenly gone. His voice held a deadly edge as he said, "Yes, I do. I said I would protect you. This is me protecting you."

Crossing my arms in front of myself, I glared back at him. We weren't going to agree on this, but for now, I needed to focus on what was important. Finding Monica had to come first. With a heavy sigh I said, "We don't have time to argue about this right now. Let's just get going and we can talk about this later."

He gestured toward the door. I walked toward it and felt him step in line behind me. My fingers wrapped around the handle, and I pulled, but his hand held the door shut.

"Claire," he said, bringing his face within inches of mine. "This knowledge is dangerous. Do not speak of it to anyone. Understand?"

My eyes narrowed at him, but I nodded. He released the door, and we moved into the hallway. As we walked through the house, I tried to focus on Monica. We'd gotten rather sidetracked, but I still had a job to do. For the moment, I needed to push any feelings or thoughts of feelings about The Superior aside.

Stepping out the front door, I followed him down the steps and into the grass.

"Where's the portal?" I asked.

He smiled, then stretched out an arm and began drawing a circle through the air. Wind began to blow, following the path of his arm. It swirled more and more violently, spinning inward toward the center of the circle. When he reached the start point again, he dropped his arm. The wind continued to whirl around, faster and faster until there was a flash at the center and a loud popping sound. Everything immediately settled. The inside of the circle fluttered as if in a calm breeze. The edge of the circle glowed a soft blue. He'd just created a portal.

My jaw dropped. "Can all demons do that?"

The Superior gave me a pretentious smirk and shook his head. "There are perks to ruling."

He extended his hand, and I took it. Together, we left the lush grass of his lawn and stepped through the portal into a knee-high drift of snow. A strong breeze blew cold air and shards of ice across my face. The land was covered in rolling hills of snow. The River rushed past about twenty feet in front of us. Squinting, I tried desperately to adjust to the sudden, blinding brightness. The Superior stepped next to me and I scowled at his nonplussed appearance. His hair was being gently tossed by the wind, but otherwise he seemed unaffected by the harsh climate.

"What's wrong?" he asked after seeing my face.

I took in his appearance while wiping tears off my cheeks. Perhaps immunity to the environments of The Otherworld was also a perk of ruling. I doubted it. No, something told me that unruffled appearance was inherent to whatever type of demon The Superior was. That thought made me think of something else. "Why don't you lose your human skin in The Otherworld?"

He was visibly taken aback by my question. "What do you mean?"

"All demons shed their human skin when they enter The Otherworld," I explained while gesturing to his body, "Except for you. For some reason, you don't. Why is that?"

The Superior stared at me for several long moments. I hadn't thought the question was that difficult, but he took his time contemplating it before he finally answered. "I have no other skin."

With a huff of laughter, I reached out and patted his arm. "Whatever you say. Now, what are we doing here?"

Reaching into his coat, he pulled out the picture of Monica. I took it and stared down at the image. My bare skin started to burn from being exposed to the harsh wind. Unsure what to do with the picture, I simply stared at it and thought, how do I find you? I stood there hoping for a sign until my fingers could no longer stand it. Nothing happened. Tucking them back inside my jacket, I shivered and stomped my feet a few times, trying to keep my blood circulating.

The Superior cleared his throat beside me. "Do you feel inclined in any direction?"

I looked around. Some distance behind us, I could see trees. Raising my hand, I pointed toward it. "The only inkling I have is to go that way, but that may just be my instinct to seek shelter."

He squinted toward the trees, then looked around as if he hadn't noticed we were surrounded by mountains of snow. "Okay," he said simply. His eyes came down to meet mine and I was surprised to see a curious light to them. Despite the pressure I knew he felt to find Monica, he wasn't pushing any of it onto me. He was willing to follow me even though I wasn't sure if it was right. Some of my tension eased at knowing he was giving me the space to try and fail.

I turned to face him and practically bounced off his chest. He wrapped himself around me then pulled me up and into his arms. Instinctively, I wrapped my arms around his neck. His lips twitched upward. "I might be able to get us there faster if I carry you."

Chuckling, I rolled my eyes. "It's not *that* far."

He took off and I was immediately thrust backward into his chest. The land flew past as he ran at an incredible speed. Seemingly unfazed by my weight in his arms, he made quick work of the drifts of snow between us and the trees. When we reached the edge, he halted and gently set me on my feet. Wiping my hair from my face, I thanked him. It honestly hadn't been that far of a walk, but this way had been much easier for me. My nose had only just started running. I pulled a tissue from my pocket then I started into the woods.

The Superior followed me as I made my way around. There was far less snow here, but I still had to push past low branches and small saplings. As I moved, I tried to think about Monica before I took each step. It didn't feel like anything was leading me, but what I did know was that I was painfully aware of the demon behind me. He said nothing as he perfectly matched each hesitation, turn, and step I made. After several minutes, I found myself being irked by the sound of his accompanying movements.

Spinning around I said, "Could you just, give me a few minutes by myself?"

My demon shadow stopped and stared at me. I expected him to resist, but he shrugged his shoulders and turned to lean against a tree. "If I sense another presence in these woods, I will come find you, otherwise I can wait here."

I thanked him, then turned back to the trail I'd been following. There hadn't been a reason I'd gone this way, but now that I had, I figured I might as well finish it out.

Several minutes later, I pushed past two massive pine trees and came to an abrupt halt. I was standing on a rocky outcrop at the edge of a ravine. All I could see to my left and right was a steep drop. The ravine spread far and wide before me. It was beautiful. I stood for several moments, catching my breath and taking it all in. Perhaps that was why I was distracted enough not to notice the other person until their hands were clamping down over my mouth.

CHAPTER 32

As one hand went over my mouth, another grabbed my elbow. Panic rose in me as I wondered how anyone had found me here with The Superior just on the other side of the trees. I heard a hiss and a gasp before I was spun around to face my captor.

"Miss Woods, what have you done?"

Relief flooded my body as I took in Gabriel's face.

"Gabriel," I sputtered, "What are you doing here?"

Normally the picture of elegance and grace, the angel before me was anything but. His eyes were wide and darting around furtively while he held his hands awkwardly away from his body. He shook them and I saw the skin of his palms looked burned.

"I came to warn you. He's so close, but..." His breath started heaving as he stepped closer to me. "Oh, Miss Woods, how could you?"

Confusion clouded my mind until Gabriel showed me his hands and then pointed at my right forearm. Color flooded my cheeks. Those burns had come from touching me. I'd been angry about the mark at first, but since The Superior had used it to save my life, I'd had a change of heart about it. Gabriel wouldn't understand that, but it didn't give him the right to judge me.

"It's not like I did this to myself, Gabriel," I answered defensively.

He stepped forward and his voice took on a dangerous tone I'd never heard before. "Did he force it on you?"

Technically, that was the truth, but there was no way I could tell him that. I didn't know the current standing between angels and demons, but I knew how Gabriel felt about The Superior. If there was a chance he could use this against The Superior to incite some kind of war, I didn't want to be a part of it. Instead, I avoided the question.

"It's only temporary. Until I find my sister."

Fishing the picture out of my pocket, I held it up for him to see. His eyes stayed fixed on my arm.

"Let me see it," he said, his words brooking no argument.

I moved the picture into his line of sight, but he shook his head and pointed at my forearm. Heaving out a sigh, I pushed up my jacket sleeve and held out my arm. Gabriel's face contorted with absolute rage. I took a step away from him.

"That mark is almost permanent, Miss Woods."

An icy feeling trailed down my back. I stared at him, not wanting to believe what he was saying. Looking down at the mark, my stomach flipped. It was darker. I hadn't looked at it often, but I could tell it was definitely darker now than it had been when I'd first seen it. My pulse started to pound.

"What does that mean?"

Ignoring my question, he began pacing. "You can't trust him. You know what he is, and he has had longer than you can imagine to perfect fooling humans. He isn't a man. Never forget that."

I shook my head, trying to make sense of his words. "Gabriel, I don't understand."

He pushed onward. "I don't have much time; he'll be coming soon. Ask him the right questions, Miss Woods.

Why is he so interested in you? Your sister? Your family? Has he told you that?"

"What do you know?" I asked, my hands clenching into fists at my sides. He knew something, just like The Superior and just like him, he'd never told me anything. "Did you know about my sister?"

He dipped his eyes away from me, all but confirming my suspicion. I shook my head, no longer having the energy to deal with these supernatural beings and their secrets.

"Do you know where she is, Gabriel?" I asked, a pleading tone to my voice.

"I do not," he said, and a pained expression crossed his face.

There was a crash in the woods. Then a wave of intense heat blasted across the ledge, knocking me to my knees. Gabriel placed a hand on my shoulder. "I have to go. Ask the right questions."

I turned to glare at him, but he was already gone.

Less than a second later, The Superior exploded onto the ledge. His face was contorted with rage. The wave of heat I'd felt before intensified to an inferno. Sweat broke out across my brow and the snow beneath my knees started melting. His eyes were a swirling sea of crimson.

"Where is he?" he asked in a tone that sent shivers skating down my body.

The heat was becoming so oppressive that I couldn't seem to catch my breath. I gasped and pressed my hands onto the ground. Instantly, the heat lessened, and I felt his presence in front of me.

"Where?" he repeated.

Looking up at him, I shook my head. "I don't know."

His jaw ticked and his eyes narrowed before me reached out to me. Gently, he lifted me to my feet. "What did he want?"

That was a loaded question and one I knew I couldn't answer with complete honesty. Gabriel's intention had been to warn me, but he'd also pissed me off by revealing he'd known about my sister. I'd known him longer than I'd known The Superior, so that betrayal stung. Leaning into my feelings of hurt I finally said, "He wanted to warn me about you."

His grip on my arms tightened as his nostrils flared. He stepped closer to me and turned his head to scan the tree line. I could feel him trembling as he tried to contain his rage.

"He said you were close by," I continued, "so I told him I was looking for my sister. He knew about her. I've known him most of my life and he never told me about her."

I let the hurt I felt sink into my words. The Superior pulled me closer, wrapping his arms tightly around me. We stood together like that for several moments. Slowly, the tension in him eased and he started to rub circles into my back. Finally, he broke the silence.

"We should probably get back."

Nodding, I moved back and watched as he opened another portal. We stepped through onto the grass of The Superior's front lawn. Chaos erupted around us. People were scrambling as vehicles drove up and around the circular driveway.

Destiny flew at us, running across the grass at a speed I couldn't quite track. She stopped in front of us with the biggest grin lighting up her face.

"We found her."

CHAPTER 33

I stood on a curb looking up at a house in Greenfield. With light gray paint and a weather worn front porch, it perfectly matched the aesthetic of the homes around it. And yet, I stared up the concrete steps and wondered how my life would change once I went inside.

Destiny climbed out of the car behind me and let out a groan. "She's not here."

Turning to face her I shouted, "What?"

Her eyes connected with mine before looking down at her phone. "They were supposed to bring her over, but they lost her. About twenty minutes ago."

The Superior rounded the back of the SUV and his eyes lit with fire. "Someone has some explaining to do."

I shivered at his voice and then felt the brush of his hand along my lower back. My instincts told me to lean into his touch, but on the ride over here I'd had time to mull over Gabriel's words. The Superior still hadn't explained why he'd marked me, nor had he said why Monica was important. After the attack at the bar, I'd found comfort in his presence and had let those things slide. Now, I looked up at him and couldn't stop Gabriel's questions from circling in my head.

Sensing a shift in my mood, he dropped his hand and said, "Don't worry, Claire. We'll find her."

He set off up the steps and I turned my attention to Destiny. The night was dark, but we stood close to a streetlamp, so I could easily see the smirk on her face.

"What?" I asked, crossing my arms and rubbing my hands across them for warmth.

She shrugged. "It's cute. Seeing you two together."

I snorted out a laugh. "There is nothing *cute* about that man. And we're not together, we're just…"

Destiny stepped closer to me, raising her eyebrows. "Just what? Living together? Sleeping together?"

My cheeks reddened at her knowing I'd slept in The Superior's bed. She hadn't seen me this morning, which meant he had told her about it and that somehow made it worse.

"Uh-huh," she said, before linking our arms together. "Come on."

We climbed the steps and when we entered the house, I was surprised to find it full of people. The small entryway was open to the living room. There was a long couch along the far wall and several chairs along another. Every available space was occupied. Everyone was engrossed in conversation and I could hear even more coming from down the hallway. I walked further down the hall, smiling at the wallpaper that looked like it was from the seventies. The hardwood floors creaked as I continued toward the back of the house.

I stepped out of the hallway and into a nicely updated kitchen. It was small, but functional and once again full of people. Some were standing around the island eating from several trays of food while others were pouring drinks from bottles set on a small table. Destiny grabbed a drink from someone and turned to lean against the counter while she took a sip.

Walking over to join her, I kept my voice low as I asked, "Who are all these people?"

"Servants of the master."

There had to be at least fifty people on this floor alone. Everyone moved with purpose, setting up chairs or arranging food on the counters. People smiled and acknowledged each other, and I felt like I was at a neighborhood block party, not an assembly of human servants.

"Why are they here?" I asked, as I watched the commotion unfolding around us.

Destiny smiled and waved at someone walking into the kitchen before answering. "Because he asked them to be."

With that, she pushed off from the counter and gave the new woman a hug. They shared a few words before Destiny lifted a hand toward me. The woman gave me a beaming smile. The two standing together were quite a striking pair. Both were absolutely stunning. Whereas Destiny had wavy red locks, this new woman had pin straight ash blonde hair. Her skin was tanned, but from the lack of smile lines around her eyes, I guessed that nothing about it was natural. Her lips were plump and pink, her teeth perfectly straight and white. She extended a hand to me, and I noticed a large golden cross hanging deep into her ample cleavage. Taking her hand, I gave a hesitant smile.

"It's so nice to finally meet you," she said, her voice carrying a rich Southern accent. "I'm Christy."

She removed her hand from my own and I said, "Claire."

Christy gave a tinkling laugh, and for some reason it irritated me. She continued smiling at me as she said, "I feel like we'll be fast friends. I already know so much about you."

I blinked back at her, confused. Looking over at Destiny she only smiled and took a sip of her drink.

"You can learn so much about a person going through their closet," Christy said, seemingly oblivious to my confusion. "We should go shopping together sometime."

She bounced up and down giddily at the prospect. My eyes widened. This was who collected my things and brought them to The Superior's house? I looked her up and down and felt a churning in my gut at the prospect of her judging my things. My face must have shown my displeasure, because Christy's smile suddenly fell. She leapt forward, grabbing my hands and holding them in her own. "Oh, I'm so sorry, I meant no offense."

I peered over her shoulder at Destiny. She was smothering a laugh with her hand. I glared at her before returning my attention to Christy. "I'm not offended," I said flatly. "I'm just surprised. I hadn't known how my clothes had gotten to The Superior's house."

This was apparently the wrong thing to say. Christy looked horrified and clamped down even harder on my hands. Her bright blue eyes looked to be on the brink of tears. "Oh, I'm so sorry, I assumed you knew! You must feel like I've invaded your privacy and please know that is not the case. TS asked me to grab your clothes and that's all I did, hand on my heart."

I blinked several times, still unsure how to feel about the woman before me. Her vice like grip on my hands was bothersome, but something she said struck a nerve. "TS?"

Christy relaxed and finally let go of me. Her fingers grabbed the cross at her neck and spun it along its chain. "Oh," she said with a small giggle, "saying 'The Superior' all the time sounds so formal."

"Is there something wrong with formal?" I asked, my lips lifting upward into what I hoped was a smile. Judging by the way Destiny was laughing, I was not succeeding.

She giggled again and waved a hand at me. "Oh, we're all friends here!"

My eye twitched as a surge of something hot and acid-like burned through my insides. I took several deep breaths and clenched my hands together. Apparently, Nancy hadn't been wrong about the feelings of possessiveness. I just hadn't experienced them yet.

I needed some distance from Christy, before I did something I'd regret, like punching her in her beautiful face. "Excuse me, I think I'll grab a drink."

"Oh, no," Christy said, grabbing my arms to halt me. "Let me get it for you. What would you like?"

"Water," I spat. Never before had that word sounded so hostile.

Unfazed, Christy gave me a huge grin and walked across the kitchen to grab it. Destiny brushed her shoulder against my own and leaned down to whisper into my ear. "You handled that *so* well."

Her words held a humor I didn't share. I glared over at her, but she only laughed.

"Don't let her fool you," Destiny said, nodding toward Christy who was now filling a glass with water from the refrigerator. "That woman is sharp as a tack."

My eyes shot over to her. "So that's all an act?"

Destiny laughed again. "No, that personality is legit. Just know there's more under the surface with that one. A lot more."

She raised her brows at me but said nothing more. I watched Christy walking back to us with a renewed interest. Stopping in front of me, she presented the glass with an elegant little bow.

"Thank you," I said, taking it from her.

My eyes drifted over her shoulder just as The Superior came into the room. I felt heat rising in me at the sight of him. He moved effortlessly through the crowd of people, acknowledging everyone with a nod or quick word. In turn, they either bowed or smiled back. I was struck by their familiarity. Despite being an all-powerful demon and these people being his servants, no one seemed uncomfortable or frightened of him. In fact, their smiles seemed genuine. I'd always assumed human servants were either bad people or people tricked by demons. Some of these people may have fit that description, but after meeting Toby and Scott and now seeing everyone here, I no longer thought that was true.

The Superior saw me and turned toward us. When he reached our little group, he moved to brush past Christy by placing a hand along her back. She jumped and then turned to look up at him. The moment her eyes connected with his, her face melted into a flirtatious smile. Acid filled my veins, and I gripped the counter as hard as I could. Closing my eyes, I focused on simply breathing in and out. Warm fingers touched my chin. I looked up to see The Superior studying me curiously.

Before either of us could speak, someone shouted, "She's here!"

"Who's here?" I asked, finally feeling back to normal.

The Superior released my chin and nodded his head toward the dining room. Everyone moved aside to allow us through, then crowded into the space behind us. I'd tried to stay in the back, but The Superior had wrapped his fingers around mine and pulled me along beside him.

He sat down at the head of the table with Destiny taking the seat to his right. The other seats were filled with people I didn't recognize. The petite woman sitting across from The Superior caught my attention. Her back was pin straight, and her hands were neatly folded before her on the table. She wore a nun's habit. I blinked at her curiously, wondering if she could legitimately be a nun or if it was a disguise.

During my musings over the woman, the room had grown quiet. I looked around and noticed that everyone was staring at me. A few gazes darted past me, and I turned to see The Superior holding his hand out to me. I gave a small shake of my head in response. He raised his eyebrows. My cheeks heated as I felt the eyes of everyone on me. It probably wasn't a good idea to reject him in front of all these people, so I took a step forward and put my hand in his. He pulled me closer and said loud enough for everyone to hear, "Would you like to sit down, My Queen?"

I looked at the full table and then back at him and whispered, "It doesn't look like there's room."

Without even blinking he said, "There is always room for you."

The blush on my cheeks deepened as everyone at the table shifted in their seats. Destiny rose and bowed toward her chair. I looked out at the crowd of faces and felt my heartbeat drumming violently in my chest. Not wanting to be the center of attention a moment longer, I dropped down into the seat and dipped my head.

Satisfied, The Superior gave my hand a small squeeze. "Now," he said in a voice full of authority. "Andrea, tell me what happened."

To her credit, Andrea barely flinched at the command. "She came to us a few hours ago. Mother Superior was not inclined to let her in due to the late hour and our beds already being full."

My head tipped in surprise. Apparently, it wasn't a disguise. How someone like Andrea became a servant to a demon was too much for me to contemplate. Looking over, I saw someone place a glass of water beside Andrea's clasped hands. She nodded her thanks before continuing her story.

"I convinced the Mother to let her stay, insisting that I could find some space. Once inside, she went into the facilities. She was dirty. She looked as though she hadn't had a proper washing in several days. I left to set up her bedding and to send word to you, sir, but she came into the room, seized my phone, and demanded to know who I worked for."

Andrea took a sip of the water, and her eyes flicked down toward the table. "I told her I worked for the Lord, but she was unwilling to accept that answer. She told me to tell whomever I worked for to leave her alone and that she was never coming back. Then she tucked my phone into her pocket and slammed the door in my face."

Shaky eyes rose to meet The Superior's. She looked at him expectantly, but when he said nothing, she said, "By the time I was able to find a phone and place the call, she must have escaped."

Whispers began to circulate around the room. Apparently not everyone had known that my sister was gone again. The Superior cleared his throat, and all conversation died.

"When did you realize she was gone?"

"Less than hour ago, sir."

The Superior let out a huff of air and snapped his attention to the man on Andrea's right. "Jules. Report."

The man, Jules, was dressed in a loose plaid shirt and an old gray baseball cap. He leaned forward as he looked back at The Superior. "Andrea called us right after she called you. We searched, but there wasn't much of a trail. We tracked her maybe a mile down the road, but things went cold from there. She's a smart girl."

"Anything from the phone or other tech?"

This time the young woman to The Superior's left answered. She had a head full of strawberry-blonde curls and a pert, pointed nose. She looked to be about eighteen years old but when she spoke, her voice was clear and authoritative. "There was no activity on Andrea's phone and Monica ditched it shortly after she left. We've still had no hits on the web and nothing on facial recognition either. Her credit cards are still dead."

As everyone was giving their reports, I started to feel like the weakest player on the team. These people were trained, and yet, even they couldn't find her. The Superior was clearly desperate when he contacted me. Once again, I wondered what Monica really meant to him.

The Superior's attention finally turned to the last person at the table, a thin man dressed in all black who sat next to me. When his eyes rose to meet The Superior's, they were completely black. A night demon. I shuddered at the sight of him and slowly leaned closer to The Superior. Night demons came from the deepest bowels of Hell. The ones on this side of the gates patrolled the edges of The Otherworld. I'd met one once before. It hadn't been a pleasant experience. I hadn't realized I was shaking until I felt the brush of The Superior's hand against my own. His fingers wrapped around mine and then his power and warmth pulsed through me. My shoulders instantly relaxed.

"Reports go around," the demon said. "Many claim sightings, but none have shown true. The others have not given up on their search."

His voice was a low growl that sent a tremble down my spine. Something in the air shifted while he spoke and all the humans in the room seemed to tense simultaneously.

The Superior still sent pulses of heat through our joined hands as he asked, "Any word on who the others are?"

The demon's attention fell to our hands. His eyes slowly raked up my body and when they came to my face, he gave me a fiendish grin. There was no flirtation in it. It was more like he sensed my unease and enjoyed it. My lips twisted in disgust.

His gaze returned to The Superior as he said, "No word on the leader. They have…many allies."

He spoke in a clipped manner. I wondered why that was until his eyes settled back on me "Many speak of *her*. Insist there is a connection."

The Superior showed no outward reaction to this information, but the air in the room grew noticeably warmer. "And what have you said in response to this?"

The night demon continued staring at me as he said, "Only connected to her demon."

His attention shot back to The Superior and then he bowed his head over the table. I was happy he was no longer looking at me, but his words tumbled around in my head. *Many speak of her.* Why were people talking about me and what did they want? Was Monica someone so special that everyone in the supernatural world was looking for her?

My thoughts were interrupted by The Superior's voice. He was commanding as he said, "Jules, you will do another sweep. Those that can help track, will. Split up along all possible routes. Andrea, contact churches in the area. See if Monica has shown up at any. I will need volunteers to check the shelters and morgues. Demons, take to the rivers and woods, accordingly."

The tension in the room broke as he finished speaking. Having been given their orders, people split off into groups and set to work. Everyone, except Andrea, who raised a tentative hand toward The Superior.

"There is one more thing of note," she said, rather quietly. Her eyes dipped to her lap, and we all waited with bated breath for her to speak. Finally, her eyes met The Superior's. "She's pregnant."

CHAPTER 34

Silence fell over the room.

The Superior let out an exasperated breath and asked in a low voice, "How far along is she?"

Andrea shook her head. "I don't know. Upon her arrival, we offered to take her to confession in the morning and she responded that she was beyond saving, but perhaps the bastard in her belly could benefit."

I started at the cruel language, but looking at The Superior and Destiny, neither of them seemed surprised. Just what type of person was my half-sister?

Continuing, Andrea said, "She is starting to show already, but I doubt she is far along. Four or five months, maybe?"

The Superior's eyes flashed to Destiny, and something unspoken passed between them. He suddenly rose from the table, and everyone acted as if that was the signal that the meeting was officially over. People started heading into other parts of the house. Destiny followed The Superior into the kitchen, but not having an express purpose at the moment, I felt somewhat out of place. Not wanting to be in anyone's way, I walked out onto the front porch.

It was cold, but after my earlier trip in The Otherworld, it almost felt warm. I breathed in the night air and wondered if my sister was still in the city somewhere. My sister *and* her baby, I reminded myself. The shocks to my life just wouldn't stop. I dropped down into a wicker chair and thought about her. Closing my eyes, I felt for my power while picturing Monica. I imagined her sitting alone somewhere feeling the same cold air under the same night sky.

My powers hummed under the surface of my skin. They pointed out a few souls around me and I sensed a portal somewhere nearby. Nothing else. No living souls. I opened my eyes and stared upward. Light pollution from the city made it difficult to see the stars. I imagined Monica like a star, shining brightly just beyond the haze. If I just knew where to look, I could see her.

The front door swung open, and Jules stepped out and rushed down the front steps. He was followed by several others, who all determinedly headed toward their vehicles. I guessed that it was the search party heading to Andrea's church.

"Lovely night, isn't it?"

My skin crawled at the voice. I slowly turned my head to look over at the night demon. He must have followed Jules' party out. His eyes were still swirls of black but thankfully he was no longer giving me that unnerving grin. To my horror, he sat down in the chair next to mine. I tried not to cringe at his nearness as I finally answered, "Yes, it is."

His lips twitched upward, but his teeth remained hidden. "It is a shame that your human eyes cannot take in all of a night's splendor."

He shifted his attention out across the neighborhood. His gaze flicked over the houses and then lingered as he looked up into the sky. He stayed quiet for a few moments, allowing me time to somewhat settle my nerves.

With his eyes still fixed on the sky he said, "Talk of you is almost as prevalent as that of your sister."

"What do they say?" I asked tentatively.

His gaze met my own and this time he smiled, showing his teeth. They were black, pointed two-inch-long needles. A shudder rolled down my spine as I struggled to maintain eye contact.

"They say you are the key to finding the lost girl."

My stomach started to roll at the predatory gleam in his eyes. I cleared my throat and said, "I don't know why they think that."

"Because it is true."

I stiffened in my chair and shook my head. In response, he tipped his head back and emitted a harsh sound from deep in his throat. It grated down my spine and as I looked him over, I realized he was laughing.

Before, I had been scared of the night demon, but now he was starting to irritate me. He seemed to want to tell me something. I wished he'd get on with it. Shifting in my seat, I asked, "How can you be so sure?"

"You are not the first of your kind that I have encountered. There have been many before you and one of the most powerful came from your own line."

I scrunched my face in confusion. "My line?"

He nodded as his black eyes swirled. "Your grandmother's grandmother was a force to be reckoned with."

My mouth dropped open. Someone else in my family had been a soul ferrier. The thought caused something to niggle in the back of my mind. Gabriel.

Why is he so interested in you? Your sister? Your family?

My family? Did that mean that Gabriel and The Superior knew about my relative? I leaned toward the night demon, questions ready to burst from my lips when the door beside him opened. The Superior stepped out and his eyes immediately fell on the two of us.

The night demon quickly swept to his feet. He bowed low to me and said, "It was a pleasure to speak with you, My Queen, but I am off to the woods."

He said the last word with distaste. The Superior gave him a stern look and then moved to block his path. "No fun in the woods," he said, his voice laced with warning.

The night demon simply bowed to him and then swept down the stairs and disappeared. The Superior watched him for a moment and then shifted his attention to me. He dropped into the chair beside me with a sigh. "Don't worry, he will not harm you."

Still reeling from the night demon's revelation, The Superior's words barely registered. My mind still whirled about my relative. Looking over at The Superior, I wondered if he knew her. My stomach knotted. He was still keeping secrets.

I wanted to confront him, but his head tipped back, and he closed his eyes. His chest rose and fell with several deep breaths, and I saw some of the tension in his shoulders melt away.

"Why does his speech change?" I finally asked, feeling that now wasn't the time to ask about my relative. "Does it have something to do with the night?"

He rolled his head to look at me. I was struck by how human he looked. His face was soft and heavy with fatigue. I wanted to reach over and stroke the locks of his hair that bordered his face.

"Being in a room full of souls is difficult for him," he explained, his eyes staying fixed on my own. "He has to fight his hunger whenever he is around humans. A tight space like the dining room earlier is very difficult for him."

"So, you're telling me that he wanted to eat us all so badly that he could hardly speak?"

He gave a small laugh, and the sound of it felt like a caress. Heat pooled low in my belly.

"Not everyone," he said with his lips still turned up in a grin. "Technically they don't *eat* humans. They rip them apart until they find the soul and then eat that."

I could feel the blood draining from my face as I pictured that horrifying image. "Please tell me you're joking."

"I am not," he said, straightening in his seat. "If you wish to see it for yourself— "

"No, no. I'm good." I shoved my hand into his face to silence him. He batted it away playfully and I smiled.

The front door opened again, and Destiny stepped out. She took in the sight of us and raised her brows. "Shall we go?"

We made it back to the estate and The Superior and Destiny went off to work. I was exhausted, but also hungry, so I made myself something to eat and settled into my bed to watch some tv.

Some time later, I checked the clock and saw it was after midnight. I cursed and made my way out of the room. Several dishes sat on a tray from my late-night snack, and I wanted to return them to the kitchen before morning. Stepping out into the main room, I set the tray on the bar, knowing I needed both hands to open the massive doors, when I was halted in my tracks.

The Superior sat sprawled in a chair by the fireplace. His eyes were glued to his phone as one hand tapped on the screen and the other pulled through his hair. The locks were disheveled from him doing the action repeatedly and yet somehow, it made him even more attractive. He was dressed down from the day, wearing a pair of sweatpants and a plain black t-shirt. His bare feet stretched out in front of him.

Clearing my throat, I approached the chair opposite him. When he looked up at me, I whispered, "May I?"

He nodded toward the chair, and I sank into it with a sigh.

"Couldn't sleep?" he asked.

I shook my head and gestured back toward the bar. "I had a snack and I was on my way to return my dishes."

He pushed himself up in the chair and set the phone down on the arm rest. He gave me his full attention. Anxiety swirled in my stomach at the intimacy of us sitting together like this. Looking down, I felt heat in my cheeks at the oversized gray t-shirt and old workout shorts I was wearing.

"What are you doing?" I asked.

His eyes darted down to his phone and a message flashed across the screen. He shrugged. "What I am always doing."

Curious, I leaned forward and asked, "And that is?"

He chuckled at my interest and then to my utter shock, he handed the phone to me. I stared down at the device in my hands. He'd left it unlocked and that level of intimacy felt like too much. "What am I supposed to look at?"

He ran his hand through his hair once again and then leaned his head back against the chair. "Just whatever comes in."

Not fully understanding what he meant, I opened the notifications and clicked on the last message. It was a text.

> Dear Sir,
> Jude stole $20 drng lst game nght. I want it back.

"Um, what is this?" As I asked the question, another text rolled in.

Sir, I have sent the latest reports for your stock portfolio.
-J

A moment later, the email alert pinged. When I opened his email, I saw the one before was from someone named Graham. I opened it and then looked at The Superior curiously. "Why is Graham asking you if he can buy a dog?"

To my surprise, The Superior groaned and leaned forward and buried his head in his hands. "Because I won't let him get one."

I chuckled. "Why not?"

"Graham finds attachment difficult," he said. I stared at the top of his head for several moments before he finally sat back up, wrapping his hands around the back of his neck. His muscles flexed as he massaged the skin and the movement brought my attention to his bare biceps. I swallowed and felt a rush of color in my face. Thankfully, the low light and heat from the fire covered it.

"He had a tomato plant once," he continued. It took me a moment to remember what we were talking about. Right, Graham. "He took amazing care of it, then he cried when the thing died in the fall."

A laugh bubbled out of me. "Wait are you serious?"

He nodded and a slow smile split his lips. "He was inconsolable. If he was that bad when a plant died what the hell is going to happen with a dog?"

I covered my mouth with my hand, but I couldn't stop the laughter that came spilling out of me. Doubling over in my seat, I was surprised to hear The Superior laughing with me. I realized I'd never heard it before and when I looked up, I saw he was smiling enough to show his teeth. Pearly white, they made his already heartbreakingly handsome face devastating.

Clearing my throat, I brought my attention back to his phone, hoping the distraction would settle the pounding of my heart. Another message appeared on the screen. "Is this what you do all day? Respond to these messages?"

He dropped his hands into his lap and shrugged. "I have over two thousand servants, demon and human. They have to do what I say but I have to be available for them as well."

Holding the phone out I said, "I always assumed you were concocting demonic dealings or stealing kids' lunch money or something."

The Superior snatched the phone quickly out of my hand and then narrowed his eyes. "I have enough money, I don't need to steal from children."

"Fair enough," I said. "So you don't do any real work?"

He raised his brows at me, assessing me for a moment before answering. "Taking care of my servants is work, but I also have an interest in real estate ventures. The same types of areas are always sought after, so it is an easily profitable game. I keep an eye on new inventions as well. Being an initial investor in emerging technologies can be very lucrative."

I held up my hand and yawned. "Please, stop."

"Am I boring you?" he asked with a wry smile before lightly kicking my foot with his own.

We sat like that for a few moments. I felt the heat from the fire brushing against my already flaming skin and I saw the reflection of it dancing in The Superior's eyes. It took me a little while to realize his foot was still touching mine, slowly tracing the back of my ankle.

I swallowed, trying to calm my libido enough to embrace this moment. He was relaxed and we were feeling comfortable together. It was now or never, so without giving myself another moment to hesitate I blurted out, "Why do you care so much about my sister?"

The shift startled him, but he quickly recovered. His face hardened and the tension was back in his shoulders. He sat up, moving his foot away from mine.

"I do not," he finally answered. "As far as humans go, she is far from praiseworthy. She has been nothing but a bother since she reached adolescence."

"Then why do you care so much about finding her?"

"I told you, because I have to."

His eyes were starting to redden, but I felt a responding tide of anger within myself. I slammed my hands onto the arms of the chair. "I need more than that. Why can't you tell me the truth?"

He matched my posture, moving his fists to the arms of his chair. "I have done nothing *but* tell you the truth since I gave you my mark."

"You're lying," I spat as I rose from my chair, "I know you're hiding things from me."

"Lying and keeping things from you are not the same things, Claire."

I lifted my arms and let them fall with a thud against my thighs. "It's the same to me."

In an instant he was in front of me, the tip of his nose brushing against mine. A wall of heat enveloped us. "Is that so? Then why don't you tell me what you were doing when Toby passed out?"

I dipped my head, not wanting to meet his eyes. I'd forgotten about that. Scorching fingers gripped my chin and pulled my face upward. I squirmed away from the look in his eyes, but he held fast. "Not interested in telling me that one, Claire? Fine, then tell me what you really want to know about your sister?"

In a voice barely above a whisper, I said, "Why do you care about her?"

"Lie," he snapped. "Why should I be honest with you when you cannot be honest with me? I will tell you what you want to know, Claire, and it is whether or not we were lovers. You want to know if I fucked your sister."

I started at the aggressiveness of his words. Attempting to pull away only made him squeeze harder. A single tear rolled down my cheek. I wanted to deny the words but something in my heart twisted. Something within me was desperate to hear the answer.

Eyes now completely circled with red, he said in a deadly whisper, "Now ask me, Claire."

He forcefully released my chin. My throat worked and my hand came up to clasp the bottom of my face. More tears fell from my eyes as I struggled to hold his gaze. I sniffled. "Have you ever fucked her?"

He sneered at me. "No. Not now. Not ever."

With that he turned, and in a blink, he was gone from the room.

CHAPTER 35

The next morning, I laid in bed and stared at the ceiling. My chin still held the memory of The Superior's fingers digging into my skin. His words, said with such venom, continued to play in my head. I understood why he was angry. He wasn't used to people questioning him, but he didn't deny the fact that he was still keeping something from me. Gabriel told me I had to ask the right questions. The ones about my sister were getting me nowhere, so perhaps I needed to shift my strategy. After several minutes of pondering, I sprang from the bed with a new mission in mind.

Gathering my toiletries, I snuck into the bathroom, took a quick shower and got dressed. Another simple sweater and jeans combination but putting myself together immediately boosted my mood. I slung my coat over my arm and took a deep, steadying breath. Making my way down the hallway, I tentatively peeked my head around the corner. There was no one in the main room. I breathed a sigh of relief and slipped out the door. Walking toward the kitchen, I maintained my vigilance. I wasn't ready to see The Superior yet.

Stepping into the kitchen, I sighed with relief when I saw only a few people and didn't recognize any of them. I walked over to the counter and ordered coffee and an egg sandwich. It was afternoon, but I hadn't had breakfast, and a caffeine headache was already starting to throb in my forehead. When my food was ready, I thanked the chef and then made my way over to a small table. After I sat down, I texted Nancy to ask if she'd heard anything about Scott. She sent a quick text back letting me know he was awake for limited time and in the ICU. That potentially complicated part of my plan, but I'd deal with it when the time came. Scarfing down my sandwich, I moved on to the second part of my plan. I grabbed a muffin off the fruit and pastry platter and headed for the front door.

When I arrived, Martín stepped out of the small side room. I plastered on my biggest smile and held out the muffin. "Good morning."

His eyes landed hesitantly on the pastry, then flicked up to my face. "Good afternoon. How may I assist you, My Queen?"

Widening my smile, I said, "I was hoping to get a car for today." I blinked my eyes rapidly, and then stepped into his personal space a bit. "And I thought you might like a snack."

I pushed the muffin toward him. His eyes widened for a moment before he gave a small nod and graciously took the pastry from me. "Thank you, My Queen. Give me just a moment."

He headed back into the security room, carrying the muffin as if it were a bomb. I sent a plea out to the universe that I would be allowed to leave, then pulled out my phone to call Mark. He answered on the second ring.

"Good afternoon, Your Majesty, to what do I owe the pleasure?"

I scoffed. "You're hilarious, Mark. How's work been?"

Looking back into the office, I saw Martín on the phone. I chewed on my thumb nail as I watched him and listened to Mark.

"Things are good," he said, "People are curious when you will return to work. I always mention you are recovering from being shot by a mob boss and that tends to shut people up."

I snort. "Billy Blake is not a mob boss."

"Semantics," Mark huffed into the line. "As for the contracts you had open, The Superior has almost closed them all."

I spun around and nearly dropped the phone. "What?"

"The Superior. He's already finished most of your outstanding assignments."

An indignant huff fell past my lips. When had the demon found time to do all of that? I balled my free hand into a fist and asked, "How have people been responding to him?"

There was a brief pause on the line. My heartbeat started to ramp up and I held my breath.

"They love him."

"What?"

"They love him. Incredibly professional, helpful, and oh so pleasant to look at. I believe Mrs. Watson has conned him into a dinner next week."

I laughed. "She would."

Mrs. Watson had been a client of mine for over a year now. A widower who lived alone in her husband's ancestral home who insisted the place was haunted. There was a familial cemetery on the property, but during several inspections, I never once encountered a lost soul. What I had found was an elderly woman who always insisted I stay for lunch and a game of Rummy after searching her house. Apparently, even a demon couldn't negotiate against that woman.

A throat cleared behind me. I turned to see Martín waiting patiently behind me. Saying a quick goodbye to

Mark, I hung up and stared expectantly at the man before me.

"A car has been summoned, My Queen."

A thrill of excitement bolted through me as he went to pull open the front door. I wanted to hug him as I passed, but after his reaction to the muffin, I decided to resist that urge and instead shouted 'Thank you' at him with a huge grin plastered on my face.

Stepping outside, I shielded my eyes from the bright afternoon sun. It was a gorgeous day. Still cold, but less windy than it had been. I heard a car engine coming down the side road. Pulling my coat tight around me, I walked down the stairs and onto the gravel. A black convertible came around the side of the house and stopped in front of me. I glowered at the driver.

Destiny smiled sweetly up at me. Her eyes were hidden behind large sunglasses and a snow-white cap sat on her head. Those wavy red locks cascaded down her shoulders onto a cream-colored peacoat.

"Hop in," she called, nodding to the seat beside her.

"Don't you have more important things to do today?"

"Yes," she said, "I do, so let's make this quick. Where to?"

I rolled my eyes at her and pulled out my phone to order an Uber. "Forget it. I'll find another ride."

"Claire, you're not leaving here without me, so let's cut the shit and just tell me where we're going."

Irritation skittered up my spine. Even if I took another car, I'm sure she would follow. Sighing, I stepped forward. Destiny slid her glasses down the bridge of her nose. "If you scratch my paint, I'll scratch out your eyes."

Hesitating, I gently lifted the handle and stepped carefully into the vehicle. When I shut the door, she pressed the glasses back up and settled her hands onto the steering wheel. "Where to?"

"Target. Then the hospital."

She nodded and took off so abruptly, the tires spat gravel across the lawn. My hands gripped the seat as I made a small squeaking sound.

"So," Destiny said after turning onto the road, "Want to talk about yesterday?"

My heart started to pound. "What about yesterday?"

"Well, I was going to say something about your future niece or nephew, but your tone makes me think whatever you are thinking about is *much* more interesting."

With a scoff, I tried to play off the tension. "I just meant that a lot happened yesterday."

We careened around a corner, and I glanced over at her. She looked perfectly at ease even though the tires had just been squealing. With a death grip on my seatbelt, I said "Can you please slow down?"

"Relax," she said, waving me off before flicking her hair behind her shoulder. "I've been driving since the day cars were invented."

That didn't reassure me. In fact, it made me more curious about who she was. "What is it you do, for The Superior, exactly?"

She snorted but kept her eyes on the road. "Whatever he tells me to do." Destiny expertly flicked the car around a tight turn and brought the car to an abrupt halt at a red light. Looking over at me, she chuckled softly. "So that's what you were thinking about."

I prayed for the light to change as I could feel my face heating under the scrutiny of her gaze. She waited, boring a hole into the side of my head with her eyes while I pretended not to have heard her.

The light finally changed, and she floored it, sending me flying backward into the seat. I was thankful her concentration was back on the road, but it apparently wasn't enough to distract her from this conversation.

"Problems in the bedroom?" she asked in a husky voice.

"What? No," I spluttered and felt my cheeks heating even more.

"By all means, please spill. I'm dying over here."

I glanced over at her. She was fanning herself with one of her hands while still steering with the other.

"What do you mean?" I asked.

We slowed down for another light, and she turned to look at me. "I'm a succubus."

Her tone was such that she seemed to think that was answer enough. Lifting a brow, I asked, "And?"

The light changed and we inched forward slowly. "Oh, I just figured you knew. Our human skin needs food for energy, but the demon underneath needs energy, too. Only our demon parts don't feed on food. As a succubus, I feed off sexual energy."

"Oh," I said, tucking away that valuable piece of information for later.

"So," Destiny said, pulling into the parking lot and starting to search for a spot. "I can feel the tension between you two and it's been driving me crazy. With all these late nights with searching for Monica I haven't been able to feed."

She found a spot and whipped the car in and shut off the engine. I breathed a sigh of relief that we didn't die and stepped out. Destiny met me at the back of the car and to my surprise, she grabbed my arm and intertwined hers with mine.

"What does not being able to feed do to a demon?"

"Makes us tired and weak." She let out a long-exasperated sigh. "And for me, it makes me horny as fuck."

She smiled devilishly down at me as the automatic doors whooshed open and we were greeted with a warm blast of air. I unbuttoned my jacket and grabbed a basket.

"I didn't need to know that," I said and walked into the store with the sound of her laughter behind me.

After shopping, we drove to the hospital. Pulling into the parking garage, Destiny abruptly halted the car outside the valet stand. A beautiful young woman with braids cascading down her back stood staring down at her phone. Destiny turned off the car and jumped out.

The woman lifted her eyes and gave us a friendly smile. "Hello. How are you today?"

Stepping out of the car and coming to join them, I watched Destiny prop her elbows onto the stand as she held out the key fob. "I'm good. How are you?"

Destiny's voice was a seductive purr. The woman behind the stand sucked her bottom lip into her mouth, trying to hide her responding smile as she looked up through her lashes at Destiny.

Shifting the bag of items in my hands, I cleared my throat a little too loudly. They both looked over at me. The woman looked abashed but there was a hint of purple rimming Destiny's irises. "You know, I can take all this stuff up by myself, and that way it frees up your time to do," I flicked my eyes from Destiny to the valet and back. "Whatever with the rest of your afternoon."

The demon's eyes narrowed slightly. "I couldn't possibly leave you all alone, so let's say we'll meet here in an hour?"

There was an undercurrent of warning in her tone, but I simply smiled and nodded. I wasn't planning to leave the hospital, but I had been hoping to get a few minutes alone with Scott. He deserved an apology, and I didn't want anyone or anything to distract me from my purpose.

I found Nancy in the emergency room, and she was able to escort me up to the ICU. In order to get in, Nancy explained to the staff that I was Scott's sister and that I'd wandered into the ER looking for him. Their eyes filled with sympathy, and I felt a twinge of guilt at deceiving them. Nancy left and a nurse escorted me to Scott's room. On the way, she explained that he was recovering nicely, but that he was on a rather large dose of painkillers and that he still spent much of his time asleep. She pushed open his door with a small smile and waved me inside. Shutting the door behind me, I turned and faced a curtain, and the unique hospital symphony of silence punctuated with beeps.

Sucking in a breath, I peeled back the curtain. The rings rattled along the metal bar, and I saw Scott's head turn lazily toward the noise. He jerked upward slightly at the sight of me, but the movement was minimal. His eyes connected with mine and I winced at the sight of him. That handsome face that had flirted with me was now a mass of bruises. Purple and red swollen patches of skin distorted much of his facial features. A brace encircled his neck, and his right arm hung in a sling from the ceiling. His left arm and right foot were also wrapped in casts.

"You should see the other guy," he said, his words coming out groggily as his attempt at a smile was lost in the swell of his face.

I had expected him to be in bad shape. Afterall, I had seen him in the trunk, but in that moment, he had been less of a person and more of a body. Now that he was looking at me and talking, he was Scott again, and I felt my heart wrench at the devastation that had been done to him. All of this was my fault. I stood frozen in the middle of the room, my hand gripping the curtain.

"If you're going to be sick, the bathroom is to your left," he said, his voice suddenly cold.

Swallowing down my guilt, I released my death grip on the curtain and stepped forward. There was a chair tucked into the corner of the room, so I pulled it over to the bed and sat down.

"I'm sorry," I said, pressing a hand through my hair, "Just seeing you, like this, I felt s—"

"Sick?" he interrupted.

"No," I said, sliding out of my jacket and pushing it onto the back of the chair. "So guilty. You wouldn't be here if it wasn't for me."

I hadn't come here to unload my feelings of guilt onto him, but seeing him like this, the emotion felt like a raging torrent inside of me. My stomach churned as I took in the damage to his body, and I couldn't stop my mind from imagining myself being the one to inflict every wound. Every spot of damage on his body was there because of me.

He looked over at me and subtly shook his head. "It wasn't your fault."

It was, but I knew this conversation was doing more to alleviate my guilt than to help him feel better. Sucking in a deep breath, I pushed away my feelings and lifted the bag off my lap.

"It most definitely is my fault, but I've brought a peace offering."

I shook the bag and smiled. He rolled his eyes but extended his hand. "What have you brought?"

Grabbing the rolling table and setting it between us, I dumped the contents out of the bag. Candy bars, bags of chips and popcorn, books, bottles of soda, mini puzzles and games covered the tabletop. Scott shifted, leaning closer to the table.

"I hope you see something you like," I said, sitting back down.

His eyes roved over the assortment on the tray, before landing on me. "Oh, I definitely see something I like."

My heart thumped at the suggestion in his eyes. I grinned back at him, happy that he was feeling well enough to flirt. "And what would that be?"

He pointed to the edge of the tray. "Hand me that Snickers and you've got yourself a deal."

Twenty minutes later, Scott was sitting with a flashing star necklace around his neck and a pile of empty wrappers on his lap. I laughed as he tried and failed again to open the puzzle box I'd bought. With a frustrated sigh, he tossed it onto the table.

"Thanks for coming," he said, his eyes connecting with mine.

I smiled. "No problem."

"Although with all the pain meds in my system, I might not remember that the Queen herself deigned to visit me."

Rolling my eyes, I brushed some popcorn crumbs off my sweater. "I am the picture of regality."

He laughed and tossed a crumpled wrapper at me. I batted it away with my hand and spat, "Hey! Keep acting like that and I might take advantage of you in your compromised state."

The moment the words were out of my mouth, I felt my cheeks heat. That hadn't been my intention, but hearing it out loud, I knew how Scott would take it. Looking over at him, I saw a wicked grin on his face. "And how might you take advantage of me?"

"Not like that," I said, climbing out of my chair and dumping several wrappers into the trash.

"Then how?"

Turning back to face the bed, I felt a twist in my stomach. This wasn't why I'd come here. I didn't want to abuse our budding friendship, but if anyone might answer my questions about The Superior, it would be Scott. His loyalty seemed far more tenuous than anyone else's I'd met.

I shrugged my shoulders and settled back into the chair. "Ply you for information."

His eyebrows rose. "What kind of information?"

Remembering what Gabriel and the night demon had said about my family, I said, "About The Superior's past."

Despite everything, I still didn't fully trust Scott. He was still a servant of The Superior and so I had to keep my questions a little vague in case he reported anything back.

To my surprise, Scott laughed. "Which part? You're going to have to be a lot more specific. He's been alive a *long* time."

"How long?" I asked, moving forward in my chair. I knew The Superior was older than he looked, but I had always been curious exactly how old he was. It also annoyed me that I had no idea what type of demon he was, but perhaps that was a question for another day.

"I don't know, but it's been a good while," Scott said. "Couple centuries at least."

"Centuries?" My mouth fell open and I was temporarily so distracted by this revelation that I forgot my line of questioning. "How's that possible?"

Scott shrugged. "No idea."

"Well, that's disturbing," I mumbled to myself. My fingers brushed my lips as I remembered kissing The Superior. It had been bad enough that I'd kissed a demon, but thinking he was some ancient being somehow made me feel worse.

"Is that all you wanted to know?" Scott asked, a laugh apparent in his voice.

"What about..." I hesitated, still unsure what I even wanted to ask. The night demon had mentioned my grandmother's grandmother, so I decided to start there. "What about past personal relationships?"

He snorted and rolled his eyes. "Checking up on the exes?"

"No," I said, "I was thinking more friendships." Or at least, I hoped that's all it was. The thought of anything more made me want to gag.

"Friendships?" Scott said skeptically, "I wouldn't know much about that. The Master is exceedingly private about his personal life. I've rarely seen him with anyone outside of those that serve him."

I mulled that over, wondering if perhaps my relative had served The Superior at some point. It was possible. I nearly smacked myself in the forehead when I remembered I had seen a record of the servants in The Superior's employ. His private journals in the library. If my relative was as powerful as the night demon had claimed, The Superior had to have written about her. The question now was how to get back into the library.

"Can you bring me my phone?" Scott asked, pointing toward a bag and breaking me out of my thoughts. Standing, I walked across the room and retrieved the device. I handed it to him and sat back down. He scrolled through something on the screen and said, "You want to know a demon's dirty secrets, you gotta ask another demon."

"Who?"

He held out his hand, "Give me your phone so I can give you his number."

I pulled out my device and unlocked it for him. "Who?" I repeated.

Setting his phone on his lap he started typing away on mine. "Vlad. He's ancient, rarely leaves The Otherworld and has spies everywhere. He's also worked for The Master for a long time. If anyone knows anything, it would be him."

Hesitating, I said, "Will he even talk to me?"

With a small chuckle, Scott finished typing and handed the phone back to me. He looked at me as if I didn't have a clue, and in truth, I didn't. "You're his queen. You can summon him and demand he talk to you."

Sticking out my tongue, I made a sound of disgust. "I can't do that."

Scott settled back onto his pillows with a yawn. The sugar high was starting to wear off. "If you want answers, you should. You should also tell him not to mention it to The Master."

"Can I trust his word?"

"If you order him not to as his Queen, he won't say anything. Demons have few rules, but they do listen to the ones they have."

The thought of trusting another demon still didn't sit well with me, but it gave me more of a plan than I'd started the day with. "Thank you."

Scott nodded, his eyes fluttering sleepily. He turned to look at me with a mischievous grin on his face. "I put my number in there, too. Just in case."

He winked and I laughed. "I better let you get some rest."

Gathering the trash and my coat, I gave Scott a soft squeeze on the shoulder and excused myself from the room. My heart felt lighter as I walked down the hallway. I still felt guilty about what had happened to him, but he was alive. He would heal and get better, and he was still willing to be my friend, despite everything I'd put him through.

Stepping out into the cold night air of the parking lot, I breathed deeply and let myself smile. I had a plan. Unlike The Superior, Vlad would answer my questions and whatever he didn't know, I would find in the journals. It was a fool's hope, but I had to have hope that something would work out. Maybe if I was able to unravel all these secrets, I could finally figure out how to unlock the power to find my sister.

Destiny stood at the valet stand. Her face was set in a calm smile despite the slightly unruffled quality to her appearance.

"Have fun?" I asked, lifting a brow suggestively.

The woman from earlier was handing off keys to another customer. She was far enough away to not hear us, but Destiny still watched her with an appreciative eye. Destiny winked at me and shrugged her shoulders. "How's Scotty?"

I winced. "He's still got a ways to go, but he seemed in good spirits."

She nodded and we turned to watch a valet drive her car up and stop before us. I was wondering if Destiny suspected anything about my conversation with Scott, but when we climbed into the car, she stomped on the gas pedal, and I was suddenly far more concerned with maintaining my death grip on the seat to think any more on it.

CHAPTER 36

The following morning, I woke early and decided to go for a walk. I donned my coat and went outside. The air was crisp and cool. Gray clouds filled the sky as I walked. I followed the gravel driveway around the side of the house. Stones crunched under my boots and birds called from the trees, but I heard little else. Rounding the corner, the main road continued further back into the property, while another veered off to the left. The path to the left ended at a large metal building with garage bays, so I went straight. Large, bare trees lined the driveway. Staring up I wondered at how beautiful they must have been a few months ago in the flush of autumn.

After some time, I spied a small sign that said 'Summer Grove' and decided to follow it. My cheeks were flushed from the cold but I didn't mind as the rest of my body hummed with warmth from the walk. I had hoped the time outside would calm the racing thoughts of my mind, but alas, the stress of my life couldn't be silenced.

The Superior and I still hadn't seen each other since our argument. Last night, Destiny and I had returned late. I'd grabbed some food from the kitchen and gone straight to my bedroom. With every passing hour that I didn't see him, the more anxious I became at the prospect. I knew it would happen eventually and like ripping off a bandage, I just wanted to see him and be done with it.

Scott had given me Vlad's number, but I had no idea where or how to secretly meet with a demon. Even if I was able to trust this demon not to tell The Superior, how would I keep him from finding out? He tracked my movements and always sent an escort with me when I left the property. I thought about texting Vlad, but that felt even less secure.

Then my thoughts always settled back on my sister. It had been almost a month since she'd first disappeared, and I was still no closer to finding her. Trying my powers in The Otherworld had been a bust and I still had no idea where a realm to listen could possibly be.

Ahead of me, there was a sharp turn in the pathway under a gnarled, wooden archway. I turned and saw the path continuing down a tunnel through tall, green hedges. Hesitantly, I stepped forward. The sound of running water caught my ear. The path turned left, and I was suddenly facing a large open space surrounding a massive tree. The hedges broke off to my left and right to encircle the space before me. There was a small man-made waterfall cascading down a rock wall and into a small pond. A small bridge spanned a narrow section of the water and led to a wooden bench under a tree. Walking over to the bench, I saw there were several flower beds, now dormant, surrounding the space. I wondered how beautiful it must be to be here in the summer.

Settling down onto the bench, I closed my eyes and let myself listen to the sound of the water. My mind tried to plague me with my worries, but I brushed each one off, trying to give myself a moment of peace. I felt a familiar brush of magic next to me and looked down to see a paper cup sitting next to me. Lifting the cup to my nose, I inhaled the sweet scent.

"Chamomile tea?" I snorted as I looked up at the sky.

My hands gripped the warm cup as I turned back to take a tentative sip. The hot liquid made a delicious path of heat through my chest.

"Thank you, Nicky," I said, smiling down into the cup.

A throat cleared from across the pond. I jumped and spilled tea on my coat. Reaching into my pocket, I fished out a tissue and started mopping up the liquid.

"I didn't mean to startle you."

I looked up and felt my heart pounding at the sight of The Superior. He walked across the bridge, his gait unhurried as he slipped his hands into his coat pockets. His clothes were all black today, making him look every bit the sexy, dangerous demon he was. He stopped at the edge of the bridge, his eyes sweeping over me questioningly.

"It's okay," I said, finishing wiping at the spill and tucking the tissue into my other pocket. My lips settled on the brim of the cup, and I waited for him to speak.

"Did I interrupt something?" he asked, still standing by the bridge.

My shoulders lifted and fell. "Just trying to find some peace and quiet so I can listen."

He nodded and took a tentative step closer. "And how's it going?"

I took another sip of tea. "About as well as you'd expect. What are you doing here?"

His throat worked as his gaze dipped away from mine. After a few moments of silence, I started drumming my nails on my cup.

Finally, he asked, "How was Scott?"

Startled by the abrupt change of topic, I stammered, "Um, he's fine. Or, well, not fine, but healing, I guess. He seemed in good spirits, at least."

The Superior nodded but said nothing. He was here for a purpose but was clearly struggling to get to it. If it had been about Monica, he wouldn't have wasted all this time.

The tension caused by our last argument was filling the silence as it stretched on and on. My own anxiety was rising at our continued awkwardness, so I decided if he wasn't going to, I would rip the bandage off myself.

"So, I hear you have a date with Mrs. Watson coming up."

His eyes shot to mine, and I saw the briefest flash of red before his lips curved into a wicked smile. "That woman is more manipulative than any demon I've ever met."

I tilted my head back and laughed. The weight on my shoulders eased and when I looked back at him, he was still smiling. With my extended olive branch, he walked toward me. When he settled onto the bench beside me, I leaned close to him and said, "She's a wealthy woman, so you better be taking her someplace nice."

Smiling, I looked over at him and my lips dropped. His face was serious as he stared down at his clasped hands. "The other night," he began.

I placed my hand over his and felt the wonderful warmth of his skin against my own. "We don't have to talk about it. I'm good to move on from it if you are."

Saying the words out loud released another weight from my chest. I breathed deeply, knowing that what I said was the truth. He'd been partially right the other night. I did think he and my sister had been sleeping together and for some reason I had needed to hear him deny it. Part of me blamed the mark for making me obsess over it, but another part of me knew it was something else. He was still hiding something. Gabriel and the night demon had confirmed that there was more of a history with my family than The Superior was telling me. I wasn't going to stop digging for answers, but I had at least come to terms with the fact that The Superior wasn't going to answer my questions. He was going to keep his secrets, and I was fine with that for now because that meant I could keep mine, too.

He studied me for a few moments, then he rearranged our hands, so his sandwiched mine. "Your hand is quite cold."

"It is rather cold out here," I said absently. Looking up at the sky, I wondered if there was supposed to be snow today.

"Have dinner with me."

"What?" I exclaimed, my head whipping back around to face him. Searching his eyes, I couldn't glean what his intentions were.

"Have dinner with me," he repeated and then gently brushed an errant lock of my hair behind my ear. Even once he'd moved away, my face still burned with the feel of his fingers on my skin.

"What about Monica?" I breathed.

His eyes immediately hardened, and his jaw ticked. "What about her?"

"Shouldn't we be out looking for her or doing *something* to find her?"

He smiled, softening his expression. "My people are looking for her. We have one new lead, but I doubt it will go anywhere. With the pregnancy, we at least know she will have to stop at some point to give birth." He shifted on the bench and slowly started rubbing his thumb against my wrist. "As far as you are concerned, I have read all the books Toby found and the best lead was the one I shared with you."

My shoulders slouched and I dropped my head at the reminder. His finger brushed along the line of my jaw. The memory of the last time he gripped my chin so fiercely surfaced, but he pushed it away with this delicate and tender touch.

"We can try again in another part of The Otherworld today, but we will still need to eat, Claire."

I turned to look at him. The wind tousled his hair as his eyes searched mine. The warmth of his hand in mine and along my jawline spread throughout my body as I took in his handsome face. His lips tipped up in the barest of smiles and I felt myself melt. Whether it was the mark, demonic magic, or something else, I wasn't going to question it.

"Okay," I breathed.

CHAPTER 37

"Destiny!"

I was going to kill her. After my morning chat with The Superior, we'd spent the rest of the day going to different parts of The Otherworld, trying to *listen* for Monica. I'd heard nothing. Eventually, I simply heard myself cursing at my powers and wondering why they wouldn't work. When we'd returned to The Superior's estate to get ready for dinner, Destiny had been waiting in my room, ready to help me with my outfit. I'd begrudgingly agreed to her help and gone to shower.

Now, I stood wrapped in a towel, dripping on the carpet as I stared dumbfoundedly down at my underwear drawer.

Destiny's head peeked into the closet. "Yes, My Queen?"

Glaring back at her, I said, "Where the hell is all my underwear?"

"Right there," she said, pointing innocently into the open drawer in front of me.

"Where's the rest of it?" I asked in a clipped tone.

She winked and shrugged before turning to leave me alone once again. Groaning, I looked back down into the drawer. There was a single lacy push up bra that I'd honestly forgotten I even owned and several pairs of black thongs. Those might have been new, but I so infrequently had reason to wear *fun* underwear that I could have forgotten I owned them.

Sliding on the bra, I watched as my boobs were hiked up toward my chin. Hastily, I shimmied into one of the pairs of underwear then wrapped the towel back around myself. Stepping into the room, I glared at Destiny. She had a devilish grin on her face. I opened my mouth to tell her I no longer wanted her help, when my door flew open.

A massive pile of dresses, shoes, and jewelry stood in the doorway. I leaned to the side, trying to catch a glimpse of the person behind the clothes, when I was met with a bright beaming smile. Christy strolled into my room and threw the collection onto my bed.

"Sorry," she said, with an exhausted sigh, "But this was all I could find on such short notice."

She wiped a hand over her brow and smiled over at me while Destiny crawled forward to examine the items. I wanted to protest, but Christy came to stand before me. Her eyes darted across my face as she said, "What were you planning to do with your hair?"

I ran my fingers through the still damp mess and mumbled, "I don't know."

She continued looking me over with an inquisitive look and then she said, "We'll decide once we pick the dress."

"I found it," Destiny called from the bed. She jumped up with a skimpy red dress in her hands. She held it out to me. The dress had spaghetti straps, a plunging neckline, and was probably just long enough to cover what it needed to if I never lifted my arms. Or probably sneezed.

"I'm not wearing that," I said darkly.

Christy came to Destiny's side and nodded approvingly at the dress. "Oh, you'd look great in that, My Queen. The Superior would definitely approve."

I glared over at her and said, "Why are you two so interested in this?"

They exchanged a look before Christy said, "It's fun. I love getting dressed up for dates."

I walked over to the stack of dresses. There were some that I immediately rejected, but there were a few that were okay. I finally found a black dress that I was willing to try on. It was sleeveless, but the straps were thick as the line of the dress plunged into a deep vee on the front and the back. There was a belt that cinched at the waist and the skirt fell loosely to my knees. There was silver thread interwoven with the black that gave the dress a slight sparkle in the light.

"How about this one?" I asked, holding the dress up for both of them to see.

Christy smiled and nodded while Destiny rolled her eyes. "So boring."

"She already has The Superior's attention," Christy said, "She doesn't need to put herself on display."

Destiny's gaze fell over Christy as she said wryly, "Like you did?"

Her fist moved faster than I would have expected as Christy smacked Destiny in the arm. I wasn't sure if hitting a demon was the best idea, particularly since Destiny's eyes swirled with purple in response. She rubbed at her arm and glared menacingly at Christy.

Trying to ignore their tension and the growing heat in my veins, I asked, "You dated him?"

Christy flicked her eyes over to me and stuttered, "Yes. Well, no, it was just once, but really it was, it was nothing."

She nodded at me placatingly, as the warmth in me turned into a burn. I clenched my teeth and felt my stomach twisting. The possessive energy of the mark pulled me to claim The Superior, to tell Christy he was *mine*. That word slammed into my mind, and I fought to push it away. Even if he was mine, I would never attempt to claim someone like that, especially not from a woman who was trying to help me.

Giving myself a moment to calm down, I excused myself and went to change in the closet. Once inside, I slipped out of the towel and into the dress. Turning to see my reflection in the mirror, I marveled at how well the dress fit me. Christy must have a fantastic eye for sizing, because the dress hung perfectly on my frame. I turned left and right to get a better view of myself.

Stepping back out into the room, Christy and Destiny gasped at the sight of me, then gave each other knowing smiles. They got to work accessorizing. Destiny threw a cropped, cream-colored sweater over my shoulders while Christy expertly applied my makeup. A beautiful gold bracelet was set on my wrist, then Destiny got to work curling my hair.

After much less time than it would have taken by myself, I stepped out of the bedroom with my look completed by black ankle boots and a long red coat. I looked ready for this date, even though my pounding pulse and sweaty hands suggested otherwise.

CHAPTER 38

The Superior stood waiting for me in the main room. When I stepped into the room, his eyes lifted to meet mine and then he gave me the most breathtakingly handsome smile I'd ever seen.

"You look beautiful," he said, his words sounding slightly husky.

Coming to a stop before him, I unabashedly let my eyes soak in his appearance. His dark hair was more tamed than usual, but still with a few errant strands that fell beautifully across his forehead. He was wearing a pair of gray jeans that fit snugly around his muscled legs. A white collar poked out inside the neckline of a black, high neck sweater. Simple pieces, but each one fit him so perfectly, that I knew I was blushing by the time our eyes met again.

"Thank you. So do you," I managed to reply.

He stepped forward and extended his arm to me. His brow lifted and he asked, "Ready?"

I was anything but ready as my pulse pounded inside my body. Somehow, I managed to nod and take his arm. Briefly, I wondered how I could possibly be here in this position, but then The Superior's other hand lightly squeezed mine. Our eyes met, and he smiled, and I felt my heart skip a beat. My mind was still a mix of thoughts and emotions, but my body clearly had a single objective.

As we walked through the house, I tried to calm myself by focusing on not tripping in my shoes. Seeming to sense my lack of balance, The Superior tightened his grip on me and slowed his pace to match my own. He did it so effortlessly that my mind jumped to wondering how many women he'd done this with. Once again that ember of jealousy lit and I immediately pictured Christy, standing beside him, touching him, and laughing. Clenching my teeth, I tried to push the feelings back down.

We walked out the front door to see one of The Superior's tinted SUVs sat idling in the driveway. He opened the back door for me and extended a hand to help me in. "What would you like for dinner?"

"Pasta." The word came out far more severe than I intended. The Superior looked at me curiously as he helped me into the back seat. He went around to speak to the driver and a few minutes later climbed into the seat across from me. His legs straddled my own and I squirmed in the seat at the feel of his warm legs along the outside of my own. I snapped my legs together and tried to position myself into not touching him.

The car started to move and after several moments of silence I looked up at him. He was staring at me. I'd grown so accustomed to him working on his phone that it felt unnerving to have his undivided attention. He leaned forward, placing his elbows on his knees.

"Something is bothering you."

Instead of asking the question that was so glaringly invading my mind, I asked, "Where's your phone?"

He looked over my face and that quietness that he so easily mastered settled over him. I could hear my heart drumming in my ears as the silence stretched onward. Finally, with his jaw clenched he leaned back in his seat and said, "For tonight, how about I won't lie to you, if you don't lie to me."

"I wasn't lying," I said with more vehemence than I intended. "I was curious where your phone was."

His face remained hardened as he looked out the window. "Destiny is handling things for a bit."

The answer came out clipped and afterward he fell silent again. His gaze remained focused out the window. I felt guilty for ruining things before we had even made it to the restaurant. Perhaps this was part of the reason why no one had asked me on a date recently. I was clearly out of practice. Swallowing my pride, I leaned forward and brushed a hand over his knee.

"I'm sorry," I whispered, keeping my head down. "I don't always find it easy to share with people."

My fingers traced small circles across his knee as I contemplated what else to say. Heat enveloped me as he leaned closer, pressing his forehead to my own. His voice was a deep whisper as he said, "I do not ask to know all your secrets, but whatever is bothering you involves me."

I pressed back into my seat with a huff. "How do you know it involves you?"

A condescending smirk flicked across his face. He tapped his forehead by his right eyebrow. "Whenever you look at me your eye twitches."

Crossing my arms over my chest, I glared over at him. His smile only grew as I said, "That's not fair."

"Why not?"

"Because I can't seem to hide any of my thoughts from you and yet I can never tell what you are thinking."

He licked his lips and brushed a finger across my bare knee. "I don't think that's true."

My heart stuttered as I imagined what it would feel like for those fingers to brush across more of my skin. I looked at his full lips and remembered how they felt pressed against mine. "Fine," I breathed, feeling my body heat from his continued contact with my knee. "How do you deal with the possessiveness?"

He tilted his head, obviously not expecting that question. His gaze turned sympathetic as he replied, "I was unsure if it was affecting you or not. You seemed rather unfazed."

"Nice to know that I can hide *some* things from you."

A deep chuckle sounded from his side of the car, and I squirmed. I felt it like a caress along my skin. Unbuttoning my jacket, I attempted to cool myself. I didn't know if he was raising the temperature in the car or if it was something else.

"I am sorry it is affecting you," he finally said.

"How do you deal with it? Or do you not feel it?" I asked, leaning forward hopefully.

With sympathy still in his eyes, he said, "I am as afflicted by it as you are. I've just had a long time to learn how to control my emotions. The feelings will continue to grow stronger until the mark is completed."

My eyes widened. The feelings were going to grow stronger? I already felt drowned by them, I couldn't possibly imagine more. As I contemplated this horrifying potentiality, The Superior started trailing his fingers along the outsides of my legs. Up and down, back and forth. My insides clenched as heat pooled low in my belly.

In a whispered voice I could barely hear, he said, "They also grow stronger with shared feelings and intimacy."

His gaze flicked upward and locked onto mine. I thought it was hot before, but now my body was positively on fire. Did he say *shared*? Did that mean he felt the same desire and loss of control that I did? I licked my lips, and his eyes immediately darted down to them. When he looked back up at me, I could see my own feelings of desire swirling in his eyes. He felt what I felt, and I didn't know how to take that. The Superior slowly leaned forward, and I felt my pulse pounding throughout my entire body.

A knock sounded on the door. "Excuse me, sir, were you planning to vacate the vehicle?"

We looked out to see a rather worried looking valet shifting back and forth outside our door. Apparently, we had arrived at the restaurant and neither of us had realized. I let out a gasping laugh, trying to relieve some of the tension.

The Superior placed a chaste kiss on my cheek and whispered, "To be continued."

He grabbed my hand, pushed open the door, and we stepped out into the night.

The restaurant was small, dimly lit, and filled with intimate tables for two. Each one held a flickering candle on an immaculate white tablecloth. Servers bustled between tables in pressed white shirts and black pants, artfully balancing heavy trays of mouthwatering looking bowls of pasta.

We sat at our table near the back, The Superior deciding to sit on my left instead of across the table. Our hands rested together on the tablecloth, and occasionally his right pinky swept across my own. His shoulders were loose as he surveyed the room around us, a small smile on his face. He looked relaxed which seemed so counterintuitive to a first date. Apparently, he'd been around long enough to no longer be nervous.

"How old are you?" I blurted just as our server appeared asking for our drink order. The Superior smiled and to my absolute shock, ordered a bottle of wine.

Once the waiter left The Superior said, "Will you be leaving your mouth hanging open for the entire meal?"

"You ordered wine," I exclaimed and then clicked my jaw shut.

"Yes, I did."

"I thought you didn't like alcohol?"

"I can appreciate the taste of wine with a good meal," he said before placing his napkin expertly into his lap. "What I could not stand was you wallowing in drunkenness, Claire."

Ouch. It was a fair assessment but that didn't mean it didn't hurt to hear. Sucking in a breath I said, "Fair enough. And you didn't answer my question."

His eyes sparked mischievously as he said, "What question?"

I rolled my eyes.

"Old."

I scoffed. "How old?"

"Why are you suddenly so curious?"

He was back to avoiding my questions, but for some reason, tonight it felt almost flirtatious. Not wanting to spoil the mood I answered him.

"Because you seem completely relaxed for someone on a first date. Just makes me think you must have been on a *lot* of dates to achieve that level of comfort."

The Superior placed his elbow on the table and rested his chin on his fist. "Should I be nervous, Claire?"

A thrill raced down my spine as I squirmed under his intense gaze. Not wanting to give him the satisfaction, I didn't rise to the bait. I leaned forward matching his posture and said, "That old, huh?"

He laughed and it was a rich, deep sound. I never would have thought him capable of such a joyful sound and once again I felt my body heating in response. The waiter chose that moment to return, and I was thankful for the distraction. He placed freshly baked bread onto the table and poured us each a glass of the wine. We placed our orders, and the waiter left.

Spinning the wine glass in my fingers, I asked, "So, do you think when we get back, Destiny will have let Graham get a dog?"

Another warm chuckle fell past his lips, and I felt his leg brush mine under the table. "She knows better than to let that happen. Besides she's busy getting ready for the exchange."

"What's the exchange?"

The Superior took a long sip of his wine. I watched his throat work and wondered for a moment if he hadn't meant to mention that.

Eventually, he said, "Every one hundred years, The Prince requires an exchange of demons. He chooses however many he wishes from his side, and I must supply the demons from this side."

"Wait," I said, leaning back in my chair. "The Prince? You mean The Devil?"

He nodded.

"So The Devil brings up demons from Hell and they switch places with some of the demons up here?"

He nodded again.

I twisted in my chair to fully face him. "And you decide who stays and who goes?" An idea formed in my mind. I took a tentative sip of the wine, giving myself a moment to ponder. Then, I asked, "Could this be why someone is after Monica? To blackmail you about the selection?"

The Superior's eyes rolled with red before he sharply said, "No."

My shoulders sagged at his immediate dismissal. "How can you be so sure?"

In a flat tone that didn't match the spark I saw burning in his eyes, he said, "No one could hope to do that and not end up engulfed in my Hell fire."

The waiter chose that moment to return with our orders. I'd gone with a simple chicken alfredo. In trying out a new restaurant I always went with the basics first. If an Italian restaurant could make a good alfredo sauce, I would be coming back to try their signature dishes. Plus, I really liked it. When I dug into my plate, I saw The Superior watching me.

"May I ask you something rather personal?"

The question surprised me, but I nodded, curious what he would want to know.

"How did you discover your Ferrier gifts?"

That hadn't been what I was expecting. In fact, I didn't think anyone had ever asked me that. Even Nancy, who had asked me countless questions about my gifts, and demons, had never asked that specific one.

"Well," I said, setting down my fork, "It happened when I was about ten. My grandmother had passed away and we were cleaning out her house. I saw her, in the house, and I told my family she was still there. At first, they thought it was sad, but the more I insisted, the angrier they became, especially my father. Eventually, they told me to go wait outside."

"I remember walking out onto the front porch. It was this big wooden thing that had green chipped paint and random boards you knew not to step on," I smiled at the memory. "And this massive hydrangea bush. My grandmother loved flowers, and that thing practically took over the entire front of the house. Anyway, I went outside and sat there on the porch and my grandmother came and sat beside me. She told me there was nothing wrong with me. She said she'd heard of abilities like mine but said that some people just wouldn't understand."

The Superior sat watching me speak, his face enraptured by my story. I took a sip of my wine before continuing.

"On the last day we were there, my grandmother told me she had a message for my father. We walked into her kitchen, and I repeated everything she said directly to him. I remember the look on my father's face. At first, he was angry. He thought I was making things up again, but then there was something in the words that made him realize I was telling the truth. And that was the first time he ever looked at me like there was something wrong with me. Like I was something to fear."

I tipped my head down to stare at my plate. I hadn't thought about that story in such a long time. My chest ached at the memory. There was my sweet grandmother's face contrasted so sharply with my father's.

"We never talked about it again. What I told my dad," I said, finally lifting food to my lips and taking a bite. The creamy, buttery taste and the smooth texture of the sauce was absolute perfection. I moaned in bliss, despite the topic of our conversation.

The Superior smiled at me over his own forkful of pasta. "Your father was wrong, to treat you that way. Your gifts are remarkable, Claire."

My cheeks warmed as I looked up at him. His words from the car suddenly replayed in my mind. *Shared feelings and intimacy.* I had just shared an intimate moment from my past that I had never shared with anyone. Licking my lips, I glanced down at the mark, currently exposed on my arm. I knew the light was low, but something in my mind still told me it looked darker. Well shit.

CHAPTER 39

We finished dinner and made our way outside the restaurant to wait for The Superior's driver. He'd offered to wait inside, but I'd needed the fresh air. After the conversation about my grandmother and seeing the mark on my arm darkening, I'd felt unsettled. I'd needed the fresh air to clear my head. Luckily, while out there, I remembered I had a book under my mattress that might have the answers I needed.

Standing in the cool air, I felt The Superior's hand clasp my own. The edges of my lips twisted upward, and I turned to look over at him. He had a similar expression, so I laughed and found myself leaning into him. His warmth was so welcoming and then I was hit with his scent which was intoxicating. He dropped my hand and wrapped his arm around me. I knew I should pull away, but I felt so at peace that a small sigh of contentment slipped past my lips. His fingers tightened on my waist as we watched his car pull up to the curb.

The Superior pulled the door open and helped me inside. I slid across the seat and then felt the heat of his body press against my own as he climbed into the seat beside me. The door shut and a few seconds later we started to move. The Superior's body touched mine from shoulder to knee and my skin buzzed from the contact.

I looked over to see he was staring at me with a heat that caused a blush to spread across my cheeks. Dropping my eyes, I tried to steady my breathing as my heart pounded in my chest. He ran his fingers through my hair and then along my chin, pushing my gaze back up to meet his.

"How was your evening?" he asked, while his eyes roved over my face.

"Good," I said, the words coming out rather breathless. I wrapped my hand around his and turned his palm upward to my lips. Kissing a slow trail along his hand, until I reached the callouses just below his fingers. I traced them lightly with my finger. Being a demon gave him an immense amount of power, but the callouses showed that he also worked with his hands. He didn't simply rely on that power. He wanted to be more, and it showed in his palms and in the exquisite lines of his body. I smiled up at him and the look he gave me was my undoing. He leaned forward and when his lips brushed mine, I felt a trickle of heat where we touched. The kiss was soft and gentle, but I wanted more.

I grabbed his shoulder with my other hand and pulled him toward me. He obliged by wrapping one arm around my waist and placing the other on my leg. His lips now pressed firmly into my own, echoing the need and desire I felt. I opened my mouth and swept my tongue against his lips. He groaned and opened his mouth in response. His hand on my leg rose higher onto my thigh, pushing the hemline of my dress up toward my waist.

His hand traced back down my thigh and then up until the tip of his index finger brushed against the hemline of my underwear. The wandering of his hand sent shudders through my body. I needed to touch more of him while my mouth continued to explore his. I lifted my fingers up and finally dragged them through the hair that had always intrigued me. It was the only part of him that seemed wild and untamed, and I was desperate to feel if it was as soft as it looked. My fingers dug into the thick, luxurious locks and I moaned as their petal-like softness brushed my skin. I immediately imagined how that softness would feel between my legs.

His lips broke away from my own and made their way down to my throat. My fingers left his hair to travel across the wide expanse of his shoulders. They were hard and toned and I couldn't wait to touch them without this fabric in the way. I leaned my head back and arched my chest upward. His lips felt like fire as they trailed down the neckline of my dress. When he reached the deep vee in the middle of my chest, his tongue briefly darted out along the edges of each of my breasts. I moaned as he slowly kissed his way back up to my shoulder. His lips found mine again, while his hands traced down my sides leaving a trail of fiery warmth behind them. I gasped and he moved further down to my sides, finding the hem of my dress and moving inward. A different heat pooled between my legs, and I groaned in protest as he pulled away from me.

"We're back," he whispered, his breath heavy against my cheek. Pulling us upward into a sitting position, he adjusted the hem of my dress and pulled a hand through my hair. I smiled at his attention and reached for the door. It was wrenched open and out of my hands.

"Thank fuck, I am dying he—"

Destiny didn't get to finish her tirade as her eyes took us in. Her irises flooded with purple, and a salacious grin spread across her face. My cheeks immediately heated as I nervously batted at my hair. I tried to step out of the car, but she pressed in toward me and sucked in a huge sniff of air.

"Oh, that's delicious," she said in a voice that was almost a purr.

"Destiny," The Superior's voice held a deadly edge, "Get out of the way."

Her eyes were almost completely purple, and I saw her hesitate for a moment, nostrils flaring, but with a reverent tip of her head, she finally stepped back. Adjusting my coat over my chest, I hopped down onto the gravel and stepped aside. I heard the crunch as The Superior joined me.

"My apologies," Destiny said, "But you are needed, Sir."

I spun around. "Is it Monica?"

Destiny's eyes barely flicked to me before she tipped her head back down. "No. I'm so sorry, I didn't mean to cut your evening short."

There was sincerity in her words. I hoped it wasn't anything too serious, but the resigned look on The Superior's face told me he was used to this. It made me wonder for a moment about his life. He spent so much of his day serving his people. We'd been gone for only a few hours and already, someone needed him again. How stressful must it be to always be needed like that?

He turned and gave me a sad smile. His fingers brushed along my elbow as he placed a kiss on my forehead. "I'm sorry," he whispered, his lips still touching my skin.

Tipping my head upward, I said, "Don't worry about it. Nothing you can do about it."

His eyes searched my face, but he offered me a smile and a quick nod. He walked me into the house, and after my insistence, he and Destiny went off to work instead of escorting me to our room. I didn't need him taking the time to walk me to our door. The gesture felt unnecessary for many reasons, including the fact that I had been ready to jump his bones in the car. I walked alone back to the room with a smile on my face. The date had been a good one and right now I was on my way to change into sweats and curl up with a dangerous book.

Translating a book with a completely foreign lettering system was hard enough without the constant drain on my energy. After returning to my room, I'd changed and gotten myself ready for bed. Curled up under the sheets, I'd found the page with the sketch of the mark and started with the first symbol at the top. Scouring the pages of the translation book took up most of my time. I made some progress, but a few symbols looked so similar to others that I had to study them more intensely. My head started to feel heavy, so I tipped it back against the headboard and rubbed at my eyes.

"There are easier ways to get me into your room at night."

A scream rose in my throat at the sight of The Superior, but the sound never came out. The weight of the demon words suddenly crashed over me. My body pitched toward the floor. The Superior was suddenly there, wrapping his arms around me and settling me back onto the bed. Waves of heat pulsed into my body from everywhere our skin touched. I closed my eyes and took several deep breaths. After a few moments, my head stopped spinning, and I was able to open my eyes again. The Superior sat next to me with his arms still encircling my waist. Looking down, I noticed he was shirtless and there were creases across his left cheek. My heart sank as I realized I'd woken him up. I opened my mouth to apologize, when I remembered what he'd said.

"Wait, what did you say to me?"

He chuckled and I felt my pulse quicken. His eyes inspected me and then he said, "If you wish to secretly read a demonic text perhaps limit yourself to a few words. Otherwise, your heart rate will again dip so low as to alert me to your activities."

I cleared my throat and gently pulled away from his grasp. "Thank you and I'm sorry. I'm still new to the effects of reading the demonic language."

He extended his hand to me and made a "give it to me" gesture. I groaned. "Is there any way you can just forget about it and go back to bed?"

Red briefly swirled across his eyes before he said, "You clearly cannot be trusted and I need sleep, Claire."

Part of me wanted to fight him on it, but the weary look in his eyes had me conceding. I handed him the book and asked, "Did you and Destiny get everything squared away?"

He looked down at the book, the raised narrowed eyes to me. "Yes, we did. Are you trying to distract from the fact that you stole from me?"

The temperature in the room rose ever so slightly. His face was hard, but I couldn't tell if he was worried about what I'd found or angry that I had it. Or perhaps both.

"I didn't steal it," I finally replied. "I borrowed it. Just like the other books."

The lighting in the room was dim, but it was enough for me to catch the flicker of red around his irises. "Those books were meant to help us find your sister. This is meant to—"

He cut himself off. His fingers drummed on the cover of the book.

"This is meant to what?" I asked quietly.

We sat in silence for several long minutes. The only sound was the drumming of his fingers on the book. Slowly, I leaned forward and brushed a tentative hand across his knee. The temperature in the room continued to climb, but I kept sweeping circles across his skin. I didn't know if I did it for comfort or to coax him into answering me, but eventually, he reached over and covered my hand with his own.

"What did you learn?" he asked.

Licking my lips, I said, "The mark is almost permanent."

I hadn't actually read that, but I had seen more evidence to confirm what Gabriel had told me was true. The Superior gently clasped my right wrist and turned my arm over. His finger traced along the mark just as it had when he'd given it to me. That time had been painful. This time, I felt my heartbeat rising and the hairs on my arm all standing on end. When he reached the end, his hand fell away, but he said nothing.

I pulled away from him sharply. "Will you not tell me anything?"

"It won't become permanent," he said, as if that settled the matter.

"How can you be so sure?"

His eyes finally rose to meet mine as he said, "You have to trust me."

I startled at his words. Part of me had come to trust him, but I knew with the gulf of secrets between us, it was still incomplete. "Trust has to be earned. You have to tell me something."

A huff fell out of him as he set the book beside him on the bed. He pressed his fingers through his hair. It was an incredibly human gesture as it caused pieces to stick out at odd angles. The sight of it brought a small smile to my lips.

"Anything else?" he asked, clearly done with the previous conversation.

Placing a finger on my chin I said, "Well there was another thing I found interesting."

He twisted in the bed, raising his knee so we faced each other. His face was blank, but I could see the tension in the lines of his body. There was something in that book that made him nervous. I wondered if I had already learned it.

Staring into his eyes I said, "There was a passage that I believe said *no lies between them*. Now, I found that strange because we both know I've lied to you."

I let the implication of my words sit between us. My gaze stayed glued to his and the longer he went without reacting, the more I started to believe it was true. A slow grin filled my face, and he glared back at me. With a sigh, he lifted the book and opened it to my marked page. He skimmed it and then turned it to me. "You see this part?" I quickly looked down to where he pointed and nodded. "You misinterpreted it. It actually says *no lies from their demon*."

My pulse spiked. "I was right? You can't lie to me?"

He flipped the book closed, with a disgruntled groan, he nodded.

Pointing emphatically at my forearm and enunciating every word I said, "What. Does. This. Say?"

"Why do you want to know so badly?" he asked.

It was my turn to groan. "Why don't you have to answer me?"

He chuckled, and the heat in the room finally started to subside. "As I told you before, lying and keeping things from you are not the same things."

His eyes fell down to the mark, and I watched a sea of emotions cross over his face. Finally, he said, "It is my first name. My given name."

The words were spoken in a hushed tone with a sort of reverence to them. I'd been so curious about what it said that I didn't think what it might mean to him. "How long has it been since you've been called this name?"

He flopped backward onto my bed with a sigh. "A long time. It might be nice to hear it again."

Leaning forward so he could see me out of the corner of his eye I said in a teasing tone, "And the name you'd hear would be?"

I grinned down at him and to my surprise he smiled back before he grabbed me and pulled me down on top of him. A yelp tumbled out of me before he pressed his lips to mine. Then he rolled us, and he was on top of me, bracketing my body with his arms and legs. His lips left mine and in a breathy whisper I said, "We should probably go to bed."

His eyes lit with wicked humor. I raised my hand and brushed it across the stubble on his cheek. "You said you needed sleep."

With a resigned sigh, he lifted himself effortlessly off me. He extended a hand, and I used it to prop myself back up. My pulse was pounding, and my thoughts were on anything but sleep, but he had mentioned needing it before. Looking at his face, I could see the dark circles.

Our gazes stayed locked as he said, "Are you sure that's what you want?"

The implication in his words set a fire licking through my body. I knew he would hear the lie in my words, so I smiled and nodded my head. He chuckled, still able to sense my deceit, but said nothing as he turned to head for the door.

I watched the dim light play across his broad back as he walked away from me. Something caught my eye. I'd seen his bare back once before and it had been smooth. Perfect. Now there were markings. I rose from the bed. "Wait."

He stopped and turned with a knowing look in his eyes. I reached out to him, wrapping my fingers around his bare bicep to slowly turn him around. His face became curious as he spun away from me. Now that I was closer, I could see the markings were scars. Two long, jagged lines ran down his back. He couldn't have gotten them tonight, so how had I missed them before?

"How come I never noticed these?" I asked, tentatively lifting a finger to brush along one of the scars. My finger had barely connected with his skin, when he spun back around. His hands fisted around my wrists and then I was airborne. My back slammed into the bed and The Superior landed on top of me. His hands squeezed my wrists, and I yelped.

"You're hurting me," I whimpered, trying to squirm out from under him.

"What did you see?" he demanded.

I shook my head, not understanding what was happening. Fire licked down my bare skin and memories of our first meeting flashed before my eyes. My body started to tremble as I tried to summon the strength to speak.

"What did you see?" He barked.

"Scars," I finally managed to reply.

He suddenly released me and rose from the bed. My body felt cold from his absence as I continued to shake on the bed. Propping myself up on my elbows, I looked over at him. His jaw was tense as he stared down at me. I sucked in several rapid breaths as I waited.

Finally, he said, "I'm sorry."

With that, he turned and left. I sat up and gingerly touched my wrists. The skin was still warm and raw from his grasp. Tears pricked at the backs of my eyes. How had we gone from making out on my bed to whatever that was? Those scars were clearly a touchy subject, and I wondered why. And why had he been so upset at me simply seeing them?

Then a thought struck me as I looked down at the book he'd forgotten on my bed. If he had acted in anger, his eyes should have been swimming in red. They hadn't been. His face had been close enough to mine that I would have seen it, but they'd been brown. Brown, wide, and full of fear.

CHAPTER 40

My alarm chimed and I quickly swiped it over to snooze and burrowed deeper under the covers. The room was still dark from the early hour and my entire body seemed to groan in protest. My mind, however, was a different story. It played back through the events of yesterday, similar to what it had done throughout the entire night.

When the alarm sounded again, I turned it off and forced myself to sit up. My eyelids were heavy as I tried to rub the sleep from them. With a sigh, I looked down at my phone. Unlocking the screen, I stared down at the now familiar contact. Vlad.

I'd stared at his name for some time last night, willing myself to call him. The Superior's reaction had seemed completely out of the blue. There was no way he was going to explain what happened, so I needed to find answers for myself. I knew we'd had a good time at dinner and after, so I didn't think it was me. Something about those scars had set him off and I needed to find out why.

Flinging off the covers, I walked into the closet to change my clothes. My body slowly went through the motions as I built up my courage. Pulling on a thick flannel and a pair of corduroys, I looked down at the number and finally hit send. I held my breath as the phone rang.

"Imir Consulting Services, how may I help you?" came the soft female voice on the other end of the line.

I stared down at the screen for a moment, thinking Scott's drug addled brain must have messed up the number.

"Uh," I stuttered gracelessly, "I was calling for Vlad."

"And who may I say is calling?"

"Claire?" The word came out as a question, and I mentally cursed myself for sounding so stupid.

There was the sound of keys clicking on the other end of the line before she said, "I'm sorry, miss, but I don't see you on my schedule."

Clearing my throat, I tried again. "I meant, Claire. His Queen."

She was silent for several long moments. I checked the screen to ensure the call was still connected. A moment away from asking if she was still there, the woman said, "Mr. Vladimir is busy doing The Master's work at the moment, but if you are in need of assistance, we would be happy to help in any way possible."

A brush off. A very polite brush off, but still a dismissal. Well, nothing worth doing was easy. I sucked in a breath and said, "I need to speak with Vlad. Right now."

"Is this a summons?"

Her words were laced with a trickle of fear. I felt disgusted with myself as I said, "Yes."

"One moment, Your Majesty," she said and then there was the sound of muffled voices. Once back on the phone her earlier cheerful demeanor returned. "If Your Majesty would be so kind as to provide a meeting location, Mr. Vladimir would be happy to comply."

Shit. I'd just hoped to get him on the phone, but it did make sense that a summons would require appearing in person. I quickly wracked my brain trying to think of a place that was in public, but not somewhere The Superior would see.

"The hospital," I said in a rush, "Have him meet me at the hospital by The Superior's estate in an hour."

The sound of clicking keys started again before she said, "Mr. Vladimir is willing to travel to any location, just remember that he doesn't do well leaving his realm."

My stomach churned at her words. What the hell did she mean by 'doesn't do well?' Before I could ask, she ended the call. I stared down at the phone and wondered if I'd made a mistake. Grabbing my coat, I left my room and walked down the hallway. I'd have to ponder that later because I had an hour to find someone to chauffeur me and then leave me alone at the hospital. Judging by the past few days, that was going to be a big ask.

I made my way into the kitchen and found it bustling with activity. At least fifty people were here for breakfast, so I hopped in line for coffee and a muffin before I spied a familiar red head.

Destiny smiled warmly when I approached her. She sat at a table by herself with a stack of empty dishes and a well-loved paperback in her hands.

"Your Majesty," she said, with a playful tip of her head.

Pulling out the chair across from her, I leaned toward her and said, "Yeah, about last night,"

She cut me off with a wave of her hand, "I'm so sorry about that, Claire, honestly, I am. Seriously, no one hates a cock block more than me."

I nodded and smiled, happy that this was going as I had hoped. "I'm glad, because I know exactly how you are going to make it up to me."

Destiny parked the car at the hospital and unbuckled her seat belt. I laid a hand on her shoulder. "You're staying here."

"What?" she asked incredulously.

Unbuckling my own belt and pushing open the door, I said, "Yep, you stay here. I'll just be a minute."

I hadn't been specific about my intentions when I'd recruited Destiny for this mission. If she was anything like The Superior, she'd have known I was lying if I'd said I was here to see Scott. Instead, I let her assume that was why we were here, and I hoped Scott would be willing to back me up if needed. Something told me he would.

"You just want me to sit in the car? In the cold?" she asked, starting to look at me very suspiciously.

"Why don't you go hangout with your friend like last time?"

Simultaneously, we both looked over at the valet stand. "Oh," I said, my hopes falling slightly at the sight of the young man standing there.

Destiny looked at me and shrugged. "He's cute. Looks kind of like Timothée Chalamet."

"Okay?" I asked, rising out of the car and buttoning my coat. "So, we're good?"

"Yep, but don't take too long, and Claire?"

I leaned over to meet her gaze.

"You're still a terrible liar."

She gave me the biggest smile and I slammed the door in her face.

I took off toward the door, unsure how much time I had. Realizing I hadn't told Vlad where to meet me in the hospital, I quickly ran through the front lobby, the emergency room lobby, and then back to the cafeteria. My hopes that he was coming started to wane, until I heard the terrible screech of a nail dragging along glass. I covered my ears and spun toward the sound. All the blood rushed from my face as I locked eyes with a night demon.

He tapped the glass twice with a long black nail, then gave me a small wave. Part of me wanted to run upstairs and throttle Scott for not having told me Vlad was the night demon I'd met the other night. Looking around, I saw a door that led out to an outside patio. I pushed open the door and Vlad was immediately by my side. Revulsion spiked inside me, and I flinched away from him.

Vlad tipped his head into a bow. "My Queen."

When he rose, I was met with two deep pools of inky blackness. His lips twitched upward into a tight-lipped smile. He sucked in a deep breath and the smile faded somewhat as he made a deep guttural sound in his throat. "Speak quickly, My Queen. You have brought me to a place ripe with souls."

I shuddered at the implication but pressed onward. "How long have you served The Superior?"

His lips twitched as if my question amused him. "A long time."

Rolling my eyes at his non-answer, I continued, "And in that time did he ever injure himself? His back, specifically?"

Vlad's head tipped to the side, and he studied me. Not having pupils to connect with, it was a very unnerving feeling to hold his gaze. "No."

Fine, this line of questioning was getting me nowhere, so time to switch topics. "You said you knew my grandmother's-grandmother. When was this and how did you know her?"

"I did not know her, but of her. She was a ferrier during the war. I'm not sure when that was in your world."

"What war?"

"The Great One."

That had to be WWI. Logically, based on my age that tracked. I had assumed she lived around that time, but it was nice to have confirmation of the exact dates to check in The Superior's journals.

"What else do you know about her?"

The demon's eyes swirled, and he sucked in another deep breath. "Not much. The Master will know more."

"Did The Superior know her?"

Vlad's lips split into a hideous mocking smile. Pointed black teeth, slick with saliva and a long black tongue completed the face that I was sure would haunt my nightmares. A shudder moved through my body as I tried to maintain his gaze.

Finally, he said, "Not The Superior then."

It took me a second to understand what he meant. The Superior wasn't called that during that time. I rolled my eyes. "Well, whatever he was called, did he know her?"

"No. Not Superior. Nothing."

"Fine," I said, sensing I was running out of time, "Whatever he called himself, did he know her?" I asked, desperation leaking into my voice. I felt so close to uncovering something useful.

Grunting as if in pain, Vlad spat out, "Yes."

I reeled back. Even though I had suspected as much, having it confirmed out loud made everything feel more real. Before I could ask anything else, Vlad suddenly doubled over and released a feral growl. His head snapped up to look at me as he hissed, "Send. Me. Away."

The look of hunger on his face sent a fresh batch of chills racing across my skin. Nodding, I said, "Thank you." I was about to release him but then said, "Not a word of this conversation to anyone. Including The Superior."

With his jittery nod in recognition I said, "You may go now."

CHAPTER 41

On the ride home with Destiny, I contemplated my next move. Vlad had given me a timeframe to look up in the journals, but I didn't have a way into his private library yet. I needed to find out where he kept those keys.

Pulling out my phone, I started scrolling through my list of contacts. With a sigh of frustration, I realized I had no one listed under 'Scott.' I didn't think he would have lied about giving me his number, so I looked again. My eyes stopped when they landed on another contact I knew I hadn't typed in. With a laugh, I typed out a message to 'Sexier than The Superior.'

Hey, do you know where HE keeps his keys?

Just in case anyone else saw it, I tried to keep the message as vague as possible. Luckily, Scott responded right away. I guessed sitting in a hospital bed all day meant he had time to talk.

Who is this?
JK. ;)
Yes, on him or in his desk.

I texted Scott back and asked where in the desk. While I waited for his reply, I leaned my head back and looked over at Destiny. She practically glowed from all the *energy* she'd been able to consume recently. "What's The Superior up to today?"

Destiny smiled. "Hoping to get a little *alone* time?"

That was exactly it, but not in the way she was thinking. Either way, if it helped me tell the lie, I was willing to go along with it. Trying not to seem too eager I sighed, "Something like that."

She hummed as she turned the car into the driveway. "He's got a busy day today, I'm afraid. Probably will be cooped up in his study for most of it, but he might not mind an interruption."

Her eyes fell on me meaningfully and I didn't have to fake the blush that covered my cheeks. I wasn't typically an open person about my sex life. Having a succubus who could literally smell my desire was something to which I was still adjusting. My phone chimed with a message as we pulled into the garage.

No can do. No one gets in there but him. You'd have an easier time trying to swipe the ones he carries.

I groaned down at my phone and climbed out of the car. Destiny and I used a side entrance to enter the house. The moment we stepped inside I could smell the kitchen, and my stomach started to growl. Destiny turned and laughed at me over her shoulder. "I guess you should grab something to eat."

Nodding, I waved at her as she headed off down one hallway and I turned toward the kitchen. Lunch preparations were already underway, but I grabbed another cup of coffee and ordered a waffle. The last time I got one, it had been amazing, and I was keen to have another one. Grabbing my plate, I settled down at a table to enjoy it and think through my options. Perhaps I could sneak into The Superior's bedroom while he was asleep. That seemed unlikely, though. My stealth skills were not the best. If I could somehow persuade him to remove his pants in my presence, I might be able to grab the keys while he was distracted. That was an enticing option. I contemplated it while I took a large bite of waffle. The sweetness of the syrup and the buttery crunch of the waffle filled my mouth with goodness. I moaned and then saw a message flash across my screen.

Are you at the estate? Sending help.

My face scrunched in confusion. I sent back a message telling him where I was. A few minutes later, a familiar blonde dropped into the chair across from me.

"Hello, My Queen."

Christy looked beautiful, as always, in a bright red sweater that had a cutout across her cleavage. Her eyes met mine with a genuine smile. I knew she had been nothing but nice to me, but the image of her with The Superior always pushed to the front of my mind whenever I saw her. "Can I help you?"

"Scott said you were in need of my skilled hands."

Her pink lips spread into a wide grin and her eyes sparked with humor. I groaned and took a long sip of my coffee. "And what *skills* would those be?"

If Scott expected me to be okay with her pawing all over The Superior to get the keys he was mistaken. I still fought the possessive feelings that wanted me to claim him as mine, but as the woman who had his tongue in her mouth last night, I felt entitled to some annoyance at the suggestion. My apprehension must have showed on my face because Christy's smile dropped slightly.

"Look, Scott said you needed me, but if that's not the case, I can just let him know you weren't interested."

"How can I decide anything if you won't even tell me what skills you possess?"

She shrugged her shoulders and moved a perfectly wavy lock of blonde hair behind her ear. My phone sounded and when I looked down at the table, I saw nothing there.

"Here," Christy said, leaning forward to hand me back my phone.

I took it hesitantly from her hands and looked down at the message from Scott.

> Christy said if you don't respond to this, I should assume you murdered her. What the hell is happening?

My eyes flicked back up to the woman before me with a newfound sense of respect. I hadn't seen her take my phone off the table, nor had I seen her type out the message to Scott. While sending him a quick reply, I said, "So what, you're like a master magician or something?"

She leaned forward conspiratorially and said with a wink, "Or something."

"Wait, why are you helping me?"

I rose from the table to clear away my dishes. Christy followed me, typing away furiously on her phone. Without looking back at me she mumbled, "I owed Scott a favor."

She didn't offer any more explanation, so I let it go. We all had our secrets around here. Setting my dishes in the appropriate bins, I set off down the hallway. Christy raced to catch up with me. "And, I said I wanted to be friends, and I meant it."

Smiling, I gave her a brief nod. I worried about Scott calling in a favor to help me. That now put me even further into his debt. I didn't like contemplating what that meant. For now, I had to focus on getting The Superior's keys.

"How do we do this?" I asked, rubbing my hands together like I was in a heist movie.

Christy's eyes looked quizzically down at me before she went back to her phone. "I'm trying to find TS. Can't very well get his keys without seeing him."

Her calling him 'TS' grated down my spine. I didn't think she was doing it on purpose, but I wasn't entirely sure.

"Fine," I said, pressing my lips together. My stomach clenched as I forced myself to say the next part. "You find The Superior and I'll meet you outside the library."

I was leaning against the library door when Christy came strolling around the corner, looking as if she didn't have a care in the world. It had been almost an hour.

"Where have you been?" I asked, my voice rising in pitch.

With quicker reflexes than I expected her to have, Christy clamped her hand over my mouth and narrowed her eyes at me.

"Shh," she whispered into my ear, "Do you want everyone to know what you're doing?"

Stepping back enough to look me in the eyes, she raised a questioning brow at me. I nodded back my understanding, and she released me. The sound of footsteps echoed around the corner and my heart sank. It had to be The Superior. We'd been found out. With a resigned sigh, I leaned back against the door. Christy grabbed a strand of my hair and pulled me toward her.

"Ouch," I spat at her.

She yanked again and gave me a scolding look. Then, in a loud voice she said, "Of course I could do that with your hair, My Queen."

Glancing over her shoulder, I saw the person step around the corner and freeze. She was an older woman with large pink glasses. When she saw Christy, her face instantly softened, and she waved.

"Hello, Mrs. McAllister. How you doing today, ma'am?" Christy said and I noticed her accent was suddenly thicker.

Mrs. McAllister nodded and then her gaze flicked over to me. Her face went a little pale, but she managed a small smile. "Fine, Miss Christy," she said before turning and continuing on her way.

When she was out of earshot, Christy thrust the keys into my hand. "You won't have long. Good luck."

A small part of me wanted to ask how she'd gotten them, but I knew we didn't have time for that. Turning to thank her, I saw she was already walking away.

"Hurry up," she said as she waved without looking back, "And remind me to book a time for us to go to the salon together."

I rolled my eyes and then turned to open the doors.

Toby sat working away at the desk. My heart swelled at the sight of him.

"Toby, you're back," I gushed.

"Yes," he said as way of greeting me. His eyes stayed glued to the desk.

Clearing my throat, I asked, "Could you open the, uh, *secret*, door for me?"

He looked up at me then, and I smiled. His blue eyes were clear and focused set behind his glasses. If he felt any lingering effects from our trip to the library, I couldn't see it. He tipped his head curiously and said, "You need the keys."

Lifting the ring in my hand, I held the keys out and jingled them.

"Ah," he said absently and leaned over to press the mechanism to open the door. He returned to his work, and I was thankful for it. I'd already caused Toby enough problems, I didn't need to involve him in anymore of my schemes.

"Glad you're feeling better," I said as I stepped away from the desk toward the passageway. He said nothing back and I stepped into the stairwell. Luckily, I had thought to message Scott for the key numbers for the gates while I waited for Christy. The question of how she'd gotten the keys lingered in my mind, but I tried not to dwell on it too much. Anything I pictured turned nefarious and got my pulse rising and my teeth grinding.

The walk through the dirt covered tunnels felt even longer than it did last time. My mind raced along with all the adrenaline pumping through my body. I wondered if The Superior knew what Christy had done. I wondered what was waiting for me at the end of all this. Would I find a detailed account of a torrid affair with my grandmother's-grandmother? Or would I find nothing? Maybe I was building it up too much in my mind, but in the claustrophobic journey through the tunnels, I had little else to distract me.

It was a struggle, but I finally managed to pry open the trap door. I climbed into the cabin and decided to leave the door open to save myself some trouble. Even if The Superior came flying up here in a rage, it wasn't like the door would stop him anyway. I walked back into the library and then found the corner with the hidden closet. My heart pounded in my chest as I stared forward.

I cycled through several keys before I found the one that opened it. Pushing open the door, I turned to see the wall of journals. I scanned the dates along the leather spines. Thankfully, the books were well organized, but the sheer volume of them made my task more difficult.

After some time, I found the early 1900s. Unfortunately, the shelf was located close to the floor. My WWI history was not the best, but I had googled the appropriate dates and knew I needed to start with 1914. I dropped down to my knees and scooted along the floor. Following the line of journals, I made it through about 1910 before the shelf disappeared behind the massive trunk.

Shifting my position, I pressed my shoulder into the side of the chest. It didn't budge. I tried a few more times, but then finally conceded that I wasn't making any progress and would need to unload the trunk to move it. Rolling my eyes, I pulled out the keys and started trying them in the lock. A quick glance at my watch told me I had been in the cabin for twenty minutes. With the time I had spent in the tunnel, I was hitting close to forty-five minutes. Was The Superior already on his way here? Shoving that thought aside, I swiped sweat from my brow and prayed the next key would be the right one.

It wasn't, but the third one was right. I popped open the lid and started pulling all the journals out. I stacked them as neatly as I could on the other side of the floor. Once I had the trunk empty, I wrapped my fingers around the side and tugged. It still wouldn't move. I groaned in frustration and kicked the side of the trunk but served to only hurt my foot. My time was running out and I was being thwarted by a stupid piece of furniture. I wondered how it could be empty and yet I still couldn't move it, when a thought occurred to me.

Reaching inside, I ran my fingers along the seam created between the sides and the bottom. I traced the wood around and around until I finally felt it. A tiny scrap of rope that blended in perfectly with the rest of the chest. Gripping the tiny piece between my forefinger and thumb, I tugged upward on it. Half of the bottom of the chest lifted up with the rope. I placed it to the side and then worked to remove the other piece.

There was a hole cut roughly into the floor below the chest. It wasn't a large space but just enough to fit a shoebox. My heart quickened as my fingers grasped the box. Dirt and dust floated to the floor as I lifted it out of the chest. Blowing across the top, I saw the colors were faded and there were no discernible markings anywhere on it.

Steadying myself, I set the box on the floor and crossed my legs. I sat in a delicate balance of time. My hesitation and fear at not knowing versus the potential flood of information that could come from lifting the lid. With several deep breaths I reached out and flipped off the lid.

Inside was a small stack of photographs. My imagination had run wild with what could have been, but a stack of pictures had never crossed my mind. On top was a black and white photo of a young man holding a small baby. They were standing in front of what looked like a two-story farmhouse. The man wasn't looking at the camera as he was engaged in conversation with another man standing to his left. Neither one seemed to be aware that the picture was being taken. Examining the image more closely, I realized with a start that the other man was The Superior. He looked exactly the same as he did now.

Why had he kept this picture? It wasn't even that good of a photograph. Maybe this shoebox contained all the photos he'd ever had taken, but that didn't seem right. I flipped to the next one in the stack.

This time, everyone was posing nicely in front of the camera. The Superior was immediately recognizable as he stood with the other people and yet still slightly off to the side. There was a different man this time and a woman and two young children in front of them. The family members were all smiling. The Superior had a slight upturn of his lips, but that was it. He looked uncomfortable and yet he'd still posed for the picture. More curious to me was that the family would want him to be a part of it. I scanned the image, looking for clues to when it was taken, but all I could tell was that it was fairly old. This one was in color but the clothes the people were wearing were not something I recognized. Looking past the people I noticed the house in the background was the same as the previous picture.

A sense of dread started to settle in my stomach. Different people in front of the same house made me think these were different generations of the same family. A family that not only knew The Superior but wanted photos with him. He cared enough to be in the pictures and to keep them, but why had he gone to such great lengths to hide the pictures?

I flipped to the next photo, and it was yet another couple standing with The Superior. The woman was absolutely beaming as she held a small baby in her arms. Her smile was infectious, and I could almost hear her laughing at the look on The Superior's face beside her. Something about her struck me and I couldn't immediately tell why. The same house stood in the background, and I almost moved to the next picture when something about it caught my eye.

The Superior stood a slight bit further away from the couple this time, so I could see something behind them. A sea of red now bloomed beneath the front window. My breath started coming in and out in short breaths as I pulled the image closer to my face. A shocked gasp escaped my lips as I threw the pictures down to the ground.

The bush behind them was a large rhododendron. The reason the woman had struck me was because I knew her. She was my grandmother and the baby she was holding was my father.

These were generational photos of my family with The Superior.

CHAPTER 42

I couldn't breathe. I couldn't think. All I could do was sit on the floor and stare at the pictures. The world around me was spinning. Gabriel had implied The Superior had a connection to my family, but I hadn't expected this. Why was he posing for pictures with my family? Why had he hidden them? I didn't know what to think, but I knew what I had to do.

Scooping up the pictures from the floor, I sprang to my feet and burst out of the room. I left the journals on the floor and the door unlocked as I ran, nearly tripping down the stairs. By the time I started climbing upward toward the main library, sweat was pouring down my face. My heart was pounding, and my head was swimming.

I burst into the main library and Toby bolted into the air in surprise. If he said anything to me, I didn't hear it. I headed toward The Superior's office with singular focus. People passing me in the hallway gave me a wide berth as I stormed forward, furiously swiping at the sweat on my forehead. The pictures were a crinkled ball clutched in my fist.

The door to The Superior's office loomed before me and the world around me faded away. I saw nothing but the narrow path forward. Slamming my hand down onto the knob, I ripped the door open. It cracked against the wall.

The Superior was standing behind his desk, searching through the drawers. Part of my brain realized he was searching for his keys, but it no longer mattered to me. His eyes took me in, and he gave me a curious and concerned look. I walked across the room and slapped the pictures down onto the desk.

"Explain this," I said.

His gaze briefly flicked down before returning to my face. I stared defiantly back at him. We had been dancing around this secret for too long. I wanted answers and I wasn't leaving until I got them.

We stood with our eyes locked on each other for several moments. I worried that he was going to deny me, but finally, he sucked in a breath and walked to the door. He pushed it closed and turned the lock. My breathing was still coming in short pants as I wondered what he was doing.

"You should sit."

I shook my head, but realized he was still staring at the door.

"No," I said, my words barely a whisper. "Just tell me."

The words came out more pleading than I intended. My eyes bore into his back. He said nothing as he finally turned and walked back to the desk. He reached underneath it, and something clicked. A picture on the opposite wall popped open. The Superior walked across the room and pushed the picture aside revealing a safe.

Normally I would have laughed at the absurdity of a wall safe hidden behind a painting, but The Superior's continued silence unnerved me. Why wasn't he saying anything? Part of my brain screamed that I was in danger, but I was too desperate for answers to listen.

He typed a code into the safe and it opened. Reaching in, he pulled out a green duffle bag and a large envelope. His eyes finally met mine as he walked toward me. They were brown and his face was impassive, but the tick of his jaw and the flaring of his nostrils gave him away. His obvious nerves did little to settle my already skyrocketing pulse. He set the duffel on the floor at my feet and then he opened the envelope.

"Please sit," he said again. There was no command in his words. It was a request filled with such concern that I felt tears starting to prick the backs of my eyes. Hesitantly, I settled down into the chair. The Superior remained standing as he pulled the contents out of the envelope.

He set a small black and white photograph on the desk. There were two young women with their arms around each other, grinning widely at the camera. Several bags sat around them as they stood in front of a car. They were both dressed in what looked like military uniforms.

The Superior's finger pointed to the girl on the right. "This is your great-great-great Aunt Annie."

I looked up at him in confusion. My desire to tell him I had no idea what he was talking about was silenced by the severe look on his face.

He continued, "She was one of the most powerful ferriers there has ever been." His finger moved to the woman on the left. "Second only to your great-great grandmother Alice."

I looked down at the pair of them and I couldn't help but return their smiles. They were my family and not only that, but they held the same power as me. I wanted to learn all I could about them.

"This picture was taken before they left for France in 1916. They traveled as close to the Western Front as they could, looking for the portals that the soldiers would use. At that time, the demons on this side were more debauched than they are now. They tormented all souls on their journey to the Afterlife. The sisters were powerful enough to stop that, so they protected as many soldiers as they could. They believed those men and women suffered enough in life that they didn't deserve to be tormented in death."

My heart lifted as I stared into their faces again. Not only were they powerful, but they used their power to help souls in need. Pride swelled within me as tears pressed into the backs of my eyes. The Superior set another photo down on top of the first. It was still Annie and Alice, but clearly taken years later. They sat in patio chairs on a wooden deck. Both older, but still smiling.

"When the war was over," The Superior continued, "They traveled back home. This was taken at their parent's house in New York. They both moved back in to take care of their aging parents. Annie married and her husband lived there as well. Together they had a son."

He cleared his throat before he continued. "The demons never forgot the work the sisters had done during the war. Alice and Annie were able to control demons with their power. As far as I know, they are the first of their kind to be able to do that."

His eyes briefly flicked to me before they settled back onto the picture. A nervous chill coursed up my spine.

"As you know, demons do not forgive, and they fear those that are more powerful than themselves. They hunted your family and on February 7th, 1925, they found them."

His eyes flicked to mine and stayed there. It was clear from his expression that he didn't want to keep talking. I didn't think I wanted to hear it either, but I said nothing and gave a small nod for him to continue.

"Alice left early for groceries that day, but just before she got home, she realized she'd forgotten eggs. Something pushed her to head back to the store, so she did. When she returned, she found the front door ripped from its hinges." He took a deep breath and then said softly, "The demons left no one alive."

I wrapped my arms around myself and shuddered. The Superior didn't seem to want to go into detail about it. Knowing my Aunt Annie had a child in that house, I didn't want to know the specifics.

"They left a warning for Alice," he continued, "So she ran. For years. Until the day she met your great-great grandfather. Something about him made her want to settle down. A few years later, she found out she was pregnant, and she knew the demons would never stop hunting her. She started looking for a solution."

The Superior set the envelope on his desk and started unbuttoning his shirt. I wanted to ask what the hell he was doing, but as he tugged his shirt from his pants, he continued, "She found a spell. I don't know how or where, but it was a lifelong binding of protection for all of her descendants."

I raised a brow, still not understanding, as he finished removing his shirt. Now bare chested, he neatly laid his shirt on his desk and then turned his left side to me. He dipped his chin and started breathing deeply. I studied his face, then something flashed across his arm, drawing my attention.

Ink appeared to bleed across his bicep, climbing up and around his shoulder before spilling across his chest and back. Pushing my chair back, I rose and moved closer to examine the lines being painted across his skin. The Superior stayed still with his head dipped as I stepped next to him. Now closer, I could see the lines on his bicep were the trunk of a tree that branched across his shoulder and the limbs and leaves decorated his chest and back. I marveled at the beauty of the piece before I noticed the words embedded into the trunk.

Tilting my head to better see, I felt him flinch as my finger grazed across the words:

"Protection to all in this tree or power unbeholden to thee."

Moving a step back, I could see that he was watching me closely. His face, normally so devoid of feeling, showed a sea of emotions. Fear and concern lay bare in his eyes. I couldn't hold his gaze as his sudden fragility was too much for me.

The Superior turned his back to me and pointed to a spot to the right of his shoulder blade. I looked more closely and gasped as I saw a name woven into the limbs of the tree.

"Monica Grace."

He removed his hand from that spot and moved to another, lower down near his side.

"Christopher James." My father's name.

The Superior turned back around very slowly. My throat bobbed as he lifted a finger to his chest, just below his collarbone.

"Claire Olivia," I said, the words catching in my throat at the sight of my own name emblazoned across his heart.

"What does this mean?" I asked, the words trembling.

His eyes searched my face, hoping that I would put the pieces together myself. For some reason, I couldn't do it. My mind was in a fog, where I couldn't see my way through all this new information. I knew something should be obvious to me, but it was all too much to process.

Finally, he explained, "It means that if any descendent of your great-great grandmother dies by the hands of a demon, then I have broken the agreement."

My fingers brushed across my name. He sucked in a sharp breath, and I found that I couldn't look away from him. "Is that why you have pictures with my relatives? As some part of this agreement?"

He shook his head, a twitch of a smile trying and failing to come to his lips. "At first, I pretended to be a long-lost family member to gain access to your relatives. I wanted to be close to them to ensure their safety."

"What happens if any of us gets killed by a demon?" I whispered.

"I lose all my power."

My eyes shot up to his. "Why would you ever have agreed to something like that?"

"You misunderstand," he said, his hands coming up to cover mine on his chest. "I dedicated my immortal life to the service of protecting your family in exchange for your great-great grandmother's power."

I shook my head. "Wait, so you're a ferrier?"

"No, think of power as an essence. Like how we are able to share power through the mark."

"So you stole her power?"

I pulled my hand from his and his eyes flashed red. "I didn't steal it."

"Why did she do this? Why you?"

He twitched his shoulders, and the tree disappeared leaving perfectly unmarred skin behind. He pushed his fingers through his hair and went to the desk to retrieve his shirt. "She did this to protect her descendants from the demons."

"And why you?" I asked again, leaning over his desk so I could see his face.

He pushed his arms into his shirt and shrugged. "That is a question I stopped asking myself a long time ago."

I felt anger rising in me as I said, "You took her power and then just left her completely defenseless? How could you do that?"

He looked up at me and I saw a frown twitch across his lips before he could hide it. "I didn't leave her."

Shaking my head, I scoffed because he still hadn't answered my question. He finished with the buttons on his shirt and came around to stand before me.

"She knew the demons would never stop hunting her or her family, so she found a spell that ensured an immortal being would always be there for them and have enough power to defend them. In order to transfer her power and complete the spell," he paused for a moment, his gaze flicking away from mine before he finally said, "She had to die."

My eyes widened in horror and The Superior snatched my hands up before I could back away from him.

"You murdered my great-great grandmother?"

Hearing the words, they sounded ridiculous. I shook my head and pulled on my hands, but he wouldn't let go. His eyes were a rolling sea of red. "I did not murder her."

"Then what do you call it?" I spat, leaning away from him. He pulled me closer.

"I did not murder her." His eyes frantically searched my own before he breathed, "You know I cannot lie to you."

A tear slipped down my cheek as I continued to stare in horror at him. "I don't know that," I said, my voice breaking slightly while I shook my head. "I don't know anything anymore."

His face fell. It was as if he had always known this would happen. This was why he had hidden it so well. He knew that I would never be able to forgive him for this.

"I can't manipulate demonic texts, and you translated it yourself. I can't lie to you and I'm not. She knew the price of the spell and she knew she would be the one to pay it."

I yanked on my hands and this time he let me go. Taking a step away from him, I wiped at the tears running down my face. "Am I supposed to believe that you did this out of the goodness of your heart or something?"

"No," he said with a sigh, dropping his hands to his sides. "I did it for power."

"And is that supposed to make me somehow feel better?" I spat. "You murdered one of my relatives."

His fist came down with a booming crack across the desk. The instant he touched it, the desk exploded in a ball of Hellfire. A yelp of surprise escaped me as I watched the desk disintegrate. In the blink of an eye, it was nothing but a pile of ash.

The Superior's gaze never left my face as he seethed out, "I did not murder her."

His voice was low and dangerous, and I felt myself begin to shiver. My back bumped against the door, and I jumped from the contact. His wrath filled gaze followed my movements. Not being able to take the intensity of his stare, I looked down at my toes.

"You know I would never hurt you."

He spoke in a quiet, tender voice. A rage built inside me, stoked by the placating tone in his voice.

"That's right," I said, my head snapping up as I glared back at him, "Because you would lose your power." So many realities started unfolding in my head. My gut twisted as my heart sank. "My sister. All this time I wondered why you cared about her, but you were being sincere when you said you didn't."

He didn't respond. He just stood there with a blank look on his face.

"You only care about power. That's the only thing that has ever mattered to you."

"That's not true," he said, taking a step toward me, but I ignored him.

"It is true. Everything you said about never hurting me, it was never about me or how you—"

I stopped myself before I said, 'felt about me.' The pain in my chest brought tears to my eyes. I could no longer deny that I had developed feelings for him. The mark on my arm now felt like a cruel irony. It had forced me to feel something for a monster and I'd been stupid enough to believe that he felt anything for me.

Lifting my forearm to him I said, "I guess this was just an insurance policy."

He moved faster than I could see. His hand wrapped possessively around my forearm. "That is *not* what this is."

Another tear slid down my face and I quickly batted it away with my hand. "I don't believe you."

He snarled at me, bringing his teeth close to my face. "I don't care what you believe, that's not what it is."

I shook my head and forced out a laugh. "Save your threats for someone whose name isn't painted across your chest."

His hold on my arm grew warm as he whispered, "The spell stops me from killing you, not hurting you, but I don't *want* to hurt you."

His knuckles brushed along my arm before he stepped away. His eyes were still a bright red as he looked down at me.

"Then what is it?"

We stared at each other for several moments before he turned away from me. "I've answered enough of your questions."

I felt a lance of pain rip through me. We were going back to this. After everything we'd been through. He finally shared something, and already, he was bottling it up again. My heart broke as I realized what a fool I had been.

The Superior walked back to the duffel bag that somehow hadn't been touched by the fire. He lifted it easily and dropped it at my feet. Without looking at me he said, "She gave me this to give to her descendant once they learned the truth."

"What's in it?" I asked curiously.

"I don't know," he replied with a sigh, "She made me give my word that I would never open it."

"And you haven't?"

The words were out of my mouth before I could think. He glared at me, and I felt the heat in the room rising. I shook my head, dismissing the comment. Bending down, I lifted the bag onto my shoulder. It was heavier than he made it look, but I wasn't surprised.

"I will find my sister," I said, reaching out to unlock the door behind me. "For her sake, not for yours."

He gave a curt nod.

"I want the mark gone."

Something flashed across his face and if I hadn't known better, I would have thought I'd hurt him.

"It may take some time," he finally said.

I nodded, shifted the weight of the bag and said, "Whatever it takes."

Walking out of his office, I set my face and wiped the last tears from my cheeks. I didn't want everyone to know what had happened between us, but the flood of emotions rolling inside me was threatening to break through with every step I took.

When I finally made it back to my room, I collapsed onto my bed and sobbed.

CHAPTER 43

Early the next morning, I stood at the end of the driveway, watching the dot of my Uber driver draw closer. I'd spent my night tossing and turning until a text chimed from my phone. It had been from Nancy. Tabitha's contact was back in town and ready to talk. She mentioned that beyond translating the mark, he'd said that he might know of a way to remove it. It sounded too good to be true, but it was late, I hadn't slept, and I was still numb from my conversation with The Superior, so I agreed. Nancy sent me the time and place, so I'd packed a bag and climbed out my window.

As the car pulled up in front of me, I took one last glance back at The Superior's estate. At first, I had seen it as a prison, dragged here against my will with an unwanted mark on my arm, fearing the people hunting me and the demon claiming to save me. In truth, he had saved me. Time and again, The Superior had come for me. Now I knew the reason why, and yet, it still didn't explain everything. His deal with my relative meant he couldn't let me die, but that didn't explain why he'd comforted me. It didn't explain why he'd held back the pain from the poison and taken the time to wash my hair. Why had he asked me on a date? My cheeks heated at the memory of the car ride home. Shaking away the memory, I pulled out my phone and distracted myself with a game.

An hour later, thanks to some lovely gameday traffic on the bridges, I was finally standing in front of Tabitha's house in Lawrenceville. Huffing out a sigh, I walked up the pathway and knocked on the door. A few moments later, the door was pulled open by a thin woman in her forties. Her eyes narrowed menacingly at me.

"Hello, Tabitha," I said, plastering a smile on my face.

"Well, well, well," she said, crossing her arms and barring my entry into her home. "Miss Too Good For Demon Lovers found herself one to love."

My smile fell. "I didn't ask for any of this, Tabitha."

"No?" she said, stepping over the threshold and into my personal space. "You just happened to get marked? A symbol reserved for only the truly blessed among us, a symbol given to you not only by the most powerful demon this side of Hell's gates but also the handsomest?"

I rolled my eyes. The fanaticism of the demon groups would never make sense to me. "Look, believe what you want, Tabby." Her nostrils flared at the nickname. The reaction made me smile again. "I didn't ask for this and if you're so jealous, then by all means go ask The Superior to remove it so he can give it to you instead."

Her eyes fluttered and a flush rose in her cheeks at the suggestion. The reaction caused a wave of possessiveness to rise within me. Despite my anger at The Superior, the mark still wanted me to claim him.

Tabitha's face twisted into concern as she asked, "Um, are you okay?"

My emotions must have been showing on my face. I pushed them back down for what felt like the hundredth time and nodded. "So do I get to come in and meet your friend or what?"

She looked me over, still unsure of what had just happened, but then she said, "If you want in, I want to see it."

I huffed out a sigh and rolled up my sleeve. A gasp escaped my lips as Tabitha fell reverently to her knees. Her shaking fingers reached out toward me and then went to cover her mouth. I looked down in horror at the sight of tears running down her face. Looking around awkwardly, I hoped that no one was around to see any of this.

"Beautiful. Just beautiful," she breathed.

"Okay," I said, slowly pushing the sleeve back down my arm, "We good now?"

Tabitha sat back on her heels and continued staring at me. Fortunately for me, a young man appeared in the doorway. He looked down at Tabitha and then his eyes rose to meet mine. My mouth opened trying to explain, but he stepped forward, extending his hand.

"I'm Ramon," he said, taking my hand in his, "Looks like Tabitha might need a minute. Come on, I'll show you inside."

He turned and headed back inside. Stepping carefully around Tabitha, I followed him. Inside, I walked down a short hallway to the right of the stairs. Ramon pushed open a door at the end of the hallway and stood to the side to let me in. I nodded my thanks as I stepped into a small home office. One way held a beautiful bay window that looked out onto the back yard. The other walls were covered with built-in bookshelves. Each shelf was filled with books, pictures, and different knickknacks. In the center of the room was a massive desk. It was ornately designed and perfectly clear except for a pair of hands clasped on top of it.

The hands belonged to a middle-aged man with brown eyes and short brown hair. The coloring matched his beard which was neatly trimmed and stylish. Despite being seated, I could tell that he was incredibly tall. He smiled up at me, but I didn't smile back as I stared down at the demon.

He laughed and it was a deep rumbling sound that sent chills skittering down my spine. "Who did you expect when Tabitha told you I could translate the mark?"

My heart started pounding as the door was shut behind me. I looked over to the window, trying to find another avenue of escape.

"I do not wish you any harm," he said, clearly reading my thoughts. "I simply wish to chat."

The demon continued to smile at me as he gestured to the chair in front of the desk. He kept his movements slow and simple so as not to startle me. His expression remained welcoming despite his imposing figure. My eyes swept back to the window as I took a step backward.

"Don't you think you deserve answers, Claire?"

That got my attention. Despite the danger of being alone in a room with a demon, I did want answers. Looking him over once again I decided it was worth the risk. I walked across the room and sat down in the chair. It couldn't hurt just to hear what he had to say, right?

He said, "I am called Jacob."

I nodded. "Hi."

"Well, Claire, let's see it."

Crossing my arms, I narrowed my eyes at him. "You already know who I am tied to, so why do you need to see it?"

He could smile all he wanted, but I knew he wasn't offering this information for free. He had a motive in this, and I needed to figure out what it was. His grin turned slightly more predatory as he said, "There are things that can be learned by the appearance of the mark."

"And why would I want you to learn any of those things?"

He sat staring back at me for a long moment. If he was hoping I would cave to the silence, he clearly didn't know how much The Superior also loved to use that tactic. Crossing my arms over my chest to emphasize my point, I glared at him.

To my surprise, he tossed his head back and laughed. It was a warm, rich sound that warmed my skin and had me smiling back at him.

When his eyes returned to mine, they held a sparkle of amusement. "I can see why he likes you. Fair enough. I will learn things, but I will share what I learn with you as well. Also, there have only ever been three queens and never having seen one in person before, I am curious." He shrugged at those last words.

My heart skipped a beat as I tried to settle my breathing. "Only three? Ever?"

Jacob smiled comfortingly and nodded. "Three with you, that is. So, you see, I would love to see a mark in the flesh. Quite literally."

He laughed merrily at his own joke, and I pressed my lips together to stop myself from smiling in response again. His demeanor was making me feel at ease and I didn't like it. I knew I couldn't trust him, but then why had I come if not for some answers?

Clearing my throat, I pushed my sleeve back and set my bare forearm on the desk. His eyes greedily took in my bare skin. His face lowered so close to my arm that I could feel his breath.

"Beautiful," he mused to himself, "Absolutely stunning."

"What does it say?" I asked sharply, keeping my focus on his features.

He ignored me at first, continuing his inspection of the mark on my arm. My eyes dipped down to it momentarily and I could have sworn it was lighter. Worry built in my stomach at the sight. Had The Superior already started the process of removing it? And why did the thought of that make me feel uneasy?

Jacob finished his close examination of my arm then leaned back in his chair. He steepled his fingers and rested his elbows on the chair arms.

"I'm sure you've noticed the mark changing."

I blinked at him. He took it as the yes that it was and continued. "The mark darkens as it grows more permanent."

It hadn't been my imagination. The mark had been changing, which meant it was lighter than before. Studying it for a moment longer I let out a sigh. I had asked The Superior to remove it, so I had to assume he was already working on it. For some reason that thought bothered me more than it should. My eyes flicked back to Jacob's, and I saw that he was watching me very carefully.

"Noticing something?" he asked, his lips pulling upward as if he already knew the answer.

I shrugged in response. He continued, "The mark is close to permanent, but from the look on your face I am assuming it is lighter than it once was. Did you two have a fight?"

My jaw dropped. Looking down at the mark, I tried to see whatever it was that he saw. He let out a small chuckle. "Honestly, I am surprised to see it's that dark."

"Why is that?" I asked.

Jacob eyed me with humor still apparent on his face. "Let's just say The Superior isn't known for his emotional intimacy."

This line of questioning wasn't one that I wanted to follow, so I changed the subject. "So, what does it say?"

He looked me over again, then said, "There is a reason that none of your friends could translate this mark. In fact, there are few who can."

Pulling my sleeve back down, I retracted my arm and leaned back in my own chair. Despite his claim that he would tell me everything, Jacob still seemed to be skirting my main question. He continued, "The mark not only uses the demon's original name, but it must be written in the language the name was given in."

I shook my head at him, not sure if he was about to give me a lecture on demon dialects, but I stopped shaking when I noticed the slight reddening around his pupils. His eyes were the same color as The Superior's. My gaze flicked between them as my pulse ratcheted up. Jacob was the same type of demon as The Superior.

His smile widened as he said, "The reason no one could read it is because The Superior's original name is not demonic. It's angelic."

CHAPTER 44

I stared at him for so long, that he started to look worried. He came around the desk and knelt before me. Gently placing a hand on my shoulder, he asked if I was alright.

My eyes were fixed on the desk as I mumbled, "So he's...? He's what?"

Jacob's hand warmed my skin as he lightly rubbed it up and down my arm. "We are members of the Fallen," he said simply. "I'm not surprised at your shock. We are not often forthcoming about our true nature."

In my peripheral vision, I saw him tilting his head as he examined my face. I couldn't move, could barely breathe, as I realized the demon I had been living with was older than the human race. The Superior had been an angel. Images of his scarred backside flashed across my mind.

"The scars," I whispered, as my thoughts snagged on the memory. He'd been so afraid that night and I hadn't known why. After learning everything I did last night, I had mostly forgotten about it.

"He showed them to you?"

I shook my head and finally turned my gaze to him. "It was an accident."

Something flickered across his features before he rose to his feet. Poking his head through the door, he called Tabitha to bring some tea. Coming back to my side, he said, "A little tea will help you in digesting these words." He settled back into the chair behind the desk. "We hide the scars beneath a powerful glamor. For him to have dropped it he had to have felt very safe."

"Why work so hard to hide the scars?"

His eyes rolled with red, and his voice lowered as he answered. "Not only were we forced to endure having our wings cut from our bodies, but we were cursed with eternal pain from the scars. This makes them incredibly sensitive and therefore a spot of weakness."

A weakness. One hidden from the world, and yet, I had seen them. The Superior had been terrified when it had happened, but what had scared him? Was it that he thought I would use them to hurt him or was it the realization that he felt safe with me?

Shaking off the question, I looked at the demon before me and said, "As if cutting off the wings wasn't painful enough, you were cursed with eternal pain? That's awful."

Jacob smiled, but his eyes remained red. "I'm glad you think so."

A knock sounded on the door. Jacob called for them to enter and Tabitha walked in with a tray in her hands. She used her hip to push the door closed and sauntered toward the desk. I wrinkled my nose at her obvious flirtation, but Jacob grinned back at her and nodded his thanks as she set down the cups and kettle. He flicked his wrist to politely dismiss her, and she glared at me, but quickly left the room.

Jacob set both of our teas to steeping and I asked, "How many Fallen are there?" He appeared to think for a moment before he said, "There are a fair few of us." Such a typical demon non-answer. The scowl must have shown on my face, because he laughed and said, "However, there are just the two of us on this side of the gates."

I sat watching the steam mist off the teacups. Combined with what I'd learned last night, this was more information than I'd ever hoped to acquire. Jacob removed the bags and then slid one of the cups across the table to me. I looked up at him and said, "Are you ever going to tell me what it says?"

He blew across the top of his cup and lifted his brows at me. "I think I will leave that information for him to unveil." Taking a tentative sip from his mug, he continued, "I do not like the demon, but I do have a healthy respect for his power and abilities."

Nodding toward the cup in front of me he said, "It'll make you feel better."

I watched him take another sip, before turning to inspect my own mug. Leaning forward, I breathed in the aroma billowing from the cup before me. It smelled of chamomile, vanilla, and honey. I took a small sip and with the delectable taste on my tongue, I took another.

"I am quite curious at this supposed *accident* that resulted in you seeing The Superior's scars."

Sitting back in my chair, I cradled the cup in my hands and thought over my response. Jacob had been quite forthcoming about the scars, but I still didn't want to share more than I had to. Deciding to deflect instead, I asked, "Have you ever shown anyone your scars?"

It was a deeply personal question that I was hoping would catch him off guard. I hid my face by taking another sip of tea. When I finally glanced back over at him, I saw that he was tracing his cup's edge with a finger. He ran it around and around, his eyes glazed over in thought.

"There have been a few," he said finally, not halting his finger or looking up. "They are hard to hide from those you love. Is that why you could see his?"

My gasp sucked the tea from my mouth into my lungs causing me to choke. I coughed hoarsely as my body bent over itself trying to pry the liquid out. Jacob came around, placing my tea on the desk and thumping his palm against my back. I kept coughing as my face reddened at his implication. There was no way The Superior was in love with me.

Jacob patted my back a few more times until I finally nodded and was able to croak out the words to let him know I was okay. I reached up for the tea, my throat now a burning ruin and gulped down the last bits of liquid to try and ease my throat. Shaking my head, I choked out, "Sorry, I just wasn't expecting that."

He titled his head to study me as he asked, "You weren't expecting him to fall in love with you or you weren't expecting me to ask it?"

I lifted my hands and shook my head. The movement made me feel a little dizzy, so I stopped before I said, "No, no, that wasn't what happened. His glamor must have been down because he'd been sleeping."

Jacob winked at me. "Ah, so you do not think it was *love* but an exhausting bout of lovemaking that revealed the scars to you?"

"What? No, that's not what I meant." I sucked in a breath as my tongue struggled to form the words. Heat gathered in my cheeks as I sputtered, "He was sleeping, in his room, before he came to talk to me. In my room. No sleeping together. No *lovemaking*."

"You must forgive my assumptions, then," he said, glancing down at his watch, "but the fact still remains that you have seen them and that your mark is nearly permanent."

"And?" I asked, struggling to force that single word out.

My head was feeling jumbled and heavy. I took a breath and felt myself falling back into the chair. Something wasn't right. I looked over at my empty teacup and then managed to raise my gaze up to Jacob's face. There was nothing but a demon staring back at me from behind that desk.

"And," he continued, leaning forward onto the desk, "That means you are far more valuable to him than I realized."

Then everything faded to black.

Sound came back to me first. There was a scraping and brushing sound. A door opening and closing. My eyelids fluttered as I tried to pull them open. The world around me was bright. When I managed to fully open my eyes, I saw that I was in a well-appointed study. There was a lush white carpet underneath my feet.

Looking down at my feet I saw ropes binding me to a chair. I found the same bindings around my arms and torso.

"Apologies for the ropes, my dear, but I can't have you running away, and I can't have anyone harming you."

Turning my head toward the voice, I found Jacob sitting in a high-backed chair in front of a fireplace off to my left. He smiled at me over his shoulder, then went back to chatting with the person standing at his side.

"Where am I?"

The words grated out as my mouth was still dry from whatever had been in my tea.

Jacob continued his conversation for a moment, then nodded to the man at his side. The man left and then Jacob came over to me. He pulled an elegant chair over from a table and plopped it down right in front of me.

"You know I won't answer that." He sat down in the chair, bracing his elbows on his knees. "This all would have been so much easier if you had just come when we first approached you."

I tried to wet my lips before speaking but found that I had very little saliva. "You sent the snake demon?"

He nodded and rose elegantly from his chair. He walked behind me to where I couldn't see him for a moment and returned with a glass of water in his hands. I glared at him, but he only laughed. "I have already drugged you to get you here, I do not need to do so again."

I doubted the sincerity of his words, but I was so thirsty. Tipping my head back slightly, I let him press the glass to my lips. Taking a few swallows felt glorious and I pushed him for more.

"Too much and you might upset your stomach." He removed the glass from my mouth and sat back down in his chair. "The sedative can have some lingering effects."

My mouth still felt desperately dry. I wanted more water, but my desire to get out of here was stronger. "What do you want from me?"

Jacob leaned toward me. "I want what I have wanted all along. Your sister."

There it was. Back to the same issue that had started this whole mess. My half-sister. For someone I had never met, she was seriously beginning to irritate me.

A sigh slid past my lips before I said, "Can't help you there. I don't know where she is."

He smirked at that and leaned back in his chair. "Your gifts can find her."

I shook my head, but when the room started spinning, I abruptly stopped. "Look, even if I have the gifts, I don't know how to use them. I've already tried."

"You have the gifts, and I can tell you how to use them."

That piqued my curiosity, but I was hoping to hide my interest from him. Instead, I asked "How do you know?"

He shrugged. "I've been alive for millennia. It shouldn't be that surprising that I've learned a few things."

"Fine," I said, huffing out a sigh, "What makes you think I would help you?"

Red rolled across his eyes for a moment and then receded. I was being brazen with my attitude and perhaps I shouldn't have been, but he had kidnapped me, so I was more than a little upset. He needed my ferrier gifts enough to kidnap me and potentially incur the wrath of The Superior. He knew something about the connection between The Superior and my sister and I intended to find out how much he knew.

Jacob tried to play that he was relaxed but his eyes had already betrayed him. "What makes you think you have anything to bargain with?"

I smiled at him. "Well, you're talking to me, which means you need me in order to do this, and if you want me to, then you need to tell me why."

He let out a small chuckle as his eyes swept over me.

"What?" I asked, shifting as much as I could against the ropes. They weren't budging.

"I never expected someone tied to a chair to think they could start making demands." His eyes sparkled with more humor as his gaze finally came to rest on my face. He studied me for a few more moments before shrugging his shoulders in acquiescence.

"I would expect my motives were obvious."

He leaned forward, offering more water that I gladly accepted. When I finished taking a few more swallows, I let myself sit for a minute. I noticed that my head was finally clearing, but I was still left with a dull headache. Despite that, sorting out Jacob's motivation was easy.

"You want to get rid of The Superior."

Jacob's eyes glittered as a small smile spread across his face. "Get rid of? No. That's rather dramatic. Replace? Yes."

I raised my eyebrows encouraging him to elaborate. He offered me more water while he continued. "The Superior has been in power for some time. Power, he has not always held."

His gaze fixed on mine as I gulped down my last mouthful of water. I willed myself not to blink as I held his stare. He was trying to see what I knew, and I wasn't going to give him the satisfaction of admitting to knowing anything.

Narrowing my eyes back at him, I asked, "What do you mean?"

"I mean he was practically a nothing demon through most of his existence." He shifted in his seat to set my water glass on the table behind him. Turning back to me he said off-handedly, "Of course that makes sense as he was a nothing angel before that."

Curiosity bloomed inside of me, and I couldn't stop myself from asking, "Wait, what kind of angel was he?"

Jacob smiled over at me and tilted his head to the side. "You mean you haven't guessed?" He let out a wonderfully deep chuckle that sent chills running down my spine. "Have you not noticed how all humans are so drawn to him?"

I nodded my head and momentarily forgot the bindings on me as I pushed forward and exclaimed, "Yes!"

"He was a muse."

My mouth fell open. The artwork. The books. Every inch of the walls in The Superior's house was covered with priceless pieces of art. How had I not made the connection sooner?

He rolled his eyes, and continued, "Everything about him is designed to draw in humans and help them find inspiration. Have you never wondered why everyone thinks he is the most beautiful bastard they've ever laid eyes upon?"

An image of The Superior's handsome face flashed before my eyes, and I nodded. I also remembered Mark and Nancy describing him as the beautiful man they'd ever seen. The thought that his looks might be tied to his nature never crossed my mind because I'd been too busy enjoying the view. I cleared my throat as I felt a slight blush rising in my cheeks.

Jacob muttered to himself, "He wasn't a fighter back then. We needed his kind to inspire others to join the rebellion. Anyway," he said, waving his hand dismissively through the air, "The reason I mention his lack of power is that obviously he found more somehow."

His eyes flicked to mine. They swirled with color, and I felt the weight of his power pressing into me. "I have searched for the answer to how he did it and I am the closest I have ever been. I know your sister has something to do with it."

I wanted to look away from him, but I knew that would only confirm his suspicions, so once again I worked to hold his stare. He was powerful and it was difficult, but I had almost a month of tangling with The Superior under my belt now. Sucking in a breath I gave him my most condescending smile as I asked, "How do you know that?"

Jacob's fingers snapped forward and locked onto my jaw. My heartbeat ratcheted upward as his grip dug into my skin.

"I know it and so do you."

Despite being able to hold a demon stare, I still wasn't a good liar. I was better at evading, so then I asked, "What are you going to do with her?"

Jacob shrugged, releasing my face. "For now, I simply wish to find her. Once I discover how she connects to his power then I will decide what to do with her."

My body relaxed ever so slightly at his words. He didn't know that killing my sister was a way to release The Superior's power. Assuming Monica had no idea, which was most likely considering her relationship with The Superior wasn't the best, that meant I was the only other person who knew. I fought to keep a smile from my face.

Jacob thought he needed me to find my sister to achieve his goal, when in actuality he just needed to kill me. There was no way I was going to let him in on that piece of information. No, I preferred keeping my life and if it meant I could get him to teach me how to locate living souls then I could come out of this kidnapping situation better than I'd entered it. I just needed to get him to believe I was willing to work with him.

Shifting in my seat, I asked, "Assuming I even believe you about that, why should I help you?"

Jacob raised his hands and said, "At this point, I would say you don't really have much of a choice. Stay tied to that chair or help find her. I have infinite time."

Glaring back at him, I said, "He'll find me eventually."

He smiled. "I have learned many things during my time in this world and I can assure you, hiding one woman tied to a chair is nothing."

I shrugged as much as my ropes would allow me. "Fair point."

Not wanting to seem too eager, I looked around the room as if I was still mulling it over. There was a small chance that Jacob was telling the truth. I mean, what reason did he have to lie? He had obviously been searching for my sister. He clearly had something against The Superior. He had also willingly given me more information about The Superior than anything the demon himself had told me in the entire time I'd been around him.

Sighing, I looked back over at Jacob. How did I end up stuck in the middle of all of this? I had a mark on my arm tying me to a demon while another one held me tied to a chair. And all of this because of a relative I didn't even know existed two months ago.

"You teach me, I find my sister, and then what, you just let me go?" I finally asked.

Jacob nodded toward my arm. "With the mark you are more of a liability to keep than to use and let go."

"It just seems odd," I said, narrowing my eyes, "You claim I have value to him, that you want to get rid of him and yet you would just let me go?"

"I told you. I do not wish to get rid of him, I simply want to discover the source of his power and take it from him. I have nothing personal against him or you, I just do not wish to be under his rule any longer."

His eyes reddened slightly as he spoke. There was definitely something more personal there, but being alive for all of human existence, they were bound to have some history. A history I now got to be a part of. Lucky me.

Seeming to sense my reluctance Jacob added, "He has not been a popular ruler. We demons are not loyal as a breed, quite understandably, but The Superior has garnered more enemies than most. What I mean to say is that there will be others who will come for her. And for you. At least I am giving you the option to help and treating you fairly."

I nodded and said, "And yet, I'm still tied to this chair."

Jacob smiled. "You haven't agreed to help me yet."

"Alright then," I said, sensing that I had seemingly mulled it over long enough. "I will agree to try and find my sister for you."

Jacob gave me a sharp nod in response, before pulling a knife from his pocket and deftly cutting through my ropes. I rose and shook his hand. With that, I entered into yet another agreement with a demon.

CHAPTER 45

I s this really necessary?"

I asked the question as I pulled on the handcuff now encircling my wrist. The metal bracelet was connected to a long chain and the other cuff was wrapped around Jacob's wrist.

He smiled. "I still don't trust you not to wander off."

Baring my teeth back at him, I snapped, "I agreed to help you."

In response, Jacob yanked on the chain causing me to stumble.

"You agreed to try and find your sister and nothing more. Do not forget, I am a demon, and I know a poor deal when I hear one."

I shrugged. "Can't blame me for trying."

"Indeed." He said with scrunched brows.

After freeing me from my chair, Jacob immediately slapped the cuffs on me. As we walked through the house and then outside, he watched me very closely. I knew he was ensuring I did nothing to injure myself and alert The Superior to our location. I had more to gain by staying at the moment, so I went along with it.

We stepped outside onto a lush green lawn. Looking back at the house behind me, I saw it was a three-story palatial estate. Yet another demon living off the perks of generational wealth. We stepped into a small side yard with a few topiaries.

"Now, to our task," Jacob said, spinning dramatically in a circle. "As a ferrier, you guide the souls of the deceased to the Afterlife. It is my understanding that there is a realm of magic that only ferriers may access that can assist them when necessary."

Furrowing my brow, I said, "I've never been to such a place."

"Do not dismiss yourself so easily, Miss Woods. As a ferrier you are tied to this realm. It seeks to aid you, to guide you, just as you guide souls. Have you never felt a spark or a pull from something outside yourself?"

I stepped back, my eyes widening as it all clicked into place. How had I not made the connection? Nicky.

My body was rigid as I stood dumbfounded. Jacob gently placed a reassuring hand on my shoulder and said, "No worries, Miss Woods, we shall learn together."

"I can't enter it. I mean, it's given me things, but it's not a place I can go to."

He titled his head, humor lighting in his eyes. "Really? Have you tried?"

I opened my mouth to say yes, but then thought better of it. Thinking of Nicky as a place fueled by the magic of my ancestors and not as a magical person never crossed my mind. Jacob watched my face closely. I could see the desire growing in his expression as he saw his words hit home.

"Alright," I said, stepping back away from him, "How do you propose I get inside?"

Jacob looked less certain now as he said, "What if you try asking?"

I chuckled, assuming it was a joke, but his face was serious. "It can't be that simple."

To my surprise, Jacob rolled his eyes. "Well, we won't know unless you try."

"Did you just roll your eyes at me?" I asked, letting the humor I felt come through in my words. Before I could stop myself, I smiled at him. Despite the situation, I found myself liking the demon before me. Without thinking I asked, "What kind of angel were you?"

Jacob's face became more serious as he said, "A general." He spoke the words quickly and then with a wave of his hand he continued, "Now, focus on the feeling and ask to enter."

Spinning in place, I closed my eyes and thought about Nicky. I focused on the brush of magic that I always felt just before something appeared to help me. Extending my hands, I could feel the brush against the backs of my hands as my mind tried to think of Nicky as a place, not a person. My breathing slowed as I pictured myself traveling through a portal. Like entering The Otherworld, I needed to enter another plane of existence, so I held all those images in my mind and whispered, "May I enter the Ferrier Realm? Please?"

The chain on my arm jerked violently, so I opened my eyes and gasped at the sight before me. I didn't know where I was, but I was no longer standing in the yard with Jacob. The world around me seemed to extend out endlessly in every direction. Light came from everywhere and nowhere and there were wisps of clouds floating by me. My body felt as though it were floating in space. The continued yanking on the chain finally dragged my attention away from the world around me. I looked down and saw that it just ended abruptly. That must have been the edge of the realm. Reaching down with my other hand I yanked back on the chain. The pulling from the other side stopped immediately.

"Claire?"

Jacob's voice was muddled as if it was coming from somewhere far away. I tugged on the chain again and said, "Yeah, I'm okay."

I wasn't sure if he could hear me, and I realized we probably should have worked out a system with the chain. One tug for yes, two for no, three for get me the hell out of here. Disregarding Jacob, I turned back around. The clouds still floated around me, but now I could also see faint, pinpricks of light like stars. I extended a hand to try and touch one, when a rough tug on the chain pulled me off balance. I landed heavily on my side.

"Claire!"

Jacob's voice still sounded very distant. I stood and dusted myself off before giving a returning hard yank on the chain.

"I'm fine," I yelled, hoping he could hear me.

I decided I should probably focus on the task at hand. Yet with a groan, I remembered that I had no idea what I was supposed to do next to find my sister. With my thoughts on her, Monica's image flashed before my eyes. Suddenly, the stars around me shifted and began to pivot and spin. Just as abruptly as it had started, it stopped, and all of the lights faded away except for one.

Staring out at it, I continued focusing all of my thoughts on my sister. The star grew brighter and brighter until there was an explosion of light. Blinking furiously, it took a few minutes for me to see anything other than black spots. When I was able to see again, I sucked in a gasp.

It looked as if she was sitting right there in front of me. I recognized her face from the picture, and I could also see the now generous swell of her stomach. She was in a small barely furnished room. Her eyes were glazed as she flicked through channel after channel on the television screen. She sat on a basic green sofa that was only a few steps away from a bed. There was also a large shotgun propped against the side of the couch. There was something slightly alarming about the juxtaposition of the lethal weapon and the bored pregnant woman.

I couldn't see anything discernible to tell me where she was. As if the realm could read my mind, the picture slowly moved outward. The number on her door flashed before me, then the hotel name sign. The images continued on and on, traveling along a pathway that led right back to where I was now standing. I knew exactly where she was. I had done it.

Now that I knew where she was, I needed to figure out what I was going to do. There was no doubt in my mind that despite his seemingly pleasant nature, Jacob had nefarious plans for my sister. I didn't know if he would figure out that he just needed to kill her to destroy The Superior's power or not, but I assumed there would come a time when he would try to kill her. I mean, why not try it and see? He had infinite time, but that didn't necessarily mean he had infinite patience.

I paced back and forth as far as my chain would allow, trying to come up with a plan. Thankfully, Jacob had stopped tugging on the other side, but I knew he would expect answers when I got back. That also presented another question: how did I get out of here? I was hoping it was something like how I got in, but I couldn't be too sure.

With my thoughts of The Superior, I looked down at the marking on my forearm. It started to glow. My eyes widened and I took several steps backward before reaching the limits of my chain. The light lifted above my arm and shot outward. I couldn't see where it went, but I felt it connect to something with a thump that shuddered through my entire body. I looked down at the light and saw that it looked like a golden rope. It gleamed and I felt myself being drawn to it.

Gently brushing my fingers across the rope, I felt a current of energy snap through me. It was an exhilarating feeling. I reached down again and wrapped my whole hand around it. The sensation intensified and an enormous rush of energy flowed over me and through me causing my feet to lift slightly from the ground.

Suddenly I was standing in The Superior's bedroom. He was pacing in front of his bed. The second I arrived, his head jerked upward, and I felt him looking right at me. I gasped and released the tether. The image fell away, but the rope immediately gave a strong pull. My head swiveled, looking around expecting to see The Superior.

I didn't see him anywhere, but the rope kept pulling me forward. Not knowing what would happen, I gulped in a breath and placed my hand back on the rope. The Superior's face was immediately there again. His attention snapped to me, and I could see that his eyes were bright red. His jaw was clenched, and I was reminded of the night I'd watched him burn several people alive with Hellfire. He looked positively murderous.

He slowly moved his left hand over his right forearm. Looking down, I saw the golden rope that was attached to my arm ended on his. He gave the rope a small tug and I felt myself pulled forward.

"Can you see me?" I asked, the words barely a whisper. "Can you see where I am?"

I didn't see any recognition in his eyes, so I gave a small pull back on the rope. A small smile spread across his lips, and I had to remind myself that I was still furious at this demon. But, if he could get me out of here, I knew my sister and I would be safe with him, at least.

"Can you see me?" I asked again, this time much louder.

The Superior turned and started pacing again. I let out a sigh and I was about to open my mouth to say something again when he spoke.

"Claire, I don't know if you are there or not, but this might hurt."

My eyes widened as I watched him wrap his hand back around the rope. I stepped back unsure of what he was doing, when his power slammed into me knocking me off my feet. My back crashed into the ground behind me, snapping my head back. Sucking in a breath, I expected to feel pain all over and realized I was perfectly fine. Reaching behind my head to where I had hit the ground, I found no tenderness there. Getting to my feet I realized my body was literally buzzing with power. The Superior had somehow sent me a burst of energy. I felt as though I had gotten the best night's sleep and pounded several Red Bulls.

The chain on my arm was yanked so violently, that I felt my shoulder pull free of its socket. A sickening pop sounded through the air. I cried out and fell to the ground, only to be dragged along as Jacob continued pulling on the chain. Yelling for him to stop did nothing, because he still couldn't hear me. I had to get out of here. Hoping I could leave how I'd come, I focused on that familiar brush of magic and imagined a portal. Pain continued to radiate from my shoulder, but my borrowed strength from The Superior was overpowering it.

A tickle of grass across my cheek told me that I had made it back into the Human Realm. My eyes flew open to see Jacob standing over me, his face alit with fury as he said, "You told him where you are, so sadly that means you have to die."

CHAPTER 46

Any positive feelings I had toward Jacob quickly vanished. Now that The Superior knew my location, he had no issues hurting me. Or at least, attempting to hurt me. He didn't seem to notice that I was filled with power from The Superior. Meanwhile, I felt as though my skin was about to burst from all of the energy coursing through my body.

Jacob dragged me by the chain toward the house. My dislocated shoulder continued to bounce across the ground. Despite the lack of pain, I knew that kind of treatment couldn't be good for the injury. I yelled out several times, but Jacob simply ignored me. When we arrived at the house, he shoved me up the steps. Before the door, he spun me around and dug his fingers into my shoulder.

"That was an unwise decision," he hissed at me. Around us, people were running in every direction. Jacob snapped his fingers at two passing individuals and thrust me into their arms. He pulled a key from his pocket and detached the cuff from his wrist. Pointing at me, he said, "Take her downstairs, find out where her sister is, then get rid of her."

"Wait," I shouted, trying to stall for time. I was ignored. Looking up at the two new faces above me, I shuddered. One's eyes shone black as night, the others were a dark blue.

Fantastic. I was in the hands of a night demon and a water demon.

In one last ditch effort I screamed, "Jacob, please."

His eyes, now a blazing red, turned back to me. He opened his mouth, but then a violent shudder went through the house. We all crashed to the ground as the house buckled and shook. Wood splintered and cracked above me as the crash of glassware sounded elsewhere in the house.

"He's here!" Someone shouted from the second floor.

Jacob shot to his feet and waved at the demons holding me. "Get her downstairs now!"

The night demon latched onto me and lifted me off the floor. As he began pulling me toward the stairs, I gave into the panic swirling in my gut and started screaming. My strength was heightened, thanks to The Superior, so I was able to pull away with surprisingly little effort. The night demon glared at me then nodded to the demon over my shoulder. I had momentarily forgotten about him. His hands latched around me like a bear hug, forcing my arms down to my sides. I kicked in all directions, but the night demon grabbed onto my legs. We started down the stairs with me screaming for dear life. I bucked hard and felt the weightlessness of my body being freed, before crashing down the stairs. My head slammed into the concrete at the bottom. Pain exploded in my skull as tears welled in my eyes.

"Get up."

The voice was gruff. Pushing myself into a sitting position, I winced at the pain in my still dislocated shoulder and the stabbing throb shooting through my head. It was possible I'd suffered a concussion from falling down the stairs, but the demons in front of me didn't seem too concerned. Placing a hand on my head, I saw that I was no longer handcuffed, but it was obvious from all the pain that I was no longer filled with The Superior's power.

"Hey," the blue-eyed demon said, snapping his fingers in front of my face. I glared over at him. "Tell us where the girl is, and we'll make this quick."

My mind was still reeling a bit, but I remembered why I was down here. There was no way I was going to tell them anything so they could 'make this quick.'

The house shook again, and a cloud of dust and a few splinters of wood crashed to the floor between me and the demons. One of them screamed as he was buried by the falling debris. While on the other side of the pile, I felt a familiar brush of magic. My dagger landed on the ground in front of me. Diving down, I managed to grab it before the other demon slammed into me. My head smacked into the concrete again, and this time I definitely saw stars. Pain lanced through me as the air from my lungs was forced out from the impact. I sucked in as much air as I could with his weight still on me, then shoved the dagger into his side.

The demon roared as I stabbed again. He seized my wrist, but I flicked the blade over and scraped it across his knuckles. He slammed my hand down and my grip on the dagger faltered. Shifting, he kicked the blade across the room and then slammed his foot into the side of my head. A scream poured out of me as pain exploded across my cheek. I kicked out at his other leg and felt a flood of satisfaction when I connected with something solid.

He spat out a curse as he hopped backward. I rolled away from him and then pushed myself awkwardly up into a crouch. My shoulder screamed at me to stop moving, but the rest of my body tingled with the awareness that I needed to fight, or I would die. My vision was blurring with tears as I struggled to remain upright. A huge pulse of energy suddenly shot through me.

I gasped aloud as I felt my body come alive with The Superior's power. The pain from my injuries suddenly dulled and I felt so full that I assumed there was power leaking out of my pores. The look on my face must have been frightening because the demon took a step backward.

A sword dropped onto the ground at my feet. Instinctively, I grabbed it, and the blade immediately lit with a wreath of Hellfire. I blinked down at the weapon, then over to the demons. They looked as shocked as I felt. I never would have guessed that The Superior could pass along that particular gift.

The demon in front of me took a hesitant step back. The other one went for the element of surprise and suddenly bolted toward me. He didn't have any weapons except for his demonic strength and speed. I had no idea how to use a sword, but I swung it at him. The threat of the fire was enough to send him twisting to the side with a pained grimace. He reacted quickly, turning in place to slam his fist into my sword arm before ducking behind me.

I spun around with the sword raised, but he was already moving. He spat at my face, and I had to raise the sword and my arm as a shield. I couldn't see him, so I took several steps backward. Despite my lack of skill with the weapon, the fire alone was enough of a deterrent.

He raised his hand to cover his eyes, when a sudden cascade of cold washed across my entire body. The fire around my sword went out and my added strength was sucked away. Crying out, my grip on the sword broke and it clattered to the floor. I dropped to my knees and wondered what had just happened to The Superior.

The water demon slammed me into the wall. He dropped me in a crumpled heap onto the floor. I couldn't stand up. My body was broken. Neither of my arms seemed to be working properly. The demon wrenched my chin upward to look into his face. He smiled triumphantly down at me.

"That was fun, but now fun's over. Where's the girl?"

If I hadn't been in so much pain, I might have laughed. I was dying on the floor of a basement because of a sister I didn't even know. A sister, who no one seemed to truly care about.

I let out a ragged cough and said, "If you get me some water, I'll tell you."

The demon considered me for a moment. Then he released my chin and took a few steps backward. A spark of hope washed over me, but then he bent down and picked up my sword. His smile turned feral as he stared down at me. "Tell me, and I kill you quickly. Don't tell me, and I start cutting you apart, piece by piece."

I tried in vain to push myself upward. My legs slipped along the dusty ground as I tried to press myself up against the wall. My dislocated arm was in agonizing pain as the demon before me pressed the tip of the blade through my wrist. I screamed. My throat was raw as tears fell from my eyes as I mumbled, "Please, stop."

The pain was so great that I simply stopped fighting. I laid there, and in my mind, I called out to The Superior. To Nicky. To my grandmother's-grandmother. I pleaded for someone to stop this demon from killing. My breaths were coming sharp and fast as tears spilled down my cheeks. Keeping my eyes shut tight, I waited for more pain and the inevitable end.

Time continued to tick by. Eventually, I pried my eyes open. An exclamation of horror fell from my mouth. My body attempted to lurch backward but was held in place by the sword pinning my wrist. My breaths were short and fast as I took in the sight before me. The water demon was an inch away from me, his face set in an animalistic snarl. One of his hands still held the sword while the other was extended to the side, with claws extended. It looked as though he had been planning to slap me, but he was perfectly still as if frozen solid.

My body shook as I slowly lifted my left hand toward the sword hilt. I kept expecting the demon to move, but he was still. Lifeless as a statue. Tugging slightly on the weapon, I freed it from his grasp and with a cry of pain, managed to dislodge it from my wrist. Sobs poured out of my body as I finally made it to my feet. I watched the demon the entire way across the room, and I even took the first few stairs backward so I could see him. He never moved and my sobbing continued as I made my way up the stairs. At some point, a memory surfaced, and I heard The Superior's voice telling me that powerful ferriers could control demons. I was crying and hyperventilating because that's exactly what I had just done.

CHAPTER 47

I reached the top of the stairs and found myself in a long hallway. There was a lot of commotion coming from my right, so I worked my way to the left. My body was working on pure adrenaline, as I had to crawl my way through the house. I hit a doorway at the end of the hall that opened into the kitchen. Looking along the back wall, I found a sliding glass door. I wrenched it open and then scanned the back yard for movement. Not seeing any, I slid the door open and stuck my head out.

There were sounds of fighting coming from the front of the house. Deciding that was not the best direction to travel, I looked toward the yard and the tree line behind the house. My options for escape were few and made worse still by the fact that I had no idea where I was. Fear and adrenaline coursed through me as I realized despite making it out of the basement, I was still trapped.

"What are you doing?"

My shoulders sagged in relief at the familiar voice. Destiny stepped up beside me. Her eyes widened in absolute shock at the sight of me. She immediately flew forward and scooped me into her arms.

"I'm trying to get out of here," I said.

"Do I need to take you to the hospital?" she asked, her eyes continuing to scan my injuries.

"Eventually," I said, patting her arm, "But right now, we need to go."

She narrowed her eyes suspiciously. "Go?"

"I know where my sister is."

Her face lit up with a smile and she squeezed me against her chest. With her mouth pressed into my hair, she said, "I knew you could do it."

"Thanks," I said, "Now can you please stop squeezing me because I think I'm going to throw up."

Destiny effortlessly flipped me to the side and allowed me to empty my stomach onto the grass. My head swam as she carried me across the property. Trees blurred past me as the sounds of fighting still occasionally reached my ear. Eventually, she halted and set me in the grass beside a car. Reaching inside, she pulled out a bottle of water and handed it to me.

"Let me grab The Master and then we can go."

She was gone before I had a chance to reply. I sat in the sun, on the cold hard ground and let my body fall back against the car. Sipping some water, I tried to convince myself that I was going to make it. I could find my sister and either The Superior or Nancy would be able to heal whatever was wrong with my body.

There was a large crashing sound and then a plume of dust floated into the air above the treetops. Destiny and The Superior burst into the clearing. I wasn't ready to see him again, but there were too many other things to worry about right now. He dove to the ground and his hands cupped my cheeks. Heat washed over me as he healed my injuries. His face was pale with a few scratches and scrapes. I could see the strain healing me was causing him. He must had been more injured than he looked, but he pressed on determinedly.

Finally, I placed my hands over his and said, "That's enough."

I could tell he wanted to protest, but he tipped backward and landed on his backside. His face was a wash of relief and exhaustion. My body was still sore, but I would be able to walk more easily now.

"Come on," Destiny said, "We've got to go."

We climbed into her car, with Destiny and I taking the front and The Superior laying in the back. I wasn't sure if I would be able to remember the exact route I saw to get to my sister, but luckily, once we were on the road, the images seemed to almost superimpose themselves over reality. I could see the turns ahead of us, so I was easily able to direct Destiny. She didn't say a word as I motioned her through each step.

When we pulled into the hotel parking lot, we both turned to see The Superior asleep in the backseat. Destiny shrugged and whispered, "Let him sleep. We got this."

She gave me a thumbs up and we quietly exited the car. It was odd to think of leaving him so vulnerable, but Destiny and I wouldn't be far away, and I doubted even as drained as he was that he could be overpowered by someone.

As we climbed the stairs, I found myself slowing. My thoughts circled in my head. This was it. We had finally found my sister. I was going to meet her. I hoped it had all been worth it.

Destiny stepped to the side of one door, waiting for me to catch up. She looked me over curiously but said nothing. With a sharp nod of my head, she lifted her foot and kicked the door in. It slammed into the wall with a resounding bang as we stepped inside.

"Who the hell are you?"

Her greeting was as cheerful as everyone warned me it would be. Monica stood in an oversized t-shirt. Her blonde hair fell in unkempt waves around her face, but her eyes were fixed on me. Mine were glued to the shotgun she had pointed at us.

Sucking in a breath I said, "My name is Claire."

"Should that mean something to me?"

I cleared my throat and lifted my hands. "I have a photo in my jacket pocket that I'd like you to see."

Monica scoffed. "No, tell me what you are doing here with *her*, or I shoot you."

The way she said 'her' made me think she wasn't the biggest fan of Destiny. The demon simply chuckled and said, "As always, such a delight, Monica."

"I don't know how you found me, but I'm not going anywhere with you," she spat.

"Perhaps not consciously," Destiny said with a hint of menace. I looked over at her hoping to signal to her that she was not helping, but her eyes were fixed on Monica.

I attempted a step forward, but Monica's eyes narrowed and the shotgun in her hands twitched. Things weren't going well, so I decided to rip off the bandage.

"I found you, because I am your sister. I want to help you."

Monica's face showed little to no reaction. I waited for her to respond, letting the pleading I felt enter my eyes.

Eventually, she said, "No thanks. Now get out."

I stared at her, dumbfounded. That hadn't been what I was expecting. I had thought she would at least be curious. Maybe she just didn't believe me.

"If you would let me show you the photo," I said again, moving my hand slowly toward my jacket.

"I told you to—"

Her words were cut off as Destiny lunged at her. Monica's attention had been on me and the strain of holding the shotgun had started to affect her hold on the weapon. Destiny snatched it quickly from her hands and pushed her down onto the couch.

"Here, get rid of this," handing me the shotgun.

I took it but had no idea what to do with it. Mentally, I pleaded with Nicky to take it away, and a moment later, it disappeared. It was nice to know that despite now knowing Nicky was a place not a person, that the magic still worked.

"I knew you were lying. You're another one of them."

"I'm not a demon," I said, walking across the room and standing slightly behind Destiny, "I'm human and I am your sister. Well, half-sister."

I reached into my jacket and withdrew a picture of my father and me. Slipping it past Destiny's shoulder, I held it out for Monica to see.

"This is what I wanted to show you. It's a picture of me and my dad. Our dad."

Monica's eyes flicked briefly over the picture and then up to my face. "I don't know who my father is."

Of course, The Superior hadn't told her either. I inwardly groaned at his inability to share any important information with anyone. How was I going to convince her now?

Destiny's fingers gripped Monica's hair and yanked on it. Monica glared fiercely at her, but surprisingly made no sound. I shuddered at the thought of what in her past had allowed her that kind of composure in the face of pain.

"You see this pretty blonde hair on both your heads?" Destiny asked, giving Monica's a tug. "You see that guy's eyes and nose? That's your stupid face, Mon, right there."

Destiny released her, and then poked the picture. "Like it or not, that's your family."

I wasn't sure how to take that last comment, but I let it go. Monica looked up at me and then back at the picture and then back to me. She took one more long look at the picture before she spat on it.

"Hey," I cried, whipping the picture away from her and running toward the hotel bathroom for a towel.

As I stormed away, I heard Monica shout, "We may have the same genes, but you are not my family."

Destiny looked over to me at the bathroom counter. "Let's just knock her out and get this over with."

I scrubbed the spittle off my picture and returned it to my pocket. Walking back into the room I saw that my sister had a very satisfied smirk on her face. Remembering that I had at one point accused The Superior of being in love with this woman, I now understood his outraged reaction.

"Pout all you want," she said when her eyes locked on mine, "I don't care who you are. You are with *him* and that means I don't want anything to do with you."

Sighing, I decided to forget the sister thing and go with a new approach. "Fine, but you won't be able to run much longer," I said, inclining my head toward her growing belly. "Sooner or later, they are going to find you. At least this way you know you won't be hurt."

"You clearly don't know him very well," she said, her eyes falling away from mine.

Destiny shoved her back onto the couch. "Don't you dare say such things about him."

Monica looked up at the demon and the two of them held each other's gaze for some time. I didn't know who to believe between them. Frankly at this moment I didn't care. I wanted to finish this job and get my sister out of here.

"Look, we found you and you're coming with us, that's all there is to it," I said, stepping closer.

Monica kicked out at me, but Destiny pressed her down and then plunged a needle into her neck. She twisted to try and grab Destiny's arm, but the demon batted her back down. Her protests continued, but they became more sluggish as whatever she'd been drugged with overwhelmed her system.

"Bitch," Monica said, her words breathy as she struggled to keep her eyes open.

"Likewise," Destiny said with a vicious grin on her face. She stepped back from the couch as Monica slumped onto her side.

"What did you give her?" I asked, concerned about the baby. Destiny waved her hand dismissively at me. "Nothing that will hurt the baby. Come on, let's get out of here."

Thanks to her demonic strength, Destiny lifted Monica over her shoulder with ease. I held the doors for her as we went. When we reached the car, The Superior was sitting upright, but still looking rather drained. He nodded at us as we set Monica down into the seat beside him. He brushed a hand through her hair that spilled across his lap. His face was set like a parent retrieving a petulant child.

I slid into the front passenger seat. We set off and I rested my head against the window. Weeks of danger, searching for my sister and learning more about my family than I thought possible were finally over. And yet, instead of feeling relieved, hesitation twisted my gut. There was some part of me that wasn't ready to be done. I was asleep before I could decide why that was.

CHAPTER 48

Four months later

S he has all she needs, but she still isn't happy."

I nodded my head. I had been hearing this for a month now. Huffing out a sigh I said, "I know, but I don't know what else to do."

The petite woman looked around nervously as she wrang her hands. This woman, whose name I'd already forgotten, had only been here for about a week. I didn't think she was going to last long. Just like the others.

"Perhaps the Master could — "

I shook my head and waved a hand to stop her. "He won't help the situation. Trust me." Fixing a fake and hopefully reassuring smile on my face, I said, "I'll talk to her."

We'd been going through this same song and dance several times over now. It was getting harder and harder to force that smile onto my face, but I did what I could. She seemed swayed by my smile as she nodded back at me.

I thanked her for her time and waved as she headed toward the main house. My gaze fell back onto the path before me. There was a small cottage situated in a beautiful clearing. Flowers decorated the railing that encircled the entire building. Lush mature trees shaded the front lawn and there was a line of hedges around the back.

The guards were milling about as always, and I nodded to each of them. A few paces away from the front porch was where I heard the yelling. I let out an exasperated sigh as the front door burst open and Monica spilled out onto the porch. Her eyes locked on mine, and I stopped in my tracks.

"What the hell do you want?" she spat as she thundered down the steps.

I stayed where I was and waited for the inevitable storm that was about to descend upon me. The guards peeled away from their stations to follow her. Monica stomped her feet toward me, her hands balled into fists at her sides. She came to an abrupt halt in front of me, her face red and her shoulders heaving as she continued to seethe.

"Why are you here?" she demanded.

Working very hard not to roll my eyes, I said, "The nurse called me. Again."

Her expression didn't change as she said, "I don't need a babysitter."

"Apparently you do," I said, motioning back toward the house, "What's going on here?"

"I'm already living as a prisoner. I don't need anyone in the house spying on me."

"They're not here to spy on you. They are here to help you."

Just then a wailing cry pierced through the air. We both looked back toward the house. A nurse stepped onto the porch with a small, squirming baby in her arms. Monica sighed and started back toward the house. I followed behind her, hoping that the worst of her mood had dissipated.

We reached the nurse and Monica scooped up her son. She walked into the house and settled down on the couch.

Slipping open her blouse, she began to feed him. I stalked in behind her and sat across the room from her.

She frowned at me, but a lot of the anger I'd encountered earlier was gone. I thanked my sweet nephew for his timing.

"When can I get out of here?" she asked, wiping a hand across her brow to brush away some flyaway hairs. She suddenly looked so tired.

I shook my head. "You know he won't let you leave." Inclining my head toward her son, I said, "Especially now that Timothy is here."

As if he understood his name, Timothy shifted in her arms and reached up a loving hand toward his mother's face. She smiled down at him, and a small swell of joy flooded my heart. I was glad to see that she was embracing motherhood so fully. We had all been a little concerned before she'd gone into labor, but then about a month ago she'd delivered her son Timothy Ryan and ever since she had been smitten.

Her eyes narrowed at me as she said, "I can't stay here. I won't."

I sighed. We'd had this conversation more times than I could count. From the moment Destiny and I brought her unconscious body to The Superior's estate, Monica had been more or less a prisoner. She was given this cottage that sat towards the back of the property. The Superior made it sound like a gift, but we all knew it for what it was. After Monica was *settled* into the house, guards were stationed around it. She was rarely allowed to leave and always with supervision.

Monica had kicked and screamed and attempted to escape as often as she could. Eventually, she hit a point in her pregnancy when such things became too difficult, and she finally conceded to staying in the cottage. When the time came for her to deliver, she was escorted to the hospital and guards were stationed outside her door. After her return, I had hoped her escape attempts would stop for a time. They didn't. If anything, the arrival of her son pushed her to try harder to escape.

She became almost feral, lashing out at anyone who came near her. We realized the confinement and caring for a newborn alone were seriously affecting her mental health. The Superior hired nannies to help her with Timothy and the care of her home. That had been a couple weeks ago, and it still wasn't going well. Monica assumed all the nannies were spies and she constantly fought with them.

Over the past few months, Monica had learned to tolerate me. I had been there to help during her labor. My presence hadn't always been appreciated, but she had allowed me to remain by her side. I think my affection for her son helped, but that still only got me so far. Monica had trouble trusting anyone and I was still tied to The Superior.

"You know he won't let you leave," I said again.

Her gaze sharpened. "How can you let him do this to me? To him?" she asked, inclining her head toward Timothy.

I rubbed my hands over my face. This was not a new conversation for us. "I can't make him do anything," I said, the words coming out rather harsh. I was so tired of talking about this with her.

"I don't believe you," she snapped.

"I don't care what you believe. It's the truth. He does what he wants to whoever he wants and none of us can stop him." The words were out of my mouth before I could think better of it. Monica's understanding of my relationship with The Superior was still limited. I didn't want to give her any further insights to potentially use against us.

She rolled her eyes. "I would imagine the person fucking him would have some sway."

I groaned. "How many times do I have to tell you? I am not sleeping with him!"

"Sorry, Your Majesty."

Bitter resentment churned in my stomach because I had no explanation for that one and she knew it. I tugged at the shirt sleeve covering the mark and changed the subject.

"Look, I just came here to tell you *once again* to stop being so mean to the nannies. And, of course, to see my nephew."

She glared over at me. "What is this, high school? I'm being mean? I don't give a shit what they think, I don't want them in my house."

"Can you honestly say you don't need the extra help?"

"Yes, Claire," she said, "I don't want them here and I don't need them."

I rolled my eyes and rose from my seat. Nothing was going to change today. "Fine, I'll suggest it to The Superior, but I can't make any promises."

"Of course, you can't," she said, an ugly sneer filling her face, "I would hate for you to have to stick your neck out for your sister to your boyfriend."

She only ever called me sister when she was insulting me. Initially, it had bothered me. Now I knew that was what she wanted, so I longer took anything she said to heart. I started toward the door, but she called out after me.

"Can't you at least agree that this is unfair?"

I looked over at her and shrugged. "Life's not fair."

Narrowing her eyes, she said, "I'm so happy I finally have a family. Now I know exactly what people mean when they say what a disappointment they are."

Smiling back at her, I said, "Likewise."

Stepping outside, I rolled my shoulders trying to release the tension that always followed me after an encounter with Monica. The spring air was fresh and uncharacteristically warm. I'd embraced the weather by not wearing a jacket over my sweater. Sucking in a deep breath, I tipped my head back and stared up at the treetops and the fluffy clouds. The sun was covered, but it was still a beautiful day.

Movement on the pathway ahead caught my attention. I looked back down slowly because I knew who it was. The enveloping heat and sense of power coming off the tall figure was unmistakable.

Our gazes locked and I felt a slight twinge in my chest. I had only seen The Superior in passing since the night we found Monica. Both of us had been at the hospital for the delivery and I caught glimpses of him when I visited the estate. Our conversations were limited to discussing my sister over text message. We never talked about that night. I'd moved back into my house and whatever had been between us was no more. Just thinking the word, *us* caused too many emotions to stir within me. I suppressed the feelings and focused on figuring out why he was here.

"Did the nanny quit?" I asked. The silence stretched between us, and I shifted uncomfortably on my feet.

Finally, he said, "No."

I nodded my head, happy to hear that the woman from earlier would at least make it one more day. Waiting for him to explain why he was here I grew increasingly uncomfortable. I started to fidget with my hands and chew on my lower lip. If he sensed my unease, he said nothing of it as he continued looking me over.

Not being able to stand his scrutinizing any longer I blurted out the first thing that came to mind. "Thank you. I mean, I never said thank you, for before, with Jacob."

His brows crinkled slightly for a moment before he simply nodded.

"What happened to him? Jacob?" I asked, hoping to get more than a single word out of him.

"He's fine now."

We were back to this. Clipped sentences and awkwardness. I didn't understand why he was the one who got to be so standoffish when I was the one who was hurt. My arms rose instinctively to cover my discomfort.

Finally sensing my agitation, he added, "I did raze his entire property in punishment."

Without thinking I said, "Perfect. I'm sure that taught him not to kidnap people anymore."

Once again, he proved that I didn't mean anything to him beyond his obligations to my dead relative. I had hoped that the time apart would have eased my pain at how we left things, but it hadn't seemed to help.

"What would you like me to say, Claire?" he asked, stepping forward as his eyes flashed with red. "Would you like me to add that I killed every one of his servants in that house? That I was so incensed that I couldn't stop myself from ripping them all limb from limb and then burning them in Hellfire? Is that what you want to hear?"

My eyes dipped away from his, but he snatched my chin with his hand and pulled my face up to look into his. "No, you don't get to demand I give you justice but then think of me as a murderer."

His face was too close to mine. I could feel all of my emotions fluttering to the surface. So that's why he had been avoiding me. I'd called him a murderer for the deal he had made with my great-great grandmother.

I swallowed and pulled away from him. His grip remained firm for only a moment before he released me. I stepped away from him, pushing down the tide of emotions that were threatening to bring tears to my eyes. I didn't like that he still had such an effect on me. My eyes dipped to the ground as I asked, "What happened to the demons in the house?"

This had been a fear of mine for some time. I had left that water demon frozen in place in the basement and I didn't know if he'd ever regained his ability to move. Worse yet, I didn't know if anyone discovered him and what I had done. I hadn't had an opportunity to ask The Superior, so I assumed now was as good a time as any.

My eyes darted up to his face to see if there was any suspicion in his gaze, but he was back to his stony expressionless face. His eyes were still red, but the color was fading.

"What do you mean?" he asked.

I shrugged, trying to play off how important the answer to this question was to me. Squeezing my arms more tightly around me, I traced a circle in the ground with my foot. "I mean, are they still his? Are they still, you know, here?"

I looked up as I said 'here' and hoped that my question seemed innocent enough. His gaze hardened at my words, misunderstanding my asking as being yet another way of judging him.

"I didn't murder any of them, if that's what you are asking," he said, his words dripping with bitterness. "But yes, they have all been reassigned away from Jacob."

A sigh of relief slipped past my lips.

"Although there was one," he said, making every hair on my body stand on end.

"One what?" I asked, my words coming out too quickly.

"One demon who didn't make it. Somehow, he got trapped in the house when it fell. I am not sure what happened, but he died."

Bile churned in my stomach. The demon had been frozen in place while the house collapsed on top of him. I'd left him there to die. Worry tangled up inside me to the point that I thought I was going to be sick.

The Superior eyed me curiously, so I looked away from him. I kept my eyes on the ground as I asked, "Is that unusual?"

"Mmm-hmm," he muttered in agreement.

There was another silence that stretched out between us. I listened to the sound of the breeze in the trees, the birds calling out to one another. Sucking in deep breaths I tried to steady the panicked thrum of my heart. I needed some time to think about what I had done, but that time wasn't right now.

After a while, I shook my head and looked up to say I was going, but The Superior cut me off.

"I need to speak with you," he said, the words tumbling out of him in an unusually anxious way.

"Okay."

"Do you still wish for me to remove the mark?"

His eyes dipped to my covered forearm, and it took everything in me to resist touching the spot. This was what I had been asking him for since he'd placed the mark on me and yet, I hesitated. My sister and her son were safe as long as they stayed on The Superior's property, but what about me? What if another demon learned his secret and came after me? If I didn't have the mark on me, he wouldn't be able to find or heal me. Then again, this would mean freedom. I wouldn't have to wonder about our connection. We wouldn't have to be together. But wasn't that the problem? Part of me was angry at him, but another part of me still wanted him. Wanted the man who washed my hair and held me in his arms. Angry with the man who never told me I had a sister. Wanted the man who let his guard down and showed me his compassion for his people and his interest in me. Angry with the man who marked me without asking and never told me why he truly cared about me.

He took my confused silence as acquiescence. "I will begin the process of removal as soon as I can."

My stomach dipped at his words. Everything in me screamed to say something, but I didn't know what.

"There is one more thing," he continued while placing his hand into his pocket. He retrieved a crisp, white envelope with my name scrawled in an unfamiliar script across the front.

"What's this?" I asked, as he placed it into my hand.

"Open it and see."

I stared down at my name as dread started to turn my stomach. Flipping the envelope over, I broke the red wax seal and pulled out a thick piece of cardstock. The unfamiliar script continued inside.

Dear Ms. Woods,

I was so pleased to hear my beloved Superior had taken a Queen. What fortuitous timing as I will be in The Otherworld soon for The Exchange. You will be my most honored guest.

I look forward to our meeting.

Sincerely,

The Prince of the Realm of Darkness

The words echoed in my head as all the blood drained from my face. I looked up at The Superior. "What is this?"

Sucking in a breath, he said, "That would be your invitation from The Prince."

"The Devil?" I spat.

The Superior winced. "I wouldn't call him that when you meet him."

My stomach dipped and I swallowed audibly. "I have to meet The…The Prince?"

His eyes were serious as he said, "Hopefully not. We have four months until The Exchange. Hopefully I can remove the mark before then."

"And if you can't?" I asked, panic climbing up my throat. I had been confused about the removal of the mark before, but now I desperately needed it gone.

He stepped forward and brushed a strand of hair behind my ear. It was a tender touch that sent a shiver through my body. His lips gave a brief smile before he said, "If I cannot, then, yes, you will be expected to be there."

I started to shake my head back and forth as my body trembled. The Superior reached out and placed warm hands on my shoulders. He trailed heat down the outside of my arms until he stopped to clasp my hands. His head tipped forward and he brushed his forehead against my own. "I won't let anything happen to you, Claire."

He placed a quick kiss to my forehead, then released me. Turning, he put his hands in his pockets and walked away.

I watched him go with a pain in my chest and a sinking feeling in my stomach. Four months. We had four months for him to remove the mark, so I didn't have to meet The Prince of Hell, and I had even less time to decide if removing it was what I truly wanted. With a sigh, I started walking toward my car. There was one thing I knew with absolute certainty. I needed a drink.

EPILOGUE

The Superior

It has been two months, one week, and one day since I last saw her. A fact of which I am painfully aware. The mark calls to me, telling me to draw her in, to fully claim her as my own. Claire does not wish it to be so, and so, I roll my shoulders to relieve some tension as I focus more intently on the paper before me.

My head chef has requested a new refrigerator. I do not know why this is needed, nor do I care. Scribbling my signature at the bottom, I place the paper into the tray on my desk. An assistant would relieve me of these tedious tasks, but I never want my human servants to think that I am unaware of everything they are doing. The freedom to do as they wish would be disastrous with some of them and so all of their requests must go through me. A pain I have laced myself with as I currently have over a thousand servants.

A knock sounds on my door. Welcoming the distraction, I say, "Come in."

Without lifting my head, I know who it is. It is rare for anyone else to come to my office. Most requests come through text or email now. My hatred for the man or woman who invented the mobile phone grows with every chime of my device.

"Someone is in a mood this morning."

My eyes flick up to see Destiny plop down into the chair in front of my desk. Her lips part into a teasing smile, but I don't take the bait.

"What is it?" I ask gruffly, my eyes returning to the paper in front of me.

"No 'hi, destiny, how are you today?' Is that anyway to greet your favorite demon?"

I cross my arms on top of my desk and glare back at her. Red rolls just slightly along the edges of my eyes. No one knows that I can control it, although I think Destiny suspects. Only when I am truly furious do I not control the amount of red that fills my eyes. After centuries of dealing with people, I've learned that it unsettles them more than words, so I use it as much as I can.

"Spit it out," I say, pushing more redness into my eyes and rolling my shoulders again.

She wiggles upward in her seat. "Well, there are a few things. Have you made your selections yet?"

I bristle at the reminder of the upcoming selection. It is up to me to decide who will be exchanged for whatever fresh demons the Devil brings with him. A process that must be repeated every one hundred years and yet always feels that it comes too soon.

"No," I finally say, "But, I have a few ideas."

She nods, not asking any follow-up questions. That means there is something more pressing on her mind.

With her eyes staring out the window she whispers, "You know he'll want to meet her."

My body tenses. Demon queens are rare and the fact that I have taken one undoubtedly surprised many. The reminder of her sends another tug through my body to find her. I clench my hands into fists to try and block the impulse.

"I am aware. I hope to sever the connection before that becomes an issue."

She turns back toward me, allowing her emotions to show on her face. "And if you can't?"

Destiny sees my struggle more than most, but it is my problem to deal with not hers. "Then I will take care of it," I say, putting an end to that conversation.

Her teeth start grating across her lower lip. We still have not come to the topic she originally came here to discuss. My patience is wearing thin.

Slamming my hands onto the top of the desk, I say, "For fucks sake, spit it out, Destiny."

My temper has no effect on her. Some days this display would get her to leave, knowing that I was not in the mood to play her games. Today, she stays put which tells me whatever she has to say she thinks I need to know, but that I won't like it.

A thought blossoms in my mind, and I let out a sigh. "Again?" I ask, keeping my gaze on my desk.

She clears her throat, and she says, "Yes. This morning."

"How much?"

I see her shoulders rise and fall in a shrug before she says, "Not enough for sex, but close enough to have been touching."

The papers on my desk suddenly combust. Now the red that encircles my pupils is purely from rage. It takes all my considerable power not to bolt out of my chair and kill Scott. He and Claire are spending more and more time together, a fact that infuriates me but that I cannot act on.

My distress clear, Destiny sighs and says, "Why won't you let me take care of this? They have no idea how it affects you and quite honestly, I find it so disgusting that I would really like to punch Scott in the face for it."

"No," I say emphatically. Then more softly I say, "She made her decision, and I will respect it and so will you."

She scoffs. "A terrible decision and one I know she will regret."

I shrug and crack my neck. "Be that as it may, it is her choice."

"It also makes you look weak," she spits at me. "Allowing your queen to spend time with a *servant*."

My tone grows dangerously low as I reply, "That's enough."

I return my attention to my desk, but then I remember I incinerated all the papers. After this conversation I am desperate for a distraction. Thinking perhaps I could work out some of my frustration at the gym, I rise from my chair. I open my mouth to tell Destiny I am leaving, when a wicked grin lights up her face.

"I have some other news you might actually enjoy hearing," she says, rising and coming to stand before me.

My eyebrow lifts in question at her. She smiles and says, "Billy Blake tried to kill his mother last night."

If I had had to guess her next words, those would never have been on my list. My brow falls as I ask, "And why do you think attempted matricide is something I would enjoy hearing?"

Her smile widens. "Because he didn't realize his mother was under your protection. When the servants guarding her informed him that you would be visiting him for recompense for this slight, he kindly offered an alternative."

My face split into a grin that mirrored Destiny's own. "And what pray tell did he offer?"

"A lifetime of service."

A dark laugh spills from my lips as the temperature in the room rises with my demonic joy. I'd known Billy Blake would be a problem from the first moment I laid eyes on him. His desire to harm my queen was not forgotten. I had been waiting for my moment to strike and I had correctly predicted his mother would be a loose end he couldn't resist tying off. Selfish and predictable, I knew it was only a matter of time before Billy would be mine.

"Where is he?" I ask, cracking my knuckles in anticipation.

"Downstairs," she says, stepping aside, "He is waiting to receive his mark and his first assignment."

A spark of excitement travels through my body as I think of all the ways I get to hurt Billy Blake. He doesn't know it yet, but Billy is going to be the perfect distraction from my thoughts. Still smiling, I reach into my desk and pull out a small golden cuff. Etched into the surface is a large sea serpent, curled into the letter 'S'. The serpent is wreathed in flames and its tail holds a small lyre. It is my sigil, and it is burned into every one of my servants and remains on their skin until their debt to me is fulfilled. I'm going to enjoy searing this image into Billy's flesh while I imagine all the ways I'm going to torture him for daring to threaten my queen. It might be excessive, but I am, after all, a demon.

Want more Claire and The Superior?

Look out for Book 2, A Fractured Soul, Coming 2025

If you enjoyed this book, please leave a review on Amazon, Goodreads, etc. Thank you!

❤*ACKNOWLEDGMENTS*❤

This book was years in the making. From one small idea about a woman being able to enter Purgatory to the story you hold today, it took a lot of time and effort, and I didn't do it all alone.

There are always so many people to thank. First of all, my family for always encouraging my love of writing. For my mother and father, who signed me up for Creative Writing Workshops and were doing the groundwork to sell all of the copies before the book was even published. For my brother, for looking at my work and always encouraging me to shorten my sentences and use less commas. Sorry, quite a few still made it in! For my sister, for giving the best constructive criticisms and for supporting me while your own life was super busy.

Special thanks to my husband for watching our kids so I could have time to do all of this. Also, when I first sat down to write this story, thank you for encouraging me to keep going and telling me that my work was worth putting out into the world. Thank you for always being my alpha reader.

Thank you to my editor, Joss, at Riveting Revisions. Your insights into my content were fantastic and I am so grateful for them.

Thank you to Salome Totladze for making the amazing artwork that graces the cover of this book. You are beyond talented, and I cannot believe someone with your history and body of work did the artwork for my book.

Thank you to Samara Saward, the best critique partner I could have asked for! Your insights and tips into my story were amazing! I hate that my process has been so slow compared to yours, but I hope that you are willing to keep reading for me, because you are not only an amazing writer but a fantastic content editor.

Thank you to Angela Thomas for being the best beta reader ever! Your love for The Superior and encouragement were the best and helped me know that I needed to publish this book. Even if other people hate it, I will always know how much you loved this story, even when it was a super rough draft.

Thank you to my amazing bookstagram community. Your support throughout this process has been amazing and I feel truly blessed to have met so many wonderful people.

Last, but certainly not least, thank you, reader for taking a chance on this book! I have poured so much of myself into this project, and I hope that each and every one of you finds something to connect with within my story. I hope you loved Claire and The Superior and that you are excited to read more. Please, if you loved this book, leave me a review and connect with me on social media. I am always available to talk about books. Also, fun fact, the page break in the book is a scrambled version of The Superior's true name. If you think you've figured it out, please send me your guess!

Elizabeth Sedell is a fantasy author who grew up in rural Pennsylvania dreaming of faraway lands filled with magic. As an adult, she still daydreams about fantastical places, but now they include swoon worthy romance. She hopes you find her characters loveable and her worlds immersive, with a touch of humor.
She currently lives in Texas with her family and when she's not reading or writing, she's trying out new recipes, attempting to grow things, or watching sports.

Connect with Elizabeth on:

Instagram: @elizabethsedellauthor

www.ingramcontent.com/pod-product-compliance
Lightning Source LLC
Chambersburg PA
CBHW031829310726
48972CB00005B/1222